Fire Within

Heart pounding, Kelsey took a step closer, ignoring his warnings. "Who's after you?" she asked, searching across the water. "Please. Maybe I can help."

Silence, gasps, desperate breathing. Then, *Yes.* That was the last thing she heard before she felt him enter her. Felt him, like a fanning breeze across her skin, unobtrusive, tender, apologetic.

Nothing in her twenty-eight years had come close to the sensations she instantly experienced. She sensed him move quickly within her, felt her chest tighten, her whole body tremble. Like burning fingers, he caressed all the way into her very core. "Amazing," she whispered, wondering how he maintained a distance of at least four feet yet seemed somehow to enter her body simultaneously. But then, he spoke within her mind, so why should this surprise her?

Touching her abdomen, she felt his fire build there, and she cried out in response, sliding to the ground. "Please," she moaned, lying back on the earth, feeling him every-where. God, he'd set her on fire, teasing her toward an unseen edge. Like some erotic torturer, he kept setting her ablaze, but he begged for her silence.

Danger here . . .

PARALLEL ATTRACTION

Deidre Knight

A SIGNET ECLIPSE BOOK

SIGNET ECLIPSE
Published by New American Library, a division of
Penguin Group (USA) Inc., 375 Hudson Street,
New York, New York 10014, USA
Penguin Group (Canada), 90 Eglinton Avenue East, Suite 700, Toronto,
Ontario M4P 2Y3, Canada (a division of Pearson Penguin Canada Inc.)
Penguin Books Ltd., 80 Strand, London WC2R 0RL, England
Penguin Ireland, 25 St. Stephen's Green, Dublin 2,
Ireland (a division of Penguin Books Ltd.)
Penguin Group (Australia), 250 Camberwell Road, Camberwell, Victoria 3124,
Australia (a division of Pearson Australia Group Pty. Ltd.)
Penguin Books India Pvt. Ltd., 11 Community Centre, Panchsheel Park,
New Delhi - 110 017, India
Penguin Group (NZ), cnr Airborne and Rosedale Roads, Albany,
Auckland 1310, New Zealand (a division of Pearson New Zealand Ltd.)
Penguin Books (South Africa) (Pty.) Ltd., 24 Sturdee Avenue,
Rosebank, Johannesburg 2196, South Africa

Penguin Books Ltd., Registered Offices:
80 Strand, London WC2R 0RL, England

First published by Signet Eclipse, an imprint of New American Library,
a division of Penguin Group (USA) Inc.

First Printing, April 2006
10 9 8 7 6 5 4 3 2 1

PUBLISHER'S NOTE
This is a work of fiction. Names, characters, places, and incidents either are the
product of the author's imagination or are used fictitiously, and any resemblance
to actual persons, living or dead, business establishments, events, or locales is
entirely coincidental.

The publisher does not have any control over and does not assume any responsibility for author or third-party Web sites or their content.

This book is dedicated to my family:

To my husband, Judson Knight, and my daughters, Tyler and Riley Knight, for their willingness to share me with my writing dream.

To my sister, Pamela Harty, an amazing agent who helped make that dream come true.

To my mother, Eleanor Knight, the first person to breathe life to the dream so many years ago by calling me a writer.

ACKNOWLEDGMENTS

There are many people I would like to thank for their generous support in the writing and publishing of this book—first and foremost my husband, Judson Knight. Without him, there would be no book. He's my best friend, confidant, and all-around hero, and his support made it possible for me to write in addition to being a literary agent.

My fabulous editor Louisa Edwards deserves major thanks and kudos, not only for really "getting" this series, but also for her great editorial suggestions, which helped make this book stronger. From the first moment she read the material, I've felt that I had a very special champion on my side. My editor Rose Hilliard is equally terrific, and I've been blessed to have not one but two editors at NAL, both of whom have taken expert care of me.

My agent and sister, Pamela Harty, is a tireless advocate for me, and has spent many years listening to me discuss one writing project or another. Thank goodness all that talk finally led somewhere! I'm tremendously blessed to have such a great agent on my side, both personally and as a member of the Knight Agency team.

Nancy Berland is a fabulous publicist, and her belief in this series has meant the world to me. Not only is she brilliant, but she also happens to be a lot of fun to dance with. Nancy, thank you from the bottom of my heart for being behind me all the way.

My wonder girl in the Knight Agency office, Samantha

Jenkins, has been a gift from God, right when this stressed-out agent/author/mother/wife needed someone to sail in and make things easier. Thank you for all you do, Samantha.

Kathy Baker's support for both this book and for me as an author has been invaluable. Thanks, girl!

I'd like to thank my e-group writer gal pals, many of whom read versions of this material and offered critique: Kath, Tas, Mel, Nephele, Micha, Blanca, Anne, Tara, Bennie, Crystal, Stacey, and Angela. Our early days together shaped me as a writer, and I am forever grateful for that time.

Mega thanks to Angela Zoltners, an amazing friend and reader, who proved invaluable in the writing of this book.

Finally, sincere thanks to the people in Wyoming who answered endless questions and have been a great resource in the writing of this series: Jeff Cunnington, and Meagan and Aron at the Snake River Lodge.

We must not allow the clock and the calendar to blind us to the fact that each moment of life is a miracle and mystery.

—H. G. Wells

Bl'alastraka
A Refarian Book of Intimate Love
Author Unknown; English Translator Unknown

VERSE ONE, SUPERIOR TEXT: The seeking of a mate shall be undertaken with all due preparation and care. A lifebond should never be contemplated as a light thing—unlike a legal union or sanctified joining, the sealing of souls CANNOT be severed. When a mate is SOULBOUND to another—LIFEMATED, as some have come to regard it—a mystery is engaged. In one aspect mystical, in another corporeal, and yet another spiritual, the lifemating process is the most sublime endeavor that a Refarian may assume. Once formed, the bond must be ever cherished and nurtured by a process of lifelong rigor.

There have been reports of other species seeking to mimic our mating rituals and bonds; the ANTOUSIANS, when first upon our soil, were both mystified and impressed to see the esteem with which our kind regarded the love bond. To this day, rumors abound that Antousians sought—indeed, continue to seek—the inducement of MATING BONDS uncommon to their kind by genetic heritage.

A BOND—even a two-way bond—may exist for a temporary purpose. This situation is not advisable, however, as such intimacy may not easily be remedied once embarked upon. One soul, bound solidly to another, has proven over time a means of inducing deep, lasting passion. The author notes that such may prove true only in instances of destined lifemates. There are extant tales of bonds unrelated to that of lifemating—wartime communication, procurement of goods, amelioration of loneliness. Such temporary joinings should always be initiated with UTMOST CAUTION.

Let the bonding ritual be regarded with seriousness of esteem and all intended respect, and if such be the case, one shall never err.

Prologue

It wasn't every day you managed to lose your king while on a security mission to an alien planet. In fact, it took a spectacularly large amount of bad luck, but Councilor Aldorsk couldn't say he was surprised. Not after the recent *series* of impetuous royal decisions, all of which had indirectly led to this moment. Every Refarian gathered on the ship's deck was concerned for the king's welfare, voicing fears they all harbored—but rarely vocalized. *What if he dies? What if he's captured? What if he never makes it back?* These were the same fears that plagued the king's leadership back home on a daily basis, only now those concerns were magnified a hundredfold because he'd taken off without so much as a security escort. Yes, Aldorsk was anxious, but, being the eldest adviser on the royal council, he simply worked to stay calmer than the others.

Before them all—and in the midst of an argument of colossal proportions—the king had shape-shifted into a ball of glowing energy in order to slip through the floor and to the exterior of the ship without being apprehended. By now the young leader had certainly arrived on Earth, and had returned to his physical form. He might even be hiking into the nearby mountains, never to return. It required an extraordinary amount of calm *not* to worry for the young man's welfare, but Councilor Aldorsk determined to put forth a brave, composed face for the Refarians knotted around the glowing center of the transport.

The young monarch's energy had left a vibrant trailing pattern on the grooved floor, finally vanishing in the exact spot where the king had last stood. The transport's captain stared at the floor along with him. "I don't think there's any structural damage," the man assessed, but from his expression he looked dubious about the situation in general.

Standing beside Aldorsk was his fellow councilor, Elder Graeon. "I don't think this is"—Graeon hesitated, squatting down to inspect potential damage to the craft—"such a very good idea, allowing him to venture to the planet's surface alone."

"He will be fine," Aldorsk insisted.

It was the ship's captain who spoke next. "If you don't mind my saying so, the king seems quite agitated lately. His frequent outbursts, the shape-shifting without restraint, and now *this*." He pointed down at the floor, which was still glowing with their monarch's energy shadow. "Are you certain he's ready for this mission? He does not seem at all himself."

"He's on Earth *now*, Captain," Aldorsk reminded them with a burst of impatience. "Therefore the mission is already engaged."

"He's unsteady," Graeon answered in a quiet voice, rising to his feet again. "I am concerned." His long black hair was tied neatly at his back, but several light strands of silver betrayed his impending maturity. All Refarian males turned silver-headed once their fertile years had ended. "He seems to grow more impulsive with every passing day."

"You know the reason for that," Aldorsk reminded him seriously. "You can hardly fault him for that which he does not understand in himself."

"We must be very protective at this time of his awakening."

Aldorsk grew thoughtful. "True, the changes in his young body are very complex, all the more because of his dual nature. Of course he's agitated. He hardly understands his transformation—much less that it's natural for his kind."

Graeon worked an eyebrow. "Perhaps he should consult *you*, Councilor. You guided his father through his own first season."

Aldorsk smiled. "I think you know our king well enough to realize that no questions will be forthcoming on this matter."

The other elder persisted: "His first mating cycle is imminent, surely—"

Aldorsk lifted a hand. "He *must* find the way on his own."

"At fifteen, he's already fertile."

"Almost sixteen," Aldorsk corrected. "What do you propose? That I urge him to take a mate so soon? He must be given time, even in the midst of war."

"It is a danger to wait," Graeon argued. "Without any clear successor, the line remains in jeopardy."

Aldorsk sighed. "It was dangerous to make this journey at all. At what point must we advise the king to remain at the palace? Hidden?"

"As you will recall, coming here was not my choice," Graeon reminded his council leader.

"No, it was our lord's."

"Perhaps he should not be allowed to make every decision until the succession is secured."

"Elder Graeon!" Aldorsk cried. "You must silence yourself. Our king is our commander."

Graeon's dark face flushed, his mouth tightening. "I love our king, as you well know, both as friend and as leader. But I worry much about his future."

Yes, they all worried about the future of the Refarian ruler, who at the moment was the very last in line after more than a thousand years of unbroken succession. But perhaps, at least just for now, they should be *more* worried that the king had arrived on an alien planet under the early influence of his first mating season.

The guy on the path ahead was up to no good, no doubt about it. He had a sample bag in one hand, and some sort of utensil in the other, and that spelled one thing for sure—illegal researcher.

"Are you taking soil samples?" Kelsey called out, though she was still a good twenty feet away from the man. She might only be fourteen (well, almost), but she felt pretty fierce and protective when it came to Yellowstone. Too many people came to the park each summer and abused the place, so her mother had taught her to be friendly but tough when she found someone doing something stupid or potentially dangerous.

Not that she hadn't just spent the entire morning hiking around Mirror Lake collecting her *own* rock and soil samples, but at least she knew how to be responsible about it. The tall, dark-haired guy on the path ahead of her, on the other hand, looked like—no, had to be—the sort who would cart truckloads of illegal samples out of the park. When she got five feet away from him, she called out again: "You're not allowed to take samples out of here without permission."

He leaped to his feet and spun to face her, but he said nothing. And when his mysterious, wide-set eyes met hers, she realized he couldn't be that much older than she was.

She lifted her chin and continued, ignoring the way the guy's dark-eyed gaze affected her. "You've gotta have a permit," she explained, drawing in a breath. "Can't take anything out of here without one."

The boy worked his jaw for a moment, seemingly searching for words, and finally dropped his hands to his sides, the apparent samples falling to the ground. "Just . . . studying," he answered awkwardly, the words accented. Was he Russian? He almost sounded like it. *Just shtudeeing.*

"Where are you from?" she asked, stepping closer to him. She had a small backpack thrust over one shoulder, with loads of her own rock and soil samples neatly labeled inside. Only she would never dream of removing anything from the park without express permission, which she'd obtained only once before—for last year's science fair.

When he didn't reply, she eyed him warily. "You're not one of those prodigies from the Thorpe School, are you?" Thorpe always beat her own high school at the fair, year after year. It would be totally like them to import some Soviet genius to their team just to dominate yet *again.*

"No."

"You Soviet or something?"

"Just"—he smiled, making her stomach flip-flop with butterflies—"stranger."

"Do you speak in full sentences?" she asked with a playful toss of her curly hair. Guys liked her long, dark-auburn hair; that's what she'd always heard.

He folded his arms over his chest, looking very much like a guy who was used to getting his way. "Sometimes."

"But not now?"

"Not now." The big smile he gave her made the flip-floppy thing in her stomach go even wilder. And the butterflies, well, they made her feel *bold*. It was weird, but true. Yeah, he had a seriously amazing smile, all right, with perfect white teeth that stood out against his dark skin—and she definitely loved the dark-skin part. He didn't *look* Russian, more like someone from Iran or Israel or Greece. Italy. Actually, come to think of it, he didn't look like any exact nationality she could pinpoint. Plus, the outfit was just a little bit funky—he had on knee-high boots of dark brown leather, and over that he wore a sort of tunic thing down to his knees, made of a simple linen material, with a long-sleeved shirt underneath.

"Where are you from? Really?" she asked, dropping her pack to the ground. "You sound Russian."

He gave her a guarded look. "Very far from here." *Vairry fahr fvrom heare.*

"But where?"

"It is not important."

"Maybe it's important to me," she said with a laugh, but he gave her a look of confusion.

"Okay, forget that. I'm Kelsey Wells," she said, sticking her hand out. He took it, his own hand closing around hers with warm confidence—and yet he released it a fraction too quickly, as if unaccustomed to shaking hands.

He said nothing else, so finally she prompted him: "What's *your* name?"

"Some call me Jareshk."

"So, Jareshk, you're, like, eastern European, is that it?" He only gave her a blank look in return, and after tossing out a few other possibilities, she finally said, "Okay, I give up. But only for a little while."

If Kelsey Wells was any indication, humans were a highly persistent and curious people, prone to leading with questions and seeking the truth. So far this reconnaissance had led Jareshk to one conclusion: He liked her species very much. Her clear, truthful eyes made him want to admit everything about his mission here on her planet. An unwise choice, perhaps, but with her relentless questions he had no doubt he would soon reveal his identity—or be forced to leave. And he definitely did *not* wish to leave Kelsey Wells, not quite yet. She brought out strange feelings inside of him—pleasurable, electric feelings.

"Want to see the samples I found?" she asked him, her eyes alight with sudden excitement. She climbed atop a large boulder beside where they stood on the wooded path, and began to spread them out. "Here," she encouraged him. "Come on and I'll show you."

He did as she invited, settling opposite her so that they sat nearly knee-to-knee atop the boulder. He wished he weren't wearing the tall boots and his Shashar robe; if he were dressed like she was, he'd be feeling her warm skin against his. As if reading his mind, she reached out a tentative hand and touched his right boot. "You must be really hot in that outfit."

"It suits me," he lied, feeling the midday sun beat down on him. The ship had been much cooler than her planet's surface.

"Yeah, I guess. If you're a Ren Faire escapee." She waved at his long robe and tunic. "Couldn't you take . . . well, the top part off? It'd be less hot."

She had no idea how her innocent suggestion caused his blood to boil. He'd turned fifteen ten months ago; he'd heard the elders whispering, talking about his D'Aravnian blood, his line's propensity for early-age mating cycles. Blushing, he stared down into his lap. There was something wrong with him, plain and simple. Mating cycles were for animals, not kings.

But it wasn't the mating urges that were making him feel things for Kelsey. It was very odd indeed, but he ached to please her. "All right," he said, jumping to his feet and pulling the robe over his head. When he was finished, he stood before her wearing only his shirt and a pair of dra-kaer pants—like her shorts, but worn beneath the overtunic.

She studied him thoughtfully. "You know, that still just looks hot to me." He swore he detected a mischievous gleam in her blue eyes.

He sighed and shrugged out of the shirt altogether, then looked to see if she was satisfied.

She stared up at him, and her clear eyes grew wide at the sight of his bare chest. "Oh, good grief!" She gasped.

What had he done? In a panic, he folded both arms over his chest protectively. "What is it? Something . . . wrong?"

He hadn't even considered the possibility that his body might appear quite different from that of a human male.

"Nothing," she practically squeaked, her face flushing visibly as she made a big show of laying out her rocks for him to see—and of avoiding eye contact with him.

In that moment, he understood. It wasn't that his body appeared alarmingly alien in some way. No, she found him attractive! He began to laugh and felt his own body flush with deep pleasure. Releasing an unsteady breath, he sat down opposite her again, keenly aware not only of his own bare chest, but also of her bare leg touching his.

"You have many rocks," he said, reaching a self-conscious hand to cover his right nipple. He felt naked, exposed—hungry for her, too, and the rushing confluence of all those feelings inside him left him feeling shy and embarrassed. "I-I do not know . . . way to describe their . . . beauty." And he didn't just mean the rocks, either; he longed for a way to express how beautiful he found *her*, as well.

"It's okay, Jareshk," she answered with a genuine smile of empathy. It was as if she knew exactly what he was feeling. "Let's just talk awhile."

And so they did, for hours and hours, it turned out, and every time she smiled at him, his heart fluttered like a bird's wing inside his chest. As a king, he'd encountered any number of odd and interesting situations, but never anything like this overwhelming and instant attraction he felt toward Kelsey.

So, for lack of a better strategy, he returned every smile she offered him, and hoped it disguised the unsettled trembling he felt inside.

By late afternoon Kelsey wondered if she would ever look at life the same again. Jareshk had already begun to seem less like a friend and more like a *boy*friend, and although it felt sort of sudden—it also kind of made sense. Her best friend, Allison Matthews, had met a guy at the mall a month ago, and he'd asked her to go with him that same afternoon, so this thing with Jareshk wasn't really all *that* strange.

The more time they spent together, too, the more his

grasp of English seemed—almost spookily—to improve. They hiked and talked; sometimes they found a spot along the lake where they simply sat and watched the play of the water's surface. "Water at my home is not so clear as this. Not usually," he told her.

"What do you mean?"

His face grew darker, sad. "It is polluted by . . . war. Our enemies."

"What war are you talking about? You should tell me where you're from; it's only fair." She couldn't help feeling angry that he wouldn't reveal more about himself.

"I don't wish to burden you with heavy things," he said, forcing his mouth into a smile, only this time it didn't reach his eyes.

Her anger melted away. "I want to know," she encouraged.

"Thank you, Kelsey," he said softly, and reached for her hand. Slowly, very gently, he threaded his fingers together with hers, and every part of her came more *alive* somehow.

They sat like that for a long time, with Kelsey's body trembling, and Jareshk holding her hand, until the day began to grow much cooler, and the sun tracked low on the other side of the mountains.

But Jareshk never said another word about his country or where he came from.

On their last night together, Kelsey sneaked out of her parents' tent and met him by the water. It was late, nearing midnight, before she appeared there beneath the moonlight. He'd been growing restless, frightened that he wouldn't see her again before he had to return to the transport. Kelsey Wells did powerful, awakening things to him, things he'd never once experienced in his almost sixteen years. It was as if every time he so much as glanced at her, his cells burned brighter, or his powerful energy blazed stronger. Two days they'd spent together, but it might as well have been a year. He felt, on a very elemental level, as if he had known her his whole life. But this feeling of a connection between the two of them transcended even that.

He had to return to the transport tonight; he knew it, but just hadn't come to terms with letting Kelsey go yet. Her family would leave tomorrow anyway, and while so far he'd avoided her questions about where he lived, or when they might see each other in the future, he knew he had much to tell her yet.

But for now, there were other, more immediate concerns, and they mostly revolved around a kiss. Both days he'd spent with her he'd longed to touch her. To feel her skin against his, to know what her hair would be like beneath his fingertips, but only now, under cover of darkness, did he finally feel free to make his move. "I wish to touch you. To *kiss* you," he amended, blushing furiously for some reason. He thrust his chest out. "I wish to kiss you, Kelsey Wells."

A playful gleam appeared in her blue eyes. "Not until you tell me where you're from."

He took another step closer, feeling his heart thunder beneath his ribs. "I think it is imperative that we kiss."

"Where are you *from,* Jareshk?" she asked. "*Really.* 'Cause you don't talk like the guys in Jackson, and I can't kiss you if I don't know. You keep not answering, and—"

He lifted his fingertips to her lips, brushing them lightly across her mouth. "I'm a visitor, like you."

"Only I'm visiting from, like, an hour away."

He glanced up at the dark night sky. "It's a bit farther to my home, yes."

"My money's still on the Soviet Union."

He studied her for a considering moment, assessing his options and strategy. If he told her the truth, it was unlikely he would get this kiss. But if he didn't, it seemed equally unlikely. Besides, he wanted her to know the truth.

He circled her, studying, calculating. The khaki-colored shorts she wore seemed no longer than his little finger. Her legs, on the other hand, seemed to go halfway to forever, all curves and shape, and just glancing at them made his pulse skitter. His whole body tightened, and he wondered if it was the result of these "cycles" he'd heard whispered about. Did he ache for Kelsey only because of something strange in his blood? Maybe humans didn't think this way at all. He felt inexplicably embarrassed, even as he felt powerfully aroused. Too aroused, he thought, with even more embarrassment.

She gave a nervous laugh. "You're looking at me funny."

"You are a child," he said, trying to argue with himself.

He shouldn't kiss her; she was too young, too human; yet he'd thought of little else for the past two days with her.

"Are you kidding? I'll be fourteen in another few weeks," she snapped, folding both arms across her chest, which only further emphasized her shapely—very *un*childlike—breasts. She was a woman. Maybe not completely, not any more than he was a man, but she was becoming one, and every cell within his Refarian body screamed that he should kiss her.

His mouth went dry. Blood rushed in his ears.

"I just want to be kissed, Jareshk. You're leaving and I'm leaving, and I've never been kissed before"—she took another step closer—"and, well, I want *you* to be my first kiss. But it's pretty simple. I want to know who you really are."

"You do know me."

"I mean, know who you really, truly are. I don't know that."

"Oh, Kelsey." He sighed, for in that moment, he knew he no longer had a choice.

"Oh, Jareshk," she teased him, stepping even closer. Her wonderful smile spread across her face, and by All's name, he *had* to kiss that mouth. He'd never been kissed either, but he wouldn't tell her that.

"I-I do wish to kiss you."

She gave a slight, encouraging bob of her head, the cascade of tight auburn curls bouncing as she did so.

Few touched him; few approached him—and certainly no one *ever* kissed the king. A droplet of rain fell on his cheek, but he ignored it, making his bold move. He'd led troops into battle already; he could handle this. The beating of his heart was worse than the night the Antousian brigade forces had cornered him in Trajsek.

Another few raindrops plopped against his face, but he brushed them away with the back of his hand. Now was the time. He bent low, seeking out her lips with his own mouth. Just a brush, a light feathering of touch. So warm, so soft as they met his. He lifted his hands and gently tipped her face upward. He kept his eyes open, because he wanted to see her expression; she had her own closed, giving herself up to him with perfect trust. On his planet, nobody trusted a near-stranger anymore. Only that was the confusing part: They weren't strangers.

Closing his eyes, he grew more intent, searching out her mouth with his tongue. He felt her hands reach upward, around his neck, her fingers running through his hair. Touching him! Caressing him! Oh, gods, he felt alive!

The kiss deepened, became hotter and deeper, and he closed his hand around her back, pulling her flush against him. Everything seemed to be swirling in around them; his power began to escalate, right in the core of his belly, and he shuddered, afraid of revealing himself. But he couldn't break the kiss—he wouldn't—but she did, pulling apart from him.

"Wh-what is that?" she asked, lifting her clear blue eyes to meet his. He shook his head, feeling fuzzy and swimmy and so aroused, all at once.

"I don't know what you mean."

She pointed upward, and as he followed with his eyes, more raindrops pelted him in the face. The transport had descended, was hovering directly overhead, silent, powerful. Purposed. He cursed in Refarian, then gazed back at her. "It's my transport. The elders have come to take me from here."

She began to shake in his arms, but clung to him. "Elders?" Her voice came out as a squeak. "Oh, God," she said, backing away from him. "You're definitely a visitor, all right." Her voice shook; her hands shook; her eyes were ringed with panic.

"I didn't want to frighten you," he said softly. "Never. I wished to keep you safe."

"Oh, my *God!* Oh, my God, oh, *God*," she babbled frantically, staring up at the transport carrier hovering directly over their heads. "I can't believe this. I just kissed you, and you're an alien. Oh, God, oh, God."

Her hand flew to her mouth, and she shoved him farther away. "You're going to go and never come back." He saw tears glint in her eyes.

He refused to let her push him out. "I *will* come back. I promise," he insisted. "I'll come for you." Then the ship descended much closer in the blink of an eye, hovering just above them.

Her gaze traveled upward, and her shaking intensified. "Y-you should have told me," she whispered, pointing to the sky. "Who are they?"

"My people. They only want me," he assured her. "They're not here to hurt you. You know there's no reason to be afraid of me, don't you, Kelsey?"

"You would never hurt me," she cried, and then with a pained sound she flung herself into his arms.

He paused long enough to bend down and kiss her full on the mouth again, this time bolder and deeper. With the elders bearing down on them, he knew what was coming: separation. And he knew what they both wanted—more of each other. He sensed the transport move even lower still, and as he pulled apart to stare into her eyes one last time, he made a decision. He would have Kelsey Wells as his own. Here, now, someday, she would belong to him completely, and he would give all of himself to her.

With an upward glance he made a second decision.

"Let's go," he commanded, as he would any of his troops under direct threat. He grabbed her hand and began running into the woods, leading her away from the ship.

"Where are we going?"

"Anywhere," he said, breathlessly drawing her into the dark, away from those who would separate them.

They ran for long moments, stumbling in the midnight woods. "My parents are going to freak." She laughed, and he tightened his grip around her hand.

"Please just run," he instructed, pulling her with him until there was only forest around them, and the only thing visible over their heads was the dark treetops.

He stopped, breathing heavily as he stared upward to confirm their safety. His people couldn't get a fix on his positioning now. "I was not yet ready to part from you."

"It's time for you to go," she answered, her voice heavy with sadness.

He would enter hyperspace later tonight, tunneling across the galaxies via an intricate network of wormholes and higher dimensions until he arrived home on Refaria in a matter of weeks. Thousands of light-years apart by her human comprehension, but not for his people, with their complex dimensional technology. He vowed then and there that he would return for her someday.

"I will find you," he promised.

"I'll just be a microscopic speck in your universe," she said, looking up toward the night sky even though above them were only the trees.

He smiled, reaching to wipe her tears. "Kelsey, there is a long-standing tie between our two worlds. I can't tell you more now, but I promise you that I will return one day. By then, you will probably have loved many human boys."

"No," she said firmly. "I don't think so."

He smiled. "You are young."

"Stop saying that!" she cried. "God, it's so annoying. You're not my father's age or anything."

He began to giggle, a strange sensation—rarely did he have the chance to laugh, but Kelsey often made him do so without even trying. "I want to show you something," he whispered, an idea growing inside of him. "Something that I want you to remember, no matter what."

She nodded, and he noticed that she shivered. "Here," he encouraged, opening his arms. "Come closer." She took another step nearer to him, and when she stood only slightly apart from him, he turned his right wrist over, allowing a silvery beam of light from his other hand to fall upon the bare skin. He felt the prickling of power, the spidery electricity of revelation—until, at last, his royal emblem appeared in the air, glowing and undulating in all its ancient mystery. It was the one sure proof of his lineage as king. He was the D'Aravni, marked as such from birth.

Kelsey's hand flew to her mouth as the bright, swirling mark moved in the air above his wrist, but she said nothing, only gaped at it. His eyes locked with hers for a brief moment, but then her gaze traveled back to his royal mark. "That's so beautiful," she whispered. "You are so beautiful."

He smiled, feeling his face flush. Something strange stirred inside of him, something that frightened him a little, a rush of desire that he'd never felt before, not even during these past two days with her. It made his hands tremble, but he resolved to keep his emblem open until she'd seen enough.

"Can I touch it?" she asked.

The heat in his body escalated again, causing the tremors to increase. He swallowed. "Yes."

She took a daring step closer, lifting her fingers gingerly to touch the shimmering, swirling mark of his power where it hovered in the air just over his wrist. First one finger, then another, until her whole hand skimmed over the surface of his energy, causing a thrill of desire to snake down his spine. Every time she touched his emblem, he felt it in his body. Everywhere. He gasped, allowing the mark to retract, pulling it back within his energy, and took hold of her. Without apology or thought, he kissed her again. His sweet, blessed human—he had to kiss her.

And she kissed him back; with everything inside of her, she opened to him, her tongue exploring his mouth, twining with his, her hands in his hair. She had to feel him—more of him—before he left her behind.

"Stop now," came a commanding voice from the darkness, slightly accented, just like Jareshk's. They sprang apart from each other, startled.

"My lord, you have made this difficult," the man said from the shadows. He spoke English, as Jareshk did with her, and as she tried to make out his face, Kelsey's heart thundered. What if this man wasn't good like Jareshk? What if he was the scary kind of alien?

"Councilor Aldorsk, you interrupt without request."

"We are overdue for departure, as my lord well knows."

"Who is he?" she whispered under her breath, but Jareshk brushed past her, touching her arm lightly in reassurance.

"Elder, I will return to the ship when my time here is done."

"You will return with me now, my lord."

In the silvered shadows, Kelsey could see the older man bow to Jareshk. She watched the discussion play out, terrified for her life, terrified at the thought of never seeing Jareshk again.

"I obey and serve the throne, my lord. You are jeopardizing your safety and your life here with this . . . young *theshta.*" The man waved in her direction dismissively.

"Speak of her with respect." Obviously *theshta,* whatever it meant, wasn't very complimentary.

Again, the man bowed, lower this time, placing what looked to be his hand over his heart, though in the darkness it was hard to be sure. "She is lovely, my king, and clearly kind to you, but your destiny beckons."

King? Why did he just call Jareshk a king?

The man stepped out of the shadows, and although she flinched to realize he was walking toward her, his eyes, once revealed by the moonlight, were not unkind. In fact, they were filled with a surprising amount of sympathy, which was probably why she felt she should trust him. She had to trust him; it was very, very important all of a sudden, just as it was critical for her to let him touch the top of her head, which the guy seemed to be doing, folding his pair of weathered hands around her forehead.

In the background, like a sailboat bobbing lazily along the horizon, she thought she heard Jareshk say something that sounded like, "Don't." *Why would he say that word?* she wondered sleepily. So heavy, so tired, so . . . ready to go home. What was she doing here? She glanced around her, and was surprised to find that she sat right in front of the lake. How had *that* happened? Last thing she remembered, she'd been asleep in the tent beside her mother.

With a jerk of her head, she glanced in every direction— first across the water, then up at the Tetons. The early pinkish light of dawn had begun to color the horizon; their campfire was cold. *How long have I been sitting here?* she wondered with a shiver. It made no sense whatsoever.

She must have been sleepwalking, she told herself, standing up to brush off her hands. That had to be it. But as she glanced down at her palms, they seemed to shine; not much, just the faintest bit, as if she'd dipped them in Day-Glo paint or something, like she'd done while working on the homecoming float last year.

Hmm, she thought with only a sluggish amount of curiosity. *Wonder how that happened?* And then she stumbled back toward the tent, ready to sleep for a very long time.

"Councilor Aldorsk, I command you to desist."

His mentor stared back at him, sadness in his aging eyes. "I must protect you, my king."

Jared knew then that the chief elder would not obey.

"Please don't," Jareshk asked simply, beseeching Aldorsk with his eyes. In horror he'd watched as Kelsey's memories of their time together had been wiped from her mind. If Aldorsk wiped his memories, too, he would never find his way back to her. It would be as if nothing had ever happened between them. Jareshk felt tears burn his eyes, and he paced the transport hallway. Must he be required to sacrifice even this? When he'd already given everything to serve his people?

He knew what would come next, felt the tendrils of his mentor's power already reaching into his mind. "Don't take her from me. Please, Aldorsk, I beg of you."

The elder's kind eyes grew pained. "Son," he said, clasping his shoulder, "the memory jeopardizes your safety. It links you with her."

"It was only a kiss!"

"A kiss that created a memory-bond between you and this human."

"Her name is Kelsey."

"My lord," his beloved councilor said, bowing, "there will be many young women . . . many kisses and far more than that. You are entering your first season; that's all that you are feeling. We can make arrangements to help you through this cycle safely. To meet your needs—"

"Don't *talk* to me about my season!" he roared, feeling his face burn at the mere mention of it. "I've not had such a thing. I will never cycle, not with someone of the council's choosing."

"Mating cycles are natural for your line, my lord. You know this, even if we've never discussed it openly."

Jareshk's stomach tightened with shame. "I will not cycle, not without Kelsey."

"She won't be the last."

"She's special," he whispered, his voice hoarse. "I don't want to forget her! I *need* to remember—I won't be able to find her if I forget."

"Your safety, my king, must always come first," Aldorsk said, inclining his head even as he closed his power around Jareshk's mind. "Forgive me, but you must forget."

Jareshk wanted to argue, to protest that he knew it wasn't his own safety, but rather the safety of the succession that the elders were so worried about. Oh, he wanted to cry out a great many things, but he could not seem to find his voice.

What did she look like? Oh, gods, he couldn't say. What color was her hair? No memory.

"Please," he implored, locking his power of intuition around one image, the only one he could seem to hold fast to, as all the others sifted away from him like sand in an hourglass. But what was it? He could not even say for sure. "I . . . beg you not to take her." He gasped, still seeking to lock on to something, *anything* that he could keep of her. There it was again! And this time he recognized the one image that Aldorsk couldn't seem to touch: her graceful human hand caressing his royal mark; then came another, of her in his arms, kissing him. Except there was a problem: The kiss was like quicksand, impossible to grasp, falling from him. If he could just recall her name, her eyes, anything! Then he could keep the memory of her; it would be *his,* untouchable. Permanent. Pure. Aldorsk's power tightened around his mind a second time, causing a flash of pain behind his eyes and a strange spasm of grief in his heart.

"There, my lord," Aldorsk soothed softly, gazing into his eyes. He dropped his hands back to his sides. "There, you are well."

"Am I?" Jareshk asked uncertainly, lifting a hand to his head. There was something precious he'd been trying so hard to remember. Wait—it was there, just below the surface, if only he could lay hold of it.

Aldorsk slipped one arm around his shoulder, walking him toward the transport elevator. "You will feel better once you rest, my king."

"Yes, undoubtedly."

"The trip to survey the mitres has been a heavy burden for you." As always, genuine concern filled Aldorsk's eyes. He'd been the closest thing to a father Jareshk had known since his own father's murder almost six years ago.

Jareshk stepped into the lift, nodding politely toward Aldorsk, but a spark of an image in his mind's eye made him stop the closing doors with his palm. A delicate hand, touching his mark. He never revealed his mark to anyone. That image was chased quickly by another, more startling one: He was kissing a woman with dark red hair. He had never kissed anyone!

Aldorsk stared at him expectantly. "My lord?"

Jareshk's head felt fuzzy, as if his memories and thoughts were suddenly expanding far too much to fit inside his brain. Had he been thinking of something? He wasn't even sure.

"I'm to bed," he said with a laugh. "I've no idea what I was going to say."

Then, like a butterfly flickering aimlessly on to its next flower, the memory of that kiss—that tender, stolen, *unforgettable* kiss—floated into the burning sun.

Chapter One

In the northern portion of the Teton Range stood a mountain as proud and immovable as the man whose revolution hid within its depths. In the grand scheme of the area, it seemed an unspectacular thing. Too small to interest climbers, too low to stand above its siblings in the region, the mountain's jagged face rose, nevertheless, in simple defiance of its averageness. It had the countenance of a warrior, with craggy heights shaped by time and element. Concealing a network of tunnels and machinery, it was Jared Bennett's most important base, crucial to the rebellion he housed within its shadow.

Today, Jared was inspecting one minuscule piece of that vast military framework, staring across a large hangar filled with a fleet of fighters his engineers had spent the past nine months testing. Sleek and black, the planes had moved stealthily along Earth's surface in test flights that had taken his pilots from California to Japan and onward over to Europe, then back across the East Coast of this country they called their temporary home.

A hydraulic lift approached, sounding warning beeps as it backed up to one plane's side. Jared's engineers stood back, waiting, as always, for their commander's approval. He mounted the steps, climbing upward toward the craft's cockpit. For a moment, he appraised the plane's design, appreciating its powerful styling.

"Tight little things, aren't they?" Jared remarked to one of the engineers, running his fingertips over the dull black surface of the wing. His deep voice echoed off the hangar's ceiling, which stood a good forty feet overhead.

His chief engineer stepped forward and smiled, obviously pleased with the praise. "We've worked hard on the design," the man said, releasing the hatch with the flick of a switch on his handheld control. "Room for two, but still light enough to go long distances without refueling."

Jared stared into the open cockpit, itching to take the craft out for a test. Even after some harrowing recent engagements, the fighter in him still needed to get off the ground again—and soon. He reached out an appreciative hand to stroke the buttery-soft leather of the pilot's seat. "Comfortable too," he said with an admiring nod.

From the cement floor below, Scott Dillon glared up at him, and he could read the warning that flared in his friend's eyes: *Don't go getting any ideas, Commander.* If his lieutenant had his way, Jared would never go up again, but that simply wasn't an option. Not only did their strategy necessitate his involvement; he also refused to be grounded like some figurehead.

Jared hoisted himself up onto the side of the craft, and was already planting one booted foot inside when his intelligence commander, Thea Haven, trotted across the hangar toward him. From the expression on her face, he could tell long before she reached him that there was a serious problem, and he swung back down to face her.

"The elders have gathered," she announced, standing at ease after he returned her salute. "They're calling you to chambers, sir."

"The occasion?" He glanced across the hangar toward the darkened assembly room where he always met with his council. Nervousness shot through his heart; the elders never convened unless something truly serious warranted it.

Thea's blue gaze darted toward Scott, and Jared had the sense that his two commanders had already discussed the matter. She seemed ready to tell him more, but then inclined her head respectfully. "Sir, they wait for you," was all she said.

Jared took his place in the data portal, sliding into the large, thronelike chair, and immediately the sensory scan of his vitals began. First his cornea, the red filter light sweeping over both of his eyes. Then, as he flattened his palms on the electrode pads, he felt a slight tingling as his fingerprints and energy readings were verified. For an answering moment, there was only the quiet hum of data renewal, and he allowed his eyes to drift shut, fighting back the wave of anxiety that meeting with his council always evoked.

In the darkened chamber, the council members began to appear in a semicircle about him. Not literally—they were, of course, back on Refaria. But thanks to technology that accessed energy packets flowing faster than the speed of light, he and the elders were able to interact in these chambers in real time, even across the vast distance that separated them. Reflexively his fingers tightened around the metallic arm of his chair. In turn, each elder made the traditional sign of respect: a slight bow, then one hand over the heart, a proud yet reverent stance. And he damned well hated it; he always did. Still, someone along the way—perhaps Scott, or maybe Thea, he wasn't sure—had reminded him that the people needed the traditions, even if he did not require them. Even if he did not want them.

Once the full council had surrounded him, he shifted in his chair in an effort to make himself comfortable, then invited them to speak.

The chief elder, Aldorsk, who had once advised his father, stepped forward into a clear beam of silvery light. "My lord," he began, his voice scratchy as he spoke slowly in their native tongue, "I feel certain you know the reason why we gather today. Indeed, you must."

Oh, indeed. He had hoped it wasn't true, but based on the furtive glances shared between Scott and Thea, he'd been pretty damned sure. Scowling, he waved for the man to continue, but said nothing.

"With all respect, the council feels the need to remind our leader that he has no heir."

"Your leader has no position," he countered, crossing one long leg over the other uncomfortably. If they wanted to force him onto a throne, couldn't they at least create one to accommodate his full height? "Your leader," he reminded all eight of them, his voice curt, "helms a small, fractured rebellion on an alien planet."

A hushed cry swept the room, heard even across the great intergalactic distance that separated them. "You underestimate the situation," the head councilman answered softly. "Need I remind you that the mitres are nearly opened? The tide in this war turns daily."

Unable to help himself, Jared released a rough growl of frustration, closing his eyes against the image of the elders gathered before him. "I am a warrior, not a king," he replied, wrestling to regain his patience. "I do not intend to take a mate."

"My lord, you have but five years left in your fertile time." This remark came from Dalnè, the youngest council member. Leave it to a woman to speak so frankly about his approaching infertility. "That is, *if* we are fortunate. Perhaps less than that."

"You make your leader sound quite inexperienced." He laughed, working to deflect the council's efforts at persuasion. "As if he does not know his own body."

"Sir, it has nothing to do with . . ." Dalnè's words trailed to nothing, and she glanced anxiously at the others for help.

Jared chose to take the lead. "I am no virgin, and do not require these *lessons* that the council seems determined to issue."

Aldorsk stepped forward, attempting to placate him. "My lord, we mean no—"

Jared continued. "I also know that any other Refarian male would have at least ten years left in his fertile time." He yielded a coarse rumble. "Perhaps fifteen. Your leader possesses a finicky, problematic bloodline, does he not?"

Blushing, Dalnè made a low bow. "Forgive me for saying what you'd rather not hear, sir." One look into Councilor Dalnè's eyes revealed her extreme agitation. It couldn't be an enjoyable task, reminding him that his fertility approached an end—and at such a relatively young age. Of course, if his council knew that he'd never passed through so much as a single mating cycle, their concerns would be greatly magnified. Mate or no mate, he should at least have experienced the fever by now; after all, at thirty, such was common for those of his line.

With a cough, he made a polite change of subject. "Dalnè, what is the weather like at Mareshtakes today?" As she glanced over her shoulder, he could imagine that she gazed out a window at their council's hidden encampment back on Refaria.

"The sun shines bright, sir," Dalnè answered with a cautious smile. "The temperature is mild, breezy."

Tilting his head backward, he tried to picture his beloved ocean, restless and rolling with waves. He could smell the brine so clearly, his heart physically tightened with the memory of it. He repeated her words like a prayer. "The sun shines bright."

"It is middle day at the moment," she continued. "Cloudless, and the tide ebbs low."

A wistful smile passed his lips. "Ah, Mareshtakes was always most beautiful at low tide." That was when the rocks could be seen, refracting the sunlight in all their glorious, prismatic color.

Six years, and he'd not been home. Six years, and he'd led this revolution from Earth, never looking back. With the war's escalation, this alien planet had been deemed the safest place for him, hidden far from his enemies back on Refaria. But he'd grown weary of the campaigns; weary enough that he did long for a mate sometimes, but not on their terms. They had but one woman in mind for him, his second cousin and trusted lieutenant, Thea Haven.

Narrowing his eyes, he allowed his gaze to travel the semicircle. "Make note of one thing," he said, his voice tightening over the words. "I do not intend to bond with Thea. Nor do I intend to mate at all."

A rumble of objection and argument erupted, but he disengaged from the portal, decisively silencing their complaints. He had listened, which was all they required of him; in the end, the decision fell to him, and his decision stood. To remain alone was the only choice for a wartime commander.

Chapter Two

The Wyoming sun slipped low on the horizon, the mountains forming long winter shadows over the lake area where Kelsey Wells studied the results of the day's geological research. *What is my next step?* she asked herself, mentally reexamining the data for the umpteenth time. She walked the length of the trail, counting off each of her steps between the scrappy, snow-dusted pines. Somewhere, here in the sedimented layers beneath her feet, had to be the answer to her puzzle, and with it the final touches for her graduate thesis.

She had first come camping here as a teenager with her parents—a few years before her mother's death, and long before her father had dragged them off to live in D.C., the hub of his political consulting universe. Ever since those earliest days, she had felt drawn to the rough-hewn terrain of this particular part of Yellowstone, almost as if this one corner of the land she loved so dearly held extra sway. No matter what she did, or how many varied landscapes she studied as a geologist, images of the Tetons' perfect reflection in the bowl of Mirror Lake beckoned her. They filled her dreams, and haunted the subconscious threads of her waking life with a pervasive sense of melancholy that she could never quite understand.

Then roughly a year ago she'd come camping here with friends from the university. That was when she had noticed a strange pigmentation to the rocks on the lake's eastern shore, and when she'd followed the trail deeper into the woods, more questions had emerged. She'd grown up here, in Yellowstone, studying the formations and tar pits and spewing geysers, and those childhood experiences had influenced her studies as a geologist. These days Kelsey spent a great deal of her life staring at the ground—was in fact more attuned to her natural environment than to the buildings in downtown Laramie or to cars or to clothing, or sometimes even to people. So when she found a potential anomaly such as the formations here at Mirror Lake, she couldn't let it go.

"Whoa, Kelse," came Ethan's familiar voice from down by the lake's shore. "Found something here! Come look." Ethan was her closest friend in the geology department. Although a self-professed science geek like herself, he certainly didn't look the part, not with his wavy blond hair and pale gray eyes and lean snowboarder's physique. The Ethan package was definitely appealing. And she knew he liked her—wanted something more than friendship—but for some inexplicable reason, she couldn't seem to shake the feeling that someone else was waiting for her. Not that she'd *found* that somebody yet, but she could never give up the nagging hope.

She trotted several yards along the shore and met him partway.

"Look at this," he announced, extending a shiny bit of silvered metal. "What do you make of this sample?"

She drew in a breath of cold mountain air. "That's strange," she agreed, seeing the way it glinted in the late-afternoon sun.

"Looks like mica," he said, scrunching his eyebrows together quizzically.

She finished his thought. "But it's denser." Scraping it into her sample bag, she marked the substance UNKNOWN and added notations regarding the time and exact location. Ethan bent back over his filter tray, sifting anew.

"You ever hear back on those samples from last month?" he asked.

"Still waiting on the lab results."

Ethan glanced across the lake, shivering as he stared into the setting sun. "We better go soon," he said, zipping his coat. "Getting cold out here. It'll be dark before long. Don't you want to go make our campfire?" They'd planned to spend the night, two scientists on a mission, but as the day wore on she noticed that he kept mentioning their tent sharing with far more enthusiasm than a mere scientific expedition warranted.

"You go ahead," she said, glancing at the shadowed mountains across the lake. Something in their stark features felt unexpectedly eerie—familiar in a way that had nothing to do with her visits to this lakeside terrain over the past year. The mountains' rugged visage, rising upward toward the setting sun, felt like a lost language that she'd once spoken fluently. She shivered, still staring, almost mesmerized.

Ethan waved a hand in front of her eyes—she'd not even realized that her thoughts had drifted so far away. "Sorry," she said, laughing in embarrassment. "I was just thinking about . . ." She didn't want to share her unsettling sense of déjà vu with Ethan.

"A boyfriend?" he prompted, his gray eyes narrowing with undisguised possessiveness.

"No." She wanted to spare his feelings; yet she had to be honest. "But Ethan, you and I are *only* friends. You do know that?"

"Sure, Kelsey," he agreed, his shoulders slumping slightly as he turned up the trail that led into the trees and toward their camp. "Course."

But then, right as he was about to vanish around the bend, he turned back. "You know, Kelse," he said. "Maybe one day you'll get tired of waiting for a guy who doesn't exist and notice the one who's right here in front of you."

He made it sound so easy to stop yearning for a soul mate, she thought as she faced the lake, letting Ethan slip away. She'd had a soul mate once—or so she'd thought. A young intern in her father's political consulting firm. That had been the only time Kelsey had actually let herself become part of the whole D.C. scene. Until one night when she walked in on Jamie and another of her father's employees, Jamie's pants down to his ankles, with the other woman wrapped around him like her very own totem pole. Kelsey had never looked back. Except to regret giving Jamie Watson the gift of her virginity. That was one gift she would have saved for someone exceptional if she had only known; even so, she often pretended that it was still hers to give.

*   *   *

Sleep came in fitful bouts for the first few hours. Ethan squished up against her back like a nylon caterpillar, and she continually edged away until her nose pressed against the tent surface, leaving her cold and lonely. Not only was he a space invader, but Ethan snored too, the loud, staccato kind that sounded like a gunshot nearly every time she managed to drift into sleep.

Still, dreams pressed closer, and so did images of the woods around them; of her running through them in a white gossamer gown, bright as fairy wings. And of a man too, following her, chasing after her. When she spun to face him, he glowed like her gown—bright, magical, tall as a mountain. She whispered his name, something foreign and strange; then he reached to touch her cheek, his fingers burning her face.

She woke in a cold sweat, shivering and fevered all at once. Lifting a hand to her face, she realized that it felt warm, as though from someone's touch. As if the forest man had truly chased her in her dreams, blessing her with kisses and that strange name of his.

Maybe it was the dream that beckoned her. Or maybe it was her curiosity about the night sky over Mirror Lake. Whatever called her, Kelsey dressed and drifted out of the tent, ignoring the mist that folded over the midnight darkness. Drawn down to the shore, she stared up at the clear sky overhead, a dazzling tapestry of lights. Moments like this made her wish she'd studied astronomy instead of geology. Beneath the full moon, the landscape gleamed, the snow-encrusted mountains jutting skyward like crystals.

Plopping onto the frozen earth, Kelsey huddled, her warm breath clouding in front of her face. *Expectant.* That was what she felt, blowing into her cupped hands to warm herself. Something about that dream had moved her, she realized, left her anticipating the extraordinary.

Drawing her knees close to her chest, she watched the sky. The Leonids were visible right now, as they always were in mid-November. Maybe she'd catch a glimpse of a dusty-tailed meteor shower, she thought with a smile.

And that was when she heard the blast—a loud, explosive sound that she thought might have been a sonic boom, and yet she knew it had to be something much greater. After the initial thunderclap, what looked like jets shot over the mountains rimming the lake's other side. Strange jets, she thought, rising to her feet. Maybe stealth fighters? Black and ominous in shape, barely visible in the night sky, they blasted across the water like a pair of twin phantoms from hell. Then they were gone, leaving a cacophonous trail in their wake, a litany of thunderclaps that still echoed off the silent landscape.

Did the fighter jets cause the explosion? she wondered, studying the mountains again. The park was a no-fly zone, but maybe the government was testing some new equipment out here in this remote area. They'd been known to do that, and it wouldn't surprise her. Still, the suddenness of it—and at nearly midnight—didn't quite add up. Besides, those jets had been moving faster than it was possible for anything she'd ever heard of to move.

That was when she saw it: a darting light just over the water, glowing like a boat's headlights. Squinting, she tried to make out the shape. It seemed to agitate, shooting first in one direction, then another, then back toward the shore where she stood.

And then the shape intensified, looming large as it made unexpected landfall, and she found herself face-to-face with a blazing wall of energy. No, she realized, not energy: a being of sorts. She gasped, staring up at him—and everything within her understood that this *being* was most definitely masculine. She thought of Ethan, asleep back in the tent, and hoped he'd heard something, that maybe he could help her. Save her. Stumbling backward, she tried to cry out, but was too terrified to form any words.

Still, she heard in her mind, like a distant whisper. *Be still.* In immediate response, her breathing came under control. She had to get to Ethan. But that thought fled her mind as the being moved closer, and she felt his energy burn low within her, like molten lava, something ancient and primal and foreign and innocent all at once. No face, no arms, no body. Only the lovely golden fire of him.

"Who are you?" She gasped. In response he retreated, the wall becoming more compact and intense. Less open. "I won't hurt you," she promised softly, terrified, but somehow desperate to keep him there all the same.

He released a quiet reverberating noise in reply, one that

she wasn't sure how to interpret. "I-I don't . . ." She hesitated, aware that breathing had become nearly impossible. "I don't understand what you're saying." When his rumbling grew louder, more forceful, she began to back away, twisting her ankle on a rock behind her. Falling backward, she stared up at him.

He had her cornered. It might be where he wanted her. Towering large, he loomed closer, and she pressed her eyes shut.

The warm sensation in her abdomen intensified, spreading through her legs, her arms, all the way up into her chest. Tentatively, she opened one eye. Was this his way of communicating with her?

A stillness resounded in the center of her being, bringing peace with it. She knew then that he wouldn't hurt her—she was certain. He couldn't possibly hurt her.

"Tell me what you want," she insisted, inching backward on the ground, trying to put more physical distance between the two of them.

Then, before her very eyes, his form began to change, drawing inward as it shimmered into the slowly solidifying image of a man. When his transformation finished, before her huddled a beautiful, black-haired man, staring back at her with dark eyes, wide-set and soulful, accentuated by high cheekbones.

Each gaped at the other for what seemed endless moments, Kelsey fearing even to blink. Her stranger wore all black—some kind of uniform—with a thick bulletproof vest. He dressed like a soldier, and as he searched her face, he obviously made calculations. Could she be trusted? Should he reveal more of himself? As he studied her, though, the wariness in his expression vanished, replaced instead by the flicker of deep recognition. She shivered, and not just because she had the sense that this stranger knew her—but rather because she felt he'd *always* known her.

But then his labored breathing grew more extreme, his eyes rolling back briefly into his head. Something was wrong with the man: Blood seeped from a huge gash across his brow. Lifting a hand, he touched the wound, then stared down at sticky red blood on his fingertips.

"I don't believe it," he half whispered, shaking his head. He seemed stunned, confused, but also very aware of his predicament.

"You don't believe *what?*" she cried, her eyes growing wide with a mixture of confusion and fear. Her words seemed to weaken him, and he bent lower, scrabbling at the earth with his open hand.

"Kelsey." He gasped hoarsely. "I won't . . . hurt you."

"No, see, how do you know my name?" she demanded, struggling to breathe as she rose to her feet. At least she could gain the physical advantage that way. "There's no way you can know my name."

The dark eyes opened, lifting to meet her own, and she saw kindness there. Unsurpassed strength. "You are Kelsey Wells," he answered, reaching a hand to his shoulder. That was when she saw the deep wound there—his left arm was nearly severed from his body, and dangled, useless, at his side.

"What happened to you?" she asked, stepping closer despite her self-protective instincts. "You're really hurt. Badly."

Her assessment seemed to steal some of his life force, and he almost collapsed, but caught his hand on the ground between them. "Too weak," he whispered. "Too weak. Can't hold form." Then suddenly the man vanished, replaced by the bright wall of energy. Only this time the glow seemed to have faded somewhat. Was he dying?

"Please," she said, drawing closer, wanting, oddly enough, to reassure the stranger. "Tell me who you are. What you are. I want to help."

Not safe. The words sounded within her mind. Glancing around them, she shivered.

"No, no," she insisted, lifting a hand to shield her eyes against his brightness. "You *are* safe with me."

Was he afraid of her? He didn't seem afraid, but as she opened her hands, he withdrew sharply. *No!* she heard him say, clear as a thunderclap within her mind. *No, not touch!*

"Okay," she agreed, taking a tentative step closer, until she stood almost at the water's frigid edge. "Okay, I won't touch you."

Never touch.

Still, she did want to touch him, burned to do it, as irrational as that thought was. She ached for more of his heat, for more of the fire he had unleashed deep inside of her body, and it seemed that touching was the only way to have more of him.

As if reading her thoughts, he again warned, *Never touch me.* Still, he edged cautiously closer.

A strange wave of defiance overcame her. "Why not?" she asked, tilting her face toward his brightness, forcing her eyes open.

Because . . . could hurt you.

"No," she said, answering on instinct, shaking her head. "I don't believe you would ever hurt me." *How can I know that?* She wasn't sure, but the certainty settled as a firm, substantial peace inside of her heart.

In reply, he released a panting sound, a rattled gasp for breath, his energy visibly dimming in reaction.

Heart pounding, Kelsey took a step closer, ignoring his warnings. "Who's after you?" she asked, searching across the water. "Please. Maybe I can help."

Silence, gasps, desperate breathing. Then, *Yes.* That was the last thing she heard before she felt him enter her. Felt him, like a fanning breeze across her skin, unobtrusive, tender, apologetic.

Nothing in her twenty-eight years had come close to the sensations she instantly experienced. She sensed him move quickly within her, felt her chest tighten, her whole body tremble. Like burning fingers, he caressed all the way into her very core. "Amazing," she whispered, wondering how he maintained a distance of at least four feet yet seemed somehow to enter her body simultaneously. But then, he spoke within her mind, so why should this surprise her?

Touching her abdomen, she felt his fire build there, and she cried out in response, sliding to the ground. "Please," she moaned, lying back on the earth, feeling him everywhere. God, he'd set her on fire, teasing her toward an unseen edge. Like some erotic torturer, he kept setting her ablaze, but he begged for her silence.

Danger here, he cautioned hoarsely; then all the heat and intensity of his touch flamed cold. Done. He'd finished with her. As quickly as he'd begun something she might dream about until the end of her days, he had withdrawn himself from inside of her.

Staggering to her feet, she reached toward him, but he spun from her, diminishing to the smallest of radiant lights. From above she heard a quiet whirring sound, and as her gaze lifted, she glimpsed a large cloaked craft almost visible against the dark night sky. It came so stealthily, so imperceptibly, she would never have spotted the thing if not for the dull humming sound that accompanied it.

And then, just like that, he soared out of sight, swallowed into the belly of the craft. The ship lifted, leaving her on the shore, and she raised her arms, still trying to reach him. He'd been inside of her, touched a yearning place where no other man had ever been—yet he'd never once allowed her to touch him in return.

"Please, sir!" came a shout.

"Out of the way!" thundered another, a voice Jared recognized as one of the medics'. A group of them knotted around where he'd collapsed on the transport floor, carefully maintaining a safe perimeter apart from him. His energy ebbed low and cool—a fact that had to be obvious to every one of the soldiers on the cruiser.

Scott Dillon's worried face appeared in his line of sight. "Jared, what happened?" his best friend demanded, kneeling low beside him.

But he didn't even possess the strength to reply. Refarian words flew about the deck, panicked cries for their fallen leader, but he hardly heard them, the pain had become so overpowering.

Yet in his delirium he remembered the girl. A human girl, maybe a woman, though younger than he. *How could she not have been frightened?* She had no idea who or what he was, but had opened herself completely. *Uncharacteristic for a human,* he thought, *but not uncharacteristic for her.* He absolutely knew it to be an essential part of her nature—but *how?* His thoughts were too confused by his injuries. Focusing his energy inward, he fought to shift back into material form.

"No, Jared," Scott urged. "Stay like you are. You're too weak to shift."

"Sir, we'll work on you this way," one of the medics assured him, but Jared was no fool—he knew that his natural form was all but impossible to treat. The sooner he could shift, the sooner they'd save him.

"Have to," he murmured weakly. "Have to change."

"If you change," Scott explained in a fierce voice, "it might kill you, Jared. Don't. Let them work on you first."

Even after so many battles and firefights, their leader's safety was sacred to these soldiers, and a hush fell over every last one of them. Finally, he sighed his assent, still thinking of the human on the earth below them. She'd offered to help, and he'd accepted—but in doing so, he'd seen things inside of her that even *she* had no idea were there. Things he doubted he'd forget anytime soon.

On the periphery of his mind, Jared sensed the vanishing darkness below—and sensed *her* there, innocent arms still outstretched. *Gods,* he marveled, feeling consciousness ebb, *the human wanted to touch me.* More than life itself, it was what she'd wanted, and she'd hardly been afraid, even though she had many reasons to be. That kind of bravery was rare in any species.

And he'd wanted to touch her back; even injured and close to dying, he'd been more than aware of that fact. So alien, so incompatible with him in every possible way, but he'd wanted every touch that she offered him.

"Next time you do that," Scott swore, pacing the length of Jared's bedroom, "I'm out of here. Or I'll kill you myself, and take the Antousians' bounty as a bonus."

"Those weren't Antousians," Jared said, closing his eyes. The cool pillow against his cheek was a welcome relief both from the excruciating physical pain and from his best friend's tirade.

"Then who the hell were they?"

"Our buddies from over at Warren."

Scott paused at the foot of Jared's bed, surprised. "Air force?"

Jared rubbed a weary hand across his burning eyes. "They caught me flying out of Mirror Lake."

"They don't know about that site," Scott argued. "Never have."

"Apparently"—Jared sighed, thinking of the hotshot pilots who had missile-locked him last night—"they do now."

Neither spoke for several moments as the serious implications of last night's events became clear. To say that Mirror Lake was crucial to their revolution would be a drastic understatement. The best of their technology had remained hidden there for at least two centuries. Protecting the mitres ranked above life itself for every last one of them fighting in this war.

At the foot of the bed Scott paced, hands behind his back, deep in thought. Finally, he said in a hushed voice, "And so they know."

Jared nodded, blistering pain shooting through his shoulder. Scott noticed him flinching as he sat up in bed. "You had no business going out on that mission, sir."

Jared hesitated, not wanting to offend his second in command. "There was no one else I'd have given the job to."

Scott's face flushed hot. "Oh, really now?"

"I couldn't risk your life," Jared continued, telling the truth. "*I* was the one."

Scott's tense voice softened. "And if you'd died out there last night?"

"You're more than capable of leading, Scott," Jared answered, feeling older than he had in a long time. The constant warfare and uncertainty of his life as leader of their rebellion had begun to take their toll on him—and on his weathered body. At thirty years old, he yearned for rest, for a peace he'd not been born into. By his tenth birthday he'd been a reluctant leader, and by his eighteenth, a fearsome warrior. Lately, though, all the years of fighting had begun to wear him down.

"Last night was"—Jared hesitated, thinking of how easily the air force jets had overtaken him—"a mistake. It won't happen again." He'd been growing careless lately, and even if Scott wouldn't say as much, he knew it was true.

Pulling a chair up beside the bed, Scott straddled it. "Tell me what went down out there."

Pressing his eyes shut, Jared willed the blinding headache to subside. Images of being shot down—his craft rolling and pitching beneath him, the black earth rising quickly—assaulted him. He'd shifted then and there, before his physical form grew too traumatized, but not before a jagged piece of the craft's torn hull had slammed him hard in the face. Not before the same piece had managed to tear through his shoulder. And those wounds had repercussions on his most basic molecular level, no matter what form he assumed. The medics had healed him, but he would always bear the hidden scars, just as he did all the others.

"There was a woman," he answered, ignoring Scott's original question. "Kelsey Wells. Her name is Kelsey Wells. She lives in Laramie. She's a student there. I want more information."

Scott studied him as he might an Antousian wellabung: one part interest, one part amusement, many parts disgust. But he would never challenge his leader. "Okay," he answered simply.

"She's critical to us now," Jared continued, even though he knew it was only partially true. *They* needed her, yes, but Jared's personal interests ran deep as well. *Far too human for you, far too unaware of this war,* his inner voice cautioned, even as another part of himself—the lonely warrior—ached for what he had felt as they formed a connection last night. For all that he'd glimpsed inside the rare woman, her strength, her beauty, her tenaciousness.

Scott drew his chair closer beside the bed. "Why?"

"I had to do it," Jared confessed, staring at the pine ceiling overhead. "I had no other choice."

"I'm not getting this, Jared."

"I bonded with her," he admitted softly, closing his eyes. "There on the shore last night."

"You *what?*" his captain roared.

"I had no choice," Jared repeated, fighting the headache that swelled behind his eyes.

"No choice but to form a bond with an alien, *sir?*" Scott cried. "In a *war zone?*"

"I had dismantled the codes from the mitres," he explained, and Scott's eyes widened, bright as lasers, the seriousness of the situation fully coming clear. They'd been working on the codes for at least two years. "They nearly captured me," Jared continued. "It's never been so close. They had me, but I think they knew the woman was there. I know they'll be back, looking for me. They might even question her."

"So she has them now? The codes?" Scott asked in a cautious voice.

"All of them, yes." Jared felt terrible guilt well within

him. What a thing he'd done to her, and he'd never even asked her permission.

"Then damn straight we need to locate her," Scott thundered. "Because I'm getting that data back."

Jared reached out a hand, clasping Scott by the forearm. "No," he commanded. "You will not. It stays inside the woman for now."

Scott's dark eyes narrowed, gleaming with an almost supernatural energy. "Why?"

"Because it's safer that way," Jared explained, leaning back into the pillows, "and so is she."

"She?" Scott sniffed the air in disdain. "You're worried for the human's safety?"

"She might have saved my life last night," he said. "And right now, she's the only one protecting the mitres. For that, I owe her everything. We all do."

Chapter Three

Kelsey slid several geological samples across Dr. Carrington's desk. "They're from Mirror Lake," she explained. "I need to know if there's anything unusual about them."

Carrington's warm eyes fixed on her. Kelsey was his star student in the graduate geology program, and he almost always took her seriously, but today she glimpsed doubt in his weathered face. "Kelsey, I'm not saying I don't believe you—" he began, but she cut him off.

"I did see something there."

"Even if you did," he continued, "what makes you think you'll find sedimentary proof?"

She thought of trying to explain her hunch, as outlandish as it would seem—but decided against it. "Could we just send this most recent batch in for testing?" she tried again, her voice filled with undisguised frustration. "Then maybe you'll come out there with me."

He nodded. "What if you do find something, Kelsey?" he asked. "What then?"

Recalling the stranger by the lake—the way he'd affected her—she could only shake her head. "I'm not sure what I'll do," she said. "But I have to know who he was."

"He?" Dr. Carrington asked in surprise, but she hurried from his office without answering further, bustling past a tall man with black eyes, who, for a moment, gave her a kind of pause. When she turned back, no one stood in the hallway at all. With a shiver, she walked onward down the polished floors, the echo of her footsteps the only sound behind her.

* * *

"She's been taking rock and soil samples," Scott said, watching Jared across the meeting table where the mitres drawings were spread. "Turned them in to one of her professors."

Jared lifted his eyes, and Scott answered his unspoken question. "She's a geology student."

Jared nodded, turning his attention back to the schematics. They'd paid for these blueprints with blood many times over, smuggling them out of the Antousian-controlled borderlands. All in hopes of gaining access to hidden Refarian technology—technology that could turn the tide in the war that waged on their own planet, and had spilled over onto Earth in the past six years. Technology left here two hundred years ago, at a time when many of the Antousians had still been their allies.

Jared studied the various chambers, the mapped catacombs, but his mind strayed again. Back to the human. All his life he'd been set apart; few spoke to him without filtering every word, which meant that few truly touched his soul. Yet she'd opened to him—and easily. *Oh, far too innocent for this conflict,* he chided himself, thinking of what a gift such innocence would be. *And far too alien.*

Should he ever form a match, there would be expectations. And, by the gods, he knew what they were, as surely as he saw Thea eyeing him from across the meeting room. Giving her blond curls a flirtatious toss, she smiled. He frowned back at his cousin, and repressed the urge to growl his dismay aloud. Equal match or not, he could never feel anything for his fellow soldier. Beautiful to a fault, she left his hot Refarian blood ice-cold, no matter how many times his council urged their mating.

"Jared," Scott snapped, glaring at his leader. "Are you listening?" No other person in their midst would dare speak to him so audaciously. But Scott was practically his brother, and knew the boundaries he could push.

"You're still angry," Jared observed.

Scott snorted, leaning over the plans. "Stop watching Thea and pay attention to what I'm saying."

This time he did growl. "Thea doesn't interest me."

"So you've said, sir." Scott inclined his head respectfully. "What's that supposed to mean?"

Scott leaned back in his seat, staring out at the woods beyond the full windows. "There's fear for your life."

Jared folded his arms over his chest defiantly. "Always has been."

"No, Jared." Scott leaned close until his piercing eyes blazed like lasers. "These chances you've taken lately have left fears within the people."

"The people," Jared repeated dully, sensing the direction this conversation was headed.

"The council."

Jared blew out a furious sigh. "I have little patience for the council."

"If you do not marry—do not have children—the line ends with you."

"The people don't need a figurehead," he argued softly, glancing again toward Thea. "They need a leader. And a leader doesn't need a lifemate." He believed strongly that he should remain unattached and focused strictly on military leadership. In fact, the thought of marrying anyone always felt *wrong*, on the most fundamental level. "I remain purposeful in my intentions."

"Then why do you keep dwelling on the human?"

Jared shuddered, staring back at his best friend, who fixed a wry smile on him. *Blast Scott and his soul gazing,* Jared mentally cursed.

Scott wasn't going to back away from the topic, however. "Well, sir?" he pressed, tapping his finger on the meeting table for emphasis.

"I will *not* marry," Jared snapped, "and if you hear rumors from the council again, tell them as much." He rose to leave, feeling his hands tremble and his heart race beneath his ribs.

"They don't know about the human," Scott answered in a low voice. "I'm asking as your friend."

Jared paced the length of the pine-paneled meeting room, raking his open palm over his short hair. It bristled beneath his fingertips, still an unfamiliar sensation. Until recently, he'd worn it long, but had wearied of the constant feel of it around his face, and so had shaved his head. It had grown out some, but not completely. He stopped before the large fireplace and studied the licking flames and the

smoldering embers beneath. The banked fire steered his
thoughts again in the direction of the human. Kelsey Wells.
He spun the name in his mind, liking the sound of it. He'd
encountered many of her kind in his tenure on Earth, many
young women with nubile, arousing bodies. Many Refarian
women, as well, who would have taken to his bed without
argument, but there was something *familiar* about her that
transcended the bond they'd formed on the shore, something that had been perplexing him ever since.

His gaze traveled upward to the fireplace mantel, where
someone had placed fresh winter flowers. Narcissus, they
were called. Life, even in this cold, forbidding landscape.
That was it, he realized, his ordinarily serious face breaking
into a full smile. Kelsey had aroused something he thought
dead in his heart. He spun to face Scott, who sat at the
polished meeting table, waiting.

"This Kelsey Wells . . ." Jared paused, trying to find the
words, and thought of how she'd opened to him. How trust-
ing she'd been—how unafraid, even in the face of obvious
danger. Her brave innocence had thawed something cold
in him, something he thought the Antousians had killed
long ago. "She made me feel alive," he said, planting one
worn boot on the brick hearth. "Very alive, I'm afraid."

Scott's dark eyebrows shot upward in amusement.
"While you were nearly dying?"

"Strange, I know."

Scott leaned back in his chair, studying Jared. "Maybe it
was all a hallucination."

Jared shook his head. "She opened to me."

"She did not."

"Scott," Jared insisted, voice rising as he crossed the
room and took his seat at the table again. "I *bonded* with
her."

"So you told me," Scott said with a roll of his brown
eyes. "All for a data transfer."

"It was something more," Jared explained hoarsely. He
dropped his voice much lower, so none of the others would
dare hear—especially not Thea. "It wasn't just me, Scott,"
he explained. "I think, well, that . . . we bonded *together*."

"Commander," Scott whispered, leaning close across the
table. "Were you insane?" Both men knew the significance

of a two-way bond with a stranger—an interspecies bond at that.

"I had to protect the mitres," Jared offered lamely again.

"But you didn't need her bonded to *you*," Scott said in a gruff whisper, shoving back from the table with an angry gesture. "And for that, my friend, you cannot offer any excuse."

"Excuse for what?" Thea asked, pulling a seat up to the table. She might have been his supposed destiny, but as she stared at him with those ethereal blue eyes, always expecting something that he was unable to give, he squirmed as usual. "Excuse for *what?*" she repeated, frustrated at the veiled looks Scott exchanged with Jared. "Listen, you two can't expect me to be effective if you're forever shutting me out," she complained.

"Commander Dillon is unsettled by my seeming recklessness," Jared answered carefully, staring at the plans to avoid his cousin's blue gaze.

She lifted a hand to his shoulder, which was still bandaged even though it was mostly healed. "How does this feel?" she asked, turning her touch into something of a caress.

"I am well," he rumbled, ignoring her hand. Finally, she dropped it away.

"Good," she said, "Because we have a situation this morning." Thea and several highly intuitive soldiers at the main base were able to communicate telepathically, which kept their risk of detection to a minimum. It was not uncommon to see Thea in a reflective position by the fire for hours, or outside on the deck, utilizing her vastly developed skills of perception. Listening, receiving, or just waiting— all through the unaided use of her mind.

"Anika and Anna are on their way now," she said.

Jared opened his mouth to question her further, but at that precise moment a pair of female soldiers entered the meeting room. All of his troops looked a bit alike, thanks to their uniforms and their military bearing, but these two were identical twins, and they shared a grim expression. Jared sensed fear—smelled it on them even before his energy made contact with theirs.

"Sir," Anika announced, out of breath. "We've been patrolling Mirror Lake."

"We were hawking it," her sister explained, black eyes fixed on him. Changelings, the twins were capable of assuming simpler forms: in this case, gliding over the lake as hawks, surveying the scene.

"Go on," Jared urged with a nod.

Anika stepped forward. "The air force is searching the lake, sir. The place is swarming with uniformed search teams and equipment." Inwardly, Jared groaned, though he kept his demeanor calm while the soldier continued her report. "But that's not the worst," she added. "They've located the remnants of your craft."

In all these years, they'd lost only a handful of planes—but every time they did, it put more of their own technology into the humans' hands. And this, of course, put them at a disadvantage, especially since the Antousians' attacks on the military installations here in the United States had increased in frequency. The humans did not differentiate between their own race and that of their enemies: Aliens were aliens were aliens in the eyes of humans. So far there had been no summit, no peace brokering—and Jared trusted the human governments very little. He was all too aware of human behavior, their defensiveness when frightened. He'd seen that much firsthand over the past six years.

But Anika wasn't finished. Clearing her throat, she revealed the one thing Jared had feared most about Mirror Lake. "There was a woman there," she continued, awkward. "On the lake's shore, before the teams arrived. She wasn't camping; she seemed to be collecting some sort of samples from the site." Apparently the camp rumors had traveled very quickly; he knew that much from the quiet blush coloring Anika's cheeks.

But it was Kelsey who concerned him at the moment, not the gossip among his people. Jared's head snapped upward, power roiling within his core. "Did the soldiers see her?"

"No, sir, she'd left already, I think."

"Good." Jared released a sigh of relief, but his need to protect his bondmate only intensified. "Very good." He instructed the twins to return to the site, to continue surveying, and to keep him posted. Thea followed them out, but not before a telling glance in Jared's direction.

As they left, Scott pulled him aside. "If they find out about the human, they'll take her in for questioning."

Jared set his jaw. "She has no idea what she's actually carrying around."

"But the data is still there, Jared," he cautioned. "If they do anything with her—to her—they could uncover it."

"Don't you think I know that?" Jared snapped.

Scott gaped back at him, but then his features softened. "You know, the bond thing," he said, wincing in obvious displeasure at the idea, "is supposed to be pretty powerful. I wouldn't trust anything it might be doing to you right now."

"I do not feel the bond," Jared answered. Staring beyond Scott's tall shoulder, he hoped his friend could not detect the bald lie in his words.

"I'm glad," Scott replied. "Because you can't afford any distractions, sir. I'll go get the data from her later today."

Jared raised a silencing hand. "*I* will go," he insisted. "She knows me. And she trusts me."

Scott stared hard into his eyes. Piercingly hard, so much so that Jared knew the man was soul gazing yet again. Jared's temper sparked at the intrusion. "Don't do that!" he barked, stepping back.

Scott dropped his gaze with a slight bow, heat creeping into his face. But he said nothing. No apology, no explanation. Jared clasped his lifelong friend by the shoulder. "Scott, I won't put myself in danger," he said. "I promise."

This time it was Scott whose temper flashed hot. "You're already in danger, sir," he snapped, turning on his heels. "I'm just trying to keep you alive despite that fact."

Chapter Four

Kelsey burrowed beneath her grandmother's quilt on her living room sofa, sketch pad balanced on her knees. From the TV in the background, a rerun of *Buffy* droned on. That stupid episode about the mayor: probably the single most overaired episode in *Buffy* history. Despite her lack of artistic ability, Kelsey had nevertheless been trying to render some sort of drawing of the visitor—as she'd come to term him—that captured his beauty. She knew all about shape-shifters, and she'd watched and read enough sci-fi in her time to understand that was what he had to be. A being didn't morph from a ball of light into a six-foot-something gorgeous man without possessing supernatural abilities. It flew in the face of every law and fact she'd learned as a scientist. And yet, somehow it felt *right*. Logical. The paradox of such illogic confounded her to no end, but the enigma always circled back to the same conclusion: The man she had encountered one week earlier had been like a being right out of science fiction, only he had also been real.

The most bewildering thing about their encounter, however, hadn't actually been his transformation—it was how attracted she'd been to *both* of his forms. That was a new one for a practical girl like her. And it fascinated her. Exhilarated her. Frightened her. It was as if he'd awakened some slumbering aspect of her soul with that strange fiery touch of his and with his raw beauty.

It had been one week since their meeting. One week of restless sleeping, of feeling her body blaze hot at the oddest moments. One week of aching for him so intently that she'd felt as though she'd go blind with need. But need of *what?* An abstract being's caresses? Was he really a man in any form she might recognize? *Insanity,* she cursed herself, slamming down the sketch pad. Despite her familiarity with the shape-shifter theory, as a scientist it contradicted everything she rationally knew about matter and energy. That was a puzzle she'd found herself revisiting all week long as well. Yet even as the scientist in her questioned, she could not deny the reality of what she'd glimpsed with her eyes. Nor could she deny that based on one brief encounter, she already had strong feelings for the man, as irrational as that sounded.

In the first day or two, she'd fantasized that he would come for her. That somehow he'd know how to find her— and that he would care to do so. But the passing days had given way to despair as she came to realize the foolish schoolgirl fantasies she'd begun harboring for an alien stranger. Yet even as she cursed herself, she wondered if there weren't some way to call him back to her, some way to let him know that not only did she *want* his return; she begged for it with every cell in her human body.

Jared stood before the mirror in his bedroom, examining himself, turning first one way and then another. After nightfall, Anika would drive him to meet with Kelsey Wells. Scott had surveyed her apartment earlier in the day, and all agreed that access would be easy. None of his officers were pleased about his going into the open, yet they couldn't argue with the importance of Jared's retrieving the information he had locked within her mind.

Given the danger, he would not visit her in his usual human form—a form that only thinly veiled his Refarian body—but instead he would morph into a temporary identity. Normally he gave little thought to such a choice; today, however, he found that it was keenly important that he choose well. Studying his appearance, he gave his body armor a tug, adjusting the outer shell of his bulletproof vest. At six-foot-four, he was a tall man and definitely a large-framed one. Kelsey, he had noted, was also quite tall for the female of her species. Perhaps she would find his natural Refarian height appealing? He smiled at the thought, pleased, and, without meaning to, blushed a bit.

Damn the human; she'd reduced him to a schoolboy, he thought with an angry scowl at his reflection in the mirror. Never before had he cared whether a woman admired his height or his size or his natural coloring, but now he found his mind wandering in that direction far too many times a day. Like now, as he studied his black eyes, his copper-colored skin—darker than he would ever reveal out in public, among the humans. The unusual tone looked too exotic for this part of the planet, he had learned, despite its general similarity to that of the Native Americans in the region. As Scott had explained, in a large American city, such as New York, he would never stand out; however, here in the mountain wilderness, his moody eyes and rich-toned skin marked him as a stranger.

With a weary sigh, he shifted a bit, diminishing his alien coloring into something paler and more unremarkable. Next, he morphed his fine cheekbones and regal nose, assuming instead a freckle-faced "cowboy" look. His black hair became sandy brown. He became plain, unnoticeable. His pride rebelled at the image staring back at him from the mirror. Not a man given to ego, he nevertheless found that he wanted to appeal physically to Kelsey Wells, wanted it more than his very next breath. Oh, he had lied to Scott this morning for sure. *I don't feel the bond,* he had claimed. The thought was laughable. Scott was right: He'd been insane to allow a two-way bond with an alien stranger. Taking a bondmate had always been a sacred ritual among his people, reserved for lovers, for lifemates. Not for alien women like Kelsey Wells, dangerous to a fault. *Why dangerous?* logic questioned. *Because you might open your heart again?*

Reaching for the bottle of whiskey he always kept in his dressing quarters, he silenced that nagging thought, swallowing a quick shot of the burning liquid. *Humans possess their share of fine inventions,* he thought admiringly, studying the bottle. But then he felt a literal tug in his spirit, a physical reminder of his separation from the human stranger, and his mood blackened again. *Indeed it* is *possible for a king to be a raving idiot,* he mused with a weary sigh. So many years in control of his emotions, his thoughts; then he'd gone out of his mind in a fleeting moment. *Irrational,* that was how he'd felt for the past days, driven by thoughts of a woman he barely knew—yet whose soul kept touching his own hundreds of times a day. *How can a man think under such conditions?* Simple answer: He could not, and Jared knew that tonight was finally his chance to remedy the situation once and for all.

Yet even with that vow, he found himself turning to the mirror once again, wondering what she would think of the form he had now assumed. A woman with auburn hair like hers would surely find a man with dramatic looks appealing—so he shifted his eyes back to their natural, dark hue with a frown. Rubbing his open palm over the top of his head, feeling the sandy-brown hair prickling his fingertips, he groaned aloud. There was no way he could make all these decisions on his own, so, hitting the comm button on his forearm, he called for Anika.

When she arrived, he formed his hands into something of a temple beneath his chin, wrestling for proper words. He knew that Anika would make an excellent consultant on a choice such as this one. She'd lived deeply enmeshed within the shape-shifter ways all of her life. She would understand his dilemma, perhaps more than anyone else within camp; and unlike some others, he trusted her to keep their conversation private.

"I go to see Kelsey Wells," he finally grunted at her, saying little else.

She stepped close and patted his thick body armor, the dress of a field soldier. "And you are wearing *this?*" she asked, tilting her dark head sideways.

"Scott insisted on the protection."

"It hardly . . . blends." She laughed. "If I may say so."

Again, he grunted. "I agree with this assessment."

She studied his features, reaching up onto her toes to gaze plainly into his face. "And, my lord, if I may further say, you resemble"—she paused, narrowing her eyes—"well, sir, you resemble *yourself.* I do not think it is safe to venture into the open in such a recognizable form."

"I am having some difficulty," he admitted, dropping his gaze to the floor between them. "I seek your advice."

"Advice about visiting the human, Kelsey Wells?"

"I find there are," he said, "too many possibilities for my form in visiting this human." With that admission, he coughed into his hand, but said nothing more, and instead fingered the button on his flak vest.

"Well, then," she announced in a bright voice, "we shall definitely make some choices."

Anika had always been his dear friend, far more than a mere military adviser. She understood him, in some ways, better than Scott or Thea ever would. Funny, but even though Anna was her identical twin, he felt nothing close to the same connection with Anika's sister.

"Yes," he agreed, daring shyly to meet her gaze, "excellent choices are necessary."

Anika's dazzling smile broadened, revealing her large, white teeth. "This will be a fine duty, my lord."

By the time they had arrived at Kelsey's apartment, Jared had on a thick cashmere turtleneck, topped by a black buckskin jacket. His hands were gloved in black wool, concealing the subtle body armor that encased his wrists, forearms, chest, and heart. Likewise, his dark jeans hid the rest of his careful protection, so that he could move safely in the open but appear fully human.

As Anika had pronounced with a pert grin, he appeared, "Both handsome and princely, while maintaining strong security."

He had complained in the face of her honesty, but smiled nonetheless. Now he found himself right outside of Kelsey's apartment, a blond-haired man with green eyes, tall, but not overly so. Nothing like the man she'd seen on the lakeshore—in fact, he resembled *neither* of the beings she'd glimpsed in him that night.

After scanning the perimeter in every direction, he passed through her front door without even a slight noise— the benefit of shifting—and began stealthily walking through her dark apartment toward her bedroom, where she was undoubtedly asleep at such a late hour. Sniffing the air, he hesitated, a smile forming on his lips. Yes, it was her, he knew, desire snaking down his spine in reaction. The Refarian in him instantly awakened at the scent of his bondmate, even as the military leader within shouted down such irrational terms of affection.

Kelsey's bedroom door stood ajar. Pushing on it with his palm, he caught sight of her there in bed, illuminated by the moonlight spilling through her windows. What he saw stirred something so forgotten within him that he felt his palms burn in reaction: the urge to touch—to be touched. Pressing his eyes shut, he refused to acknowledge how many years it had been since he'd come this close to wanting a woman—really *wanting* one, rather than just availing himself of that which was offered to him. *Gods, so beautiful,* he thought, taking a tentative step closer. Hair like gypsy's jewels, the dark red visible even in this half darkness. Blinking, he allowed his vision to heighten, so that he instantly gazed upon her as if in clear daylight. He breathed her in, held her scent in his lungs, then released it.

Sprawled across the covers, she wore only thin cotton panties and a camisole—even in the dead of winter. Had she been feeling the heat like he had ever since their encounter? Her skin appeared flushed, and her nipples jutted outward like prize beads beneath that cotton. Studying her fully formed body, he felt his groin tighten in immediate reaction. *This isn't natural, this kind of coupling,* a political voice warned, but he recognized it as belonging to Scott Dillon, and ignored it altogether.

Tugging off his gloves, he slid them into his jacket pocket and took another careful step toward her bed. Cautiously, he settled onto the edge of it. "Kelsey," he whispered, lifting his rough fingers to her cheek. Soft, like a flower petal—the kind that might easily bruise—that was how her skin felt. He blinked in surprise.

"Kelsey Wells, wake," he urged in a whisper, not wanting to terrify her. He could have done the job without disturbing her—should have done—and yet he couldn't seem to stop himself. Her sleepy eyes fluttered open, then widened, but she didn't move. She lay there in the dark, gazing up at him, unflinching despite his unexpected appearance in her room. A slow, delirious smile spread across her face, and he stroked her cheek again, tracing his fingers down to her lips, amazed. She caught his hand in her own after a moment, their fingers twining in silent unity.

"You came back," she answered finally, drawing in a breath. He couldn't help but smile in return, his heart hammering a frantic rhythm; his reaction had nothing to do with his reason for being here, and everything to do with his soul's deeper intentions.

"I knew you would come," she whispered, brushing a hand through her tousled hair. Only then did he remember that he had not shifted back to the man she would recognize. Yet she still knew him.

"Are you surprised?" He cocked his head sideways as he studied her. By All's name, how had she known he would come? He'd not believed it himself until today.

"I thought it would be sooner." Sitting up in bed, the tumble of wild auburn hair spilled across her pale shoulders.

"Ah," he breathed, a hushed sound in their darkness, "you were giving up on me already?"

"Not yet, no," she said, still smiling.

"Perhaps you would have if I'd taken longer," he suggested, allowing his doubts about true love to solidify between them. She should know he was no naive prince, nor a young man in search of a feckless enchantment. "Perhaps you would have forgotten."

"Are you making fun of me?" she asked, the radiant smile forming into a look of frustration. "I don't understand any of this. I don't even know your name. In fact, I don't even know what it is you've made me feel at all."

"I wasn't being cavalier." He stared into her eyes, searching them. He wanted her to trust him—to grasp that, just as she'd understood by the lake, he would never hurt her. At least not intentionally.

"I could have run," she whispered, and he swore that even in the darkness emotion glinted in her pale eyes. "I could still run now."

"You could," he agreed, brushing a long, spiraling lock of hair away from her eyes. "But I would follow." As if in reply, he felt the bond between them constrict, drawing his chest tighter than a drum. He recognized the sensation as Kelsey's pull on him, magnetic and unshakable.

"I want to know your name." She sounded almost angry, all the tenderness and joy he'd seen in her moments earlier replaced now by pained frustration.

He nodded, lowering his voice. "You could not pronounce it." That was the most truthful answer he could give—rather than the much easier one of his assumed human name.

She tilted her chin upward, eyes flashing with challenge. "Try me."

He laughed, then stated his Refarian name as rapidly as

he could. Not just his name, but his *full* family name as well as his formal title, all of which together comprised a long sentence.

"Well, that is"—she hesitated, laughing awkwardly— "mmm, kind of challenging, actually."

For a moment she attempted to repeat it, stumbling painfully over several of the syllables, and this made him smile. He had no doubt that Kelsey Wells rarely backed down from a challenge. "You may call me as all the others here do," he suggested gently. "Jared Bennett."

"That sounds a little like it."

"A bit."

"Jared." She tried the name out on her tongue, almost like she wanted to see if it really did fit him. "Jared Bennett. Jared." Touching her lips, she hesitated, then lifted her eyes to meet his. "I like it."

Strange, but he felt his face flush hot at those words. "I am glad." He wanted her to like the name; he wanted her to like everything about him. They fell silent, not out of awkwardness but rather because of overpowering emotion. *Do your work and be gone, Jared,* the warrior demanded. *Much is at risk for your people,* the king urged. But then, lastly, the *man* begged for another course of action entirely. *Take her with you, damn it. Take her.*

"Kelsey," he began. "I'd like to show you something."

"Your ship?" she asked breathlessly, clear eyes widening. "I'd love to see it, would love to know more," she rushed, squeezing his hand.

"No, not my ship," he said, suppressing a smile. Kelsey had no idea how very human his life here on Earth actually tended to be. "But someplace important to me—and to my people."

"Who are your people? I know you must be some sort of . . . alien, a shape-shifter, right?"

"You have many questions," he observed, tracing his thumb over the back of her pale, freckled hand. "You are a scientist, I am told."

"How did you know—"

"I know much about you," he explained.

Her whole expression changed, her voice growing husky as she said, "I imagine you do." She leaned in close, cupping his face within her hands, drawing his lips toward her own. "I haven't ever felt anything like I did the other night," she said. As she brushed her lips over his, he felt his entire body grow taut in reaction. Unfamiliar with the precise sensations, he felt her gain control of him, a fact that perturbed him on every level. Without meaning to, he pushed her slightly away.

"I wish to take you from here," he said. Frowning at her, he wiped the back of his hand over his lips.

She seemed not to notice—at least, not exactly—saying with a shrug, "All right." Releasing his hand, she slipped off the bed, scooping up a discarded pair of blue jeans and a sweater. Standing beneath the slip of moonlight, her figure appeared even more supple and curvaceous than it had there in the bed. Shimmying into her jeans, and then her sweater, she seemed oblivious to the painful arousal she'd caused in him. "Okay," she said with a warm smile, "let's go."

Just like that. No questions, no doubts or interrogation of him. Gaping at her, he wondered why she wouldn't be afraid. He felt the burden of the acts he had committed, the blood shed by his hands. A distant part of his mind ached to warn her against himself. To send her a thousand miles in another direction, away from the warrior and king.

But instead, he whispered the truth. "I need you," he said, holding his breath lest she flee right away. She did not, but turned to him, smiling as he rose to his feet. "So I beg your forgiveness for what I do next," he said, capturing her hard against his body.

A man could do only so much harm in his quest to find love. That was what Anika had whispered in his ear right before taking flight. Alone in the car with Kelsey now, Jared turned that phrase over in his head, gripping the steering wheel of the Suburban until his knuckles grew white—until the blue veins stood out, stark against the blanched skin. Damn it, he knew he was lying to his heart, making promises that could never be kept. The bond between Kelsey and him would have to be broken. Tonight. The leader within him would see to that fact, even as the man inside raised bitter fists in objection. It had to be done, for everyone's safety.

Beside him, Kelsey slumped sleepily against the window,

his winter scarf still wrapped solidly around her upper face and eyes. Her deep auburn hair spilled over her shoulders, waves of it that caused his fingers to burn. Kelsey stirred in her seat with a quiet little murmur and sat up. She clutched at the blindfold, but Jared caught her wrist, gentle but firm. "We're still driving," he informed her coolly. He was determined, if he accomplished nothing else by carting her off to their camp tonight, to master his careening emotions.

She nodded, silent, and he instantly regretted the stern tone he'd taken. Softening his voice, he asked, "Are you all right?"

"I'm blindfolded and in a car with an alien who might— or might not—want to hurt me," she growled with a toss of her hair. Well, this human clearly did not like playing captive. Without Anika accompanying them, perhaps her fears were intensified.

"This action is for your safety," he told her, frowning. *And because I couldn't resist bringing you back to my compound. God, I'm behaving like a fledgling experiencing the first flush of hormones and bodily urges.*

"Oh, right." She snorted. "It's definitely key to this whole enterprise that I be taken as a *hostage!* Hello? Hostage? Do your people have a word like that?"

He suppressed a smile. "Actually 'hostage' works quite well, thank you."

"You think this is funny, is that it?" she cried. "This isn't funny at all."

"I think you are beautiful." Where had that come from? *Silence, you idiotic and brainless king.*

Well, her reaction did nothing to quash his growing burning for her. Her full mouth parted, forming a quiet *oh* sound.

"I mean, you are, of course, very beautiful," he persisted, training his eyes on the road ahead. Silence curtained between them, and in a burst of awkward anxiety, he turned on the radio, and U2 blasted loudly from the car's speakers. Feeling with her hand, she touched the button, silencing the music.

"Then why wouldn't you kiss me?" she asked, turning toward him even though she could see nothing. "Back at the apartment? It didn't seem to do anything for you."

"Kelsey," he protested softly, feeling his chest tighten

with unwelcome tenderness for her. His bondmate. *She could be yours, Jared,* a wooing voice promised.

She answered her own question. "I guess I'm beautiful, but not very exciting," she said, turning back toward the window and wrapping a long, spiraled lock of auburn hair around her forefinger. "It's that whole sister vibe, which is pretty much the lifelong thing I get from most guys, which just *happens* when you're almost six feet tall."

"I make decisions based on pragmatism," he answered, reaching a hand to clasp her shoulder, aching to transmit some sort of tenderness to her. She jumped at the contact, but he did not withdraw. Instead, he curled his long fingers slowly through the hair along her nape so that his heat threaded into her body, opening up the physical connection as well as the ensuing flood of sensations he knew would accompany it. "Such is the way of all leaders."

Shivering beside him, she pressed on: "What kind of leader are you?" Only then did he recall that she knew nothing about his identity—nothing important, at least. She had no idea of the war between their two worlds, or of the rebel forces that he led here on her planet.

He withdrew his hand from her shoulder. "What kind of leader am I?" He laughed hoarsely, working to cover his misstep. "Right now, a fairly stupid one." The less she knew, the better for her safety.

"Who do you lead?" she insisted. "Do you mean your people?"

Blowing out a heavy breath, he focused on the road ahead, training his eyes on the yellow centerline and the clear arc his headlights arrowed into the blackness ahead. Maybe if he didn't answer, she would let it go.

"Tell me who it is you lead!" she cried, grasping outward with her hand and feeling for him.

"My people, yes," he answered. "We are in a war, and . . ." What more could he tell her? Knowledge would place her in extreme danger—and him as well, not to mention many millions of others.

"And you're leading these people from here on Earth?" she questioned, leaning back in the seat. "What sort of war? Who are your enemies? Are you fighting us?"

"Humankind is not the enemy I fight." Partial truth and partial lie, but it was best that way.

"Why are you here, then?"

"My own planet is in chaos, Kelsey," he answered, grief stabbing at his heart. "The war has raged for a long time, and taken a brutal toll on my species. The people we fight would destroy every last one of us. They are genocidal and cruel and despise my kind." As he spoke, he found that it felt right to open to her with the truth. It comforted him in some strange way that he didn't bother to question. "I am the last in my line. All the rest were either murdered or died in battle. So now it falls to me."

She didn't answer at first, only nodded, sitting ramrod straight in the seat beside him. Perhaps so much information had overwhelmed her? She had no experience with such things. But she surprised him, whispering softly, "Why does it fall to you? That's a huge burden for any one man."

His breath caught at her words, choking him with years' worth of unexpressed pain. Stealing a sideways glance, he saw that she'd turned toward him and was waiting.

"You may have a bad habit of taking hostages," she continued, a tender expression on her face, "but I do know you're a good man."

He ached to warn her, to tell her of all his horrible deeds. To remind her that he could spill her blood and drain it from her body with one lift of his hand. *Murderer, changeling, king, freak.* All the descriptors applied and in equal measures, but never *lover* or *husband* or *lifemate.* These words were the property of other men—ones who led easier and less complicated lives.

"A good man," he repeated dully.

"I knew it within moments of meeting you, Jared."

"You make many assumptions based on little fact."

"I know what I sensed that night," she insisted, reaching to dislodge the blindfold with her free hands—hands he had intentionally left unbound so she could retain her rightful sense of freedom. "I knew then that you were someone I could trust. And I know that now." She reached a hand to touch his where it gripped the steering wheel.

He did not react, did not move—and did not push her away. With a sniff, he said, "You should not reach such conclusions so very easily," then turned up the radio full-blast to drown out any answer she might have given him.

Chapter Five

Jared pulled the Suburban up in front of a large, rustic cabin perched on a mountain peak. Their winding approach had proven difficult, with the vehicle's tires spinning and spitting gravel on the unpaved drive. At one point, the rear wheels had become entrenched in a deep snowbank, then spun out on the ice, but Jared, obviously used to the terrain, never flinched. They had driven at least four or five hours from Laramie, and he'd never mentioned the blindfold again, not once she'd removed it. She had seen some highway signs since then, ones for Bondurant and Pinedale and other towns in the western part of the state. By her calculations, they didn't seem to be all that far from Jackson.

After shifting the SUV into park, Jared stared at the brightly lit cabin in front of them, but remained silent. Exhaling slowly, like a man deep in thought, he rubbed one large palm over his closely cropped hair. Somewhere along the drive, the blond hair had again become black, the green eyes again the lovely dark ones she had seen before.

Two men emerged from the cabin's interior and walked toward the vehicle, but Jared raised his hand, issuing some sort of sign, and they immediately retreated, closing the cabin door behind them.

Jared watched them, his dark eyebrows hitching together in an unreadable expression. She followed his gaze to the cabin's brightly lit windows; inside, even though it had to be at least three or four in the morning, she could see people moving about. For a moment, she had the laughable notion that perhaps Jared wasn't an alien at all, but rather some perverse underground cult leader. Wait, weren't there supposed to be alien abduction cults? She thought of one in particular, where a whole houseful of people had committed suicide while wearing running shoes, and prayed that nobody would ask about her footwear.

But the seriousness she saw in Jared's eyes reminded her of all the weighty secrets he'd shared with her. Of his people being pursued to extinction by their enemies, chased from their homes, wandering across the galaxies. No, this was no laughing matter for Jared Bennett; of that much she was certain.

"Are we going to go inside?" she asked, curious about his life here, even as she felt a tiny constriction of fear.

He nodded. "In a minute. This is my home, you must realize," he said. "It is strange, having you here. I wanted it, but still . . ."

"Why strange?" She wanted her presence to feel natural to him, to feel *right*.

"You are innocent of many things, Kelsey," he said, giving her a pensive smile. "I am wrong to draw you into my world. I have been selfish in this."

"I chose to be here," she reminded him. "You didn't make that choice for me."

"But I drew you into our conflict," he argued, the sadness she'd glimpsed in his eyes morphing into something darker and unreadable. "I apologize for this. And also because some may not appreciate your presence here. Nor my bringing you into our camp." He looked into her eyes. "Just know that going in."

"I see," she answered in a cool voice.

"Only because they wish to protect me." He cupped her cheek within his large, calloused hand. "Do you understand this, human?"

"I'm not sure."

"Some of my people would have me sit apart from our struggle, alone and out of danger, while they take all the risks," he explained, dropping his hand back to his lap. "I'm not comfortable with that."

"No, I can't imagine that you would be." She smiled, and this time she was the one to reach out a hand to touch his cheek. His face was beautiful, sculpted and formed like a classical piece of art. She thought of Minoan sculptures, or Greek, perhaps. He possessed a hewn warrior's visage, tough but surprisingly graceful as well: strong, high cheekbones accented by the long, noble nose, the copper-colored skin. Slight scarring along his left cheek and his forehead—which only made his features seem more angular. But then those soft, full lips. Those lush black eyes with the long feathered lashes. The combination of rough leather and velvet softness in this one man's features made for an unabashedly sexual blending.

She noticed a small pendant stone, black and shiny like onyx, on a thin leather cord at the base of his throat. Despite his turtleneck, he'd made a point of displaying it. "What's this?" she asked, reaching to touch it before he could caution her, but quickly withdrew her hand. "It burned me," she exclaimed, laughing in surprise. "Your pendant almost burned my hand!"

"It does that if you're not careful," he agreed with a smile. "That is, unless you're the wearer of it."

"No, now, see, I'm a geologist," she said, incredulous. "Stones don't *burn* people. Not like this, not when they're worn as jewelry."

"You're obviously not a geologist on *my* planet." He laughed, stroking the black, gleaming stone between his fingertips. "This was a gift from my people. It was once set in my father's"—he hesitated, seeming to catch himself, then continued—"in my father's vaults, long ago. Before the war. When we arrived here, on your planet, those I command gave it to me as a gift. They had brought it all that way because they wanted to remind me of what I fought for."

"And if I were to touch it again, would it still burn me?" she asked, working to mask her curiosity.

"It's called a strake stone," he told her. "Very rare, even on our planet." Reaching behind his neck, he unfastened the leather cord that held it in place. "Here," he said, "you may wear it. For now." With a gentle motion, he brushed her hair off of her nape, gathering it across her shoulder. She was aware of his warm breath fanning against her cheek, then her neck, as he bent to fasten it. He had an earthy scent too, ironically enough, one that she hadn't noticed back at her apartment. "There," he said when he was finished. He gave a satisfied sound of approval as he studied her. "Yes, you wear my stone well."

Staring down at the gleaming rock, she dared to touch it. This time, though it was warm, it did not burn. "Your people obviously love you."

He nodded. "I am nearly all that remains of the old ways," he said. "This is difficult for some."

"You're right." She laughed. "Your people *aren't* going to like me very much." He reached for her hand, their fingers threading together. She loved the rough feel of his hands against her own; loved how warm they were. The man absolutely radiated heat—that much she'd realized from the beginning; perhaps his stone pendant took its cue from him.

"But they must respect you," he said, setting his strong jaw. "I will require it. Demand it, if need be."

The dark determination in his face led her to an odd thought: He seemed to be speaking about far more than her visit to his home tonight. Or even about his people's general reaction to her—he seemed already to be forming a place for her within his world. And it felt familiar, this determination, as if she'd always heard him promising that his people would treat her with respect.

Jareshk. The name whispered in the hidden places of her mind like the faint tinkling of a distant wind chime. *Jareshk . . .*

"Here," he said, reaching for the pendant. "Best that you keep this hidden." He tucked the necklace down inside of her sweater, and for a moment as his fingertips grazed her breastbone, each stared at the other. This time, *he* reacted like one burned, quickly withdrawing his hand.

She shivered, staring away from him and again toward the large cabin. It had to be at least five thousand square feet, seemingly hewn from the mountainside itself, facing the valley below as if it stood at attention. The structure looked to be four stories deep, down the side of the jagged peak. It had several tall observation towers, built into the structure, and long, covered porches along the front and sides. Wood and mortar, accented by large windows—probably so they could carefully keep guard in every direction, she guessed. It was a dream cabin, the kind she'd always secretly wished her father would purchase and keep somewhere in the northern part of the state so she could hide away with her research or a book.

"You like it," Jared said, catching something in her expression, something she knew she couldn't hide from him even if she tried.

"It looks like a home," she whispered, feeling a sudden pang of loss. Her father had moved them to D.C. when she was sixteen, immediately after her mother's death. It had been a lonely time, a time when she'd ached for the land of her Wyoming childhood. And she'd never quite found home again.

He nodded, but said nothing more. They fell quiet, studying the structure, wrapped in their own thoughts. How could she feel sorry for herself when Jared had traveled so far from his own world?

"What is your race?" she asked, suddenly needing to know. "Where are you from? At least tell me that before we go inside."

"I am Refarian Arganate," he said, whispering the words like a holy prayer of sorts, his pride in his heritage obvious.

"Where is that?" Planting both hands on the dashboard, Kelsey leaned forward in her seat so that she could see the sky overhead; she wanted to imagine that she could glimpse his planet with her naked eyes. Or maybe she was just trying to reassure herself that she really was on Earth, the only planet she had ever known.

"Quite far from here." He draped an arm around her shoulder, pulling her close until their heads inclined together, both of them staring through the windshield up at the sky. "How I wish I could show you. The scientist in you would find my planet very beautiful and wondrous. There are many things there that you do not have here on Earth."

For a moment, the whole thing seemed ludicrous— laughable—until he turned his black eyes upon her, and she glimpsed a strange shimmer of energy within their depths. And she also noticed that, overall, in some imperceptible way, Jared did not appear human.

"God, you're beautiful." She sighed appreciatively. And this . . . this, the man seemed to like very much. His serious expression softened, the full mouth parting with a husky, masculine laugh. Or was it almost a soft growl of pleasure?

"Indeed," he purred, stroking his chin with a thoughtful expression, his fingertips lingering on the black stubble of beard that had appeared there in the past few hours. "We like that you find our natural appearance pleasing. Yes, we like this very much."

We? What was with the "we" thing? But before she could tease him—or even ask—he seemed to grow quite self-conscious, fiddling with the button on his buckskin jacket and avoiding her eyes.

"Did I say something wrong?" she asked, confused, but he refused to meet her gaze. Maybe it was a cultural difference, some misstep she hadn't intended. "Jared?" she pressed.

"I show myself to very few," he finally explained in a low voice, still refusing to look at her. "Perhaps no humans ever."

"Perhaps?" She had to know the answer, had to know the truth. She leaned closer toward him. "Yes or no, Jared?"

"No humans." He released a low rumble of what she interpreted as pleasure. "Never shown myself to a human until you."

She recalled her first glimpse of him on the lakeshore the other night—already it seemed like years ago—but said nothing. She understood that he meant *all* that she'd seen, both of his selves. It was somehow an intensely personal experience, one that she felt certain he couldn't translate for her. It was the only explanation for the fact that this rugged warrior, a man whose forceful strength of spirit she'd felt firsthand, had been reduced to such an awkward, shy gesture, this fiddling with his jacket.

She captured his hand, stopping the anxious motion. Then, slowly, he dared to lift his eyes until they met hers in the darkness. "Kelsey Wells was the first to see me."

"Knowing that," she whispered, feeling surprising tears sting her eyes, "only makes you all the more beautiful to me."

"Commander," Thea announced tightly, avoiding Kelsey altogether as she clasped his forearm the moment he entered the cabin. "May I have a word?"

"In the morning," he said, shaking off her grasp. His cousin and her expected tirade would have to wait. At the moment, Jared reflected, the idiot king had but one objective in mind: bringing Kelsey into camp and introducing her; then, perhaps, taking her down to his quarters for a nightcap—that is, if he couldn't shake some sense into his bond-impaired mind. He had hoped the human's hold on him might lessen with proximity, but it seemed that every passing moment with her only intensified their connection. Then he'd even bestowed her with his family's strake stone, without so much as placing a time limit on the gesture. Any ordinary woman might interpret that kind of gift as a mating pledge. And he wasn't entirely sure he hadn't meant it as such.

As they passed into the main entry of the cabin, Thea persisted, flanking him. "Jared, please," she urged. Kelsey remained close on his other side, following his lead. Others lined the entry hall and made bows of respect, inclining their heads. He returned the gesture, but perhaps with even less gusto than he normally would, because their shows of respect embarrassed him with Kelsey present.

Thea wasn't going to back down. "Commander," she pressed, "it is urgent that we speak tonight."

He rounded on her, unable to prevent the quiet growl of protest that sprang from his chest. "We have a guest," he reminded her, speaking very precisely.

She answered rapidly in their native tongue, an idiomatic Refarian laced with cutting terms, complaining about Kelsey's presence, arguing that he had placed himself—and all of them—in unwarranted jeopardy.

And he shot back in Refarian, employing simple, plain words. "I am leader," he said, bending low so he could stare meaningfully into his adviser's eyes. Thea blinked back at him, visibly trying to calculate the risks he'd brought upon himself. Softening his voice, he added, still in their shared tongue, "Trust the human, cousin. Trust me."

"I trust you completely," she said, "except in matters of your heart." Words that were shot through with import—words that accused even as they cast doubt.

"Cousin," he said firmly, "your leader's heart is his own affair." Marrying Thea had never felt right—he'd tried repeatedly to explain it to her, this sense deep inside that he could not lifebond with her, nor even marry her.

"The *king's* heart is the affair of his people," she retorted testily, then turned upon Kelsey—who definitely dwarfed her—and stuck out her hand. "I am Thea Haven," she pronounced in precise English, her words tinged with an elitism born of their bloodline. "I am cousin to the king."

At no other time in their lives had Jared ever wished to thoroughly pound his cousin into the damnable ground. If there'd been one word he had hoped—prayed, in fact—that Kelsey would not hear while in camp it had been that single blasted one: *king.* And of course Thea would have guessed as much; she knew all too well his aversion to pomp and titles and all the discomfiting traditions with which his bloodline had been cursed. She also knew that, deep down, his heart wanted nothing more than to be loved for itself, for its commonness—and not for the nobility of the blood that flowed through it.

Jared flinched, waited, held his breath—did anything to gauge the human's reaction. But then sweet Kelsey—his blessed human—smiled regally and took Thea's strong, pale hand. "I'm Kelsey Wells," she answered without blinking. "I am honored to be here tonight as guest of your king. And I am honored to meet you as well."

Kelsey never once glanced his way, but instead waited to see what would happen next; it almost seemed that protocol and its many requirements were not unfamiliar to her. The warrior felt himself breathe a bit easier, even though the *man* wondered desperately whether Thea would manage to frighten Kelsey away from him.

For her part, Thea's reaction to Kelsey was interesting. A look of grudging respect came over her countenance; clearly, she'd meant to intimidate or shock the young human, but Kelsey had gracefully passed Thea's first test. And his loyal lieutenant was nothing if not rigorous in her testing of those who kept her king's company.

Placing his hand gently in the center of Kelsey's back, Jared guided her down the hallway. "Let me show you about the place," he said.

In his wake, Thea pressed behind them. "Jared, we still must speak," she persisted. "It is urgent."

He wondered if it was something more—if she had a report for him, or if something beyond Kelsey's appearance here at the compound troubled Thea tonight. "I will meet you in the boardroom momentarily," he answered, striking a formal tone. "Once our guest is settled."

"I would prefer to take the discussion to the exterior," she answered with a steely-eyed look. Inwardly he groaned; this had nothing to do with politics and everything to do with pressure both from the council and from Thea that they form a match.

"Outside, then," he agreed, his hand never leaving Kelsey's back.

Jared stood, both of his booted feet planted on Hooded Rock. This particular promontory provided a most spectacular view of the valley; unobstructed by pines or other trees, it opened onto a cold, windswept panorama, one that Jared treasured. He'd left Kelsey inside, sitting in the upstairs den by the fire; she'd looked weary, and he had knelt there, apologizing. Even now, his fingers and body burned to touch her; he yearned to kiss her on this very rock. The image felt real somehow—as if it had already happened, and he shivered, feeling as if Kelsey must be standing right behind him. But when he opened his eyes, he found Thea, not Kelsey, standing back on the trail.

She took a step closer. "Jared." On her lips his name suddenly became a husky promise. Stepping up onto the rock, she faced him. "My lord, I needed time alone with you," she began, unfastening his jacket. Once it fell open, she slid her palms inside, easing them underneath his sweater.

"Do not do that!" he snarled, turning from her. He was more than accustomed to Thea's temptations, but tonight he had little patience for her ploys. "Your king wishes to be alone," he announced, intentionally positioning his title between them.

"Oh, cousin." She laughed, her voice lilting and breathy as again she stepped closer. "There are many things you wish for, but you don't wish to be alone. Not anymore. You haven't wished so for a long while. And it's become evident that I need to be bolder, now that the"—she hesitated, making a small sound of revulsion—"human is among us."

"We wish to be alone!" he thundered, taking another step apart from Thea. "Leave us."

"Well, *we* wish to be with *you*, sir," she countered, slipping her arms around his waist and holding tight from behind. Uncharacteristically, her physical touch caused him to burn a bit. A strange, unfamiliar sensation in reaction to his cousin—almost a kind of magnetism. She slid one hand low onto his abdomen, stroking his stomach, which caused his groin to tighten in instant reaction. The sensations were all wrong—and not only because of Kelsey. Jerking apart from her, Jared growled his dismay.

"What are you up to, Thea?" he barked with a low, protective rumble. "What game is this?" And why, with as much as he already cared for Kelsey, would Thea be arousing him at all? He had a bondmate—why would his cousin be stirring his blood, now, after so much time? Unless . . .

Pressing a hand to his eyes, he groaned, shaking his head. He understood precisely what his cousin had done to him, the spell she'd attempted to work. It was manipulative, by the gods. She had to be desperate. Opening his mouth to reprimand her, he felt an answering thunder in his loins— which he realized was Thea pressing much closer behind him once again. With a roar, he spun upon her, and just as he had guessed, she stood before him, transformed to her most natural form—she, the only person other than himself on this planet capable of such a transition. The only other royal among many hidden Refarians here on Earth.

She purred at him, moving closer, all bright and glorious, radiating power and sensuality. Transmitting promises of love and seduction.

But it was more than her natural form, which shouldn't have possessed such a strong allure all on its own, beautiful as it was. It was something she was *doing,* somehow. Then, as she brushed her golden body up against his, sidling close, he understood with perfect clarity: "You've brought the fever upon yourself," he replied in a hushed voice. "You're in your mating season."

Yes, came her answer, shimmering across his skin. *And you like it.*

"You're trying to trick me into mating!"

Falling into their shared language, she spoke inside of him in a silky voice. *It was the only way. I have to help you see that I am the one.*

"We will never form a mating bond," he told her plainly. "Never, Thea."

Her Refarian words flickered through his mind like a threat. *Then the line will end with you.*

For a fleeting moment, the husky sound of his native language almost aroused him. Almost, but then again, not even remotely—he knew it was just the impact of her mating season, working to put some sort of spell on him. "I command you, Thea Haven, to make the change!" he cried. "Do not remain at this game." Damn it all, her erratic mating impulses were starting to cause his brain to fog up.

Obeying—since, after all, she remained his follower and his cousin—she transformed back into the petite blond he was accustomed to seeing here on Earth.

"I'm having you carted over to Base Ten until your cycle is over." He shook his head, seething. "And I'll think long and hard as to how we will recover from this embarrassment."

She stared up at him, blue eyes welling with tears, and for a tiny moment Jared pitied her.

"You bound yourself to a stranger." She wiped at her eyes. "After so long, you gave yourself to an alien and a stranger." His heart protested, and he longed to explain that Kelsey meant so much more to him, already, than those words conveyed. "I thought it wasn't true," she went on, "that you would go for the data and then return, and then . . ." She released a quiet sob.

"Even now, in your season, you don't affect me, cousin," he replied, his voice becoming gentler. "How much less, were we to have mated?"

Bowing her head, she replied, "But you have *always* affected me."

Cupping her chin in his palm, he lifted her face until their eyes met. "Because I am your king," he answered without a trace of pride or sarcasm. "No?"

"No," she answered, shaking her head. "Because you are like me. Which means I'm not alone when you are near."

He closed his eyes, feeling compassion for his distant cousin—understanding the isolation that came with their exotic and dying bloodline. "There will be someone else who makes you feel that way."

"That's not true, Jared," she said, their families' golden aura enveloping her—even without the change. "You have always been the one for me. But now it seems you have made your choice, and she is another."

"You know the purpose of the bond I formed with her," he argued, even though he knew he was being dishonest, and that his intentions regarding the human seemed to be changing by the moment.

"The purpose doesn't matter anymore," she answered flatly. "I don't see you backing down now. Do you?"

He could not answer, not without wounding Thea's heart and pride even more.

"As I suspected," she said, tilting her chin upward with a resolute gesture. "But can she even produce an heir for you, Jared? I find that quite doubtful. And so, as I said, the line will die with you."

"I do not know what will happen with the human," he said. "Time will reveal the answers, cousin." He put his back to her. After a moment he both sensed and heard Thea making her retreat. When he was certain he was alone, he slid to his knees and stared upward—homeward. Silent and gaping at the sky above, he wondered how a future with Kelsey had become such an inexorable fact— or how it seemed that, even as the warrior had promised to sever the bond with her, the man had clearly mapped his own destiny. He had chosen to mate.

Chapter Six

Jared climbed to the upper story of the cabin, searching out Kelsey, whom he'd left in front of the fire in the den. He'd chosen to share one of the most intimate places in his whole compound with her; in fact, only his personal chambers were more important to him. The den was where he often strategized or meditated; he took no meetings there, but instead reserved it as a place of stillness. With its stacked stone fireplace and panoramic, windowed view of the surrounding mountains, it had seemed the right place—a pure one—to introduce Kelsey to his life here on the mountain.

Thea's words to him had been true, as had his own inner admission: He no longer intended to break the bond he shared with Kelsey. No, the thing he wished was far more troubling indeed: He hoped to *solidify* their connection. And thus he'd allowed the fantasies to begin, fantasies of leading her by the hand down to his chambers, where they would drink whiskey before a roaring fire. Slowly, they would fall together there in his room; he would gaze upon her, unhindered and slow. His fingers would find their way through every auburn curl, along every soft, rounded curve of her human body. He would woo and win her, binding his body to her own . . . until somewhere in the process, he would retrieve the data as well. Then at last, with duty honored, he would make love to the human yet some more.

As long as they could keep the war at bay, he would hold her there in his bed, loving her and mating with her. Fine plans indeed, he thought with an audible rumble of expectation as he arrived on the upper-floor landing. His heart leaped a bit in his chest as he caught her scent from down the hallway.

But upon entering the den, he discovered that his beguiling bondmate had collapsed into sleep, curled up on the sofa, fully clothed. She'd obviously tried to wait for him, but had lost the battle. Humans required a great deal more sleep than Refarians. On average, he netted three to four hours of rest a night, but he understood that her kind became irritable and diminished unless they slept for much longer periods than that.

Dropping to his knees, he studied Kelsey as he had done earlier in her bedroom, this time with the luxury of a much closer and less hurried inspection. He found that the woman sparked an immense amount of curiosity within him. He had not been so near a human before, at least not for such a prolonged period of time. And so he studied her closely, noting the fine physical details that he'd previously missed: the delicate curving of her lips; the scattering of freckles all across her forehead and nose like stardust; the alabaster tone of her skin, so different from his own darker hue. He even held his hand to her cheek, thrilling at the contrast between their disparate colorings. Damn it all, but he found it evocative that she was alien, and that he had no idea of what precisely to expect in bed with her. That she smelled different from other women he'd been with. For a fleeting moment, he recalled Thea—how her season had briefly magnetized him—and a new yearning birthed within him. He desired to cycle with Kelsey.

That thought caused heat to rush from his cheeks and upward to the very crown of his head. Ever since he had come of age and learned that his line experienced mating cycles, he'd been ashamed—mortified that the agonizing taint, purged from all but the most royal of Refarian bloodlines, still haunted his line. He'd determined then and there never to succumb to a mating season, and had successfully managed to avert the fate without problems. Yet as he watched Kelsey sleep, his blood raged hot at the thought of coupling with her during his season. It felt so utterly right that his hands began to tremble with the urge.

Almost as if she knew his thoughts, Kelsey stirred, rolling away from where he knelt beside her. Again, his face flushed hot, and he dropped his head in pure shame. Ani-

mal instinct. She would never accept that in him—how
could she? He cursed whatever base thing inside of him
had brought it out even now. Still, as he watched her sleep,
an eerie shadow of memory fell between them once again,
as it had repeatedly done ever since that first night he'd
been wounded. This desire to cycle with her . . . it felt
familiar, as if she were part of this ancient urge fanning to
life inside of him. With a growl of dismay, he shook that
thought aside. Humans knew nothing of Refarian mating
calls.

But then a fleeting image imprinted in his mind—her
pale, freckled hand touching his royal emblem. *Impossible!*
He had never shown a human his brand, and only a trusted
few Refarians had ever seen it at all. Certainly no one had
ever touched it.

Perhaps it was just the aftereffects of Thea's seduction
attempt, he told himself uneasily, rising to his feet. Searching about the den, he found his favorite fleece blanket
draped over one of the chairs, and covered her with it,
bending down to tuck each of the edges about her as he
did.

Turning to leave, he glanced at her one more time before
flicking off the lamp. The morning would bring truths, desperately needed truths, and he prayed that Kelsey Wells
would forgive him when she learned of his deception.

Kelsey woke to find sunlight filtering through a case-
ment in the ceiling, clear morning sky visible overhead. A
royal-blue fleece blanket covered her—one she didn't recall falling asleep beneath. Perhaps Jared or someone else
had covered her in the night? She stretched, pointing her
toes, and for a minute wondered if it had all been a bizarre
dream. Alien compounds and warrior kings and middle-of-
the-night secrets. She even returned to her recurring fears
that Jared might be some kind of cult leader. She was
contemplating that, along with the possibility that maybe
the whole "warring species" idea might be just a code
phrase for some strange variety of terrorism, when a soft
voice startled her.

"You're awake, I see."

Only then did Kelsey notice a striking, dark-haired
woman sitting by the fire, legs crossed. "He doesn't usually

allow any of us here," the woman offered. "Well, perhaps I should clarify. Our lord would never forbid us to come. But we all know that it is his place."

"But he let me in here," Kelsey said, planting both feet on the floor, curious as to who the large-boned woman was.

She gave Kelsey a brilliant smile. "Oh, I imagine he wanted you here, Kelsey Wells. That he wished to show you something of himself."

The woman waved her closer. "Come," she urged. "Sit with me by the fire. I am Anika."

Kelsey rose and, taking the blanket with her, approached the fire. "Are you Jared's cousin too?"

"An adviser," she said. "He has sent me here to watch over you until you wake."

Kelsey bristled at such protectiveness. "I was fine," she said, pushing a lock of hair behind her ear.

"Of course you were fine," Anika agreed with a firm nod. "But our commander knows our world here is unfamiliar to you. He wishes you to be comfortable." Another large smile. Anika's appearance was odd, different from Jared's: She possessed the same dark hair and eyes, but her skin was much fairer. She almost had the look of a dark-eyed Viking: the same strong bones, large teeth.

"It's all a bit"—Kelsey hesitated, wrapping the blanket around her shoulders as she settled by the fire— "overwhelming, actually."

"Of course," the woman agreed. "Our lord *is* overwhelming—is he not?"

That was one way to describe the spell Jared had managed to cast over her in one week's time. She stared into her lap, avoiding the alien woman's questioning gaze. "It's all very strange," was all Kelsey admitted.

"Our war is not known to most humans," Anika continued. "This would be strange, I am sure. As would engaging in a relationship under such terms."

"A relationship?" Kelsey asked, glancing upward in surprise.

Anika's open face brightened with what could only be described as amusement. "Is this not what brings you to our camp?" she pressed. "A relationship with our commander?" She gestured toward Kelsey's throat. "And it seems you wear my lord's strake stone." Kelsey glanced down, surprised. The pendant had obviously worked its way free from beneath her sweater during sleep. She could offer no defense as to her reason for wearing it, but tucked it back beneath the turtleneck hastily.

"He wanted me to see this place," she said, though she knew something far deeper had led her here with Jared. "That's all."

"A place that he regards with the utmost level of security? A place where he has never once brought an outsider? Where only the highest ranking officers *ever* visit? Yes," Anika concluded with a firm nod. "This is highly unusual for our leader, and you must know it."

For reasons that Kelsey couldn't understand, she wanted to confide in Anika. "We only met once before," she admitted softly, trying to form logic out of such an illogical attraction to the man. "At the lake."

Anika gazed at her. "You believe in the possibility of true love," she observed after a searching moment. "I sense it. And you have waited for someone for a period of many years. And yet you question? It seems to me that your feelings were anticipated for some time, Kelsey Wells. Perhaps it was their fulfillment that has confounded you so much."

Kelsey shivered, but said nothing. There was nothing she *could* say upon being analyzed in such a penetrating manner. After a moment of gauging Kelsey's reaction, Anika turned back toward the fire. "This morning, our commander meets with several key advisers," she said. "He hopes to see you in two hours."

Kelsey glanced down at her rumpled sweater and jeans, and felt painfully self-conscious. "I have nothing to wear."

Anika laughed, a warm bubbling sound. "Ah, a familiar refrain the universe over," she said, regarding her with a sideways glance. "We appear to be the same approximate size. Perhaps I can help with that."

Jared stepped out onto the deck where he'd finally discovered Kelsey after searching for her inside the cabin. She leaned against the wooden balcony railing, her chin propped in both hands. "And so it is morning," he said.

"A beautiful morning," she agreed, giving him a reserved smile. She wore an ice-blue ski sweater that matched her eyes in brilliant vibrancy, obviously some of Anika's doing, as were the formfitting Refarian uniform slacks that Kelsey wore. *Blessed Anika and her love for her king*, he thought, forcing himself to gaze into Kelsey's vivid blue eyes, *not* at her curving hips.

"Has your time been pleasant so far, here in my camp?" he asked, taking a position along the balcony edge with her.

"Pleasant?" Her smile broadened. "Wow, that seems awfully formal, don't you think?"

"Formal? I did not mean it so." He suddenly felt himself a boy, quivery and unsure of himself—as uncertain as he'd been the day of his coronation. Gods, how he wanted to say just the right thing with this human! It seemed suddenly to matter a very great deal.

She shrugged. "Well, I guess for a king, you're not too terribly formal, not really."

"I-I have some trouble with your language."

"You're great with English," she disagreed. "That's not it. It's just . . . you could have told me that you're a king." Her tone was contemplative as she stared across the sun-dappled valley. "You could have trusted me."

"It has nothing to do with trust," he said, forming clouds with every breath. "I usually save that information when I can," he admitted. "Not that I can very often, since most everyone in my life knows precisely who I am. And always has."

She turned to him, and when she did he saw flecks of gold reflecting the sunlight in the depths of her blue eyes—something he hadn't noticed previously. Blue teased with green, mated with gold, taunted the king.

"Why didn't you want me to know?" she asked, making a sweeping gesture with her hand. "You brought me here to show me your life."

He sidled up to the railing, draping one arm over it, studying her. She raised a crucial question, and the answer was simple—but he wasn't sure he wanted her to know just yet. "The element of surprise," he answered, locking his eyes with hers in challenge, "is key to any battle plan."

She folded defiant arms across her chest. "This is not a battle, and I'm not your enemy."

Her denials brought out something playful and flirtatious within him. "Ah, so you say, my human."

"*Your* human?" She laughed, giving her long curls a toss. "I am not your pet either, thank you."

Cocking his head sideways, Jared studied her, confused. " 'My human'—this term conveys affection. Not ownership."

"*My*," she replied. "In English, 'my' means ownership. Belonging."

"You do not wish to belong to anyone," he observed. It was true, and from the beginning he had found her independent spirit more than a little alluring. Yet a part of him also longed for her to understand—to acknowledge even—that they were bonded on the deepest level. "You wish to be alone in life, perhaps?" he pressed.

"It's not that I-I don't wish . . ." she hesitated and he saw the faintest crimson invade her cheeks. Then she blurted, "It's that, well, that I—"

He lifted fingertips to her lips, silencing her awkward attempts at a reply.

"Your heart longs for much, Kelsey Wells," he interpreted, tracing the outline of her soft, delicate mouth. "But you are strong and independent. I like this in you. Very much. I admire it as well."

She met his gaze, her eyes watering unexpectedly. "It's gotten me into a lot of trouble in the past."

"You have not loved strong men," he observed. "Who could handle this trait in a woman."

"I loved a man once." She turned from him. "Or I thought I did. And he wanted to have me all to himself, wanted me to sacrifice the things that were important to me. I think he wanted to own me, in a way."

"Humans own others?" This revelation he found confusing, as he did not believe such was common among her kind here in the western part of this planet, at least not at this point. "A man may *own* a woman?"

"He wanted a relationship with me, but only on his terms," she clarified, laughing softly. "And I was willing . . . for a while. Until he hurt me."

He felt an irrepressible flash of fury: That any man might have hurt his bondmate awakened the warrior in him. His hands clenched at his sides, his full body tensed, and it was all he could do to suppress an audible growl of protection.

But he managed, forcing himself to grow calm again before answering.

"My human," he said, intentionally invoking the warm term again, "this is an endearment. It conveys strong affection. Tenderness, if you will. These cultural things are sometimes difficult."

"Oh." Her eyes widened, and she blinked, swallowing visibly. "Tenderness. I get it."

He smiled at her, noting that her pupils seemed to dilate in emotional response to his explanation. "Perhaps 'my Kelsey' sounds better?" he suggested in a gentle voice.

"Probably less *Star Trek,*" she agreed, her nose crinkling as she smiled. "If you don't mind my saying so."

Reaching out his hand, he cupped her face, surprised yet again by the pristine softness of her skin. "My Kelsey," he whispered, "you look very beautiful in the morning light. This soldier should be so blessed every day."

She dropped her head, self-consciously fingering the stone that glinted there at the base of her throat. The strake's presence had electrified him from the moment he'd first seen it on her this morning. Not that she'd have laid the pendant about carelessly, but still, the look of its dark beauty against her skin had caused him to tremble with an unfamiliar sensation—the thrill of having claimed a mate. *She has never agreed to such a plan, Jared. Move slowly,* a voice warned. But the man inside refused to back down, and the thought of proceeding cautiously seemed an unbearable task. Perhaps he could at least steal a kiss this morning? He took an intrepid step closer.

The wind kicked up around them, sweeping a twined curl of auburn hair across her face; he reached, carefully tucking it behind her ear. The color in her cheeks deepened as he made his move, resolving that he would finally kiss her. Although he remained well aware that those inside the cabin might see him do so, he closed the small distance still separating them, and turned her face upward toward his.

At that precise moment, Scott burst out onto the deck, followed by another of his soldiers. "Commander! We—" The first soldier gasped, and Scott glanced from Kelsey back to Jared and then to Kelsey again.

Then, apparently understanding whom the woman in his

arms obviously had to be, Jared's best friend actually had the gall to scowl at him. Bitterly. Then he coughed, and all the while Jared couldn't seem to activate his brain to simply release Kelsey from his grasp.

It was the other soldier who spoke at last, murmuring, "So sorry, sir," with a bow. "My apologies." Then the man bowed even lower, the greatest show of respect.

Jared returned the gesture and rolled his eyes at Scott, who still stood gaping. Like himself, Scott was keenly curious about humans—but probably more quizzical about this particular woman Jared had actually brought into camp. "In a moment?" Jared prompted Scott when he did not turn away.

"Commander," he whispered, and turned on his heel without another word.

Jared watched them go, wondering if he'd made a mistake in not introducing Kelsey to Scott at that moment. But he wanted to do so later, when his lieutenant could spend time with her. When he might better understand his commander's attraction to the alien woman.

After both men had left them, he turned back to Kelsey. "I've asked them not to do that," he told her.

"Do what, exactly?"

"Oh, bowing and treating me that way," he said, rubbing his jaw. "But I think they need it, even if I don't."

"Everyone needs to remember the reasons for what they do."

This concept resonated deeply, and he nodded. Perhaps Kelsey might understand the reasons behind the bond he had forced upon her. Perhaps she might accept it—and forgive, even as he begged her forgiveness for having gazed so deeply into her soul during that quiet flash of a moment. He wanted to believe that.

Then he reached for her hand and closed it in his larger, darker one. "Kelsey, there is much you do not know," he began, "about the war I fight. You will learn more in time, but . . ." She squeezed his hand, urging him onward, so he continued. "I need for you to meet with my cousin, Thea Haven. You saw her last night."

"As if I could forget," she said.

He had no doubt that Kelsey had recognized Thea's possessive jealousy from the moment they'd entered the cabin. The last thing she probably wanted was to spend more time in her company. "I need you to trust my cousin," he urged. "She is a good woman and a good soldier."

"Even if she didn't like me very much?"

"She liked you fine," he disagreed. "She doesn't trust humans. But she's the one I need to pair with you because of her intuitive abilities."

"Why would you want me with her?"

Jared dropped his head, his black eyebrows drawing sharply together. "Kelsey, I had to leave something in your care," he admitted, his voice thick. "That night, at the lake." Across their bond, he sensed how her mind raced— an object? a weapon? She had no idea of anything that he'd left with her.

He answered her unvoiced question. "Not an object," he said. "Nothing like that. Information."

"Where? I don't know of—"

"Sweet human, please forgive me," he whispered.

Sweet human, please forgive me. Forgive him for what? Fear began to choke Kelsey's thoughts, because his apology seemed to portend something dark, frightening. Gauging by the stricken expression in his dark eyes, she guessed she wasn't far off base. "What did you do to me?" she asked in a tight voice.

"The night of my crash," he began, but then halted, staring into her eyes. "Kelsey, that night something fantastic happened between us. We both know that."

Setting her jaw, she only said, "Go on, Jared. Tell me what you did to me."

"I left important information inside of you, for protection," he said. "Information that I feared would fall into enemy hands."

"I see," she said, disturbed by his formal, distant attitude.

"I-I fear that you won't understand."

Her heart softened at the words. He wasn't acting odd because he'd done something horrible to her—he was afraid of somehow losing her. That she wouldn't understand a split-second decision when he was horribly injured. "I did tell you that I wanted to help," she reminded him. "That night. Remember?"

"But it wasn't fair to you," he said, staring out across the valley. "I placed you in danger. Terrible danger."

"That's why you came for me," she said, suddenly understanding, and she couldn't fight back the wave of disappointment at realizing that he'd come for data—not for her.

He turned back to her. "Sweet Kelsey, I came for many reasons," he said in a husky voice. "Most especially for *you*." Had he known her thoughts? Read her mind? His words were deeply melancholy, the tone one of wistfulness—the kind one used when talking about lost dreams.

"You're going to take the information and then send me away," she answered, realization dawning. "Back to Laramie. Aren't you?"

He set his features. "You do not belong here."

"I belong nowhere else," she argued. "I belong by your side." Unexpected tears stung her eyes; she thought of the past week—how it had felt to be away from him—and her heart clenched.

His black eyes narrowed. "I never denied that you belong in my life."

"Just that I couldn't be here with you," she said, and for some reason, she thought of her father. Of his constant inaccessibility, and of the job in D.C. that always ranked ahead of her in importance.

Jared leaned close, hoping none of his soldiers would see him brushing a kiss against her forehead. "I send you away for your protection, Kelsey," he said. "I'm not safe."

"I don't want to choose safety."

"You will be missed back there," he argued, imagining that with her presence at Mirror Lake after his crash, there would be many questions should she vanish, not to mention that she would be missed by her family. "Police will get involved, perhaps federal agents. It could expose me."

"We could cover my trail," she said. "There's only my father, and he lives far away. I can make this work."

"Kelsey, stay today." He rubbed his jaw, studying her. "Tomorrow even, but then you must go back."

She'd be damned if any man—alien leader or not—was going to make unilateral decisions for her. She'd had enough of strong men and their choices on her behalf. Twenty-eight years as Patrick Wells's daughter had ensured that.

"No freaking way," she snapped at him, clutching at his

pendant where it rested at the base of her throat. "You are not just going to send me away like some child!"

He shook his head. "You are far too intelligent to be disregarded in that way," he said. "I would not. But I also must make decisions based on my knowledge of this war. Such decisions are different, Kelsey, than one-sided choices on your behalf."

"Please, whatever I need to know, tell me," she urged again. "I'm strong. I can handle whatever it is."

"Tonight," he said, with another glance around them, back inside the cabin. "My people wait for me now. But tonight we will be together."

With those words, he vanished inside the house, and eight or nine hours suddenly seemed an insufferable period of time to wait to see him again. *Powerful men,* she mentally cursed. She had always promised herself she would steer clear of them. And then what did she do? Like some silly storybook dreamer, she'd gone and fallen in love with a king.

Chapter Seven

Night did come. Eventually. But not without behaving like a tricky, coy thing, managing to stretch hours and minutes endlessly for most of the day. At least, it seemed that way to Jared, who spent the time deliberating with Scott about a new penetration plan that Anika had been devising, a way to get inside the Antousians' camp without detection. Between that, his advisers' concerns about his crashed aircraft, and rumors that their enemies had infiltrated the highest ranks of the U.S. president's security, his day had dwindled to nighttime at the pace of Antousian gorabung torture. And this was precisely why he had no business with a bondmate, he thought grumpily as he endured his final meeting of the day.

Even as Scott and Anika argued, he listened quietly, returning to his discussion with Kelsey out on the deck. How he'd wished they could have been completely alone at that moment, so he could have cautiously—tenderly—explained the bond they'd formed with each other. But at least his confession about the mitres data had been a solid beginning: Soon Kelsey and Thea would sit together and work to retrieve the information stored in Kelsey's mind.

He could have done Thea's job himself, at least in theory—after all, he was the one who'd left the data within her. Beyond that, he'd gazed right into her very soul when he'd formed the bond in the first place. But his gut told him that a true intuitive, someone with the highly developed skills Thea possessed, not a low-level intuitive such as himself, was the right choice in this instance. No matter how attached he was to Kelsey, he might be too clumsy, might even inadvertently hurt her somehow. No, it was worth the emotional risk of pairing Kelsey with Thea once his cousin returned from Base Ten. Perhaps after cycling, Thea would be calmer and less threatened by Kelsey.

But that thought prompted another, less pleasant one: How would Kelsey feel when she learned that in forcing a bond with her, he'd invaded her innermost thoughts? That he'd seen Jamie Watson, who had crushed her heart at such a tender age by betraying her with another woman. He'd watched as her mother had died, two days shy of Kelsey's sixteenth birthday, leaving her alone at a time when a girl most needed a mother. He understood those emotions; he'd lost both his parents at age ten, and been left to decipher far too many family and leadership puzzles all alone. Even worse, he'd lost his beloved protector, Sabrina, a year later, when they'd been separated by conflict. She'd been as much a mother to him as his own birth mother had been, and he'd never stopped grieving that loss. He'd always prayed to find her again, but had finally given up when he'd been exiled here on Earth.

Did he love Kelsey already? Perhaps. But if he did, he knew it had much to do with how intimately he'd gazed into her heart. So how could he admit to her that he knew her much more deeply than he'd so far admitted?

Wiping rain from his face, Jared entered the firelit main room of the guesthouse, an older stone structure dating back at least seventy-five years. As soon as he made his entrance, his soldiers nodded to him, leaving him alone with Kelsey, as they had been instructed to do. Darkness had fallen, and she stood by the fire waiting for him, bathed in the glow of the flames. He wished she were bathed in nothing else, he thought, and his body tightened in reaction to the image.

"I promised you nightfall," he breathed into the shadows between them, every part of his body electrified by longing. "That we'd be together. I could hardly think of anything beyond that promise all day."

Slowly she turned to face him, her spiraling curls worn loose and long across her shoulders. He loved those curls;

they weren't the soft, wavy kind. They had a life of their own, and every time he'd seen her with her hair down, his hands had burned with the need to touch them.

She laughed huskily, teasing him with her eyes. "I have no doubt that you're a man who keeps his promises, Jareshk."

With that one word, his mind filled with an unshakable image, just as it had the previous night: her pale hand caressing his royal mark. *"Jareshk?"* he repeated, his heartbeat quickening. It wasn't possible—she had no way of knowing that name. Or *did* she? "Why did you call me Jareshk?"

"I'm not sure," she said, her auburn eyebrows drawing together in a perplexed expression. "It just kind of . . . came out."

He pressed a hand to his eyes, feeling unsteady. "You used my childhood name," he explained, swallowing hard. "A name you could not know."

"I just heard it in my mind."

"No one has called me Jareshk since I came of age at sixteen," he told her, not able to express the loneliness that had dogged him then. "My parents called me that, as did my protector, Sabrina. But then, for reasons no one precisely understood, including myself, I refused to answer to it years ago," he said. "Without reason or explanation, I no longer allowed any of those who served me to address me by that name. And yet now you call me Jareshk, and I burn inside." He shook his head. "I do not understand my own reactions."

"Maybe you didn't like the name," she suggested gently. "Maybe it was just as simple as that."

"No, Kelsey," he said, feeling something roar to life within his soul, "my feelings for you are the farthest thing from simple!" He cupped her face within his palms roughly, needing to see into her eyes. "This attraction," he breathed, "is too familiar."

"Like we've been together before," she agreed, feeling his grip on her tighten.

"*Do* we know each other, Kelsey? Is that it?" He searched her face with a look of utter desperation. "Did you know me . . . somewhere before?"

Slowly she lifted her hands and closed them over his. "I

think I've always known you, Jared," she said, expressing a thought that had been catching fire within her for days. She knew this man; everything within her recognized him. "And you me."

He nodded. "I have seen something in my mind." He dropped his hands, and turning his wrist over, rubbed the underside of it thoughtfully. "I must know what it means to you."

She nodded her encouragement, and very carefully he raised his other hand; a silvery beam of light spread through the air, falling on his open wrist until an undulating sphere of energy appeared in the air between them, lighting the darkness. She gasped in wonder at the exotic beauty of it. "This is my royal emblem," he explained, his eyes never leaving her face. "I am marked for life by it."

Her whole body quivered, her hands trembled, and she had to touch the swirling mass of color and light. "I know this," she said, carefully lifting her fingertips toward his mark. "I *know* this, Jared! I've touched it before."

Her skin made contact with his power; the energy of it coursed into her body; then memory exploded out of the darkness and into her being, and Kelsey fainted.

All these years, Jared thought, *and we never knew.* All these years, and they might never have remembered again, not if destiny hadn't had its way with them. Holding her head in his lap, he wiped at his eyes, whispering her name over and over in an effort to wake her. Remembering what it had felt like the first time she'd caressed his mark, the way his entire body had quivered in reaction. It had been the most sensual, erotic thing he'd ever experienced in his young life. To be touched that way, the intimacy of it; few could possibly understand how erogenous his royal emblem truly was—that when she stroked it, she stroked *him.* More than that, her gesture had made him feel how she loved him.

And he'd loved her already then too; it had been so easy to love her, from the very beginning.

No wonder their newly formed bond held such power over him! Taking a mate was a rite of mystery for his people: How much more so now that he understood what Kelsey truly meant to him? He couldn't remember much, not yet, only refracted glimpses. Mirror Lake, some rocks . . . but enough to know that bonding with her had completed something crucial inside of himself.

She stirred at last, blinking bleary eyes up at him as she came back to consciousness. "I'm confused."

"I know," he soothed, stroking her hair. Did she remember, as he did? Something had obviously made her faint, but still he chose his next words carefully. "It was too much," he said, "too fast."

"Did you remember too?" she asked, wiping at her own eyes.

He bowed his head, unable to find words, then finally whispered, "Yes, love. I remembered a little. I remembered *you;* oh, gods, how I remembered you." The rain on the rooftop brought even more memories rushing to the fore. "It was raining—"

"—by the lake!" she finished for him, bolting upright. "Yes, yes! And you kissed me, there in the rain." She lifted fingertips to her mouth, brushing them over her lips in wonder. "You were my first kiss! You were the one."

His own memory was so vivid, he could *feel* her mouth against his, could almost see the way she'd looked, but not . . . quite. He reached for a lock of her hair and slowly rubbed it beneath his fingertips, hoping the texture would awaken more memories.

"I had never seen anyone so lovely in all my life," he said, feeling everything shift inside him. His mind, his memories—it all seemed to be coming into alignment. "I wanted to take you with me. I promised I'd come back for you."

"Just like I said, Jareshk," she said, resting her cheek against his shoulder. "You're a man who always keeps his promises."

"Unless I am prevented from it." He felt anger roil inside of him. How dare his people have done something like this—and *who* would have done it? He could recollect nothing but the dim awareness of what he'd lost, nothing more. "I am so sorry," he said.

She pulled back to stare into his eyes. "Did *you* make me forget?"

"No, Kelsey, but one of my people obviously did." He could think of only a few Refarians capable of erasing a memory bond, and he recalled that one of them had been on board the cruiser that summer he ventured here to Earth. The summer he had been coming of age. "And I will learn who did this."

"Was it because I'm human?"

He rubbed a tired hand over his eyes. "Because they wished to protect me." He sighed. "It's always been the same with my people." He used his limited intuitive ability to grasp within his mind, seeking whatever remnants of memory still remained. He knew he could use his bond with Kelsey—the same damn bond he was supposed to break—to search out her memories, as well.

With that thought came another, as the present came rushing back with perfect clarity: Kelsey was not a child any longer; nor was he on the verge of his awakening. She did, however, contain data lodged deep within her mind that put both her life and his rebellion at risk. Who and what he was had already caused her enough pain, and in that moment he vowed that he would not cause her more.

"Kelsey, it's been a long few days," he said softly. "I will walk you to the main cabin so you can rest."

"It's still early . . ." she protested, but he leaned low, brushing a kiss against her cheek.

"I have some people to see." Yes, he would meet with his elders in the coming days, but it was more than that. If tonight had convinced him of one fact, it was that he couldn't hurt her—not any more than he already had—by revealing the bond he'd created with her the night of his crash. Especially not when he'd become convinced that it would have to be broken for her own protection.

Chapter Eight

The stranger searched the landscape with black eyes. Eyes that had seen bloodshed and warfare rip this very parcel of ground apart. Eyes that knew this dark earth, stained red with the blood of humans and aliens and hybrids alike. But back in *this* past, the lake still reflected the azure sky like a child's dream. Standing within the mitres' chambers, he stared out through the portal at the shimmering images of an Earth long vanished, except in his memories—until now.

Moving through interdimensional space as one might step through a sliding door, he left the mitres in his wake, stepping fully into prewar Earth. A bitter smile pulled at his lips. They'd called what they were engaged in then a *war*— they all had. What simpletons they'd been. They'd never conceived that the horrific events to come would make such an idea laughable, ridiculous. They'd been like children playing war games, nothing more.

The stranger's smile transformed to a scowl as he thought of the man who had caused the war's escalation. Jared Bennett, their supposed leader, had called the blight down upon them all. That was why he had to pay with his own blood—and why Jared had to be stopped now, he thought, squinting up at the snow-covered Tetons. Drawing the clean mountain air into his lungs, the stranger stirred the hatred in his heart, allowing it to fuel his intentions. He would not acknowledge his ties to this land, to this very place, nor would he acknowledge the memories. No, his mission had brought him back ten years into this past, and he would remain focused on that, he decided, walking out of the woods and into *their* present.

"She waits, my lord," Anika whispered in a low voice, pressing Jared toward the back stairs that led to his quarters. His chest constricted in anticipation; like yesterday, today had seemed interminably long while he suffered through war council meetings, including one with the elders where it required everything within him not to accuse Aldorsk of treachery.

Taking the steps two at a time, he found himself in the lower hallway, surprisingly anxious. The day had provided ample time to question, and to even doubt his sanity for allowing their bond to continue, but at last the night had come—again. Another night with Kelsey, only he wasn't sure he could be so strong this time. The urge to complete their mating was physically and spiritually overwhelming, and growing stronger with every day their bond was allowed to remain intact.

Pausing outside his own room, he hesitated, lifting a hand to the pine door. For a moment he sensed her energy radiating into his fingertips, then farther into his body. Only with a bondmate was such a thing possible. The effect on his Refarian senses was so sharp that his eyes watered in reaction. Without waiting another moment, he pushed open the door.

There, by his hearth, she sat on silken, jeweled floor pillows. Crimsons, azures, rubies. He'd never seen them before, but then again, his people spoiled him far too much. Undoubtedly Anika and her twin sister, Anna, had made a point of spreading them on the pine floor of his bedroom, treating him like a Refarian king, not a rebel leader in exile. Kelsey glanced over her shoulder at him, her skin golden in the firelight.

"They said I should wait here," she said, her voice husky with promise.

"They were most definitely correct," he said, closing the distance that separated them. He tossed his jacket onto the bed, along with the flashlight he'd used walking up the trail from the stone guesthouse. "Are you comfortable?" he asked.

Kelsey watched as Jared shrugged out of first his coat, then his pullover sweater. For the briefest moment his shirt rode upward, revealing a taut, muscled abdomen that somehow she had never fully expected. The sight was luscious, and she ached to reach out a hand and stroke his warm, bronzed skin in appreciation. He never seemed to notice, walking right past her toward his dressing area. "Would you like a glass of Scotch?" he asked. "Nothing like a drink by the fire."

"Sure," she said, suppressing a giggle.

"Very sorry, but I have no ice or water handy," he said. "Will you take it straight?"

"Of course." The notion that Jared had immersed himself in human ways enough to have discovered whiskey amused her to no end. Apparently some cultural things proved no problem at all. He returned, bearing the bottle in one hand and two glasses in the other. With a flourish, he poured a drink for her, and it struck her that he was attempting to court her in whatever way he had discovered was common in human culture. Then, after pouring his own, he sat beside her on the lounge pillows. It seemed that sitting on the floor was customary for his people, especially as they relaxed, she reflected.

He settled in front of the fire, one hand loosely holding his glass, the other planted on the pillows between them. Out of the corner of her eye, she kept watching the hand, wishing it would edge closer to her. For a painfully long time neither spoke, until she began to feel her face flush hot, and she searched desperately for something to say. That was when he tossed back the rest of the whiskey with a quick shot. "I wish to touch you," he told her, without a trace of shame or self-consciousness.

"Okay." What else did you tell a bold alien?

He knelt then, turning until he faced her. "I wish you to touch me as well," he continued. "I wish it very much." She swallowed hard, and nodded.

"Kneel," he urged her, taking her hand and drawing her upward. "Here, like I am doing. Face me." She found herself forming almost a mirror image of him. "Ah, yes," he whispered, slipping his hand around the back of her neck. His long fingers combed through her hair. "Just as I suspected. My awakening memories only make you all the more beautiful."

"Are you remembering more?" Kelsey had been fighting to retrieve her own memories all day, but so far she could only touch shadowed thoughts within her mind.

"Bits," he agreed, his expression growing serious. "But not enough to satisfy me." Then he smiled and said, "I think only *you* can do that, Kelsey."

Feeling suddenly shy, she avoided his piercing gaze, and glanced around them at all the jeweled pillows. Kelsey had the feeling that she'd landed in some prince's harem. "This place is amazing," she whispered, pointing around them.

"Ah, my people," he said, dropping his head. "They spoil me too much."

"How?" she asked, as he pressed his lips close against her throat, kissing her there.

"They know how I love a warm fire at bedtime," he said.

"That's hardly spoiling." She panted as his strong arms wrapped about her waist, urging her backward onto the pillows.

"Well, all these pillows are new," he said softly in her ear. "But one or two of my people know just how I feel about you."

They rolled onto their sides then, still touching and exploring every inch of each other. Reaching a tentative hand to stroke his cheek, Kelsey outlined the small scars there. For the first time, in the firelight, she noticed lines around his eyes. This surprised her—almost as much as the nearly imperceptible shots of silver-gray that the firelight caused to gleam in his hair.

"How old are you?" she asked, and he glanced upward, surprised. She ran her fingers over his bristling hair. "There's silver in your hair."

With a deeply self-conscious gesture, he lifted his hand as if he meant to shift his appearance, but she stopped him. "No, don't change it," she said. "It's lovely."

"I didn't want to be dishonest," he admitted with a hesitant smile. "So I kept the gray. I wanted you to know about our age difference."

She wondered if perhaps he was a great deal older—if his species aged on a different timetable altogether. "Just how old are you then?" she asked, bracing herself for some shocking revelation.

He rolled onto his back, staring at the ceiling in contemplation. "Old enough to know that I can't afford to feel the things you bring out in me. No warrior can."

"You're still a man." She watched the emotions that played across his serious face.

He cut his eyes sideways, meeting her gaze. "I am thirty."

"Geez, Jared!" She began to laugh, relieved. "I thought you were going to tell me you're, like, four hundred years old or something. That's only two years older than I am."

"But they have been hard years," he explained, rolling back onto his side to face her. "Destructive, aging years, Kelsey. *Very* aging years."

She sensed that there was more—something important he withheld from her about his age, or their differences—but she also understood not to push him. "How is it I know so little about you?" she asked. "And you know so much about me?"

"Does that matter?"

"I-I'm not sure." He nuzzled at her neck, nipping her there with his teeth. A strong voice inside urged her to trust him—to have faith, even though he seemed so unknowable.

Wrapping his arms around her waist, he drew her close to his side. "You do know me, Kelsey," he answered, almost as if he'd heard her thoughts. "Already better than most in this camp."

"I want to be closer."

Graceful as a wildcat, he accepted her invitation, rolling her on top of him. Her strong thighs closed around his, and she felt his coiled power beneath her hips. And that wasn't the only thing she felt. *Oh, boy, not by a long shot.*

A slow, devilish—and decidedly human—expression formed on his features. In fact, he seemed quite pleased with himself. And with his size.

"Is *that* honest too?" she teased, rocking against him.

"I do not understand this humor."

"Like the silver in your hair," she explained. "Is this"—she paused, lifting up so she could caress the hard ridge that jutted from within his jeans—"*all* you?"

His lips parted, his eyes drifted shut, but he said nothing

at first. Then, after a quick reply in his native language, he groaned, "All Refarian, all me."

She outlined the bulge, rubbing it harder, and noticed that his body seemed to tense in reaction. "Poor human men," she said. "But lucky, lucky me." She laughed, growing more intense in her stroking, and this caused him to cry something in Refarian, and while she couldn't understand the words, they aroused her wildly nonetheless.

"What does that mean?" She sighed, arching her back.

"I said, it's important that my anatomy meet"—he paused, eyes sparkling as he unsnapped the fly of her jeans—"all *human* requirements."

She giggled, daring to slip one palm beneath his shirt, feeling the flushed heat of the flat, muscled abdomen she'd glimpsed earlier. "You'd know that answer better than I."

Lifting his hips in invitation, he purred, "Quite compatible, I am certain." His dark eyes narrowed to catlike slits as he tugged on the zipper of her pants.

She reached a hand to cup his cheek, feeling the bristling of his beard stubble, the warmth of his skin. He blinked beneath her examining touch, but did not squirm or flinch. That was when she realized what he had done: he'd allowed himself to be in the prone position, allowed her to be the one in control. Their physical positioning couldn't be an accidental choice, not with a warrior like Jared. No, he wanted her trust. And he wanted it badly—badly enough to risk assuming the vulnerable role in their first genuinely physical encounter.

Their eyes locking, she began to shiver uncontrollably. Between the way his body had begun to tease her into a fevered state, and her uncertainty about what he was truly inviting her to do, she couldn't seem to stop the trembling. Then, quiet as a Sunday-morning snowfall, she heard him in her center. Heard his words. *Feel me! Touch!*

And if she hadn't been sure of the invitation, he gave a slight, affirming nod, urging her to continue. Sliding both palms farther beneath his turtleneck, she found the rough casing of body armor and gave a little cry of frustration. He made several quick motions with his wrist and it fell open, exposing his chest, his stomach, his body. He shrugged out of his turtleneck, then discarded the body armor, revealing a golden-brown chest dusted with only a few silken hairs, and those low on his abdomen, threading their way downward into his jeans, suggesting a predefined path of exploration like a well-lit runway at night.

But she chose the opposite direction, caressing his warm chest with both hands, feeling his nipples bead with arousal at her touch. The longer she touched him, the more his chest heaved with uneven breaths. He licked his lips, swallowing visibly, his moody eyes drifting shut. For some reason, she recalled her first image of him from a week before: the blazing wall of power, erotic, bright, burning. Nothing like the much more physical man she straddled and stroked at the moment.

"This isn't even your body," she whispered, staring down at him. It was such an eerie feeling, this overpowering attraction—but to what? To whom, really? His dark eyes fluttered open again, fixing on her. Studying his handsome face, she continued, "Or, it *is* your body, but it's not your *only* body. Is that it, Jared?"

His black eyebrows narrowed. "It's one of my bodies," he answered in a soft voice, his chest rising and falling visibly. Beneath her hand, she could feel his heart's staccato, frantic rhythm.

She kept her open palm positioned right there, over his heart like a pledge. "Who is the golden one?" she whispered. "The one you showed me . . . that night?"

He slid his own hand over hers. "Me as well."

"Are there others?" She had to know, had to understand this man who had touched her very soul.

He hesitated, watching her with a wary, guarded expression. But then something in his face changed, softening. "Many others, Kelsey."

"Then how can I possibly know you?" she cried, feeling tears burn at her eyes.

Clasping her strongly by the waist, he steadied her, saying, "*This* is me, Kelsey. *Me*." His dark eyes searched her face, begging for her trust. "You see me. You feel me. Why does the form matter?"

"Because it does," she said, touching his face, outlining his strong cheekbone, then trailing her fingertips along the straight line of his nose. He had a beautiful, ruggedly formed face, and it literally caused her breath to catch as she touched it in appreciation. "It matters completely to me."

Words that he'd heard before, spoken by another woman in another time on another planet: the memories swam to the surface, causing a sharp stab of pain behind Jared's eyes. He blinked, trying to focus on the woman he held now, a woman whose eyes were open, accepting, who did not judge a man for choices he'd been forced to make. *But she does not even know of those choices.* He pressed his eyes shut, fighting the flood of images, of Lahrae's long black hair spilling down to her hips. Images of a young warrior who longed to love her, but feared his feelings more than the war he found himself fighting. If only he'd understood the reasons behind his fear of loving Lahrae: that Kelsey had been ripped away from him so traumatically.

"What's wrong?" Kelsey asked, caressing his cheek. "Jared, I don't want to hurt you."

I don't want to hurt you, love. I do not. Lahrae's voice, Lahrae's words in their shared Refarian language. The refrain of a woman who yearned to love a man who refused to be loved. Until it was too late. A man who had already loved once, but been made to forget—no wonder he had been unable to love Lahrae.

"I just want to see you," Kelsey whispered in a hoarse voice. He allowed his eyes to flutter open, and found her blue-eyed gaze fixed on him. "That's all, Jared. To see *you.*"

His answer came out gruffer than he intended. "You have seen my core selves."

"Core selves," she repeated, searching his Refarian features. "How many are core?"

Maybe if he could make her grasp his dual identities, she could understand him. But he did not answer, and instead released a guttural sound, one that instantly caused her to shiver atop him. "This is me," he growled, and he felt the fire between them grow cold as he rolled her off of him. She spilled awkwardly onto the pillows beside him, sprawling there with a soft gasp of surprise. "You'd best learn now that I am not given to sentiment."

She turned on him, clutching one of the pillows against

her chest. "I don't believe that," she insisted, her voice rising in anger. "You're crazy if you think I buy that for one minute! It goes against everything you've told me since I got here."

Staring at the ceiling, half praying for guidance, he made a simple grunt of displeasure, but said nothing more. One week was damned fast—too much control, too much power given into this alien woman's strong hands—and it terrified him.

"I do not like this hold you have upon me," he snarled at her, rubbing his hand along his jaw. "It is too powerful for a stranger." Although he, of all people, understood that they'd ceased to be strangers that night one week before.

"In what universe am *I* the stranger?" she shot back at him, then hit her forehead with the heel of her hand. "Oh, *that's* right—that would be your universe. On this planet, last time I checked, *you're* the alien."

Kelsey Wells had spirit—true backbone—and it instantly penetrated all his old fears about love and abandonment. "I stand corrected." He gave a grudging smile. "Smarter minds obviously prevail in this relationship." To punctuate the apology, he bowed slightly in respect.

"So you're admitting it's a relationship now?" she said. "One minute, I'm just a stranger, but now I'm part of a twosome?"

"You confound me, Kelsey Wells."

She set her jaw, blue eyes flashing with fire. "Hey, maybe it's time someone did."

"These emotions, this connection . . . I find it most confusing," he admitted seriously, adjusting his jeans so that his erection didn't hurt so damned much. Bad strategy, falling into a disagreement with the human at such a prize moment as this one.

She knelt before him, leaning in close until her steady gaze locked with his own. "Tell me what this is between us," she insisted, her voice growing softer again. "I think you know what's really happening here. I think you can explain it to me. And I don't think it has anything to do with data you put inside of me or even our past together. This is about right here, right now."

Such trust—both in her statement, and shimmering in her firelit eyes—and something about seeing that complete trust there unraveled him. It caused all his poise and self-possession—his attempts to gain control over his skittering emotions—to crash down around him like shattered ice.

Leaping to his feet, he cried, "I have bound you to me! *That* is what I have done!" He began pacing before the fire, the agitation in his heart swelling. "I have taken you and mated your soul to my very own. And for one purpose, Kelsey Wells. To preserve information that might save my people. And yours." Gazing up at him, she remained in the kneeling position, there on the pillows, like a captive offering herself to him. "That is the sort of man I am—that is the sort of man you are dealing with here. I've taken you against your will, by the gods. And not only that. I allowed you to give yourself to me in return. That is not the behavior of an ally, but of an enemy. And yet—we are mated. We are fully bound to one another, human. Mystical, pure . . . and yet utterly, utterly *wrong.*"

Her features hardened. "When?" she demanded. "When did we . . . mate?"

"The night of my crash. *That* is what happened there, Kelsey," he said, punctuating each word with his finger in the air as he paced before the fire. "*That* is why we can't stop hungering this way—not because of love or tenderness or attraction. Not even memory! Because I forced my will upon you."

"Forced?" she whispered, and he dropped down before her, so that he was kneeling just as she did.

"And yet you think you care for me," he continued, schooling his features into a cold, fearsome expression. "You think me beautiful? A man you might love?" He couldn't seem to halt the fury, the deep pain, so long etched into his heart, and now that she'd uncorked it, it seemed like acid, overflowing onto the gentle, strong human before him. "You think me a man who might not harm you, given the chance? If so, you think wrongly! Perhaps now you understand."

Frowning, tears pooling within her eyes, she studied his face and whispered the one thing he least expected: "I don't think that I could love you," she said in reply. "I *know* that I could."

With a rough sound, he rose and strode from the room like a firestorm, all quake and thunder and fury. Sprawling on the pillows, Kelsey watched Jared's retreat, shocked. Her mouth still felt swollen from his kisses, her body still ravaged by his fever. But even as she blinked back tears— tears caused by his horrible admission of how he'd taken her against her will—the quietest of voices argued that Jared had not told her the full truth. *There is more to this situation,* the scientist within her resolved. *There is much more to this man you've already come to care for—and who has obviously come to care for you.*

In her heart, she heard his words from last night in the car: *no other human.* She was the first and only one on her planet whom he'd ever allowed to glimpse him. And what was all this about their souls being mated? She had to know more, had to understand what he had revealed.

Rising to her feet, she went out the same door he'd used, past the sitting area and into what appeared to be his dressing room. There, bent over the sink, the alien warrior stood, shirtless, splashing water on his face—a face that could be described only as ashen. Without looking up at her or even meeting her gaze in the mirror, he demanded, "Why do you follow?"

She stepped closer, her eyes fixed on his reflection. "I think you care for me."

He made a slight groaning sound, as plaintive and despairing as it was angry. "I have told you what exists between us."

"But it isn't *all* the truth," she pressed, reaching a hand to touch his bare shoulder. A long mark graced his back, running down along his shoulder all the way to the small of his back—a jagged, angry scar, and for some reason, she felt the need to caress it. Lifting delicate fingers, she traced the outline, and he visibly flinched, jerking upright. His blazing eyes locked with hers in the mirror.

"Kelsey, it has to be the truth," he said in a low, pained voice, much like the sound of a wounded timber wolf, baying at the moon. "Human, it must be. I must lead this revolution," he continued. His voice assumed an even, placating sound. "I must be focused. Not distracted by someone as . . . perplexing as you."

"Are you not allowed to love?" she asked, cocking her head sideways and studying him in the mirror.

This comment seemed to garner a strong reaction, his

black eyes flaring bright with harnessed energy. Alien eyes, masquerading as human.

"I am allowed whatever I choose to venture."

"Oh," she said, her hand withdrawing from him to flutter to her collarbone protectively. "Then you must not want to love me."

A terrible broken sound erupted from his chest—something foreign and decidedly inhuman—and he swept her into his arms with unbridled force. She could barely breathe, feeling his strong ribs pressed hard against her, feeling the untamed rhythm of his heart. With every moment that unfurled between them, he seemed to become more alien. Less human. The change aroused something primal within her.

Murmuring words that she did not recognize, he ran his strong hands all over her body, almost as if he needed to feel her shape. Her substance. He made another cry, a harsh, angry sound. "If I am not careful, Kelsey Wells," he confessed, pressing his lips against the top of her head, "I *will* love you. It is what I fear most right now."

"Why is that something to fear?" she argued, wrapping her arms around his lower back, holding him close.

"Because no man has ever slain me."

Suddenly, she understood. "But a woman has."

He turned, pulling free from her arms, again putting his back to her. Kelsey followed. "Was she . . . bound to you?"

"Never," he said, their eyes locking in the mirror. "Never before have I taken a bondmate. Never a mate."

"Why not?"

He didn't answer, so she reached to touch his lower back again, feeling the thick scar beneath her fingertips. "I can't imagine anyone refusing you."

With the unexpectedness of a snow squall, he whirled upon her, shape-shifting in the flare of an instant to the fiery, blazing ball of energy she had first seen on the lakeshore a week earlier. He shot past her, back to the bedroom, hovering over the pillows where they'd been lying together only moments earlier. Swallowing hard, she followed him, taking cautious steps toward the place where his radiant form blazed in competition with the flames in the fireplace—not touching the floor or the ceiling, but occupying nearly the entire space between both boundaries.

"Jared," she said, keeping her voice calm as she measured out her steps. He wanted her to be terrified, wanted to demonstrate that anyone in her right mind would be afraid. In fact, he seemed eager to prove that point to her.

The hearth behind him was little more than a dim candle compared to his wild brightness, towering high over her—much higher than he had that night at Mirror Lake.

"Jareshk, did this frighten the woman you loved? The one you wanted to bond with?" she asked, craning her neck to take in the full height of him, fury and all. But the brightness proved too much, forcing her eyes shut.

Would you *mate with this?* he shouted inside of her mind, the words searing her heart. *Willingly?*

"Yes."

Then you are insane!

Forcing her eyes open, she gazed upon him, refusing to flinch—refusing to back down or away. "I have never seen anyone more beautiful in all my life."

The roaring storm grew hushed, still. Like Christmas Eve on Main Street back in her hometown, all expectant and magical. *Beautiful,* he repeated, and she shivered, feeling his deep, shocked pleasure.

"Oh, yes, Jared," she said, smiling. "Amazingly beautiful. Just as I told you before."

The golden fire of him suddenly burned a deep russet, almost the color of her hair. In some elemental way, she recognized that he was blushing. Feeling her compliment to his very core.

Kelsey. He sighed, but said nothing more. *Lovely, lovely. Human beautiful. Strange.*

As with the first night, she realized that to keep his true form, he had to sacrifice his facility with human language. So she chose to stand before him, as quiet as she felt him to be, and gaze upon him, watching the reddish hue morph back to the recognizable blaze of fire. Reaching out one hand, she wanted to touch him, but again like the first night, he admonished her: *No touch!*

Why was he always so adamant that she not touch him? Maybe he was, in some way, like that stone that he wore, capable of blistering her with a single touch.

She held her palms out to him, opening them. "Then touch *me,* Jared. You touch me . . . like that other time.

When we . . . well, when we made the bond, like you said. I want to feel that bonding again."

Her eyes were closed against his wildness, but she sensed him whispering within her soul at that moment. Some sort of promise, or assurance, or pledge. She didn't think to question it, because at that precise moment, the low burn began—just as it had that first night between them— winding its way up her legs, parting her thighs, searing her until her lips opened with a quiet *ohhhhh* sound of pleasure. The closer he pressed within her, the more she could feel his memories. She saw unearthly sunsets and flashes of people in his life—dark-haired men and women and his beautiful cousin. Then she saw, oddly enough, an image of herself.

Now he's in my heart, she realized, feeling him burrow in, his soul pushing upon hers. Her nipples grew erect within her bra, pressing against the thin silk. He eased farther apart from her, careening toward the far side of the room, but she understood somehow that he wished her to lie down on the large throw pillows. A single alien word whispered through her consciousness. Instinctively she knew its meaning: *Open.*

"Open?" she repeated. "Open what?

Then she felt him tease her, coaxing her open. Her soul, her body. She arched beneath the seduction, lifting her hips, her eyes drifting closed again. One by one, she unsnapped the buttons of her sweater until it fell open for him, revealing her human body. She stripped out of her bra, and he sighed across her skin—all the while keeping his distance on the other side of the room.

Sitting up, she managed to open her eyes and stare at him, and without ever allowing her gaze to waver, she slipped out of her jeans until she stood before her lover in nothing more than her panties.

He whispered a few words within her spirit, then her name, which sounded a bit like "Kelsha."

Down! he urged. *Pillows.*

So she obeyed, spreading across the silken throw pillows, flat on her back. At that precise moment he moved, now hovering directly over her against the ceiling. His fire overtook her in the space of a single heartbeat, snaking across her abdomen, coiling about her loins and tightening. She bucked her hips upward, crying out loudly. His fiery fingers reached between her legs, inside, touching, caressing, working their way to the very center of her being.

She couldn't breathe; couldn't think. There was just so much of him, all inside of her, and she couldn't stop shaking, her entire body shuddering. "More!" she cried, bunching silk within her hands, her back arching. "Jared, more!"

And he obviously sensed her longing, moving quickly apart from her—no longer hovering over her body. From across the room, even with her eyes closed, she knew he was shifting again, closing the distance that separated them with one quick stride. "Kelsey," he moaned, falling upon her. "Kelsey, Kelsey."

His body was hot to the touch, burning her fingertips as she ran them over his strong, muscled shoulders, his dark forearms.

For a moment, he tugged at her underwear, scowling in deep and obvious consternation. A low growl rumbled from his chest, something primitive that she welcomed from him. Taking one fingertip, he used his power to separate her from the silken material.

"This . . . patch," he observed, stroking the silken red hair that graced the area between her legs. "It is red. But blond some, too."

"You've never been with a redhead, I take it." She gasped. His eyes lifted to hers, mischievous with desire, and he teased his fingers through the thatch of auburn curls that had caught his fancy, dipping his fingers into her wet warmth.

With a satisfied, slow smile, he told her, "I like red. Everyone knows this." In response, she shimmied back against the pillows. "Yes," he said, pressing a burning kiss against her abdomen. "I definitely like red."

"And I like you out of those jeans," she shot back.

Glancing down with sudden self-consciousness, he seemed almost surprised to discover himself still dressed. With a flick of his wrist, he unsnapped the Levi's and snaked right out of them until he stood before her in all of his glorious naked form. *Wow, so the alien warrior goes commando? Good to know.*

"You are quite naughty, human."

"How could you hear that?"

Pressing his long, sinewy body on top of her smaller one, he nuzzled her, slipping right between her legs. *Because I could,* he answered with a heady little sound inside her soul.

"Is this because we are bound?" she managed to pant into his ear. "Because we're tied together, like you said?"

"No, Kelsey," he whispered, pulling her back into the pillows, spread like an offering to the king. "It is not because we are bound," he managed to groan, desire and heat reaching a mad crescendo inside his body. He would do anything to take this human, anything to mate with her, anything to satisfy this pulsing intensity that the bond had created in his Refarian bloodstream. *It is far more than the bond,* he told himself. *It is Kelsey—you have fallen for the human. You feel love.*

With that inner admission came another. He could no longer hold back: He would bed her tonight, no matter the cost. Even if such a joining would mean they could not go back, could not reverse the bond that had been formed.

"Then why, Jared?" She gasped as he pushed between her legs. "Why can we not stop these feelings? This fire?"

"Because, sweet Kelsey." He sighed, knowing that his next words *would* be true, once they had completed what they'd already begun a week ago. "We are more than bond-mates," he said. "A bond is beautiful, powerful. Special. Sacred. But this is more."

"What more is it?" she asked, breathless.

"I believe we are destined," he whispered in her ear. "I wish you for my lifemate."

Oh, my goodness. Kelsey drew in a breath as he pushed against her opening like sculpted stone sheathed in silk.

For long seconds he hesitated, hovered there, pushed a bit, pulled back. "Jared!" she cried aloud, clutching at his broad shoulders.

Drawing in ragged breaths, he stared down into her eyes. "We'll never have this moment again," he told her huskily. "Never can we go back."

"I don't think I want to," she said, stroking his hair, his shoulders, needing all of him.

Sucking in gulps of air, he worked to steady himself, then, cupping her face, whispered, "Until we seal our bond, it can be broken, sweet Kelsey. Do you understand? After, we are bound forever. If we cross this boundary, if we take this step—"

She pressed her fingertips against his lips, silencing him. "Then we become lifemates. Don't we?"

He nodded, closing his eyes. "You speak truth," he whispered, swallowing. "And perhaps we should wait. Too fast, too soon."

"I won't wait," she insisted, clasping his hips and urging him onward, feeling something strange boil in her blood. Something that she understood was the very alien compulsion to mate.

"Yes, love." He sighed, and then did something unexpected. He whispered a line of poetry into her ear, something about changing states with kings. *Shakespeare!* she realized with a giddy laugh. "Yes again, my love," he purred, and then, without another word, plunged deep inside of her.

At first they rocked quietly together; then they intensified their motions, crying out, pushing, chasing each other's need to the very brink of ecstasy; later, as they neared the end, they couldn't stop cradling each other's faces, showering each other with sweet kisses. But neither spoke a word; neither wanted to communicate that way. Jared began to feel Kelsey's soul; imperceptible at first, the softest brushing of hers against his—but then the sensations intensified until he lost himself in it, seeing the beautiful purples and crimsons of her energy. Drinking in her scent, drawing it deep into his lungs with every thrust he made into her human body.

At last, he could no longer hold back—and judging by the way she moaned beneath him, she didn't want him to. He allowed the bond between them to finally roar to life—allowed it to solidify hard within his chest as it took root forever. Alien bound to human. He belonged to Kelsey Wells. For the first time in his adult life, the solemn, lone warrior no longer stood on his own.

Afterward, they stepped silently into his bath and he drew warm water for them in his large, claw-foot bathtub. Sliding in after him, she slipped backward against him, sated and drowsy in his strong arms. Neither seemed to want to speak at first, seemed only to require the quiet. She nestled back against him, and he took the large sea sponge and began using it along her arms, stroking her with it.

"Jared, I have a question," she asked after a time, startling him.

"Yes, love."

"How is it that you're two people at once?" she asked, and his throat constricted. Did she still wonder about him? It was too late for fear or doubt, he wanted to tell her, but he had said that before they made love. Very carefully, he framed his answer.

"I am Refarian. I am also of the House of D'Aravni. That is my royal line, and I am the last," he explained hoarsely. "The being you saw at the lake—in this bedroom tonight? That is one self. The man who holds you now is the other. There is a duality, you see."

"So . . . let me get this straight," she said, leaning back against him with what sounded like—could it possibly be?—a happy and satisfied sigh. His heart began to thunder until it seemed to leap into his throat. "You are partly of this royal house, but then you're also a Refarian. Is that right?"

"A Refarian changeling," he clarified, swallowing. "That's how I shape-shift."

"What does it mean to be part of this royal house? Are you your own, unique kind of race?"

"I am two men." He pressed a kiss to the top of her head. "Both at once."

"You're a changeling, and then you're this other . . ." Her voice trailed off, and within her spirit he sensed a constriction: truth realized. "Well, you're their king."

"I am their *leader*, Kelsey," he whispered, brushing a wet, curling tendril back from her cheek. "That is all that matters now. I lead this rebellion and I fight to save my people. And yours."

"But these people here fighting with you," she continued, "every last one of them considers you their king."

"Yes, Kelsey, what you say is the truth," he answered finally, his voice thick. *Please don't flee me; please don't fear,* his heart begged of her. "Even in exile, I remain their king."

"And it's, like, a unique race—if I understand right? You're not quite Refarian?" she asked, leaning back, close against him. "Or, no, that's not it. It's that you're Refarian, but something else too."

"Refarian and something else," he repeated. "This is correct." Arganate D'Aravni. But he would not try to explain the complexities of his unique and strange genetic heritage tonight.

"So you are both men at once," she repeated, her voice thoughtful. "You have two bodies, not just one, like I do."

He reached for the sponge and slowly worked it across her shoulder. "Yes, sweet human," he said. "You are right again."

He held her closer than an ion's meter, felt her ribs beneath his splayed palm, the measure of her breathing. Did it increase? Did it strangle with terror at loving one of his bloodline? Somehow, if he could only draw her inside of himself, closer, up within his chest or into his blood or even his cells . . .

And then he waited. One heartbeat lay down upon another, upon another, forming a frantic, uncertain rhythm. Expecting betrayal. Awaiting abandonment. Lahrae had stared at him, mouth agape, unable to conceive that Jared could be two men simultaneously, that one self could peacefully coexist with the other, belly-up to each other, yet both equally real. And she had feared his fire, the same fire that he felt banking in his loins even now, here in this very tub. The same fire that had *not* terrified Kelsey when they'd made love for the first time.

Yes, another heartbeat thundered down upon another, upon yet another, until . . . Kelsey leaned back against him with a sigh—a full, pleased sound of safety—and threaded her smaller fingers together with his strong dark ones.

Until Jared Bennett knew, at last, that he loved well. That he loved a woman who did not fear him.

Chapter Nine

Stepping into the bathroom doorway, aroused and naked, Jared stared at Kelsey. Her thick curls cascaded over the porcelain edge of the tub, and even in the candlelit semi-darkness, he could see a slow, tempting smile form on her lips. He had slept with many women in his time—many beautiful Refarian women and even a few Antousian hybrids back in his wilder days—but he was certain of one thing: No woman, not of any species, had ever appeared so worthy of the title *queen* as did his sweet human at this moment.

He'd intended to check with Scott about a few things, but had been derailed by the sight of her reclining in the tub. Extending one pale, lightly freckled hand, she beckoned him, and soap bubbles dripped from her fingers onto the thick bath mat. Smiling up at him, covered in shimmering foam, she appeared to be one of the legendary *lalastra* from the myths of his home planet. Like Earth's mermaids, the *lalastra* lived in the sea and were considered by Refarians to be mystical, erotic creatures, capable of luring unsuspecting men into the very depths of obsession—to their deaths, even, in pursuit of the creatures' sensual thrall.

As if by unseen force, he moved toward the bathtub, feeling his groin tighten with a spasm of desire. *"Mlashk lalastra,"* he breathed huskily.

"What does that mean?" she asked, running her tongue along her bottom lip as he took another step closer. Her gaze dropped low, her eyes widening slightly at his undisguised arousal.

"Mermaid," he explained, staring down at her possessively. "I called you my tempting, seducing mermaid. In Refarian, of course."

She held the sponge close, almost protectively against her chest. "You think I'm tempting?"

He dropped to his knees behind her, at the head of the tub, and leaned over her so that his mouth grazed just behind her ear. "Human, you are quite a temptress," he whispered, nibbling at her lobe. "I have discovered this about you already." She shivered at his words, or perhaps at the feeling of his warm breath against the nape of her neck. "I have discovered that you are not nearly so innocent as you seemed upon first notice," he added, pulling her strong human scent into his lungs, drinking her in until he felt dizzy with it.

Reaching back over her shoulder, she touched his jaw. "Well, I *like* to tempt you," she acknowledged in a low voice.

He gathered handfuls of her thick, twined curls. The dampness had caused her auburn hair to tangle into an erotic display of beauty. "You tempt very well, fiery one," he groaned with pleasure, pressing his lips against her shoulder, sucking and licking at the wet skin there.

She turned so that her radiant eyes locked with his. "No, Jared," she said. "It's not just temptation. I plan to follow through on my promises."

"Ah, indeed." He slipped his hands from behind her, cupping both of her full, round breasts in his open palms, stroking his thumbs over her puckered nipples with a relentless motion that caused them to bead even harder beneath his fingertips.

In answer she moaned, a loud, almost indelicate sound, and arched back into his grasp. He reached lower with one of his hands, parting her legs, then pressing fingertips upward, into her. "And, human," he asked, fingering her slickness, slow and deliberate, "what do you think of this? Good temptation or no?"

Planting both feet against the porcelain rim of the tub, she raised her hips with a stabbing cry of pleasure.

"Perhaps this is not good," he assessed, nuzzling her. "Maybe I should stop?" He made a pretense of releasing her, and she reached back over her shoulder, grasping for him with a flailing hand as he leaned low, whispering in her ear. "Tell me, dear Kelsey," he said, feigning seriousness, "shall I cease this action?"

Panting, she managed to grab hold of his hand, crying out, "Jared! What . . . do . . . you . . . *think*?"

A deep, rumbling moan of pleasure escaped from his chest. "I think you like being with this Refarian," he answered in a gruff voice, laving her earlobe with the tip of his tongue. "I think you *like* being the king's mistress. Yes, you seem to like this very much."

"Mistress?" She sounded almost alarmed, her whole body stiffening at the word. He cursed his nearly but not quite perfect command of English. *"Mistress?"* she repeated.

"Lover," he rushed to correct, pressing his eyes shut at his mistake. "Lover. The king's *lover*," he hastened. "Mistress means . . . Well, it's not quite right, is it?"

She gave a shrug. "If you plan no true commitment, then yeah, mistress would be accurate, sure." Her voice was quiet, wounded—cool, even—as she stared into her lap. His hand between her legs suddenly seemed that of an invader, not of a welcomed lover. "Kings throughout the ages have kept mistresses," she continued. "So what should stop you?"

"Kelsey, I fear . . ." He hesitated, trying to think clearly in English amid a muddled rush of Refarian words. He shook his head to clear it, clasping her by the shoulders with a gentle gesture. "I have chosen the wrong word in your language, I am certain. *Mistress* is not the same as *lover*, is it?"

She glanced up at him, her face drained of all its usual rosy beauty, and simply shook her head.

"My wording is inaccurate, then," he said, rising to his feet as he shrugged out of his bathrobe. He swung one long leg over the side of the porcelain tub. Sliding down into the warm water, he faced Kelsey, noting the slight hurt in her expression. Never taking his gaze off of her, he made a great show of drawing each of her legs around his hips, tugging her close until his groin made contact with hers. She lazed back in the tub, apart from him, with only her legs wrapped close about his waist.

"We are committed, Kelsey," he assured her huskily.

"More than committed. It is as I said before: We are mated now, sweet human. You are mine." He felt a possessive growl rise up from within, something primal that he'd never once felt with a lover before, not even with Lahrae. "Mine," he repeated with a wondrous grin, thrilling at the sound of the word, at the sense of belonging—and of belonging *to*—another. *Mine, mine, mine,* he wished to cry, but managed to quell that nearly uncontrollable urge. "We are mated; we are lovers; we are bonded," he proclaimed in a rush. "I am yours and *you* are *mine.*"

"Geez, Jared." She laughed, cutting her eyes at him. "And I thought my ex-boyfriend had possession issues." She gave a little, delicate snort of amusement—and yet also seemed pleased by his possessive streak.

He ran his palm over the top of his head. "Jamie Watson wished to own you," he observed, feeling guilty. "I am not like this man."

"How did you know his name?" Her graceful auburn eyebrows shot upward in surprise.

Without meaning to, he had just betrayed his secret. "Love," he whispered, "we are here. We are *now.*"

"Tell me how you knew Jamie's name," she insisted, sitting upright in the tub. "I never told you what his name was."

"Does it matter?" he asked, snaking his arms around her waist, determined to redirect her to more immediate and corporeal pleasures.

"Yes." Her voice had become hushed, her expression equally intense. Her blue eyes fixed on him, seeming to flash golden-green with emotion; he could see it even by the candlelight here in his bath chamber. "It totally matters, Jared. How did you know?" Her long, spiraling curls hung heavy with dampness, but her scorching gaze was anything but subdued. She pinned him with it, fire flashing from the very depths of her clear eyes. "I met Jamie years after I met you—you couldn't know his name."

"I saw it," he confessed, running both open palms over her muscular thighs, then skimming them underneath until he clasped her shapely bottom in both hands. "I saw it in your mind. The night of my crash." He'd dreaded her knowing that fact for the past week, but now that they were truly bonded, he felt an exhilarating freedom with this woman. Felt that she should know and sense all that he had kept inside of himself, that she should uncork it as if he were her very own genie—and then she would own *him*, as well.

Her face fell, her expression becoming grave. "I see." She pulled back from him, drawing her legs back against herself.

He stopped with his act of body worship and leveled his gaze at her. "You are angry?"

"It's a little personal, don't you think?" How had they gone from nearly making love one moment, to falling into a lovers' quarrel the next? "I mean, what?" she pressed. "You know everything that's inside of me? I don't get to tell you anything myself? Just like that"—she snapped her fingers to illustrate her point—"it's all yours?"

Odd, but he felt his entire body tremble in reply to her question. His heartbeat accelerated; his throat tightened. "We *are* personal," he said, surprised by the way his voice betrayed his feelings. He clasped both of her hands, placing them on his own dark-skinned thighs. "*This* is personal, Kelsey."

"I should've had some choice in the matter," she answered, looking away from him. Then, tears glinting in her eyes, she turned back to face him. "What else did you see?"

Ah, now this question—this one he had dreaded most of all. *What else did you see, foolish, idiot king?* The answers were too myriad even to address.

He tilted his chin upward, seizing control of the moment like the commander that he was. He even allowed defiance to enter his tone. "Many things," he answered. "I saw many things inside of you, human."

She leaned closer, placing an open palm over his crazily pounding heart. "Many *personal* things?" she pressed.

He lifted an eyebrow in challenge—and yet he had no wish to cause her even a moment's pain. "Many *Kelsey* things," he told her, his feelings for her coloring his confession. "Many, many facets to the woman I now love."

She nodded and, chewing on her full lower lip, seemed to think on his answer for a long moment. His heartbeat's tempo took yet another spiraling, upward turn until he could feel the very blood coursing through his veins, could feel the muscle in his chest pumping to keep pace with the emotional intensity between them. Just when he'd begun to wonder if he'd shattered everything between the two of them, she glanced upward and searched his face. Her irises seemed large and black, the emotion in her eyes palpable. But he did not blink beneath her scrutiny, and for long moments they regarded each other. Such strangers they were in one way, aliens completely, and yet fully mated despite that fact.

"You love me?" she asked thickly after a few searching moments.

He bowed his head, smiling. "Sweet human, what else could you possibly think? I loved you years ago, and I love you now."

"Why didn't you tell me you'd seen all those things?" She didn't try to mask the hurt in her voice. "If you'd just told me . . ."

He shrugged, wishing he had an apology to offer, but there was none. There was only the truth: "I wished you to love me, Kelsey." There, he had said it. "I had already glimpsed everything—it could not be undone. I wished you to believe me a good man, insane as that may now seem."

"Jared!" she cried, leaning close—much closer. She slid upward, climbing onto his lap with a burst of heartfelt exuberance until the water sloshed over the rim of the tub and he had to groan with the sudden weight of her upon him. She was not a small woman, not by even his own species' reckoning. "Jared, I do love you. Already. I did from"— she paused, cupping his face within her soft palms and turning it upward until his eyes locked with hers—"well, from the beginning, I think. But you should have told me." She shook her head, tears welling in her cool-eyed gaze again. "I really wish you had before tonight."

"Before we mated," he finished.

"It's a trust thing."

He felt with her now as he often did with humans: unable to reason out her reaction. "You are angry about this seeing inside of you," he observed, feeling confused, "but not about my forming the bond?"

"I told you that was okay. I told you I wanted to help that night, remember? But this . . . this is you seeing *into* me."

"Isn't that what lovers do?" he asked, and meant it. Maybe the timing had been wrong, but damn it all, he'd gazed into her as surely as if they'd been mated lovers already. "Don't they see each other's hearts? Very souls?"

She dropped her head. "I wouldn't know."

"You know *me* now, Kelsey," he promised, taking her chin and tipping it upward until their eyes met again in the dim light of the candles around them. Beyond her shoulder an array of tapers stood along the ledge of the tiled wall, their flames licking at the otherwise dark room, creating lyrical shadows in every direction. "Did you not see inside of me?" he asked, curious. He had wondered—frantically wondered—what she might have seen within him by the lake.

She shook her head, her expression becoming unreadable and sad, but her tender gaze never left his face. "Only images, tonight while we made love." She stroked his cheek, tracing the outline of his scars. He wanted to flinch beneath her close scrutiny, but willed himself not to. "No, I didn't see inside of you, not really. But maybe one day I can."

"I wish you had."

"I've felt you, though," she said, her voice growing much softer. "All week. It's become more and more intense."

"That is our bond," he agreed, staring up into her eyes. The blue in them had all but vanished, replaced by bright green. "You opened to me—did you know that?"

She shook her head, confused. "What does that mean? To *open?*"

"Most of my species would guard themselves," he explained. "Without even meaning to do so. You . . . opened. There is not another word for it." The language barrier between them agonized him—he longed for his native tongue in a way he'd not done in years.

"When you appeared, there at the lake after your crash," she said, seeming to choose her own words carefully, "I was terrified of you. But I was drawn to you too. It was weird, Jared. I wanted to be afraid, but I couldn't be, not really. I felt your goodness. I'm sure some lost part of me remembered you, but it was more than that—much more. It was like down inside of you something beautiful attracted me. Something beautiful and very, very appealing."

He remembered the way she had responded as they'd formed the bond; how the physicality of it had aroused her. But had it been something about him as well? "Ah," he whispered, and searched for the right words, but seemed unable to produce another intelligent syllable in English. So he repeated the only ones that came to mind: "Ah, Kelsey."

She bent down to kiss him full on the mouth, almost as if sealing something between the two of them. As he sucked on her lower lip, teasing her with his tongue, she tasted sweet, like the whiskey he'd served her earlier—and she even tasted Refarian somehow, infused with the intoxicating kisses he'd been giving her all night long, and perhaps because she truly was a part of him now. He clasped her face in his hands, and she coaxed his lips open, her tongue darting into his mouth, twining with his own.

She was so close upon him, he could feel the warmth of her breath tickling his cheek, and her steady heartbeat beneath the palm he'd splayed across her back.

"Jared," she groaned in his ear as he cupped her bottom, holding her firm atop his groin. His erection pressed into her thigh, and he ached with need for her. Gods, how he wanted her—more than earlier, more than during the past week. His heart and loins thundered with his desperate hunger for his mate.

"Jared?" she whispered in his ear, her voice a coquettish, seductive sound.

"Umm?" he managed, feeling her lift atop him slightly. Her hand slipped between them, closing about his erection. He cried out at the intimate touch.

"I'm going to do something," she warned him with a vixen's laugh right in his ear, never relinquishing her hold on the hardened length of him.

"Okay." The word came out all breathless and desperate. Damn it all, he had no control with this human! "Do . . . what?" He gasped, practically begging, as she gave his erection another tantalizing stroke, her thumb lingering on the vein underneath until he growled.

Her moody eyes narrowed with desire, and she positioned herself squarely on his lap, over him. Then in one swift, aggressive move, she sheathed herself over his hardened length. Against the back of his neck, the faucet knob pushed into the base of his skull. He braced his feet against the tub's ledge as she rocked atop him with a furious motion. This time it wasn't gentle or beautiful; this taking of hers was fierce and binding. She wanted to seize something from him—just as he had taken from her soul that night at the lake. Men and kings and rulers all wished to dominate him; never did he submit. But this lover of his . . . he yearned for their bond to be equal—he yearned for her— and she needed to take him. With a muffled groan of pure pleasure, he closed his eyes and let himself fall under her control.

Her thighs tightened, pulling against his, and her fingers clawed at his shoulders. Water swelled over the sides of the tub, sloshing onto the tiled floor. Over and over he moaned her name, whispered it, prayed it, breathed it. All the while he felt something unfamiliar rising to a crescendo in his blood, something that could never be denied. But he ignored the siren song of that thing, focusing only on Kelsey, right here, right now, atop him. He could feel the deepest place inside of her, like a slick, grasping caress. Unrelenting, she continued to move atop him, gasping, throwing her head back in ecstasy.

On and on they went for long, aching minutes. Kelsey wrapped her arms around Jared, pressing her abdomen flat against his. Her breasts moved against his face, and the bristling of his shadowed beard scraped at her nipples. She didn't care; she had to have all of this man who already owned so much of her. He'd wanted her to love him, and she did, completely, but there was a possessing that also remained here. Beneath her, his skin seemed darker than before—*he* seemed darker, more ambiguous. "What"—she gasped as she rocked atop him—"did"—more movement, her pushing down atop him—"you . . . see?" she cried out, her own orgasm ripping through her core as she felt his burning essence fill her.

She cried, and he gasped, his face twisting into a glorious wince of pain and bliss. He grasped at her, his large hands steadying her atop him. He'd slid down into the tub beneath her until he was in a contorted position that didn't look even remotely comfortable—but her alien made zero complaints. Now they stared at each other, almost squared off into a battle of wills, his chest rising with ragged breaths.

"I saw that you are unique," he answered, panting. "I saw a kind, good, strong woman—untouched by the evil I've known all my days." He paused, his sensuous eyes narrowing. "I saw that you possessed every quality my heart has secretly longed for in a wife." *Wife?* But then again, what else was a lifemate? "I saw," he said, easing her off of him, "that humans, despite this war I'm embroiled in, are good and noble people—that is, if they are like you, my love."

She pitched forward, tears suddenly coming unbidden. She leaned against him, feeling his hands trace her backbone, caress the whole of her body. And she wasn't certain why she cried; maybe it was realizing that he knew her through and through. Maybe it was that she could never know him in the same way, not without this alien ability of looking into someone's soul. Or maybe it was just that she felt—despite how he'd invaded her initially, against her will—full trust for him. And there was a tremendous relief that came with that realization.

She should feel robbed of something; should have felt, as she had at first, that she wanted to take something from him in turn. But what she felt, here with the warmth of the lapping water around them both, with his muscled, warrior's body beneath her and his strong arms around her, was something unexpectedly alien: the complete, abiding, perfect trust of belonging to another. And she did belong, not just to Jared as a mate or a lover, but here with him, right in his arms. Somehow across the twining, circuitous paths that searched the galaxies, her soul mate had come to her.

"On Refaria, we have an understanding of time that is different from yours," he whispered, petting her hair with a gentle gesture. "It flows, forward and backward; sometimes it folds sideways or makes a contortion." She sniffled loudly, her face still buried against his sinewy shoulder. "But the main thing time does is that it brings us to the place where we belong."

I belong with you, she thought, closing her eyes. She hadn't belonged anywhere in such a long, long time—not really. Hot tears squeezed out, rolling down her face and blending with the warm bathwater. *Oh, I so belong here.*

"Some of my people even believe time to be a mirror," he continued in a whisper, "reflecting all our infinite possibilities, in multiple dimensions."

She pulled back to look in his eyes. "I have studied physics," she reminded him, sniffling. "So I'm familiar with hyperspace theory."

"But I'm talking about more than theories, Kelsey," he continued. "What I'm getting at is . . . the way you felt you could trust me? That you seemed to know me? Not just now, but when we were children? Perhaps on some other planet somewhere, you already did. Perhaps you beheld the future, folding onto the moment—and knew I was your mate."

"I recognized you." In all his glorious, terrifying beauty, she had definitely known him. It was all beginning to make sense, even to a scientist like herself.

"And I you."

Then, breaking into a surprising, boyish grin—almost lopsided—he traced his fingertip over her breastbone, outlining a constellation of freckles. "I even knew these."

She leaned upward onto his lap and touched the fanned edges of his almond-shaped eyes. "And I knew these."

"We knew each other," he affirmed with a nod. Somehow, when he put it in great philosophical terms like that, his seeing all her secrets no longer seemed such a very big thing after all.

Chapter Ten

Jared left Kelsey soaking in the tub, a half-dazed expression on her face; their interspecies mating had obviously taken quite a toll on her human body. Blissful, celestial, holy, the joining had nonetheless been exhausting for her system—as had all the emotional interactions between the two of them. Kissing the top of her freckled forehead, he promised to return soon with a surprise, and she sank down into the frothy bubbles with a smile on her face. Just as he'd suspected: The woman loved surprises.

Mirror Lake had been a surprise—the ultimate one for her—yet she'd welcomed him with open hands and heart, then displayed that same lack of inhibition while making love with him tonight. She'd even begged for his fiery other self to touch her. Rarely had Jared felt that kind of deep, resounding acceptance, not in all his thirty years as a dual being. In his most natural state, none dared approach; people feared him, revered him, and if he were critically injured, they attempted to cure him. But none had ever longed to touch him in D'Aravnian form.

Not so with Kelsey. She had wanted his fire to roam all over that luscious curving body of hers, caressing, teasing her—and had never once counted the cost. Perhaps next time he might dare to move even closer. She would be safe, he promised himself, swallowing hard; he could dance near his love, keeping distance enough not to harm her. Just at the thought of it, the bath towel he'd swagged around his hips tented upward with lustful enthusiasm, and he made a rough rumble of desire. *Silence, man, or you'll frighten her,* his calmer side cautioned. *This is all new to her. She does not yet understand what you are.*

Rubbing an open hand over his hammering heart, he worked to center his thoughts. The plan. He had to focus on the plan, which had formed in his mind as a way of expressing something *human* to Kelsey. One thing Jared had come to understand during his six years on Earth was that her species valued their pleasures. Not just the physical-ecstasy kinds of pleasures like the two of them had shared tonight, or life's greatest pleasures, but the simple kinds as well. Food, drink, sleep: Humans enjoyed even the most mundane elements of their existence, and when denied them, they chafed and grew irritable. His own life was a rugged one, with long hours of soldiering and dismal prospects for peace, but he wanted Kelsey to know something better in his arms. He wanted her first night joined with him to be one marked by all the sorts of indulgences that he imagined must matter to her.

And so his plan: He yearned to draw his exotic lifemate up into bed and *feed* her. Feed her little bits of chocolate and cookies and grapes, even give her sips of that blasted whiskey he loved so much. Then, after this royal banquet, he intended to massage her feminine toes with some kind of lotion or oil—but where to find such things? Warriors kept no chocolate, no lotion.

Passing by the bathroom door again, he watched Kelsey adjust the faucet with said toes, and he smiled. She possessed beautiful, delicate feet, ones that required adoring. A quick glance at his bedside clock showed the time to be just after midnight, which meant that only watch patrols were about, and possibly Anika, who rarely slept more than an hour or two each night, seemingly powered on bottomless reserves of energy. Ah, his dear Anika—when it came to doting upon her king, she was perhaps the worst in this camp, he thought with a devilish smile, as he slipped into his long terry-cloth robe. Yes, she would know exactly where to find what he needed.

Jared crept into Anika's room, the hall light arcing across the pinewood floorboards. In the top bunk, her twin sister, Anna, sprawled on her stomach and snored, one pale arm dangling over the side listlessly. In the lower bunk, Anika had folded herself into a neat, quiet ball, sleeping without making any noise whatsoever. Squatting beside Anika's bed, he gave her shoulder a nudge. Her eyes snapped open, then widened in alarm upon finding her commander bedside at such a late hour. He lifted a finger to his lips, indicating quiet. "All is well," he assured her, and relief washed over her features. He gave her a warm smile. "But I could use a little help."

"Certainly, my lord." She sat up, all business, without missing a beat—always the disciplined soldier. "Tell me how I may assist you. Is it further help with Kelsey Wells, sir?" she asked.

Did he look as shy and absurd as he suddenly felt? He had no business here, pawing around for such common things. Had he lost his mind? Anika might be his dear friend, but first and foremost she served within his military ranks.

"It is . . . nothing," he answered, his smile turning downward into a frown. "I shouldn't have wakened you. Back to sleep, soldier." He rose to his feet, but Anika followed.

"Please, my lord," she insisted, bowing slightly. "I wish to help with the human." The bow deepened, became a low gesture, and she placed one fist over her chest in pledge. He could trust this woman; there were few in all his elite forces more loyal or more deserving of his faith than Anika. Only Scott ranked higher as a friend and confidant. "Please, Anika," he whispered hoarsely. "Rise."

She obeyed, pulling up to her full, willowy stature. "Tell me how I may help," she urged again, turning her open, kind face upward toward him.

"I require chocolate," he grunted—rather unpleasantly—folding both arms over his chest. The robe fell open then, revealing his bare skin beneath, still flushed with the afterglow of mating. Anika averted her eyes and he added, "Very fine chocolate."

The edges of Anika's fan-shaped eyes turned slightly upward with joy. "Chocolate, my lord?" Oh, this pleased his lieutenant—pleased her quite a bit, in fact, from what he could see. Among his people, those who attempted such workings were called *lalalosungs:* a mellifluous term for those with a sneaky habit of matchmaking.

"Lalalosung," he accused, his frown beginning to tug into a smile.

"Courting king," she shot back at him, eyes gleaming. For a long moment each regarded the other in challenge. Then Jared burst into rumbling peals of laughter—couldn't have stopped himself if he'd tried—until, on the upper bunk, her twin sister stirred. Anika yanked him by the hand, pulling him beneath the bunk and onto her bed before Anna woke and discovered her commander standing in their bedroom. He nearly slammed his forehead into the frame of the upper bunk, but fortunately missed the wooden beam by an inch or so.

Once they were settled and Anna's snoring had resumed, Anika leaned close, smiling at him. "My lord, did you know that humans consider chocolate to be a sort of love token?" she whispered, her voice assuming a conspiratorial quality as she crossed her legs. "Some even say it's an aphrodisiac."

Strange, but he felt himself blush at her remark. "Yes, I have heard this."

"I wasn't sure if you knew that, sir." She leaned under the bed to retrieve a small box of private things, depositing it on the mattress between the two of them. When she removed the lid, there in the middle of the trunk sat a golden, perfect box, like the most royal case of jewels. GOD IVA. Was this the name of a human god? He cocked his head sideways, heightening his vision so he could better read the lettering: GODIVA. Ah, a single word. Yes, he had heard this term before here on Earth, though where precisely, he could not recall.

"They make delicious, wonderful chocolate," she promised him, her dark eyes growing wide.

Nodding toward the gilded box, he asked, "How did you procure this?"

"I have my ways," she answered cryptically, sliding the unopened box across the bed toward him.

"This seems a prize item," he protested, pushing it back toward her with his fingertips.

She shook her head, beaming at him. "Take it," she sang, again slipping the box across the bed like a golden pawn. "It's your mating night, my lord."

He opened his mouth in disbelief. The woman knew!

Somehow, blast it all, his adviser knew they had crossed the ultimate barrier together. "How did you—"

She took his hands, closing them beneath hers atop the box. "I would recognize that look anywhere," she replied. "The look of a man who has taken his lifemate."

He gaped back at her, puzzled. "The robe?" he suggested, fingering the terry-cloth collar as if it would provide all the explanations.

"You might have taken the human as lover, but not mate," she dismissed, beaming at him.

"Then?"

"You glow, my lord," she trilled, gesturing toward him. "From the inside, all the way out."

He gazed downward self-consciously, and there, beneath his open collar, he could see the golden hue that emanated from his bare, muscled chest.

"Ah," he agreed softly, "so I do."

"And I have a queen. At long last," she said, clapping her hands together like an innocent child. "My king and I *both* have a queen." Unexpected tears gleamed in her sparkling eyes, visible by the doorway light. He bent low and brushed a kiss of gratitude across his friend's cheek.

Anika was right: He had a queen. At long last, he did have a queen.

Kelsey retrieved a fire-warmed towel from where it hung on a rack by the corner hearth. She'd visited many posh places with her father over the years, but she wasn't sure she'd ever stayed anywhere with a fireplace in the *bathroom*. This one was made of stacked stone and stood in the corner, gas logs burning low.

No wonder the alien loved fires, she thought. Like some great mythological being, Jared *was* fire. It coursed in his body, powered through his loins, ran in the man's blood. Lifting a hand to her flushed face, she marveled at how he'd brushed fever across her cheeks just by kissing her there. Every place he'd touched glowed afterward—no, it burned. Not with a painful sensation, but a pleasurable, arousing one. It was as if he'd pushed right up inside of her with his other self, the vibrant one made of pure shimmering gold, and stroked her into fiery oblivion. No man had ever touched her that way. No other man ever could.

Smiling at the memory of their lovemaking, she caught a sideways view of herself in the mirror. Here she stood, half-naked and in a man's bedroom suite, and she felt . . . unashamed. Gorgeous. For once, she was with a man who wasn't shorter than she was—or even a similar height—but one who actually stood many inches taller. It was a remarkably feminine sensation.

Even though she and Jared had been apart for only a few minutes, she felt impatient for his return. He'd said something about a surprise—what, exactly, she could only imagine when she was dealing with a man capable of flying over water in the form of a glowing orb. Yeah, that whole fire thing would be *so* easy to explain to her father and to her friends. She thought of Ethan and his persistent scientist's habit of investigation. If he ever scented the first idea of who Jared was, he'd never back off until he'd figured the whole thing out. She'd just have to make sure Jared Bennett never once intersected with her real life. Besides, despite what he'd said earlier today about returning to Laramie, she had no immediate plans to leave him here.

Then she had a sinking thought: She had been here at Jared's home for two full days. What if her father had been phoning her? Or if Dr. Carrington had been trying to track her down with the lab results? The voice of responsibility tried to make itself known, but for once she kicked it back into the corner. She'd been responsible plenty of times. In fact, she'd spent her entire life being responsible. Her father wasn't exactly consulting her on his love life these days, so she damn sure wasn't going to ask his opinion of Jared. What would Patrick Wells have to say about the Refarian king, rebel leader extraordinaire? She winced; a time would come for facing her father about all this. Thank *God* it wasn't tonight.

Jared's footsteps sounded on the pinewood floor outside the bathroom. "You should come back in here," she called out. "It's warm by this fire, Jared." The alien loved his fires? She'd fire him up, all right, she thought with a mischievous turn in front of the mirror.

She heard him pause outside the door, then hesitate. "Jared, I'm waiting!" she sang out flirtatiously, ready to seduce him all over again. "Oh, I have a sur*prise* for *you*."

She allowed her towel to slip to the floor and pool around her ankles.

And then every delirious thought died: A man she'd never seen before appeared in the doorway, a man with threatening, hooded eyes.

She shrieked, lunging for a bath towel, and shouted at him: "Who the hell are you? I'm naked, for God's sake! You can't just come in here without knocking!"

He made no reply, but his vacant eyes locked with hers— cold, lifeless eyes, blacker than night. Eyes that in that split second Kelsey knew reflected his very soul—and what she saw in them was death. And suddenly her nakedness hardly mattered, not when her very life hung in the balance.

Lunging toward the door, she tried to escape, but he seemed to anticipate her move, and slid wordlessly to block her exit. Her next thought was to run, to just get past him somehow, but she couldn't seem to budge, or even breathe, despite gasping for air. The moment was like something from her most terrible nightmares: Time froze, suspended endlessly before her. There was only the sound of blood rushing in her ears, and the sight of the dark man staring back at her as her mind worked to arrive at a plan of escape. She took a step forward. Who the hell cared if he blocked her path! She'd get past him. Jared would be here soon.

Jared! she cried out with her spirit. *Jared!*

Then, oddly, the man stepped aside, as if he would simply let her pass. She didn't have time to worry about her nakedness, racing toward the door, but before she could even reach it, the thing slammed shut in her face.

From behind her, the intruder spoke her name. It was then that she heard the voice, a sound that seemed to echo from the depths of some soulless abyss, reverberating off the emptiness of space. "Kelsey Bennett," the man said. "We meet again."

Jared took the stairs two at a time, balancing the chocolates and a tray of cheese in one hand and a bottle of champagne with a couple of glasses in the other. Last year Scott had hidden the champagne in the far reaches of the refrigerator for Victory Day, that long-hoped-for time when the Antousians would bow down before the Refarians in defeat. Jared had borrowed it for tonight's occasion, knowing he'd have the bottle replaced before his friend ever missed it.

Jared reached the landing and paused, resituating the items into a somewhat more elegant arrangement before taking the remaining stairs to Kelsey. On the landing's right side stood a cavernous den made from rough-hewn stone and wood. Designed by the architect to resemble a cave, the intimate room housed a movie screen and digital stereo system, and Jared never knew who of his elite officers might be discovered there, night or day. With a self-conscious glance, he hoped he would find himself alone on this stealthy mission of his.

Instead, a familiar, deep voice sounded from the hidden darkness. "I've been saving that bottle." There, leaning back on the leather sofa, sprawled his best friend.

Jared gave him a guilty smile. "It's not like I won't replace it."

Scott swung both feet to the floor, peering out at him from the semidarkness like a cunning night creature. The room was punctuated only by the muted flickering of the television's blue light, and Scott's energized eyes caught the gleam, reflecting it back at Jared.

"You're up late," Jared observed.

"I was watching over my commander." Scott's eyes turned golden with emotion, glowing like embers in the darkness.

"You weren't here when I went upstairs."

"I sensed you prowling about, and came to investigate."

Jared turned away, making to leave the room. "I don't need that kind of watchdogging."

"You need me to kick about five levels of common sense into you!" Scott snarled, jumping to his feet. "Have you gone mad? She is human! *Human,* Jared. They are your enemies."

Jared rounded on his friend. "They are my protected."

"They are hunting your *ass*!" Then, seeming to catch himself, Scott muttered, "With all due respect, sir."

"Only a few hunt me."

"Her people are hunting you, Jared," he maintained. "Don't fool yourself. They hunt you and will keep on hunting you until they have you." Scott's eyes blazed golden-red, then orange. Rarely did his friend's emotions flare visibly, only when he was at his most agitated. "The humans don't care what you're doing for them. I don't know why you bother."

Jared stiffened. "We have a mission here, and that mission hasn't changed," he answered, his voice formal. "We protect. That is why we came."

"We came to hide you," Scott countered.

"To protect," Jared repeated, lifting his chin. "That is the mission."

"And your safety is irrelevant?" They'd had this same damnable conversation before—on numerous occasions. His chief adviser had very specific ideas about his commander's safety, but they bordered on smothering Jared.

"If I died tomorrow, Scott, would you carry out my mandate?" he asked in a serious voice. "Because I need to know your position."

"Yes."

"The humans do not understand us, but that does not make them our enemies."

"You don't belong with her."

Jared sighed, depositing the tray on the coffee table, and then the champagne bottle and glasses next to it. "This has nothing to do with Kelsey."

Scott snorted. "It has everything to do with her," he countered. "The woman is one of them. For all you know, she's a spy."

At this assertion, Jared smiled. "Scott, she is no spy."

"You don't know that."

"Trust me." He laughed. "She's not a spy."

"She was there the night you were shot down," Scott reminded him. "That was pretty convenient, don't you think?"

"You don't know her."

"Excuse me, Commander—but you do? It's only been a week."

A quiet hush overcame Jared in an instant. "A week spent under the deep sway of a soul bond." He couldn't possibly explain to Scott about everything they had remembered.

Scott's eyes grew large, the golden-orange flaring bright in their depths again. "Gods, you mated with her!" he cried, circling closer. "Tell me you didn't. Tell me you still plan to break the bond." Scott's eyes brightened to laser points, flickering vibrantly.

"Watch yourself, Lieutenant," Jared admonished, pointing to his own eyes by way of explanation. Scott blinked back at him, clearly unaware of how hard and fast his power had been escalating. "Your eyes," Jared said gently, and Scott dropped his gaze. Beyond his soul gazing, the hybrid soldier possessed other, more dangerous gifts, ones he always struggled to keep in check when among his comrades.

Pointedly studying the floorboards, Scott repeated his question: "Did you mate with her, sir?" His voice had assumed a chastened tone, his black eyebrows knitted together in worry as he waited.

Jared considered his reply. Scott Dillon had been beside him since boyhood, always loyal, always prepared to fight. From a biological standpoint, the two men should have been enemies; from a philosophical one, however, they stood together—always had.

"Yes, we are mated," he admitted quietly.

Scott made a flourishing bow. "Congratulations, my lord," he said, his voice hoarse and filled with emotion. "I wish you many years of happiness together."

"I wish you approved."

Scott shrugged, sadness filling his dark eyes, brown again—no longer flaring with energy. After a moment of regarding his king, Scott whispered, "I do too."

Chapter Eleven

Kelsey Bennett. The intruder had called her Kelsey *Bennett*! Her mind whirled—why would he call her by Jared's last name? They weren't married yet; besides, she'd never seen the man before in her life.

He studied her, taking a step closer, an expression of mingled hatred and fascination on his dark features. Kelsey fumbled to grab a bath towel from beside the sink, bunching it in front of herself protectively, but then it slipped, revealing the soft curve of her breasts before she could secure it again.

In reaction, the man arched an eyebrow suggestively, but made no comment.

A silvery scar divided the black hairs of that right eyebrow, creating a sharp furrow before the mark sliced upward across his forehead, vanishing somewhere in the black, wavy hair atop his head. That scar had to be important—she knew it, though the reason why seemed to float just beyond her grasp.

"To think that Jared couldn't protect you," he observed in a hushed voice—a threatening one. Had Jared tried to stop this invader on his way into the bedroom suite? Was Jared out in the hall, hurt? "To have failed you, of all people, sweet Kelsey." He shook his head, clucking his tongue. "The man always lacked wisdom, but this? It surprises even me."

"Let me out!" she cried, giving him a serious shove in the chest, but he didn't even budge at the impact of her frame against his. He released a low chuckle, but that was

all. She had to get past this guy, whoever he was, and into the bedroom. Again, she lunged at him, but this time he caught her wrist in midair, and the towel gave a small lurch, dropping low. He gazed downward, a lustful expression on his face as he examined her.

"Stop it," she spit. The adrenaline was rushing so furiously throughout her body, she felt light-headed and dizzy.

"You don't like that?" he asked, clearly enjoying this game with her.

Grabbing a brush from the counter, she hurled it at him, but he easily deflected her makeshift weapon with his forearm.

"Kelsey Bennett, I'm not going anywhere," he said, releasing a throaty laugh at her expense. "Not with a show like this one to enjoy. God, you always were quite the spitfire, and I admire that in a woman."

Once more, she searched past him, wishing Jared would return. Was he injured? She tried feeling for him within their new bond, but only emptiness echoed back across their separation.

She turned on their enemy. "What have you done to him?" she demanded. "Tell me where Jared is."

The man said nothing, but took a step closer. He possessed a pantherlike gracefulness, giving the impression not of movement as he circled inward upon her, but rather a kind of fluidity—and this despite his towering height. He was Jared's size, perhaps even taller, with the same exquisite dark eyes and rich-colored skin. Gauging by those looks, he had to be Refarian—at least based on what little she already knew of that species' physicality. Few of their kind seemed to be fair-skinned or light-haired.

"What do you want?" she demanded, raising to her nearly six feet of height and staring him in the eye.

The man did not reply, but instead acted as if he had all the time in the world, his sinister gaze roving the length of her barely concealed form. First her legs, then upward toward her hips, the hooded eyes registered every detail. Then his gaze trawled even farther upward, lingering. Invading. *Provoking.* Still he said nothing.

"You have no right to be here!" she said firmly, working to seize control of their interaction.

"On the contrary," he purred, leaning languorously against the marble countertop. "I have every right. In fact, I'm more than a little entitled, my dear."

"Jared will be back any minute," she told him, trying to sound forceful, but her words only came out raspy and shrill. The stranger smiled, a smug look coming over his features as she wrestled to readjust the towel.

He folded powerful arms across his chest. "Don't bother with that on my account," he offered, again lifting one eyebrow almost as if to taunt. "Besides, my business isn't with Jared."

"Who are you?" she tried again, feeling her hands tremble as she clutched the towel close.

"You may call me Marco," he drawled, "though I'm surprised you don't know me." He studied her, shady eyes narrowing.

"I've never seen you before in my life."

"Well, Kelsey Bennett." He shook his head, releasing a slow, rumbling laugh. "It's been far too long for *me*." He gave her one last appraising look. "Far too long. But trust me, I'm more than pleased to see you again."

From the bottom of the stairs Scott heard his commander cry out, a pained, raw sound, the sort he rarely heard from Jared, or indeed from any soldier off the battlefield. Springing to his feet, he hit the comm button on his forearm, signaling the highest distress code among their ranks. "Jared!" he shouted, and another wounded howl of agony rang out from the steps below. Scott stumbled, taking the steps three at a time until he tumbled to the bottom, and there in front of his bedroom, forearms braced against the door frame, Jared Bennett stood bathed in the clean blue light of an energy field.

"Commander!" Scott cried again, pulling up fast. His gaze darted to the bedroom's interior, but he could see nothing—and then back to Jared, who appeared uninjured. "What's happened? What's going on here?"

"They have her," Jared rasped, his voice eerie in its quiet. He stood dangerously close to the undulating energy field, attempting to look past it into the room. "I can't see anything. But they have her; I feel it."

"We have to get you to safety, Commander." Any of their enemies might be here, but that blue swirling helix was the telltale sign of only one: the Antousians. "Sir!" Scott barked again, wrestling with Jared, who shrugged him off as he would a small insect.

Scott did not back down. "We must secure you," he demanded, but Jared wouldn't budge, instead moving even closer against the undulating bands of energy. "You are in danger, my lord!" Scott shouted at his friend, but Jared seemed to be in a kind of shock, immovable.

"They took her," Jared repeated, his voice a dull whisper. "My mate—they have her."

"Sir, please," Scott begged, wrestling with Jared. "She may still be inside. We must get you to safety. Your protection, sir, is paramount. You know that!"

Jared turned to him, and for a long moment their eyes locked, silent intention passing between them. Scott knew what would happen next, felt it ripple across the surface of his perception before Jared actually made his move.

Jared glanced away from him, and then with a seamless, fluid gesture, shifted form, converting to pure energy. Scott took a staggering step backward, Jared's heat almost singeing his skin before he had time to process his king's powerful change.

Jared's fierce form rose toward the ceiling, expanding, towering, filling the area outside the bedroom doorway. A loud roaring sound—like a great freight train bearing down on the hallway—hummed through the air as Jared hurled himself at the banded doorway, blue sparks shattering in a bright arc around them. On the stairs, Scott heard the approaching thunder of footsteps, and quickly recognized his comrades' voices in the din of soldiers' cries: Anna, Anika, Thea, others. Still facing the doorway, he lifted one hand to halt them as they arrived, and they lined up just behind him.

Scott's own weapon was cocked and ready, and he knew that the soldiers behind him were heavily armed as well. All watched—all waited, breath held, as over and over Jared launched his full D'Aravnian form against the power grid. Scott felt his friend's pain shooting through the air around them. Smelled the blistering sparks of the Antousian bands, sizzling off of Jared's own power—which had to hurt, no matter how much energy was banked within Jared at the moment.

A secondary unit of soldiers came pounding down the steps. "There's nothing, Lieutenant Dillon," the lead officer reported from behind him. "No sign of any penetration here, sir. No sign of unauthorized entry." It seemed impossible: How could Antousian forces have broken into Jared's quarters, the most secure place in the whole compound? Antousians were plenty skilled at subterfuge, but there were too many inuitives in this cabin who would have sensed them. Besides, no one would've gotten past Scott's honed sensory perceptions. He could sniff out any Antousian who came within half a mile of them; at least *something* good had come of his mixed heritage.

Jared released a high-pitched wail as he flung himself yet again at the barrier, this time twining his energy with that of the Antousian force field, pressing, pulsing, joining his blazing swath of power with that of his enemies. Just behind him he heard Thea gasp, whispering Jared's name, her voice stricken. She of all people knew what this desperate bid to dissolve the field was costing their king. In front of them all, Jared's magnificent golden power battled with the blue, nestling in, burrowing, becoming one with the swirling helix.

Scott had watched Jared destroy enemy armies in this form, moving over them like a hushed kiss, taking their life that easily. But when raw energy met another kind of raw energy—well, that was another story altogether. Scott swallowed hard, unexpected fear seizing him. For a moment, the familiar color of Jared's power faded, matching that of the Antousian bands of blue energy.

"We have to stop him," Thea hissed, low enough that others wouldn't hear, but perceptible to Scott's heightened hearing.

"What's he trying to do?" he asked her, his eyes never leaving his king.

"He thinks he can rupture the field with his own power," she said, grasping Scott's arm like a vise.

"Can he do that?" he asked, feeling her grip tighten. "Is it really possible?"

"Maybe," she said, "I'm not sure. But we've got to stop him, Scott. *Now.*"

"Or what?" he asked, watching the dynamic surge of energy in the doorway brighten unexpectedly.

"Or this is going to kill him."

Outside in the hallway, Kelsey heard noise, scuffling. Shouts. Then a roaring sound that she recognized as coming from some sort of weaponry—something meant to blast open an entry to Jared's room.

"You won't be able to fight them all off!" she insisted, pressing against the bathroom door, but she needn't have struggled so much. This time, Marco let her slip past him and into the main bedroom.

"Try if you want to," he called out after her, "but they won't hear you."

She fled toward the hallway door. She had to get to Jared! But as she reached it, bands of flashing energy circled in a serpentine pattern within its frame. She could not see past the barricade into the hallway, and it gave off visible sparks, even without her touching it. Grabbing her jacket, she hurled it against the force field to test it. The smell of melting nylon filled the air as the jacket sizzled, then collapsed in a blackened heap on the floor. Behind her, Marco ambled into the room with the same kind of relaxed cowboy's pace she'd observed earlier. He seemed to feel no fear or need to rush, and clearly he wanted her to know it.

"We're locked within a suspended dimensional zone," he explained matter-of-factly. "Not a soul can hear you, Kelsey."

"Jared!" she screamed, trying to reach him through the shimmering blue boundary.

"I wouldn't touch that if I were you," Marco cautioned. "Not if you want to live."

"I'm in here, Jared!" she shouted across the barricade, pacing back and forth in front of the doorway.

"I repeat: No one can hear you," Marco said in annoyance, stepping right behind her. "Well, except me. You and I are alone together, tripping along, just the two of us." He reached out a hand, touching a loose lock of her curls, rubbing it between his fingertips.

She rounded on him. "Tell me what that means," she insisted, out of breath. "What is this dimensional thing you keep talking about?"

He let his hand drop away and shrugged. "An in-between place." Glancing past her at the undulating blue helix, he added, "You have the Antousians to thank for that device."

"Are *you* Antousian?"

He snorted, sauntering past her. "I'll choose not to take that as an insult."

"Then you're working for someone else?" she asked. She could hear a loud keening sound on the other side of the barricade.

"I work on my own."

"You have to work for someone," she said, spinning to face him. "I know that much."

He tossed her clothes across the room with a rough gesture that sent them sprawling at her feet. "Get dressed. Now."

"Are we going somewhere?" she asked, glancing at the doorway. "Seems to me that you may have me imprisoned here, but there's not exactly any way out, either."

"I'll be utilizing interdimensional space to transport you where I want to," he said. "Don't worry; Jared will never see it."

Dazed, she slipped to the hardwood floor and stared into Jared's hearth. Only a while earlier, they were making love, right here on these same pillows. She ached for Jared, feeling violated, frightened. What if they'd come this far together, only to lose each other so soon?

Her body felt cold and numb, and she began to shake all over. Beside her, Marco knelt, pressing her clothes into her hands. Strangely, his expression had softened, grown less caustic—he actually assumed a surprisingly soft tone and said, "If you dress, Kelsey, you will feel better."

"Don't tell me what will make me feel better!" she snapped, turning from him to stare into the fire. She could hear his footsteps recede, and when she was certain he was no longer watching, she began putting on her clothes.

My mate . . . Enemy has mate. The thought drove Jared, propelled him into the energy, forced him hard, hard, hard into the helix. She might be on the other side! She might be just beyond his grasp. His body stung from the sharp pelts of the enemy's energy field, but he was stronger. Had to be stronger. Had to reach Kelsey. Behind him, he sensed others. Ahead of him—on the other side of the barricade— he sensed something too. *Mate?*

Battling, he spun open their bond, grasping for her. *Not recognize energy form.* That thought crystallized. *More alien now. Alien to Kelsey. No: Can't feel mate either. No mate.*

Bond?

There should be her voice in his head; he should feel it. With a humming shout, he burrowed deeper, chanting her name. Simple, pure, purposed.

Kelsey! Kelsey! Kelsey!

Must reach. Kelsey. Mate!

Kelsey knelt in front of the fire and listened to the snapping sizzle of some sort of weapon as it made contact with the Antousian barricade. Perhaps rifle fire? Something popped and hissed each time it tried to penetrate.

Behind her, Marco paced. "Are you dressed yet?" He sounded annoyed; whatever Jared's soldiers were trying to do, Marco clearly didn't like it.

"Are you in a hurry?"

"He will never break through," Marco replied, staring at the doorway. Despite his words, for the first time since his arrival, she glimpsed a slip in the man's relaxed confidence. "It's not possible, not even for him."

She spun to face him. "What makes you think that's Jared firing the weapon?"

Marco glared down at her, a cruel sneer turning his lips upward. "You don't know your own husband very well, do you?"

Husband—there it was again, Marco's belief that she and Jared were married. "Why do you think he's my husband?"

"Don't try to lie to me!" he snapped.

She blinked back at him, her whole body trembling with fear. "I don't know where you got your information," she said, hearing the sounds beyond the doorway intensify, as though her would-be rescuers had grown more determined. If she could just stall this Marco, then maybe Jared and his soldiers *would* break through in time. "But it's not correct."

"You are Kelsey Bennett. Wife of the leader of the rebellion. I know you very well, my dear."

"Nothing you've said since you got here makes any sense."

Reaching into his pocket, he pulled out a small object and tossed it toward her. It clattered at her feet with a tinkling sound. A worn, golden wedding band gleamed in the firelight. "Take it." He grunted with a nod. "It's yours." This seemed to amuse him to no end, and he even repeated it to himself, under his breath, with a dull laugh, *"It's yours."*

Retrieving it from the floor, she drew it into the palm of her hand. "This could be anyone's," she said, feeling confused, but also registering a sharp pang of recognition. She'd seen this ring before, *known* it. Jared's words from earlier in the bathtub came back to her. *Time folding inward on itself.* Like this Marco's scar, how she'd known *it* too.

"Look inside," he said. "There's an inscription." She lifted the ring up to the light, and there glinted a date—three months in the future. And there was an inscription: SONNET 29:13–14. The very one Jared had whispered in her ear tonight as they gave themselves to each other for the very first time, joining as lifemates.

Speechless, Kelsey closed her fingers around the ring, holding it against her chest like a treasure. She didn't understand its meaning, although she had an idea of it, and yet she knew that *nothing* could mean more to her at this moment. "How did you get this?" she asked, feeling all the color drain from her face. "How come you have it, not me?"

"Time, my darling," he said with a soft chuckle. "Time. And right now, we have all we need, thanks to this device." He produced a small handheld instrument—smaller than a digital camera, or even a very compact cell phone.

"You tell me what this means!" she said, gesturing with the ring.

"Put it on your hand," he ordered. "We're leaving." Beyond the perimeter, what could be described only as a supernatural hum intensified, causing the hairs on her neck to stand on end. "Your damn husband is making headway," Marco said with a nod toward the door before yanking her to her feet and spinning her hard against his chest. "We're leaving now!"

A doorway seemed to open—not the one to the room, but from somewhere else, another dimension. Kelsey felt heavy, impossibly heavy, and light splintered into prismatic shards in every direction. Although the wedding band was already priceless to her—she didn't need anyone to confirm its significance—she allowed it to clatter to the floor of Jared's room. As it fell, a chiming *tink-tink* resonated in the air, the sound itself forming a giant glowing oval around them, expanding with all the power of a mushroom cloud until the bright door in front of them opened. Like Alice with her Mad Hatter, the two of them went tumbling through it.

Jared's pulsing energy swirled in union with the Antousian helix, seeming to fuse with it. Scott's heart pounded in his chest; he'd watched Jared Bennett take many risks over the years, but never anything as bold and dangerous as this attempt to break through the field. The man loved his human mate with a mystic kind of depth—if Scott had doubted it before this moment, he would never doubt it again.

Thea took a step forward. "I'll join my power with his," she offered, dropping her pulse rifle to the floor. "See if that will be enough to break through."

"Get through to him, Thea," Scott warned, their eyes locking briefly. She gave a comprehending nod, taking several steps closer toward their king. Jared would have noticed her if he'd pried himself loose from his struggle long enough, but he remained locked into the helix, battling to pierce the damn thing.

Still in her physical form, Thea took another step nearer to their commander, and spoke to him in clipped, urgent Refarian; then, just as Jared had, in the whirling flash of a moment she transformed into her flaming, natural form. Scott's forearm came up to shield his eyes as others around him did the same. It was too much, all that naked power, bright before their eyes.

Bowing his head, Scott listened and waited, rolling out his sensory skills: his scenting, his awareness, his hearing. Every one of his gifts opened to its fullest extent—all except his gazing, since he had to keep his eyes shut. He sensed the dangerous battle that Jared and Thea waged, felt Jared growing weaker with every passing second. He could hear bits of communication between the two of them, preverbal and fragmented, as it always was for them in their energized forms. They argued; Thea begged him to cease; he shouted at her something primal and plain, understood by only the two of them.

The atmosphere in the hallway rippled, like a slow, cautious wave rolling over the air, and grew instantly hotter, singeing Scott's sweater sleeve. Then everything closed up, growing many degrees cooler, and the Antousian barricade dissolved. With a heavy, painful thud, Jared morphed back into his physical form and collapsed in a heap before them all, gasping, naked. His robe had vanished, probably consumed in his Change.

Beside him, Thea sat panting; she had morphed back into her uniform, but then again, she hadn't expended nearly the amount of energy that Jared had.

Sprawled facedown on the floor, Jared sucked in gulps of air, his naked body still glowing and gleaming with sweat. Scott got a good look at his friend's back, at the long battle scar that ran from the upper left shoulder all the way to the lower back, and at the other smaller scars snaking across his torso. The full extent of their leader's battle marks always unsettled him, reminding him as it did of every battle they had fought together. From beside him, Anika rushed forward protectively, producing a jacket. Dropping to the floor, she swept it over their leader's backside. "Here, my lord," she whispered, covering him. He collapsed, face-first, onto the pine floor in a spasm of coughing.

"We have to get him into the bunker," Scott ordered, coming back to the moment. "The Antousians could still be here." Sweeping past him, a team of soldiers took Jared's quarters, weapons raised.

"They're gone," Jared panted, weakly raising his head until his eyes locked with Scott's. "They took her."

"She could still be inside," Anika soothed, touching his shoulder. "Let our team look."

Jared roared, his gaze sweeping the group of them still gathered there. "They have *taken* her! I felt it the moment the barrier dissolved." He struggled to sit up, but in another spasm of coughing he pitched forward until his forehead came to rest against the floor. "They have taken my mate," he whispered in a hoarse voice. "How did they know about her? *How?*"

It was Thea who crawled closer to him. "Jared, we will find her," she said, her voice calm, but Jared appeared almost crazed, eyeing her with a maniacal stare.

Scott knelt low, taking Jared's arm. "Jared, I'm getting you into the bunker."

Jared shook him off. "No!" he thundered, but Scott wouldn't yield, and wrestled Jared to his feet. Complaining the entire time, Jared struggled with him, battling him—as if he, Scott, were one of the invaders—but with Thea's and Anika's help, they forced open the door to the bunker in the hallway outside Jared's quarters. They'd installed the panic room adjacent to Jared's quarters for security breaches just such as this one.

As the group of them shoved him inside, Jared lunged like a wild-eyed beast, forearms lifting, wrestling toward the hallway. Finally, in an act of pure desperation, Scott slugged Jared across the face hard, sending his king sprawling against a high shelf of munitions that rattled with the sheer impact of Jared's muscular, solid frame.

Jared gaped back at him, eyes widening. "You struck me," he said, rubbing his jaw in disbelief.

Anika secured the bunker door behind them, and turned to face them both. Only the three of them stood in the darkened room, surrounded by shelves of weaponry—four-foot thick walls separating their leader from the potential danger that remained somewhere outside. Anika assumed a guard position in front of the door, hands behind her back. At the moment, Scott knew she answered to him, not to their flailing king.

Jared raised his own hand, ready to battle Scott, but in his weakened condition, Scott easily overpowered him, slamming him hard against the bunker wall.

"J'Areshkadau!" Scott shouted, employing Jared's most personal Refarian name. "J'Areshkadau," he repeated, breathless as he stared his friend down. "You are out of your mind."

Jared's lungs sucked at air, his bare chest rising and falling, a sweaty sheen gleaming on his naked body. "You have never once struck me." He seemed dazed, shocked, blinking back at Scott. This recent battle had left him depleted not just of energy, but also bereft of the physical here and now. Scott had seen this before in the man; that keeping his natural, energized form robbed him of something . . . *tangible.* He became like the energy itself, and returning to the material realm after a long time in his Change left him confused and disoriented.

Jared glanced around them, blinking. "My lord," Scott said, softening his tone, "security has been compromised." He kept Jared pinned against the wall, one forearm positioned squarely under his chin. "You are not in body armor. Your mate is taken—from your own bedroom. Don't you see that the Antousians wanted you too? That they came for you? If you won't think of your safety, sir, then I must."

Jared stared up at the ceiling, wrestling for breath, but said nothing. "Here," Scott said after it became obvious his commander would no longer resist, "take my clothes."

He shrugged out of his sweater, tossing it to Jared, but it dropped, unused, to the floor. The air about them shimmered as Jared shifted until he stood in full battle gear, compliant, body-armored to the hilt.

"This should meet your approval," Jared answered, his voice numb.

Scott gave a nod, taking a step apart from his king. "It's safer."

Jared glanced to Anika as if seeking help, then back at him. "I mated with her, and then they just . . . took her," he whispered, tears glinting in his eyes. Scott felt his own eyes sting—never, not in all the years he'd known and followed this man, had Scott ever seen him cry. Yet the brightness of unshed tears filled Jared's dark eyes. "I left her unprotected," he repeated. "And they took her."

"We will get her back," Scott vowed with a vigorous nod. "We will search until we do. Starting tonight."

"She knows nothing of this war, nothing of my enemies," Jared said, dropping his head into his palms. "My God, what have I done to her?"

Scott braced a hand against Jared's shoulder, but said nothing. In his deepest heart, however, he prayed that Jared had retrieved the mitres data in the midst of his union with the human woman. He prayed it not just for Kelsey's benefit, but for all their sakes.

Chapter Twelve

Blue shot outward, a cobalt ring of light that rippled, becoming larger as it fanned into an elliptical pattern surrounding Kelsey. A slipstream of fractured images flowed, a luminous ribbon unfurling midair like a fast-projected film strip. Blinking her eyes, she tried a glance around the room, but could see nothing past the spinning arc of imagery.

It was as if some force had magnetized her to this unknown spot, pinning her like an anxious, drunken butterfly. She felt almost dizzy, watching the procession of memories and unrecognizable futures swirling past her eyes. They came in chaotic order: her mother swinging her in the backyard when she was just a tiny girl; snuggling between her parents in their bed one nameless Saturday morning; her hollow-eyed mother dying in the hospital.

More pictures followed, faster than she could identify them, so fast they caused blinding pain behind her eyes, yet she couldn't force herself to look away. Not until she saw where the images were leading. Mercurial patterns of her past unfolded, one upon another—sometimes reaching out to touch an unknown future—and then the visions would recede, leaving behind a concrete past. Her father hugging her at graduation . . . a stolen kiss from Jared on the bank of a darkened lake . . . next Jamie Watson, stripping her out of her slinky black dress on inauguration night . . .

Wincing, she watched the spiral change and lurch forward by several crucial chunks of time until the memories—obviously plucked right out of her mind—became almost current, showing her father across the table from her at the lunch they'd had last week. Lifting a rubbery hand into the air, she actually tried to touch his face, but the fading hologram looped past her, part of a larger cobalt spiral that seemed to physically ring her where she lay on the hard, cold floor.

The coil accelerated, then slowed, landing on a single image, one that caused all of her stupefied senses to come fully alert. *Jared.* But not as she knew him now, with the short-cropped dark hair and the slightly scarred face—no, this *other* Jared wore his hair long, pulled back into a sleek ponytail, significant strands of silver and gray threading through his natural black. This was Jared from the future— somehow, this stream of time had folded inward, touching her other self's memories like a shadow of foreknowing. *Some of our people even believe time to be a mirror . . .* Those had been Jared's own words, earlier, and gasping at the scene unfolding before her eyes, she knew she was glimpsing a future that she'd not yet lived. She pressed an icy hand to her breastbone, working to still her frantic heartbeat.

In the unfolding vision, this Jared stood proud as a king: defiant, rugged, fearsome-looking, his face lined with age and deep scars. But older. So very much older. And hardened in some significant way. His right eye had a strange look to it, half closed like that of a journeyman prizefighter. As he spun to face her, she caught a better look at him: The eye was blinded, its natural almond shape marred by a vicious scar.

She lifted a hand—or tried to—yearning to feel her lover's weathered face. Such pain and suffering were etched into his dark features, she could hardly breathe with what she saw. She worked her mouth, desperate to cry out to him, but no sounds would form. Why couldn't she comfort him? He turned from her, and as he moved, his strong, confident gait seemed altered from what she knew, less steady. A slight drag to his right foot punctuated each of his steps—the aftereffects of an old injury, perhaps?

Whatever scene unfolded, he stood, one hand on his hip, surveying, while with the other he unfastened his ponytail, allowing the graying hair to fall across his shoulders. He continued watching for something or someone, glancing in her direction ever so briefly—and that was when the full truth hit her with a freight train's vengeance: This Jared wasn't nearly so old as she'd first thought, yet his body had been ravaged. The war had eaten him alive, one battle at a time. Tears began seeping out of her own undamaged eyes as she watched him move through a crowd . . . doing what? She couldn't tell, but there were soldiers all about him; he shouted something, and his soldiers reacted, dispersing. Then, across the gathering, he lifted his eyes. His one good one—beautiful and dark as ever—locked with hers, and words passed between them.

Do it, love. That was what he transmitted. *Do it,* now! His features never changed, never shifted or altered. She ran hard. With all the life in her lungs and body, she hurled herself through the pressing throngs, her feet slapping hard soil, dust rising around her. To her left, then to her right, she saw blood and bodies and destruction in every direction. And yet she ran. *Go, love! Go now!* She ran because he depended on her to do so. She ran because in some very crucial way, her husband and beloved lifemate could *not.*

Kelsey slapped the smooth floor with her open palms, transfixed in whatever location she'd been transported to. What was happening to her? What did these images even mean? Again, she tried to open her mouth to cry out, yet her jaw wouldn't move. Her lips wouldn't move. *Suspended.* That was the word her captor had used: He'd said they were suspended in interdimensional space.

Then, in the unfurling strip of time, she saw *him.* The terrifying one with the shadowy features and the cruel scar across his forehead. Marco. He spun upon her, trying to make her cower, but she wouldn't back down. She experienced her other self's memories as if they were her own; in some elemental way, as irrational as it might be, she understood they *were* her own memories now. She was certain of it. In those memories, she watched Marco move closer, something in his hand. *A weapon brandished, silver.* Her heart beat out an insane rhythm. He had the weapon trained on her! Panting, she cried out, screamed something in a language she did not know. One word, over and over: *J'Areshkadau! J'Areshkadau! J'Areshkadau!*

Marco meant to kill her. He lifted the weapon, bore down upon her . . .

It's been too long, my dear. The lip curled back; he reached toward her, ripping something from around her neck, something precious beyond measure. The *tink-tink* sound of her wedding ring, clattering to the floor of some-where cold and echoing, like a science lab—yet dark as a hidden burial chamber.

The fabric of the future and the present wove together with an eerie, resounding silence, making her light-headed and woozy. Kelsey sat up, groping in the darkness, and felt Jared's strake stone burn her hand, the familiar leather strap rough beneath her fingertips. But she'd left the pen-dant in his bathroom, on the sink when she took the bath. Still, she felt it burn into the flesh of her palm as she held it to the floor, unwilling to relinquish the precious item—sure as if it were happening *now,* not to her future self. A black boot came down upon her fingers, and with a gasp she withdrew her seared hand, the strake stone ricocheting off of Marco's boot until it clattered across the metallic floor. And there, in the darkness beside it, spinning like it meant to decide all their fates, stood her wedding ring—ripped from the neck of her *future* self, in a *future* time so many years from now. That was the last memory Kelsey felt sear into her mind before feeling the world teeter away from her once again.

Facedown on a cold polished surface, Kelsey came slowly to her senses. One hand was sprawled above her head, her torso twisted painfully atop something bulky that jammed into her rib cage, and only after several head-throbbing moments did she identify it as her other hand. Her whole body felt like a withered husk, as if the firestorm she'd just traveled through had sapped her dry on the most microcellular level.

Beyond her she heard heavy breathing and a rustling sound. But she couldn't force herself to move and investi-gate. She released a soft groan; in answer, the hollow echo of footsteps on tile neared her head. A hard boot nudged at her shoulder.

"Wake up." That voice she remembered: Marco, her cap-tor, the man with the vile and terrifyingly empty eyes.

With a sluggish turn, she managed to rotate her head so that her gaze fixed on his boots. "Why?" she asked, and though she meant it as a defiant question, it came out more garbled than rebellious.

Above her, he chuckled softly to himself. "Such spirit, Kelsey Bennett," he said. "Such determined spirit. Just like your husband. You two definitely had that much in common, despite your other differences."

"You know . . . nothing about Jared and . . . me," she managed to sputter through a spasm of coughs, and this protest seemed to enrage him.

"Wake *up!*" he growled, giving her a more forceful shove with the tip of his boot.

She pressed her eyes closed and willed the man to disappear. Or if not that, then she willed the blinding migraine that had exploded behind her eyelids to subside. With a soft moan, she managed to roll onto her side. An explosion of light came into view, all of it muted blue and low-wattage, but still bright enough to pierce her eyes after her plummet through the darkness. Marco dropped to the floor, crouching beside her with a look of grim satisfaction on his face.

"Yes, fair Kelsey," he purred, brushing several loose curls away from her eyes. "You are mine now." He allowed his fingertips to graze her cheek, and the gesture was invasively tender. She slapped his hand away, which only made him laugh, a deep, rumbling sound. "My little spitfire," he said with a shake of his head. "Even after so much time."

She struggled to sit up, the entire room swimming, until she pressed the heels of her palms into her eyes with an agonized groan. Once during her freshman year of college she'd drunk way too many Bacardi and Cokes, insisting with each refill that the alcohol wasn't affecting her. The next day she'd paid for her foolishness with the most nauseating hangover of her entire college career; she felt something approximating that memory right now.

"I think I'm gonna be sick," she managed to mumble, shivering with the sensation.

Marco reached inside his jacket, and then, with a movement of his hand, produced a Sprite. "This will help." She had the idea that the soft drink had been something else entirely just one moment earlier. Greedily, she popped it open and sipped from it, praying that her stomach would stop its uncertain roiling. So he was helping her now? She didn't bother to question his motives, not with the way her stomach flip-flopped acidly.

"Dimensional illness," he explained, rocking back on his heels to study her. "It happens."

She made no attempt to answer him, but after a time,

her stomach began to still itself and the headache improved a little. Only then did she begin to steal glances around the room where she'd found herself. Everything in it gleamed: polished steel and ceramics, instrument panels of unnamed type (that did not look to be of earthly origin, either), and then a warren of tunnels that ran off this main room in several angled directions, vanishing into darkness.

Marco paced the room, stopping momentarily to enter some kind of data into one of the dimly lit panels, but said nothing more. It seemed he was giving her time to recover her senses. "Where are we?" she asked once she'd battled away the overpowering nausea. If she could figure out where he'd taken her, then maybe she could devise a way to escape. All those tunnels and open shafts had to lead somewhere, after all.

"Don't play coy with me," he replied, his voice tightening over the words like a vise.

"I'm serious—where are we?"

"You know exactly what this place is," he insisted. "*He* brought you here the night he proposed to you."

"I have no idea what you're talking about." Proposed? He clearly thought that she and Jared were married already—and that the proposal had happened here, which it hadn't. Jared had essentially popped that question in the bathtub earlier tonight, not in this cold set of chambered rooms.

Scrutinizing her with his black gaze, Marco narrowed his thick-lashed eyes. "Your plan won't work, lovely Kelsey," he said. "I see what you're up to, and as ever I admire your tenacious strength, but trust me—you will fail."

"Marco, you know what's going on, but I'm in the dark here," she said. "If you want something from me—and you obviously do—then you need to bring me up to speed on things. First of all, you keep talking about Jared like we're married, calling me Kelsey Bennett, and you're just flat wrong."

"Quiet!" He spun on her like a black hawk, and he raised his arm. Suddenly some sort of supernatural pall descended on the room. It was as if he'd called upon the elements, causing shadow to fall upon them both. She shivered, blinking up at his face, a hardened mask of fury. "You will tell me everything, Kelsey, and you will start with your name."

She tilted her chin, a plan beginning to form. "No."

The fury intensified and her enemy swooped low. "Then you will yield to me!" he thundered, and grasped her face roughly in his calloused hands.

Marco held her head between his palms with an unrelenting force. "What is so important about this time?" he asked. "Why did he choose now?"

"He?" Kelsey asked, genuinely confused. "Now?"

"What was Jared trying to accomplish by choosing this particular time to send you back?" he pressed. "What is so critical about now?"

"I-I don't understand." Thoughts raced one after another through her mind, but one thing was clear—as she'd first suspected in Jared's bedroom, this man was not from her time; he was obviously from some future where she and Jared were already married. Probably that same time she'd glimpsed earlier, the one where Jared's body had been ravaged by the war. While all of these courses of thought defied science and logic, the foundations of her world, she reminded herself that Einstein himself had thought time travel possible, at least in theory. Perhaps it was more than just a theory for these aliens.

"Kelsey, he targeted this time, this day," Marco explained, with a strange kind of patience—as if they were coconspirators. "I need to know why."

Kelsey smiled in victory. "I'm not telling you anything."

All pretense of partnership dissipated. "You're so pathetic. Both of you." He sneered. "Your precious husband sacrificed everything to protect the location of the mitres. His family, friends, even his throne." He shook his dark head derisively, one fingertip reaching to trace the outline of his scar. "And then at the very last moment he got careless. Betrayed its location by sending you back to now."

Kelsey gasped. "What do you mean?"

"I mean I followed you. To these chambers." He paused, sweeping his arm about them. "The mitres. And after you prepared to use the weapon, I stopped you."

The muddled images she'd seen while passing through interdimensional space suddenly pulled into focus. "You killed me. In the future."

"Not quite," he whispered. He dropped his hands away.

"In the end, your king couldn't protect the mitres." His voice grew hushed, almost seductive. "And he couldn't even protect you, the one he valued most of all."

"That's not true." Kelsey shook her head forcefully.

"Are you so sure? You weren't there." He reached out and touched a stray strand of her hair, causing chill bumps to rise on Kelsey's skin. "There were only the two of us, my dear. I enjoyed sifting your mind to learn his pitiful plan." She thought of what she'd seen in the slipstream, how Jared's future self had urged her to run. All the experiences and emotions of her other self pulsed through her body *now*, in *this* time, causing tears to sting her eyes. She owned the memories now; they were her own, sure as if she'd lived them. She felt a lifetime's love for her warrior husband; he'd counted on her with his very life to accomplish whatever plan he'd devised. And she'd failed him!

Kelsey's breath caught in her throat, and she flinched as Marco let his fingertips linger on her face, tracing a path down the skin of her neck. "But you were strong. You shut me out, at least from that area of your mind." He looked at her significantly. "I couldn't learn why he chose this time, but now *you're* going to tell me." His fingers stopped at the base of Kelsey's throat, and she could feel her pulse throbbing beneath his large hand. His black eyes met hers with a maelstrom's force, and she couldn't make herself look away. *Why does he have such immense power over me?*

"And then you're going to draw him here, out into the open." He let his hand drop.

Oh, God . . . he's here for Jared. To destroy him, before that future can happen.

"I don't even know who you are," she choked.

"True. But I know *you* extremely well, Kelsey Bennett." His dark eyes flared for a moment with an emotion she couldn't read. "It's one reason that I've come."

Kelsey met his gaze and tried to form some kind of plan. She had to protect Jared at all costs, had to lure this stranger away from him. She shivered because somehow she knew that part of Marco's mission was to end Jared's life, and then to set about changing the course of the future in his *own* ruinous way.

And with that, she made a fateful decision.

Chapter Thirteen

Jared had experienced grief many times in his thirty years, until now believing that he'd identified all its faces. He'd known the sorrow of sending a friend out on an aerial mission, never to see her return; he'd held a comrade on the field of battle as he drew his last breath; he'd mourned his beloved cousin, Valyre, after the soldier's disappearance on a recon mission when they were both twenty; and then there had been his parents' deaths. Barely ten on the day of their murder, he had swallowed his grief when destiny had first laid the responsibility of leading the Refarian people at his feet. Yes, he had endured grief's season a thousand times over, and thought himself a man accustomed to it—inured to it, even.

But nothing, nothing in the vast emptiness of the universe and all its fickle dealings, had ever prepared him for this moment of absolute loss. His bedroom stood empty before him, all the promise of the past hours wrenched from his hands like the plaything of some cruel god.

His chambers hummed with complex power—they all felt it. He had ushered the soldiers away, holding back only Thea and Scott, since otherwise the powerful imprints left vibrating in the room's atmosphere might be disrupted. Now only the three of them remained—Thea because her skills of intuition were the most refined within the compound; Scott because as an Antousian hybrid, he had ways of seeing unlike any of them; and Jared because he was bonded to Kelsey as deeply as was possible between two souls. Together, they three held the best chance of winnowing through the energized impressions here to produce some trail of evidence.

Thea knew he'd mated with Kelsey tonight, though she said nothing to acknowledge it—and for that, his heart thanked his cousin. From the moment they'd joined their power within the helix, his thoughts had been open to her. She'd expressed her grief at his choice then, as they united in their energized forms; nothing more remained to be said. Now she served not only her king, but the one he'd taken as queen—*her* queen as well.

Kneeling in the middle of the floor, her face drained of color, Thea reached with all of her senses. She hummed slightly, both arms wrapped around her body, rocking as she knelt on the same pillows where he and Kelsey had made love not long ago. He wondered what private moments might be unveiled to her, but the time for propriety had vanished along with Kelsey.

Pausing in the room's center, Scott scowled, turning first one direction and then another. "What do you see, Lieutenant Dillon?" Jared deliberately forced his manner into that of leader, not a desperate lover.

Scott said nothing, but resumed his pacing. His sensory abilities always involved movement, a physical outworking of the man's interior life. Only Jared sat, quiet and still. "One man," Scott finally told him in a whisper. "He came alone and he left with her."

Jared swallowed hard, urging Scott on with a firm nod. "What else? I need to know, soldier."

"Refarian," Scott continued, narrowing his eyes as he gazed about the room. "Full-blooded, sir, no doubt about that." Scott paused, sniffing at the air like a timber wolf. "Rogue all the way."

Jared's hands clenched at his sides. "Why?" he cried, no longer able to control his simmering emotions. Why would this man have taken her? Why *now*, of all nights? On the floor, Thea's humming ceased, and he lowered his voice again: "Tell me, Lieutenant Dillon, of this man's motives."

Scott met his gaze with a forceful expression, one that spoke of endless loyalty, boundless commitment to his king. "They are obscured from me, my lord," he replied, "but I promise you I will discover his intentions."

Jared swore aloud, leaping to his feet, and pushed past

Scott and across the room. He cursed his own lack of intuitive abilities, an innate skill that his warrior's life had never allowed him to nurture. "Where did he take her?" Jared wondered aloud. "And *how* did he?" It was the question each of them sought to answer. There had to be knowledge here within the room, if they could only discern it.

On the floor, Thea stirred, lifting her pale eyes to meet his own. "The man has a name," she said in a quiet voice, "a secret name that no one else knows."

"Tell me," Jared said, dropping to the floor beside her.

"Marek Shaekai. It's his Refarian birth name," she said.

Scott shook his head, not recognizing it. Neither did Jared. Thea stared into the fire. "He knows you, Jared," she said. "Extremely well."

"I've met no one by that name."

Scott shifted on his feet, rubbing the bridge of his nose, and said, "You might know him as someone else. Maybe by his human name."

Marek Shaekai. Jared turned the name over within his mind. Bracing his hands on the mantel, he swept his thoughts over his comrades, the Refarians who had served him these many years. Who had left his ranks disgruntled? Who had spun damaging rumors about him? Not a man or woman in his corps.

"What does he look like, this Marek?" he asked, already knowing that if either of them had seen an image of the man, they would have reported it.

"Dark," Thea answered. "I see only darkness, cousin."

Scott murmured his agreement, but offered nothing more.

Thea turned where she knelt, gazing up at him. "You should try to reach across the bond to her," she said, unable to disguise the anguish the words caused her. "Your connection with her is very strong, Jared, and wherever he's taken her, you might be able to . . ." Her voice trailed off, and she swept her gaze toward the hearth, the words unfinished.

"You're right," he agreed, bowing his head. What he didn't say was that for the past minutes he had repeatedly been spinning his energy toward Kelsey, bringing more and more of his soul's force to bear. But in return he felt nothing. Sensed nothing. The resounding emptiness was the cause of his despair.

Still, he had to try again, and closing his eyes, he quieted his mind. *Focus—she needs your focus, warrior. Her life depends on your discipline.*

And so, in his heart's center, he conjured the image of his beloved's blue eyes, her fiery hair. Then, fanning the energy inside of himself, he centered on her soul, the vibrant magentas and purples and blues he'd glimpsed as they'd mated.

The bond did not come to life in answer—not precisely. Yet he *did* sense something in the room, something of extreme importance.

Behind him! Whatever it was lay on the floor behind him. Jared wheeled in the direction of the object he sensed, dropping to his knees. Beneath the bed, he detected the object that seemed to burn into his consciousness.

"What is it?" Scott asked, pressing behind him.

Jared knelt there, grasping with both hands beneath the dark wood of the bed frame—pulling with his intuition to identify the clue he had detected. His palms met dust and hardwood, but still he swept his hands, feeling, reaching . . .

Until his open palm centered on something cold and solid—yet smoldering like all the stars overhead at night.

Marco held Kelsey within his grasp, his hands crushing her face in a rough gesture. She could feel the tendrils of his power reaching into her mind, yet she had no concept of how to resist such an invasion. With every shred of her will, she worked to block him, focusing all her mind's reserves against his alien prying. Perhaps she succeeded, or perhaps her captor didn't discover what he sought, but with the same maelstrom's power she'd felt invade her thoughts, she sensed him retreat.

But he never once released his physical hold on her. "Tell me why this time matters," he insisted, yanking her closer. "Why was it targeted?"

She could think of only two reasons why their future selves might have deemed this date of monumental importance: It was the night of their mating, and Jared's data still remained lodged within her mind. But she wasn't about to reveal either detail to her captor, not if she could help it.

"I-I don't know," she whispered hoarsely.

"How can you not know?" he shouted, tightening his grip upon her. "You are his trusted. You are his wife!"

"No," she said. "No, I'm not." There, maybe if he would finally accept the truth, he would relent, she thought hopefully, but the roar that erupted from the man's chest silenced any wishful thoughts on that count. "It's like I already told you. We aren't married—not, uh, yet."

"You've been lying to protect him." He met her eyes intently, and she could almost *feel* him drawing things out of her, some part of her mind giving way to him.

She began to shake. "No, it's the truth!" she cried, wondering if her plan had been such a great idea after all. But she'd felt that the revelation might gain his trust somehow, and now there'd be no turning back. "I am telling you the truth."

He made a low sound in the back of his throat. "Kelsey, you are such a disappointment to me. To think how many years I've admired you."

"I've never seen you before tonight," she tried. "How do you even know me? None of this makes sense to me. I keep on telling you that I don't understand!"

"You understand that I am here because of Jared." She trembled in his grasp, but said nothing. "You understand that you have something of priceless value to me," he continued. "Do you not?"

The creeping nausea returned, and she whispered, "But what is it?"

Releasing her, he rocked back on his heels and sat in thoughtful silence, clearly considering his next move. She didn't dare flinch, even though she desperately wanted to scurry backward, to distance herself from him as much as she could.

Tapping his fingers on the cold floor, he seemed to reach a conclusion. "You are not yet married," he said. His eyes shifted from hers in slight hesitation, and Kelsey was struck by the odd notion that his incorrect assumptions about who she was at this point in time had been disconcerting to the man—and on a deeply personal level. It left him seeming strangely vulnerable.

She seized the moment. "I hardly know Jared Bennett," she lied. At least, it was a half-truth.

He furrowed his brow in thought. "None of us understood how to set the mitres precisely," he reflected, obviously speaking of her future self. "Perhaps our calculations—*your* calculations—were wrong."

"My calculations?" she asked numbly.

His black eyebrows shot upward. "It was you who taught us how to use this weapon."

She glanced around them both, at the dimly lit chambers. It looked more like a science lab than a weapon. "What kind of weapon?" she asked. "Biochemical or nuclear?"

He actually laughed. "Far more devastating than that, my dear."

"Then what?" she demanded. "If you don't tell me a damn thing, then how can I possibly answer these questions? You're an idiot if you think I can."

He didn't flinch at the insult, but rose to his feet, walking to the center of the room, and placed both of his hands on a large, liquid-filled tube. It glowed with a phosphorescent color, and as he touched his palms to it, the bluish green changed, morphing to a dark, cloudy consistency—as if it had reacted in some fundamental way to Marco's nature.

"We stand within the mitres," he said, his voice formal. "Capable of altering time, creating portals of entry and exit throughout eternity and space; this is the revolution's greatest weapon. Jared Bennett's greatest weapon. And only one in our midst possessed—excuse me, possesses," he corrected with a light flourishing bow, "the power to harness it. You, Kelsey Bennett." He continued to use her married name, though it seemed as much out of long habit as from any confused or darker motivation.

Kelsey was beginning to understand. She stated what she had already begun to surmise within the past hour. "You used it to travel back from the future."

"I passed through a portal, designed by you, Kelsey— and arrived from the future to this point in time."

She was a geologist—granted, she had delved deeply into geophysics as well, but she found it difficult to imagine herself capable of such advanced and technical calculations. Without even intending to, she voiced her doubts aloud. "How could I possibly have done that?"

He spun to face her. "You alone could harness the power of the mitres. You alone were the one capable of it."

"Why me? I'm a geologist."

He cocked his head sideways, appraising her. "You really don't know, do you? I would sense your subterfuge, but there is none in you." Refusing to reply, she waited for him to reveal more; at last, he did continue. "It was not only the knowledge you possessed of physics and the geology of this location that gave you the ability," he said, sweeping his hand about the chamber, "but the data that Jared fused with your mind."

Fused? *Fused* sounded permanent, not like temporary safekeeping, as Jared had described his actions by Mirror Lake. An uncontrollable shiver swept down Kelsey's spine.

"You came here a week ago?" she asked. It would have been the night after she had first encountered Jared by the lake.

"Precisely."

"Maybe it wasn't the right date," she speculated, although she didn't want to go giving this man any ideas, either. But maybe their future selves had meant to stop the data transfer—perhaps that had been the intention.

"Or perhaps you miscalculated on purpose—to deceive me."

"You're dealing with universal laws of physics, Marco, not exactly something to go tampering with." She frowned, unable to contain her derision. "How far back did you travel in time, anyway?"

He stared at her—through her—ignoring her question. "Or perhaps this time *was* the intention," he mused, black eyebrows hitching upward. The ugly scar became more pronounced with the gesture, the white striation stark against the natural black hair of his eyebrow. "Perhaps now is, in fact, the pivotal moment. Perhaps only my assumptions have been incorrect."

Shit. The man was smarter than he appeared to be—very smart, with a mind that seemed to be calculating faster than she could outthink him.

"Now I see that my strategy has been all wrong," he said, whirling his full attention back upon her. "My focus has been on the wrong Jared, the one who tried to send you back in time. We cannot know what my enemy was thinking—his thoughts are as lost to me as that time will ever be." He slipped his hands firmly about her face again, clasping her hard. "Yes, the other Jared is no longer of any importance," he said dismissively, "and so now I will learn all about *your* Jared."

Marco closed his eyes, and an electric sensation shot through Kelsey's mind, followed by a report of immediate, searing pain. He flinched, and his expressions altered repeatedly as she felt her mind being sucked of something, almost as if a giant vacuum were engulfing her thoughts. And then, just as suddenly, the sensations stopped. His eyes flew open, growing wide.

"You have spoken the truth," he whispered fiercely. "You are *not* Kelsey Bennett. Not the wife of the leader of the rebellion."

Kelsey drew in a sharp breath, bracing for his next words as he dropped his hands.

"However, I see now that you are extremely important to the Refarian ruler. You are his bonded lifemate, and that means one thing," he said into the hush. "*Your* Jared will be simple to defeat."

In the center of his palm, Jared held the gold ring, staring into the circle of it as he might a scattering of mystics' reading leaves.

"What is it?" Scott and Thea demanded in unison, each trying to see the object he held close inside his palm.

With a mystified shake of his head, he extended his hand toward them in explanation. "A wedding band."

"Whose?" Scott said, kneeling beside him. "Who in hell's name would have left a ring in here?" They had purchased the cabin from its builder; no one else besides their team had ever lived within the large home.

"Marek did," Jared answered, his gaze never leaving the object. Against his skin, the gold burned like a strake stone, almost scalding him with its supernatural energy, but he wasn't about to relinquish the object.

"How do you know that, Jared?" Thea asked, gazing over his shoulder and into his palm's center.

"I saw it. Him. *And* her." It was the vision that had sent him to his knees, searching. Oh, yes, he had seen Kelsey here on the floor, naked and frightened, had seen her clutching this same band in her pale hand, unwilling to relinquish it. But what had it meant to her? That he did not yet know.

As he turned toward Thea, the air crackled with energy and came alive around him. The floor shifted beneath his feet as he caught a glimpse of Kelsey in front of his bathroom mirror with nothing but a towel wrapped around her beautiful body. Before he could make sense of it, the image dissolved and faded into another: Kelsey on the floor of his bedroom, a threatening stranger towering over her half-naked form.

He jerked his head toward the center of his bedroom, as if he might actually see her sprawled there, and flashed on the strangest vision of all. He saw someone who looked very much like himself, but older, harder. Scarred. Ruined. Jared dug the heels of his hands into his eyes and began to shake as the air all around him cooled unnaturally. What was happening to him? What had happened in this room, intense enough to leave a visual imprint in the atmosphere?

Jared looked up slowly, lifting his face out of his hands. "I . . . I'm getting things . . . off this room," he told them, wheeling his gaze about. "Things that might help us find Kelsey."

Scott placed a strong hand on his shoulder. "What sorts of things, my lord?"

"Emotions . . . images." Not that such a discovery should be surprising—only surprising in that he, a nonintuitive, should see so much.

Jared closed his eyes. *Grief . . . a solid wall of grief. Terror. Delirious ecstasy . . . more grief.* The impressions washed over him in rapid succession, almost like watching a fast-forwarded movie, the images were that vivid and fast. But of all the sensations swimming through his mind, one in particular kept surfacing out of the murky depths: terror. Kelsey's terror shooting like ungrounded electric current all about them; it was the starkest, most recent imprint he was picking up.

A sharp wave of nausea knotted his stomach, and he buried his face in his hands again, willing the room to stop its spinning. He had to quiet himself, no matter how difficult—especially because he recognized the emotions in this room.

And he'd felt this kind of raw, confused terror only one other time in his life.

Chapter Fourteen

When Jared was twenty-six, just two years after his arrival on Earth, he'd become embroiled in a ferocious firefight somewhere over the open spaces of Idaho. Air force jets had closed in on him, much as they had done recently near Mirror Lake, chasing him with patient resolve. He'd been sure he would die. If not for his craft's advanced engineering, which allowed him to evade missile-lock repeatedly, he *would* have been killed. Still, in the face of the American crafts' continuing onslaught, his plane's propulsion system had eventually lost power, sputtering and lurching until in one heart-stopping moment he had found himself free-falling straight toward the blackened expanse below. With no other alternative, he ejected into the night.

Scrambling through brush and grass and blackness, his body gashed and broken, he stumbled until almost sunrise, trying to make his smashed comm system work and praying that the base had tracked his descent. As the first pink light fingered across Earth's sky, Jared glimpsed soldiers appearing out of the morning mist, and he'd thought himself rescued. Collapsing in a heap on some farmer's open field, he gasped his gratitude, until he realized that it wasn't rescuers who had him, but his Antousian enemies. He hadn't even possessed the wherewithal to make his Change.

Hours later, beaten senseless and within an inch of his mortal life, Jared found himself kneeling before his greatest enemy: the Antousian warlord Veckus Densalt. Leader of the Earth conquest, Veckus wished Jared dead more than he cared for intelligence or blood debts—or even that he finally had the Refarian monarch within his grasp. Veckus lusted for one thing: vengeance. So for three interminable days the warlord had extracted it, Jared's captivity a study in depraved torture. In fact, he still bore the scars on his back and face and upper thighs; the initial beating had been but a dress rehearsal for the bloodthirsty Antousian's true skills at torment.

During that long darkness, Jared moved in and out of a death dream, rank visions passing through his beating-muddled mind. Images of formless Antousians and silver-eyed devils and winged creatures buoyed him through timelessness. Still, always at the edge of awareness he sensed protection—perhaps from those winged creatures he swore he glimpsed in his fever dreams, or perhaps from the shadow men hovering near; he never knew. By the third night, when Scott finally managed to locate him and send in retrieval forces, Jared's spirit had set to wandering the midplaces; he was certain of it. But his soldiers did come, and although the terrified dreams still tormented him even now, he *had* lived. Thanks to Scott Dillon. And perhaps thanks to some divine force that still breathed purpose into his existence.

But even without the dreams, he could never shake the horror he'd known for those three days, which was why, as he sat on the edge of his bed now, the stench of Kelsey's terror felt so familiar. And he'd be damned if his blessed lifemate would experience anything approximating the suffering he'd known at Veckus's hands.

"Thea, I need you to help me." Both soldiers had been waiting on his word while he held the band, fielding the impressions it radiated.

"Is it something with the ring?" she asked, dropping heavily beside him on the mattress's edge.

Staring into his open palm, he nodded, turning the band over in his hand. "This belongs to Kelsey," he explained, speaking from instinct rather than factual knowledge.

"But . . . I don't understand. It's a *wedding* ring."

He nodded. "Yes, I know. It's inscribed as well. Look." He extended the band to her. "It's worn down some, but hold it to the light. You can still read the inscription."

She did as he instructed, lifting the ring to eye level and

squinting. " 'Sonnet twenty-nine, verses thirteen to fourteen,' " she read, her pale brows furrowing in confusion. "I-I don't understand the significance of this, Jared."

In answer, he folded both arms over his chest and began to recite the Shakespearean poem from memory: " 'For thy sweet love remember'd such wealth brings—that then I scorn to change my state with kings.' "

"Does that mean something to you?" Scott asked.

Jared met his friend's questioning gaze. "It's our wedding vow, I believe," he answered, feeling an unstoppable wave of grief rise up within his chest. Grief for a beautiful future, stolen like some intricate, fragile snowflake lost forever in a harsh wind.

"What the hell?" Scott asked, his fair face flushing with emotion. Thea gaped at Jared, stricken, but he alone remained calm, a center of focused purpose amid the tumultuous emotions passing between them all.

He looked from one to the other of his two most trusted soldiers. In a soft voice, he said, "It's *our* sonnet, given by me to Kelsey tonight." Thea's blue eyes welled with tears—she understood; without another word of explanation, she understood exactly in what way he'd "given" that verse to his mate. "And apparently," he continued, drawing in a steadying breath, "the day we were married, it served as part of our wedding vows—three months from today. Take a look at the date inside the band."

"Three months from *today*? Sir, your words make no sense," Scott answered, placing a firm hand on his shoulder. "You're upset. Grieved—"

"No, Lieutenant, I am perfectly rational about this. I saw it." He indicated the bedroom with a sweep of his hand. "Saw it all here, in this room—*and* there in the future. This ring belonged to another Kelsey, years from now, and somehow it was brought back to *my* Kelsey from that time. I saw myself, older somehow—and I saw her, older too." For a moment, Jared had to drop his head; the graying man he'd glimpsed had been a diminished shadow of himself, ravaged by years of warfare. His wife's bold and strong spirit had been like a beacon in that future, his other self's true sustenance.

His two advisers exploded in dispute and challenge, but with a lift of his hand he silenced them. He met his cousin's confused gaze and extended his open palm with a resolute gesture. "Lieutenant Haven," he said in a calm and determined voice, "I require your help."

Ashen, she stared at his hand wordlessly, and it lay between them, an unanswered question until he explained his plan. "I need your power, cousin," he told her gently. "It's the only way I can do what I must."

Hesitating only one moment longer, she extended her own trembling, pale hand to him. Before their fingers had even locked together, the tendrils of his cousin's immense energy had already begun to twine with his own, giving him the strength he hoped would enable him to reach Kelsey across the expanse that separated them.

Kelsey sat on the smooth floor of the mitres chamber, leaning against the tiled wall. She drew her denim-clad knees close against her chest, making herself as small as possible—almost willing herself to disappear—as if an auburn-haired, nearly six-foot-tall woman could *ever* escape notice. Without being obvious about it, she stole glances around the place, trying to get a better fix on her location. Was she underground? On Refaria? She hadn't a clue, because the catacomb-like place didn't seem to possess a single opening to the outside world. It reminded her of her grandparents' farm in Montana, where she'd once seen a basement fallout shelter left over from the 1960s, still stocked with dingy soup cans and dusty supplies. Only this weaponry complex—for surely that was what it had to be, even if that revelation had come from Marco—was the sort of place that sent people *into* shelter. It didn't provide it.

Kelsey studied the large, luminous tube in the middle of the main chamber's floor. It held no meaning for her, no relation to anything she had ever encountered as a student of the physical sciences. Yet apparently ten years from now she knew exactly how to operate the damn thing. She let her gaze slide over other parts of the chamber, squinting as she followed the trail of a dark, narrow hallway until it vanished into blackness. Maybe the way out was down that hall? With a surge of hope, she knew she had to break away from Marco somehow, at least long enough to see if her freedom lay at the obscured end of that tunnel.

She lifted wary eyes to study her captor. Marco sprawled

against the wall opposite her, his lean frame imposing the strength and weight of an armed fortress without so much as twitching a single muscle. His long legs extended in front of him with a casualness that belied whatever purpose had dragged them both to this alien place. His calculating black eyes locked with hers in challenge, and one dark eyebrow shot upward, daring her to question his motives.

She dropped her chin onto her knees and fixed her eyes on his weathered black hiking boots—anything to avoid that cold, vacant stare. One of his boots had a long gash along the side, the kind a penetrating knife might have left in the middle of some struggle, and as she stared at that slash of leather, she thought of his scar. Again she wondered why it felt so familiar and significant.

Glancing upward, she studied the way the silver line sliced through the otherwise silken black hairs of his eyebrow. With his waving black hair and sultry-eyed appearance, he was just the kind of guy she and her girlfriends might have ogled from afar. He possessed the dangerous, graceful looks of the unattainable, the sort of bad boy she would never dare to pursue. Not if she didn't want her heart smashed into thousands of pieces—she'd encountered his kind before. Then again, Jared had the same kind of breath-stealing good looks about him too. But in every plane of her lover's face, every realm of his heart, Jared transmitted goodness. Strength. This Marco's dangerous beauty made her shiver like she would in the middle of some sudden snow squall.

"You study me," he observed, that eyebrow cocking upward in question again.

She countered, "How'd you get that scar?" and locked her eyes with him in challenge. Unflinching, he stared back at her for a long, thoughtful moment. Against the wall, he stiffened, as if he meant to come after her, but she refused to cower. Just as suddenly, their battles of wills softened, and he released a breath, settling into his watch again without another word.

But she remained undaunted. "You're not going to answer me?" she pressed.

He released a low, soft chuckle. "I owe you no answers, my dear."

"Oh, so . . . what? You just get to snatch me from the

bathroom half-naked, send me flying through God only knows what that was earlier, but I can't ask about a scar?" She snorted with ironic laughter. "No, I'm sorry, but I think you owe me plenty of answers."

His black eyebrows drew together with a focused expression, but he said nothing, only retrieved his weapon from a side holster—a silver pistol unlike any she'd ever seen before—and gazed down the barrel at her.

"That doesn't intimidate me."

His full lips pulled into an amused expression. "It would if I fired into you."

"No, that would just kill me," she answered, trying to sound nonchalant. "But it still wouldn't intimidate me."

This statement, for some inexplicable reason, earned her a grudging look of appreciation. He lowered his pistol and immediately reholstered it. "I don't believe I am ready to kill you, Kelsey." He lifted a thumb to his marred eyebrow, rubbing it with a thoughtful gesture. "Why do you mention the scar?" he asked, searching her face.

"It's important." She'd felt the undercurrent of knowing in those first moments when he'd taken her captive. She sensed it even more so now. "Tell me why." If she could get control here, be the one in command of this situation, then maybe she could control *him*.

"It's an odd question, Kelsey," he answered, his hard gaze never leaving her face. "Again, I wonder why you ask."

"Maybe the scar is part of all this."

His expression darkened, and she swore that the dusky skin of his face reddened as well, but he said nothing more. No answers, no reasoning behind what they were doing here in this strangely lit chamber, only a heavily drawn and oppressive silence.

Well, she wouldn't let him think it mattered to her. She dropped her gaze again, and began to trace her finger in little circular patterns on the smooth floor. "Well, if *that* question's no good, then here's another one," she said. "What are we doing here?" Maybe being direct was better with this enemy. "Other than your plan to destroy Jared Bennett, that is."

He tilted his head sideways. "I liked the first question better."

He seemed to gaze at some distant point, a surprising mixture of emotions flashing across his features. Sadness, regret, emptiness—all those passed over his dark face, and he made no effort to disguise them from her. Then, just as quickly, he grew guarded again, his expression steely and harsh as his gaze bore down upon her. "Yes, Kelsey Bennett, I do indeed prefer the first question," he said, his voice assuming a formal tone. "And yet I shall answer the second one." He shifted where he sat on the floor, sitting more upright. "We're going to call Jared in a few minutes and have him meet us here."

"Why are you waiting at all?" she demanded, leaping to her feet. Jared would come, marshaling all the soldiers at his disposal, before he'd let this man touch her. "Why not just call him now?" She stared down at him, unable to suppress her fury and fear another moment.

Only the subtlest shading of surprise even passed over his face. "Ah, well, there's reason to my madness." He folded his muscled arms across his chest. "I want to give him time to know you're really gone, because his fear for you will be his weakness."

"Of course he knows I'm gone!" she cried in frustration, pacing the floor. "You kidnapped me from his freaking bedroom!"

With unexpected swiftness, one dark hand shot out, clasping her ankle like a strong manacle. "I want him to feel your absence," he said calmly, holding her fast. "To experience the truth of it in the marrow of his bones. Only then will I allow him to know the full measure of his defeat. Now," he said, his voice edged like a knife blade, *"sit down."*

"So we can wait for Jared to know 'the measure of his defeat,'" she taunted, trembling as she sank back against the wall opposite Marco.

"I wish the battlefield to assemble well," he answered with a nod.

And for Jared to realize that I'm as good as dead? She shivered at the thought, but forced herself to focus on getting Marco to talk—to reveal some hidden detail that might help her escape.

"Why do you want to destroy Jared? You *must* be Antousian."

Marco had told her at the outset that he was Refarian—but from what she already knew about Jared's people, why would any of his own kind wish to see him dead?

"Antousian?" He let out a deep, gravelly laugh, something she never expected. "No, I told you before—I'm Refarian. Just like you and Jared."

She would have sworn that her heart stopped beating beneath the ribs of her chest, turning instead to a chamber as hollow as the one all around her. Then with a violent lurch, it began to hammer an erratic, crazy tempo, the room nearly fading to black around her.

Finally, she found her voice again. "Like *Jared,* you mean," she corrected with a swallow. "You're Refarian like *he* is."

Marco's eyebrows drew together in confusion as he studied her. "Like you, Jared—all of you." Awareness grew in his expression. "Kelsey, don't you know what you are? Surely you know by now."

She felt hot tears begin to sting behind her eyes, anger roiling hard within her. "What kind of game are you trying to play with me?" she demanded.

"I was merely answering your question as to my genetic makeup." He cleared his throat with a wry laugh. "I did not expect to bump into something so . . . awkward, shall I say, as your not knowing which species you belong to." He bowed his head dramatically. "I do hope you'll forgive my indiscretion."

"What you're saying . . . it can't be true. It's impossible." Her hands began to tremble uncontrollably, the tears still prickling her eyes.

"Kelsey, it is very much possible, because it is who you *are.*"

"I have human cells," she insisted. "Human blood! My father is Jordan Patrick Wells. My mother—"

"He changed you."

"My *mother,*" she continued, "was Erica Marshall Wells—"

"When Jared left this mitres data inside your mind, Kelsey, it changed you on the most basic cellular level. I'm sorry, but you *are* part Refarian now." His voice had assumed a quiet, soothing tone. "Between the soul joining and the mind bonding, and the presence of his data, it

transformed you. So you're part Homo sapiens and part"—
he chuckled—"Homo Refarius, I guess you'd say, since our
genetic codes are more than ninety-nine percent the same."

"No, you're wrong." Kelsey shook her head adamantly.
"There's no way you could even know this at all."

He studied her with a sympathetic expression. "Actually,
I know firsthand that it *is* the truth."

"How?" she rasped.

"Because I came to serve as your protector—pardon, I
will come to serve two years from this time." He met her
eyes with a steady gaze. "Both you and Jared—it was what
I was bred and engineered for. I vowed my allegiance before the high Refarian council, pledging my service, my
indenture, my very blood to the throne. So, you see, I know
a great deal about you, Kelsey—apparently more than you
know about yourself. I am sorry if my revelation shocked
you."

Swiping at the tears, Kelsey buried her face in her knees.
She didn't want Marco to know that his bizarre tactic was
unnerving her so badly. Yet something deep within her ignited at his words, and she knew that they were true.
Slowly, she raised her head and found Marco studying
her coolly.

"Then why are you here to destroy Jared now?" She
couldn't help the pleading tone that had entered her voice.
"Why have you kidnapped me? If you're our protector,
then—"

"I *was* your protector." She swore a note of compassion
softened his words.

"But you just said it was what you were bred for," she
tried to argue, hoping to appeal to some forgotten sense of
purpose in the cruel man. "Why would you hurt us then?"

Marco rose, brushing off his faded jeans, and began to
slowly pace the length of the chamber. For a long moment
he seemed to consider his reply, bracing his arms on the
tiled side of the mitres' walls. Finally, he pivoted to face
her, meeting her eyes with meaningful intensity.

"I'm here because that's what Veckus has asked me to
do, Kelsey," he answered quietly. "And I serve him now,
not Jared."

*   *   *

Jared pressed his eyes shut and allowed Thea's power to bolster his own. He'd sat still for several silent moments, seeking the necessary strength to forge a spatial bridge with Kelsey. He caught foggy glimpses of her while he waited, of her sitting on the floor of an unknown location, and the need to place her in time and space made him almost wild. Made the wait unbearable. As his eyes searched for her in the darkness, he could almost recognize the room, but the outlines were just too vaguely defined, shaped only by mist and shadow. So he'd waited, allowing the buzzing energy to build within him before he pushed forward toward her. But now Kelsey pulled into focus, the haziness around her parting like summer storm clouds over the valley.

Stepping across the bridge—immersing himself within their bond—he walked toward her, kneeling beside her on the floor. But she was busy talking, and even though he kept repeating her name, she couldn't hear him.

Kelsey. Kelsey, sweetheart, he tried, forcing a semblance of calm into his words.

She continued with her conversation, unaware of his presence. He was little more than a mist to her. Or a ghost. That thought sent an unsettling shiver up his spine. If only he could make out what was being said—or whom she was talking to.

She buried her face against her knees, fighting back tears. Who was hurting her? His heart rate soared, and he spun first in one direction, then another, seeking Kelsey's tormentor. Nothing to be seen! No discernible forms around her. At last she became quiet, so he tried again. Placing a tender hand on her back, he began to rub her shoulders. With every caress, a blazing fire built within his abdomen, then his hands and legs, until at last he swore that his raging power would overtake him, inciting his Change. But he tamped down his restless energy, focusing only on his life-mate, until at last she lifted her head, glancing around her as if she expected to see someone. She had felt his touch! He saw little goose bumps shoot across her arms. He hadn't ignited their bond, not yet, but he was very close.

Stepping around her, he knelt on the floor facing her. He placed his hands on top of hers, whispering her name like one of the mystics' sacred chants.

Kelsey . . . Kelsey, he called to her, offering a breath of golden life. A tether of safety. A promise of his protective love.

No answer.

The heat that had begun in his belly now radiated outward until it seemed to explode within every part of his body—until he burned, maddeningly so. He spoke across their soul bond, propelling himself across distance and space, right into her immediate presence: *Kelsey, my love. My mate! Hear me! It is Jared. J'Areshkadau! Love, love . . .*

His energy careened uncontrollably, his Change nearly unstoppable in its pulsating demand—but he clenched his teeth, refusing to allow his fire's engulfment.

Again, Kelsey glanced around her in confusion, unsure of what she had seemingly sensed. With a hopeless gesture, she buried her face in her hands. Gently, he placed his hands on top of her head, allowing the heat and energy that had been building inside of him to flood her.

Kelsey dropped her hands to her sides, her eyes meeting his desperately—and the connection between their two souls roared to life.

Jared, are you really here? With her eyes she implored him, their blue depths radiant with hope.

No, I'm using our bond. This is something . . . like a vision. I am within your mind and soul right now—with you in every other way but the physical.

Jared looked around them and instantly noted her location: the mitres chambers. Of course—now he understood its pressing familiarity. *Why are you here?* he asked. *Who has brought you?*

Oh, Jared . . . . he works for your enemies—someone named Veckus? His name is Marco, and he's not from this time—

I know, love.

You can't come here, no matter what, Jared. Send Scott. Send any of your people, but you can't come.

She sounded hysterical, and he forced calmness into his own words. *You know I will come for you.*

No! she cried out. *No, don't you see? You're the one he wants. It's why he took me.*

Jared glanced about the chamber again, and this time noticed a figure—a rangy, broad-shouldered man, well over six feet tall, with shadowy features. Her captor paced the length of the chamber slowly, studying Kelsey where she sat on the floor. Jared rose to confront him; he raised a fist, ready to kill the man in order to protect his love.

Then he remembered: He wasn't even there—had no recourse at all, not yet—and was powerless to help Kelsey until he got there. He knelt in front of her again, and saw that tears streamed down her face.

Please, Jared. If you come, he'll kill you. It's what he wants.

He cupped her face in his hands and pressed his lips against her forehead. *Shh . . . nothing's going to happen to me. I will be fine. We will both be fine, sweetheart. . . .*

She pulled back, looking up into his eyes. *He was our protector, but something went really wrong. I don't know what.*

Suddenly darkness began to form around Kelsey and he felt himself being pressed away from her. Marco towered over her now, staring down at her, talking. What was the bastard saying?

"Kelsey, what's going on?" came this Marco's voice, deep and throaty, echoing as if from the bottom of a stony canyon. The words were furious, cruel; Jared raised a fist again, ready to battle the man to the death, despite the distance that separated them.

But before he could challenge his enemy or even offer Kelsey a last assurance of protection, darkness overcame her. And everything within Jared's mind and spirit faded to black.

Chapter Fifteen

"This is taking way too long." Scott crouched in front of the bed, where Jared slumped, eyes half rolled back into his head. "He should've pulled out long before now."

"Don't you think I know that?" Thea tried not to panic, and placed a hand to Jared's flushed cheek. "God, he's burning up." She shook her head, trying to understand her cousin's fugue state. "Something's definitely wrong here."

For the past twenty minutes Jared had been sitting beside her, his hand clasped around hers, but his mind and soul transported to somewhere else entirely—a place where no one else could follow.

Scott planted both hands firmly on Jared's shoulders. "Jared," he said, but there was no change at all. Scott turned back to Thea. "You've got to do something about this."

"Like what, Scott?" she hissed. "I don't even know what *this* is, all right?"

She wriggled her hand out of Jared's sweaty-palmed death grip, and turned to face him where he slumped on the bed. His dark eyebrows were furrowed in deep concentration, as if he were intercepting a very intense conversation held another galaxy away. She drew her face within an inch of his and gave him a gentle shake, whispering his name. Then, for the first time since they'd linked power, his expression changed, as some unidentifiable emotion flashed across his features. His eyes grew wide, his eyebrows hitched upward, and he began growling loudly in apparent denial. It was the instinctive sound of an enraged Refarian changeling. Bracing herself, she wondered what might come next.

"No," he whispered hoarsely, focusing on an unseen spot across the room. "No. Kelsey! *Kelsey*," he cried, and then his eyes flew open, darting as he gasped for air.

"Jared!" Scott released his shoulders and dropped to the floor in front of their leader. "Tell me you're all right, sir." Scott made no effort to mask the fear they felt; Thea had cursed them both as fools for even letting Jared attempt such a dangerous tactic. It was one thing to make a connection when one's bondmate was in close proximity, but Kelsey might be anywhere by now. Traversing long distances could put his spirit in jeopardy, for all they knew.

"I saw her," Jared gasped at last. Springing to his feet, he began to move about the room, a study in coiled fury. "Ready a transport," he commanded.

Scott gave an answering nod. "Already done and awaiting orders."

"They're holding her at the mitres," Jared continued. "We must get there at once."

Thea reminded Jared that a retrieval team, not his own presence, made the most sense. When he again insisted on personally accompanying the soldiers, she pressed the issue harder. "I don't understand how you can put yourself in that kind of danger," she said. "All these insane chances lately, cousin—"

But he cut her off. "There is no other way this time." He turned to her, his face a mask of composed leadership, meeting her gaze head on. "The mitres data remains lodged within Kelsey's mind. *I* am the one who placed it there—and *I* am the one who left this human vulnerable, exposed to our enemies, of whom she knows *nothing*." Deep blotches of color stained his face, and he drew in a shuddering breath before continuing. "I am the one who must retrieve it—and I am the one she is counting on." He reached for his pistol where it lay on the mantel, and holstered it before turning back to them, his black eyes blazing with emotion. "*Now* do you understand the stakes this night, cousin?"

And without awaiting an answer, he strode out the door.

A nagging thought teased at Marco's mind, one that gained substance the longer he observed Kelsey. She sat exactly where she had for most of the past thirty minutes: leaning against the wall opposite him, her face lowered. And deathly still. When at first her questions had ceased and she'd buried her face against her knees, he'd assumed she was simply crying. But now his suspicions grew rampant.

She and Jared weren't married yet, so he didn't know if their bond was anything like it became in the later years of their relationship—or if they had even discovered their unique gift for communicating over vast distances yet. But what if they had? And what if she were trying to make that connection right now?

"Kelsey, what's going on?" he demanded.

"N-nothing," she stammered, face still buried in her crumpled jacket.

And he knew. He was across the room in a breath, and with a rough jerk of her arm he yanked her to an upright position. "You were trying to reach Jared."

She shook her head in denial, but he recognized that dazed look; he'd seen it on both their faces too many times over the years *not* to recognize it.

"Kelsey, I know exactly what you were doing." Answering fear flickered in her intelligent eyes.

God, she thought he might actually hurt her. That he could ever hurt her—even if he tried. No matter what had happened between them all in the past eight years, wounding her in *any* way was something he remained incapable of doing.

In the chamber a week ago, he'd nearly aborted his entire plan after accidentally crushing her future self's hand beneath his boot. She'd cried out in sharp, undisguised pain, and the mission had all but ended before it had even started. For five full minutes he'd struggled to recover his stupefied senses enough to sift through her thoughts. He'd been gentle with the woman, as gentle as he could be; even so, she'd believed he might kill her at any moment. She, the only woman he had ever loved. But by the time he'd left her behind, shaken and dazed, he hoped she understood the truth: that even with all their painful, twisted history, he would never willingly harm her.

However, Jared Bennett was another story entirely.

"What happened to make you turn from us?" *this* Kelsey whispered, strong as steel—yet delicate as a newly budded flower. There it was: that dichotomous beauty he had always found so fascinating in the human. And, yes, she was human,

although her story was as complicated as he'd indicated; he'd
been honest about that much. Still, he'd twisted things somewhat in an effort to keep her under his control; he'd done it,
and begged her forgiveness in silence the entire time.

Closing his protector's eyes, Marco willed himself to regain his composure. Thinking too much about his past
never led to any good end these days. He had to stay focused, had to accomplish his mission, and he refused to
yield power by dredging up things that should remain
long-forgotten.

When he looked again, he found Kelsey studying him,
waiting for some kind of answer. Her gaze more than any
other had always had the capacity to unsettle him. So of
course it had that exact effect right now; against his will,
his cheeks burned hot beneath her examination. After so
long, just one look from her could still cause his heart to
lodge solidly in his throat, and his mind to play wayward
tricks; he moved to block the impressions he kept reading
off of her. Better to seal off his intuition. Better to fall
back on uncomplicated warrior's strengths right now.

"So, now that you and Jared have shared *communion*—is
he on the way?" he asked with forced coolness, brushing past
her. She remained silent, until at last he began to laugh. Of
course Jared was on the way—that was how connected they'd
always been. No one needed to remind him of that fact.

"Well, at least that will save me a phone call," he said,
and felt something like a shiver of anticipation run
through him.

He hadn't stood face-to-face with Jared Bennett—any
version of him—in more than four years.

Kelsey wasn't entirely sure what she'd just seen in Marco's eyes, but she would've sworn she sensed some kind of
fondness for her. Maybe she had more to do with this situation than she'd initially guessed. And if so, then maybe she
could get a few answers from Marco: answers that might
help Jared. She rose slowly from the cold floor and felt her
knee throb from sitting in one place for the past hour—she
had an old skiing injury, and when she kept still for too
long, it always began to ache.

He moved his large frame to block her. "Where do you
think you're going?"

She didn't flinch. "I just want to stretch my legs. Is that okay?"

At last he gave a nod of agreement, stepping backward from her.

"You'll never be able to fight them all, you know." Kelsey smoothed her hands across the front of her rumpled sweater. "They're too powerful. And you're just one man."

He looked at her and laughed softly. "I think it's really quite the opposite, my dear."

She stepped closer to him, and suddenly felt incredibly small next to his towering frame. "What does that mean?"

"I'm a full-blooded Refarian." He cast his eyes down for a moment and seemed to struggle with something. Then he looked back up at her, his expression completely unreadable. "And that's what makes all of you weak. Jared, the others, are corrupted by their human interactions. Weakened."

"Well, then I must be the weakest of all—and I still don't believe what you told me earlier."

He arched an eyebrow. "Why not?"

"A change like you're describing, on a cellular level, isn't possible. I don't even have to be a scientist to know that."

"Would you have said it was possible for one person to leave complicated designs and coding within another's mind?"

"I don't know that he did that," she argued. Although she had only Jared's word, she did believe he'd actually done what he claimed.

Marco shook his head slowly. "Kelsey, you are just more human than the others. That's all. But you are one of them. It was part of why the people rallied . . ." Marco's voice trailed off, and he began shaking his head as he stared at her. "My God. You really don't know any of this, do you?"

She met Marco's cold eyes with determination. "Tell me what you were going to say."

"Okay." He pulled his face within mere inches of hers. "You were his bride," he whispered, his eyes raking over her face heatedly.

"I already know we were married," she stated impatiently. "You told me that earlier. You *showed* me the ring!"

"No, Kelsey, I mean you were his *bride*. You are the

beloved of Refaria—more valuable to the revolution than even the king. You are the one the rebels rise to follow. Because of your humanity. Because you are both human and Refarian, as a result of your change. You were prophesied to him years ago—hasn't he told you? You were foretold by the mystics. In every way possible, you are their queen, and they are pledged to you."

And with that simple statement, Kelsey felt her entire universe shift on its axis, and she collapsed to her knees.

Marco watched Kelsey slide to the floor and shook his head in disbelief. How was it possible that she didn't know any of this? He thought they'd learned about her hybrid DNA long before she and Jared were married. The mitres data wasn't simply within her mind; it was permanently fused inside her brain, making her not only the queen—but the revolution's true weapon. It had been why she alone could operate the mitres ten years in the future. This ignorance of hers gave him a distinct advantage; he wasn't going to spend this time before Veckus arrived educating her.

But when she slowly raised her eyes to meet his, and he saw the wild look in them, he felt something shift and come alive within his chest. Her eyes had always been like two deep pools that he could lose himself in. Find himself in.

She continued to stare up, begging him with those same lovely eyes. "Tell me the rest," she breathed at last.

The urge to guide her, to make her understand her purpose, was compelling—he'd spent too many years fulfilling his duty as their royal protector *not* to feel it. Obviously, she and Jared didn't know their true destiny. And he was painfully aware of just how vulnerable it left them all.

Did they know about Veckus? Valyre? Thea?

He shook his head, clearing his thoughts. He could not do this—he had a mission to complete.

He coughed into his hand, furrowing his brow. "The rest?" he asked, feigning ignorance.

"How can I be the one they follow? I saw Jared in the slipstream, when you took me through the time portal! He was alive—I saw him. He was alive and leading his people. Leading *me*!"

"Yes, that's true," he agreed with a sigh. "I never said

the people didn't follow him. But the one who drew humans and Refarians together and bound them as one . . ." He shook his head slowly, fighting a wave of melancholy as he recalled the way their future had gone. "Trust me, Kelsey, it was you."

"Trust *you?*" she cried incredulously, raking fingers through her hair. "*Trust* you? *Please!*"

He hadn't even noticed his choice of words. How could he ever expect her to trust him? Trust had departed between the three of them so long ago. Well, not the three of them; between the two of them and himself.

"What purpose would it serve me to lie about such things?"

He extended his hand to her, intending to help her to her feet, but she ignored it. He wasn't sure how to read the look on her face. She dropped her head, bowed it almost, and remained on her knees. He tried to see her expression, but her long auburn curls formed a curtain, hiding her face from him.

"Kelsey, please get up," Marco said, extending his hand again.

She kept her head lowered. "Please, Marco . . . just don't hurt him," she whispered.

Again, he felt the spark of something come alive within him, but he willed it to die. "I follow Veckus now, Kelsey."

She shook her head slowly, gaze lowered to the ground. "I'm begging you. Please don't hurt Jared."

Begging you.

And then it hit him, nearly driving him to his *own* knees.

The woman he had called queen was kneeling before him—bowing before him—begging for her husband's life. One with such a noble and beautiful spirit was reduced to kneeling before a traitor, before him, of all people, the man who had betrayed her. He closed his eyes against the sight of it.

God, how had it come to this?

The memories engulfed him in the space of a heartbeat, catapulting him through time as surely as if he'd activated the mitres. Time dissolved completely until, vivid as this moment, he stood before Jared, the terrible gash in his forehead throbbing incessantly. Jared might as well be standing here in the mitres right between them both; his voice sounded that clearly in Marco's ears: and so did his own.

"*I'm begging you not to do this, Jared. Please,*" Marco had said. "*My lord, please. Not this. Anything but this.*"

And Jared had stared down at him, despising him. The man he'd called brother. King. Turning his back on him after their years together. It was never supposed to be this way!

"*Get up, Marco.*" *Jared's breathing was labored and heavy.* "*Now.*"

"*I was wrong. God, I* know *how wrong I was.*" *Marco sought his king's pardon with his eyes, imploring him to listen to his heart, not the evidence.*

"*Wrong?*" *Jared roared in disbelief.* "*You tried to kiss my wife. Your* queen! *In my own bedroom. And when she resisted, you struggled with her. How wrong could I be about those facts? What don't I understand?*" *Jared's large frame bore down upon him, threatening something far worse than mere coldness.* "*Tell me, Marco,*" *he thundered, so loudly the walls of the great room had echoed the words back at them,* "*why did you kiss my wife?*"

And Marco had no answer. None whatsoever to offer the man he loved more than any other. Casting his gaze downward in shame, he felt his face burn with it.

Jared's voice became as cold and crafty as an Antousian's. "*So you don't deny it.*"

"*I-it wasn't like that, my lord,*" *he finally stammered, still not daring to raise his eyes to meet those of his king.* "*Please hear me.*"

Jared cupped his chin, forcing Marco to meet his gaze. "*Look at your face,*" *the king said, reminding him of the gash.* "*Look at the proof of your deeds. She is my mate, my life. You were my friend.*" *Jared's voice had become a hollow imitation of its normal sound, filled with dark emotion.*

"*It was . . . a misunderstanding.*" *Jared dropped his hand away, and Marco immediately inclined his head*

lower, deepening his posture into the lowest, most ser-
vile of genuflections among the Refarian people.

"You told her," Jared shot back at him, gesturing
furiously, "that you've been in love with her for more
than a year. Did I misunderstand that?"

Marco remained silent for a long moment, wondering how he could possibly explain what he knew would
sound insane. Keeping his head bowed in reverence to
his king, he wondered how Jared could ever understand the truth of what his life had been like for the
past four years. An intuitive, always in their presence—
and therefore always so near the bond that wove between the two of them. Oh, it would have to sound
crazy, no matter how he attempted to defend himself.
How could Jared ever understand his torture during
the past four years? That somehow, impossibly, he'd
begun to feel their connection. All that tenderness, all
the love and desire that spun between Jared and Kelsey
had been slowly winding its way into Marco's own
spirit and mind.

God, he'd never meant for it to happen, hadn't
wanted it or asked for it. He'd begged for the temptation to be taken away. With all his soul's strength, he
had tried to will their damn bond away. Every day for
those years he'd shamefully lusted for and loved his
king's wife—his own queen. What sort of monster did
it make him? He hated himself, so he could hardly
expect his best friend to feel any differently. And of
course it would sound insane to a low intuitive like
Jared. No, there was no point in explaining at all, because Jared would never believe him.

Jared's furious gaze never wavered. "Did I misunderstand, soldier?" he repeated, his voice like acid.

"No, my lord," he finally replied in a defeated voice.

Jared blinked back at him. "I trusted you with her,
with her very life. God, with my own life—and you
betrayed me. You betrayed us both!"

Marco came to his senses, rallying to attempt a defense. "Won't you at least hear what I have to say?"

"No. I want you out of here."

The words had torn into Marco's very spirit—he had
no other purpose in life than to serve the two of them.

"I don't want to leave either of you," he'd said quietly, daring to meet Jared's furious, blazing gaze.
Jared stared down at him, shaking his head bitterly. "You already have." Then he had turned on his heel and left Marco there, kneeling before no one.

But when Jared had turned his back on him that night, he had left a great void, because Marco had no other purpose than to serve his king and queen.

"Kelsey, please get up," Marco said, extending his hand again.

"Not until you tell me you won't hurt him," she said. "You don't have to do this. We've already changed the future, you and I. Tell me what went so wrong. We can fix it. Together."

"Shall I remind you again that I no longer serve Jared?"

Kelsey gazed up at him, suddenly seeming very small. She lifted her hands in front of her in desperation. "You can still make a choice, right here, right now."

Marco was silent for a long moment. "That's not really true, Kelsey."

Her eyes flew to his own, fear growing on her beautiful features. "What do you mean?"

"I made contact with . . . our people after I came back in time."

"*Our* people? You're Refarian—you said so yourself."

"The people I serve," he corrected.

"So this Veckus knows."

"The people who answer to him know. And they're outside right now."

"Then this is all a setup." Kelsey clutched her hands to her chest.

"Trust me," he said, shaking his head at the further irony of his word choice, "Jared Bennett can defend himself."

"Why would you do this to him? At least tell me that much."

There were a lifetime of answers Marco might provide, but he decided on the path of honesty. "Because, Kelsey, long ago Jared Bennett gave me no other choice," he said.

Then he left her there, just as Jared had once left him, kneeling in front of no one.

Chapter Sixteen

The silent transport hovered in midair, a small dark blot against the starry sky above the Refarians' position by Mirror Lake. Unlike the massive battle cruiser, the transport served in critical moments when speed meant everything. Only eighteen minutes had elapsed since Jared first issued his summons to Scott. Now, sheltered behind a massive outcropping of stone and boulder, Jared and his most elite soldiers strategized their best approach toward Mirror Lake and up the steep incline to where the mitres chamber lay hidden deep within a rocky cleft along the cliff's side.

A soldier appeared just beside Jared and pressed night-vision glasses into his hands. "Four of them on the ledge, my lord," he said. Jared leaned onto his elbows, feeling his bulletproof vest pull across his shoulders as he snaked on his belly along the cold ground to gain a better view. It was nighttime, so they'd opted for their darker wear, especially since the snow around the lake was still spotty. If it had been the dead of winter, they'd be in their winter whites, but tonight they'd darkened their faces with charcoal, worn their usual black uniforms, and were moving in complete stealth as they formed their position behind the rocks. They looked like a Refarian sniper squad, which, in effect, they were. Once they'd gained a solid fix on the enemy encampments in the area they would begin to take them out, some by teams, some by long-distance weaponry.

This was what they trained for: to overpower their enemies at times of critical warfare. Adrenaline flowed in every soldier present, empowering their minds and bodies, awakening their Refarian senses totally. And while none of them relished being called into action like this, the troops serving him wouldn't be as deadly as they were if they didn't welcome warfare. He'd never forget one dying soldier's last words, years ago back on Refaria. It had been after a blistering battle outside the city, one that had lasted for three solid days weaving in and out of abandoned buildings, and ultimately into a decimated cluster of housing units. By the time the fighting was over more than eighteen hundred Refarian soldiers had been killed. Jared visited the field hospital, trying to comfort the wounded and critically injured.

One young man on the brink of death had waved him closer, and pulling Jared's ear down to his mouth had whispered, "I never imagined having such a grand time dying, my lord." The young soldier's death less than fifteen minutes later had crystallized something critical for Jared that day—his people welcomed a fight. They wanted to battle the Antousians who had robbed them, raped them, and seized their world from them. And if it meant dying in service of their king and home, then so be it.

Today was another such day, Jared mused, accepting the night-vision glasses from the young Refarian corporal crouching beside him, waiting for his word—any word—to pass back to Lieutenant Dillon.

Jared settled down on his belly and observed the distant terrain through the field glasses. After a moment, two Antousians stepped into plain view on an exposed portion of trail that led to the mitres, and Jared adjusted the register on his glasses; he wanted to verify that he'd read their energy correctly. Antousians had a noticeably cooler reading than Refarians, showing up a dull blue-green, while Refarians, on the other hand, tended to glow a vivid golden green. The two species' energies registered very differently on the spectrograph, as differently as they did in all other matters, it seemed.

Behind him, Jared sensed two more of his soldiers edging their way toward his position. "Commander, Lieutenant Dillon urges us to move in," one of the newly arrived soldiers informed him. "He wants to lead a team in *now,* sir."

Without lowering the glasses, Jared shook his head in disagreement. It required a soldier's mastery of discipline, but he instructed the men to return to Scott with one directive: "We wait," he said, and prayed that Kelsey had the time they needed to mount a stunning counteroffensive.

Kelsey watched Marco vanish into one of the three dark passageways that led from the mitres' central chamber to God only knew where. She stared after him in shock. He hadn't bound her or tied her head to toe, he had simply *left* her. Almost as if he wasn't sure what to do with her now that he had her in his alien grip. Well, she decided, it wasn't her job to remind him that she was his captive.

Yet some strange, quiet voice whispered that he still cared for her—and for Jared—despite whatever had gone wrong between them all. If he'd truly been their protector, then surely his current plan contradicted every aspect of his training. Maybe *that* was the real reason he'd left her here unguarded, she thought with a surge of hope.

She listened to the echo of his retreating footsteps grow softer and softer, and when she could no longer hear them, she leaped to her feet. If he thought she was some kind of weakling who was going to take being kidnapped without a fight, well, this Marco had another think coming to him. Marco—and Jared—had both said the mitres data was embedded within her mind. This obviously wasn't the moment to put that data to use, even if she knew how, but it certainly meant she had a bargaining chip. Would anyone really want to see her dead if she was the only one with the means to operate this weapons system?

Clasping her hands to her head, she tried to focus her swirling thoughts. She needed to choose a tunnel, any tunnel that might lead to the exterior. But if there really were a way to escape, would Marco have left her unbound? No time like the present to find out. With nothing whatsoever to go on, she chose the left tunnel and sprinted into the darkness.

Kelsey felt her way along the smooth wall of the passageway, taking stumbling steps through the darkness. If an opening existed in this dimly lit path she'd chosen, surely she'd find it. But she felt nothing; her hands found nothing. The tunnel seemed to go on and on without end, and the farther she went, the darker it became. A whole lot darker. She'd never before feared the dark, but her heart now slammed inside her chest, so hard she could barely breathe from the impact of it against her ribs. She was terrified, but she swept thoughts of death and torture and time travel out of her mind, forcing everything within herself to focus. And yet step after step after step continued into the blackness, and it seemed like she would be swallowed up completely by an ocean of nothing.

Jared! she cried out to him, becoming frantic as she swept her hands about the walls in wide circular arcs. *Help me! Jared!* They had connected earlier, and then Marco had shouted at her and she'd lost that momentary flicker of communication—maybe they could connect again. She centered her mind, working to access that place where they'd found each other before, and cried out desperately to him again. *Jared!*

Kelsey, came his answer, quiet and focused somewhere within her. She stopped clawing her way through the inky black chamber.

Where are you? she asked, feeling tears well in her eyes. *I'm lost, Jared. I'm here, somewhere . . . the mitres . . .*

We're nearby, outside. Tell him nothing. Does he still have you? He sounded breathless, but very much in control, and just the sound of that composure stilled her own breathing a little bit.

You're outside here? she asked.

Yes, we're holding a position on the western side of the lake.

Which lake?

Kelsey, you're at Mirror Lake, he told her. *That's where the mitres are located, along the shore, up on the cliffs.*

So many things came instantly clear with the abruptness of a camera shutter's snap: meeting him fourteen years ago, his crash, the anomalies in the geology of the region, the data that he'd placed in her mind. Everything revolved around Mirror Lake—only it *wasn't* the lake. *That's why you came here, why you were at the lake.* She gasped. *Because of the mitres.*

It's everything to our revolution right now.

And so is the data inside of me, she finished.

Yes.

She couldn't read his voice—and she needed to know his meaning. Had it only ever been about the mitres technology? She felt a wave of hysterical anguish bubble up within her, as if, in the space of a moment, all the events of the past week were finally overtaking her. How could she even be sure that he loved her, and that it hadn't been only about protecting this place? Maybe that was all it ever had been about, so long ago.

Of course it wasn't just about the mitres, he whispered fiercely.

I know.

Do you? he insisted, sounding almost angry. *Because you should know it!*

His fury, so pure and intensely focused, had the strange effect of arousing her, even now in the midst of their danger and separation from each other. But she forced all thoughts of his gorgeous Refarian body and their physical needs for each other far from her mind.

Jared, you're in danger. Someone named Veckus—your enemies, they're here. It's not just Marco—

It's all right, love. His voice softened again, growing low. *I know.*

Marco's not working alone. He's talking about this Veckus and . . . and—

Jared cut her off, obviously sensing her fear. *Please, love, I know it's difficult, but try to let me calm you. I can do that, you know, and then I can help you out of here.*

I don't under—

Just let me calm you.

And then, like a faint whisper, something of Jared—of his very spirit and essence—breathed across her soul, assuring her, touching her. It was his voice. Maybe. Or it was his song—she wasn't sure. Whatever shimmered through her in that moment, it belonged to Jared and it filled her with a settled peace.

There, he said. *Open your eyes now.*

She'd braced herself against the chamber wall, pressing her eyes closed while he reached into her core. Now she stood, trembling, her legs weak beneath her, afraid to look around her. But when she dared to open her eyes again, instead of the blackness of the chamber she was met by a golden wavering mist, enveloped by it, really. The entire tunnel filled with a nimbus of light that radiated around her, warming her from without and within, and then there, standing in the very center of the tunnel, was her lifemate. Not physically, of course; he was walking her soul or whatever it was he'd done a while ago. Only the connection with him was manifesting much more strongly this second time around, probably because he was just outside the chamber.

She flung herself into his arms. *I knew you'd come.*

Even though you begged me not to. He laughed gently, folding her against his muscular, strong chest. It was as if no physical separation existed between them, even though she knew that one did. Selfishly, she wanted to forget that fact, wanted nothing but the safety and strength of her lover's arms, and so she clung to him. He was real; this moment was real. She'd be damned if actual reality would wrench him out of her arms yet again.

I'm going to get you out of here, he reminded her, slowly pulling back to stare into her eyes.

She'd already forgotten how warm his dark eyes were, the exotic almond shape of them, the way they flashed with undeniable energy and heat. Alien eyes. Her mate's eyes. *You're beautiful,* she breathed—silently, she thought. Until he whispered back: *So are you.*

You came for me, even though it was the last thing you should've done! she cried, suddenly remembering the truth of their circumstances again.

He glanced around them, running his fingertips along the wall. *This isn't the right tunnel,* he said, ignoring her protests. *It's not the right way to get you out anyway—nor the best way.*

You could've done this for me from your camp, she reminded him.

He turned back to her, blessing her with such a loving gaze that she felt the breath leave her lungs. *You knew I couldn't leave you here,* he said, his voice filled with the same emotion she saw glinting in his dark eyes. *Not with all that you mean to me, and not when I'm the one who put you in this situation.*

Marco wants you dead, Jared, she reminded him seriously. *Please be careful. Please don't put yourself in any more danger than you already have.*

But all he said in reply—as vague as he usually was when answering her questions—was, *I am protected. Don't worry, sweet human.*

But are you in danger?

My whole life I've been in danger. I wouldn't let that keep me from defending my lifemate. He took her by the hand. *I'm here to show you how to open the chamber portal,* he explained, leading her quickly back down through the dark hallway she'd just traversed. *I can't open it for you, not from the outside, but I can show you how to use the codes that are already within your mind.*

She ran with him, holding fast to his hand, not bothering to question whether they were walking physically or if he was simply moving within her thoughts, laying out a plan for her escape through their psychic bond. It took only a few seconds to return to the central chamber—a path that had taken her several long minutes to traverse on her own in the darkness.

In the better lighting, the flickering vision of Jared dimmed. *Close your eyes again if it will help,* he instructed her. Taking her by the shoulders, he pressed her down to a sitting position on the floor. *Here,* he urged, *close your eyes and listen to me. Watch.*

Scott leaned against the boulder beside Jared, using his natural Antousian skills at power manipulation to circle his commander with a ring of protection. Jared's eyes were pressed closed, his hands clasped tightly in his lap, and his head lolled back against the boulder as if he were asleep.

Objectively, Scott understood why Jared had chosen to connect with Kelsey in the middle of their recon, and yet *sub*jectively, he felt panicked and protective. Here they were, deep in the backcountry at three a.m., enemies all about them, and their king had chosen to form a spatial bridge with his lifemate. So Scott watched over the man, all his senses opened wide, and prayed that their commander's plan for opening the mitres would work. A mist rolled slowly over the lake, haunting as a specter in its foggy progression, the full moon slicing through it like a searchlight. Its atmospheric appearance did nothing to ease the creeping apprehension that had settled over Scott's mind.

Thea appeared beside them, crouching low. "They've located a nest of Antousians on the southern end of the lake," she said, rattling off coordinates, and then with a curt nod toward their commander she asked, "How long will *that* take?"

"He's getting her to open the chamber," Scott explained in a terse voice. "Talking her through it."

Thea gave a nod of affirmation. "We have to get those codes out."

"She's his lifemate, Thea," Scott said. "You know that. It's not just the data that's important to him."

"You don't have to remind me," she snapped, rocking back on her heels.

"When this night is done, just remember that things have changed," Scott cautioned, knowing that of everyone in the camp, Thea would have the hardest time supporting Jared's choice of a mate. "And be sure your judgment won't get clouded tonight. If you feel that it's compromised—"

She waved him off. "I'm a soldier, first and foremost."

"Good. That's what I wanted to hear," Scott said with a nod, and turned back to his watch over their king.

Veckus himself had come. A surprise, but not wholly unexpected, given the importance of this particular mission, Marco thought, hiking down the back path away from the mitres' entrance. Jared's soldiers would soon be massing at the foot of the trail, laying down an encampment. But they would be far too late. The Antousians had been granted plenty of advance warning to assume their own positions, and this far into the backcountry of Yellowstone—a good twenty-five miles' hike up any of the trails that led here—no rangers would hear their exchange of weaponry. Or the screams of a dying rebel king. That thought caused Marco to shiver, and for a moment he pressed his eyes shut, lifting a dangling birch branch out of his way on the path.

"About time you arrived," came Veckus's familiar rasping voice from out of the darkness. Even though he couldn't see the Antousian warlord, Marco sensed him hovering at the darkened edge of the trail.

"I've had work to do," Marco responded, lifting his chin into the air. This was no time for attitude from his leader, not tonight. He was delivering a prize jewel, the king of Refaria himself—so he'd be damned if Veckus didn't show him a little more respect.

"You arrived almost an hour ago," the alien hissed, reminding Marco of a reptile in his vocalizations. He always reminded Marco of a reptile: a reptile in human form.

The shadows seemed to part, when in reality Veckus only took two steps forward into the clear shaft of moonlight limning the mountainous trail. The blond man sneered at him in greeting; truthfully, it was a delighted smile on the face of the alien, but somehow, like all the other gestures on his humanized face, it looked *wrong*.

"What took you so long, Marco?" The leader spoke in smooth Refarian; he was fluent in the language, which was common for Antousians who, like Veckus, had been raised on Refaria.

"I've been with the queen."

This elicited a soft hissing sound from Veckus's lips. Even though he was an Antousian-human hybrid (which meant that his physical form was human), his voice patterns still reflected his natural Antousian genetics. Unlike so many other hybrids of his kind, he cleaved to his heritage of origin, despising the need for a human body that had been forced on all the Antousians who survived the viral plague.

"Do not refer to the rebel human as *queen*. Do not show her that honor."

Marco inclined his head respectfully, but inside he wondered why Veckus even bothered. She *was* the queen—just as Jared was king—and whether Veckus honored the title or not hardly mattered when it came to logistics. Still, the warlord preferred to refer to Jared as "the rebel leader" or even, on his less generous days, as "that rebel idiot."

"I believe we were clear on our mutual objectives," Veckus stated carefully, lifting his chin until he stared Marco in the eye. "Our plan is to lure the rebel leader into the open, and thereby end this insurgence once and for all."

Although Marco's heart rate sped up crazily, he forced himself into a posture of steadiness. "Of course. Our mission has not changed."

"Good. I wouldn't want to think that your Refarian . . .

ways"—he spit the word with undisguised distaste—"had somehow obscured your judgment."

"I'll give you Jared Bennett," Marco vowed. *And you'll give me a better future.*

"Yes, so you will keep the rebel whore inside the mitres until Jared is dead," Veckus said, his mouth pulling into an ugly mockery of a grin. "Then you'll bring her to me."

"What are your intentions for Kelsey?"

"Don't worry about that." Veckus's eyes narrowed, and the telltale odor of deception filled Marco's nostrils.

"You promised she wouldn't be hurt," Marco cautioned, his voice rising slightly. "That she would be freed once Jared was dead."

"You will have her in the end," Veckus promised. "Our plan remains in effect." The odor of betrayal grew rancid about them, the vilest possible stench. *This* Veckus didn't know all of Marco's myriad intuitive skills. "So are we still agreed?"

"We are agreed," Marco said, and tried to ignore the sickening spasm that his stomach gave when he turned away from the alien.

Bargaining with a devil, never a good idea, he thought furiously, and began his hike back to Kelsey's side.

Marco entered the chamber and found Kelsey deep in a trance again, her hands clasping the coiling unit in the center of the chamber. One instance of connecting with Jared had been bad enough—two were unacceptable. The core energy inside the coil's tubing had already changed color, altering from its cool luminous blue to a bright golden orange. She was powering up the unit! Preparing to open a portal!

"What," he roared, grabbing her by the upper arm, "are you doing?" She kept her hands locked about the cylinder, and so he jerked her harder, sending her sprawling onto the floor of the chamber. The tubing remained a golden-orange hue, indicating that the dimensional space around them was becoming unstable; a portal could be opened, but without her continued interaction with the unit, the energy inside would cool again eventually.

Satisfied that he'd interrupted her in time, he rounded on her. "I trusted you," he hissed as she stirred on the floor beneath him, shaking her head as if in a daze. "I left you here unbound. And this is how you repay me? What did you think to accomplish?"

"I was trying to escape, you imbecile."

He folded his arms across his chest. "I see that my trust was misplaced."

"Don't you dare talk to me about trust," she spit, slowly turning to gaze up at him. "You have violated every one of your vows. You're a stranger to me, and you betrayed us."

There it was again: that gut-wrenching reminder of his betrayal and the beautiful, perfect relationship he had long ago shattered to bits. "I'm sorry," he mumbled before he caught himself.

"Sorry?" She struggled to her knees and speared him with a cold gaze. "You kidnapped me and threatened to hurt us," she countered. "That is not a relationship based on trust. We don't trust you—I could never trust someone like you! You protected us once, and now look at what you've become. You're trying to destroy your own king."

"J'Areshkadau Bnet D'Aravni," he hissed, pronouncing the leader's true Refarian name with slow and acid precision, "is not my king. He has not been my sovereign for more than four years."

"Do they fire protectors?" She sneered. "They what, just rescind your vow? Tell me, Marco, exactly what the Refarians do with the likes of you."

He brushed past her, refusing to succumb to memories and feelings of love that had never died for him, not in all these years. Those eyes. So blue he could spend forever in them, worship her by the simple act of gazing into the most unusual eyes he had ever seen. Not now; it was too late for these feelings, such wrong, tortured emotions that had led him to such a wrong and dreadful end.

"Exactly as I thought," she said with deadly intensity. "There's no place for you in any dimension. You're a traitor."

"Stop it!" he roared, spinning to face her. He wanted to cover his ears and silence her accusations. He wanted to proclaim his love for her, even after all these years. "Just stop it."

She kept at him, though, accusing, needling, torturing, but somehow he used his power to block the words. Or maybe it was just that the truth of her words was so unbearable he couldn't even process them.

He grasped her by the arm angrily, yanking her to her feet. "You're coming outside with me," he snarled with a glance back at the coiling unit. "The easy way. We'll let the unit cool again." The power still raged orange, indicating the possibility of a time portal opening. He'd deal with that later.

Retrieving the remote unit from his jacket pocket, he depressed a button and the gateway to the chamber's exterior opened. He glimpsed the darkened outside world open before them: the lake below, the rocks, the shards of moonlight reflecting in the creeping mist. Behind him he heard Kelsey gasp aloud at the wonder of the bridge he'd woven, but he had no time to tell her of the true laws of the universe.

Chapter Seventeen

Kelsey sat shivering on the smooth rocks outside the mitres, tucked neatly into a cleft of the cliff face where none of Jared's soldiers could possibly see her. She considered leaping to her feet and waving her arms wildly, since Marco would have to kill her if she did that. And she knew Marco didn't want to kill her. In fact, she suspected he just might be having serious doubts about this entire kidnapping plot of his. He squatted beside her, studying the winding path below them through some kind of night-vision binoculars. She'd never seen anything remotely like them before—tiny and compact, they apparently enabled him to see long distances.

They enabled him to track the assent of Jared and his team, and she wanted to snatch them right out of his hands and send them careening over the cliff ledge. Still, as she studied Marco in silence, she couldn't shake the strangest, most inexplicable sensation: that as much as Marco frightened her, and as much as she'd just argued to the contrary, she might actually be able to trust him. She even felt the slightest bit of kinship with the man, sitting beside him in the dark.

She shifted position on the rocks. "Where is everyone else you said would be waiting for us out here?"

"Around," he answered coolly.

"So, Jared is going to get here and then you're just going to"—she stared at the strange metallic weapon holstered at his side—"*what?*"

He remained silent, his eyes hidden behind the glasses. She rubbed her arms, trying to warm herself. She wore only jeans and a sweater; their hasty departure hadn't allowed her to find her jacket.

Marco rocked back on his heels, dropping the glasses away from his eyes. Apart from when he'd taken her through the slipstream, this was the closest she'd been to him physically. She wished it weren't the dead of night—how late was it anyway? Two a.m.? Three? She had no idea. And she wished the moonlight weren't blocked by the scraggly tree branches overhead. Knobby pines sprouted out from cracks in the rock face, growing tall despite the unforgiving terrain. Kelsey leaned forward, wanting to see Marco's eyes. For some reason, she felt it was important that she get a genuine look at him. A close look, the soul-staring kind.

He seemed to know what she was doing, and dropped his gaze to his hands. "We will stay here for now," was all he said, his voice stern.

She decided to try a new tack. "What's going to happen to *me*? I get that you're out to destroy Jared, that you have some master plan and all that. But what about me, huh? Where do I figure in?"

He glanced sideways at her, his eyes hooded and dark. He opened his mouth to speak, then closed it again, looking away from her across to Mirror Lake shimmering in the moonlight below them. It was hard to believe that on the very far side of that large body of water was where she'd first seen Jared's light. It had been little more than a week since she'd met him there and felt the pure magnificence of all that he truly was. She would die before she let Marco or any of his gathered conspirators hurt Jared.

She sat up taller on the rocks. "You're just going to ignore my questions, huh?"

"Kelsey." He sighed heavily, his eyes trained on the path below. "I can't answer these things. You know that."

Maybe if she could distract him then that would buy some time. "How about other, less complicated questions?"

"Like what?"

"Like, are you planning to use the mitres? Is that why we're *really* here?"

"No, apparently"—he rose to his feet, peering through the night vision glasses and around the large wall of rock— "I should leave that maneuver in your capable hands."

"I wasn't trying to use the weapon." When he made no further reply, she attempted another angle with the man. "Tell me more about what you were saying, about my being—what did you call it? The beloved of Refaria?"

Nothing but stony silence, his face an inscrutable mask of indifference.

If she could only find a way to distract him, or to somehow appeal to Marco's ingrained sense of loyalty. "So, you won't answer that either," she said.

Resting one forearm on an outcropping of rock, he bowed his head and remained quiet for a long moment. At last he turned his head sideways and met her gaze in the darkness. His black eyes, so empty and lifeless before, nearly blazed with energy. "In our future you were worshiped, Kelsey. By the Refarians, because they yearned for a queen, and by Jared because . . ." His voice trailed off, and he just shook his head, saying nothing for what felt an eternity, until he finished with, "We all worshiped you, Kelsey." His voice had become hoarse. Choked. Full of emotion. But then he looked away, shuttering his features and setting his jaw.

How ironic to think she was learning these things now, at a time when her only thought was for Jared's very life. *Jared's life.*

Her heart thundered within her chest, and it was hard to suppress her mounting sense of panic. Her palms were sweating, and she could hear the sound of blood rushing in her ears. *What am I supposed to do?* They all needed her to do something—and now. She took deep breaths, trying to get her equilibrium back in check, and in response an excruciating pain hammered in her head. It had begun when she'd traveled through the slipstream, and been there vaguely ever since, intensifying when Marco had invaded her thoughts earlier in the mitres.

What a weird sensation that had been: painful, like something being sucked right out of her. In its wake, a dull throbbing had intensified to what was now a blinding headache. She rubbed her eyes, trying to still the pain.

Then she had the oddest memory. And she *knew* it was a memory, something that had actually happened, not a fleeting impression.

"What if he doesn't come back, Marco? What if this is it?"

His voice, strong and reassuring. "He'll be here, Kelsey."

They were sitting on a rocky outcropping. Not here, somewhere else. Nighttime . . . and he was surveying the landscape with the same binoculars.

"I can't feel him. Not at all," she cried quietly.

He looked at her and pressed his hand over hers. "He'll be here. He will always come back for you, Kelsey."

"I *can* trust you," she announced quietly.

Marco dropped the glasses, staring at her dumbfounded for a full five seconds.

"Please tell me I'm not wrong," she implored.

"I am your enemy," Marco insisted, straightening himself where he sat. "Make no mistake about that fact."

"No." She shook her head with conviction. "I don't believe you."

His voice rose. "You *need* to believe it, Kelsey."

"You might, but I don't, not anymore. It goes against everything that you are."

"You have no idea what kind of man I am." He laughed wryly. "What I'm capable of." She realized those words were familiar, though it took her a moment to place them. And then it hit her—Jared! He had used almost those identical words to describe himself earlier that evening.

"I know that there was a time you would have done anything for us," she said softly.

"Once." His voice seemed sad, lost.

"Whatever Jared did . . . to make you turn from him—" His angry glare cut off her plea, his eyes flashing with fire, and then he stood suddenly. He grabbed her arm, jerking her roughly to her feet. At that exact moment, Kelsey heard a rustling behind them. Marco glanced quickly in that direction, shoving her ahead of him.

"I want you back here. Now." He dragged her toward the concealed mitres entry, and this time he did bind both her hands and her feet so there would be no hope of escaping.

Marco stood with Veckus at the highest point of the trail, obscured from the Refarian soldiers advancing below them. They'd ascended a hidden back path, hoping to go unnoticed, but he'd been observing them from the very beginning.

"They're almost here," Marco stated calmly, studying Veckus's features. Unbelievable—here it was ten years earlier, and Veckus looked exactly the same as he did in the future. He stood with two other men—Antousians, no doubt—whom Marco had never seen before. All three observed the path below.

"Well, well, Jared will be very surprised to see how the tables have turned." Veckus sneered. "The mitres and the fallen king, all in one day. Not bad work."

Marco bowed his head slightly in acknowledgment. "I am only following your future orders."

"You follow well," he said, his eyes narrowing in appreciation. Veckus would be considered quite handsome by many people on Earth, but when Marco gazed at the tall blond, he only saw ugliness and hatred.

Veckus reached for Marco's field glasses, and over his comm system he ordered another unit of troops to make the ascent. "They will be here very soon, yes," Veckus said, lowering the glasses. He turned to Marco. "And where is Jared's *human* now?"

"Inside the mitres," he lied.

"Bring her out."

Marco hesitated. "She's not to be harmed." He met Veckus's gaze pointedly. "You do remember that?"

Veckus shrugged indifferently. "Well, Raedus's directive has changed slightly. We're to get rid of them all."

Marco stared at the warlord in disbelief. To the Antousians, their sworn word meant nothing and was ever shifting to suit their current needs.

Veckus's hand twitched against the pulse gun holstered at his hip. "Yes, we'll just have a nice little group execution and be on our way," he said with a smile.

They would not hurt Kelsey. Marco would not allow it.

"Kelsey was never to be harmed." He gave the Antousian a forceful shove in the chest. "That was our arrangement from the beginning."

Veckus brushed off his jacket with a scowl of distaste. "Well, I'm a bit troubled by the idea of one dethroned and exiled queen left as a rallying point. I want this rebellion quashed once and for all."

Marco thought a quick moment, as priorities shifted and realigned in a nearly forgotten way. "You should wait behind the rocks," Marco told the hybrid calmly. "We must protect you at all costs, my lord."

Veckus nodded in agreement. "Of course. Best to maintain the illusion that it's only you."

Marco chose not to correct the hybrid's false assumption that Jared thought he acted alone. Nor did he see fit to inform him that the king and queen had formed not one, but two spatial bridges within the past hour.

Veckus and his flanking soldiers took a position behind the rocks where they'd hidden before.

And Marco knew exactly what he would have to do, because even after all his long history with Jared and Kelsey, he had come to understand something crucial about himself this night.

He realized that he had never fully turned away from his queen.

"Come with me, Kelsey. Now." Marco knelt beside where she huddled on the rocks, quickly loosening the ropes that he had tied her with.

"What's happening?"

As the bindings fell away he pulled her close to him— so close that she could feel his hot breath fan against her cheek. "Go to Jared," he whispered in an urgent voice. "There's an unused trail off to the eastern ledge, and if you take it, that portion is unprotected. All their attention is trained on Jared's advancing units on the south trail."

She stared at him in silent shock, and he squeezed her upper arm tightly. "*Now,* Kelsey," he said, his voice husky. "Before I change my mind."

She nodded, moving to the ledge, but he pulled her back by the hand. "I can't protect you here, Kelsey," he reminded her in a low voice. "You know that. But Jared can. Get him and get out of here."

Chapter Eighteen

Kelsey scrambled down the dark hillside as quietly as she could, hoping to reach Jared before his enemies did. She became more and more frantic as she made her way down the trail, wondering how she'd ever locate him or even any of his soldiers in the midst of such darkness. As she slid down the path, her foot caught on a hidden piece of brush that sent her sprawling forward roughly onto her hands. A sharp pain immediately shot through her wrist, and she was pretty sure she heard the snap of a broken bone. But there was no time to think about that now.

Get to Jared. She trained her thoughts, forcing herself back to her feet. She glanced quickly over her shoulder, searching for any sign that she was being followed.

Focus, Kelsey. Keep yourself together. Finding Jared is the only thing that matters. As she stumbled down the path it seemed as if she were floundering in an ocean of darkness, groping for some unseen shore. If only she had a light of some kind, anything at all to guide her.

Then she remembered one singular advantage that she had over their unseen enemies.

"You've no business here at all, Jared," Scott insisted with an uncomfortable glance up the dark trail. "Or have you already forgotten the details of your capture a few years ago?"

"You know I'll never forget." Jared kept his voice emotionless with an effort.

"I'm the one to lead the team in, Jared, not you."

"Is that your opinion or your sense?" Jared never liked

being taken out of the action—and now, with Kelsey's life in the balance, he liked it even less than usual.

"Both," Scott said.

Jared studied the steep cliffs, the rocks above them on the trail silvered by moonlight. They had no idea what waited for them at the top of the winding path. "She needs me," Jared whispered.

Scott clasped his shoulder with an intensity of affection that Jared rarely saw in his friend and lieutenant. "She needs you alive, J," he said, giving Jared's bulletproof vest an adjusting tug. "You *know* you've got no business on this mission. Period. I should have made you stay behind at the compound to begin with." Scott never minced words when it came to leadership, one reason Jared knew he could trust him with his own life and, more important, with Kelsey's.

Jared's hand hovered against his comm button as he contemplated his next set of commands. Every soldier waited, at the ready. He trusted Scott's instincts, especially at a moment when his own skills felt so impaired by emotion, but his fear and worry for his lifemate were immense, and his need to fight for her was nearly overpowering. That made it impossible to stay away when he understood the intentions of the enemies she faced up on that trail.

Still, as leader he also knew his own safety had to take priority. "Anika and I will return to our position by the lake," he finally agreed. "If anything happens, you signal for us immediately. Do you understand, Lieutenant?"

Scott nodded his agreement. "Be careful, Commander."

Jared glimpsed the flicker of worry in his friend's dark eyes. "You're the one who needs to be careful," he reminded the Antousian softly. "I'm entrusting my queen into your hands."

Marco studied Kelsey's descent through his binoculars and wished for at least the tenth time that he'd simply gone with her. What purpose could he possibly serve by remaining? Although he knew the answer to that question: He had to end what he'd started by leading Veckus to the mitres in the first place.

He rocked back on his heels and continued watching Kelsey's halting progress through the green haze of the night-vision glasses. Humans registered with a midlevel en-

ergy reflection, whereas the Antousians' thermal register
was always brighter, and the Refarians' the brightest of all.
Then of course there were Jared and Kelsey, another story
altogether. Kelsey's register had always been completely
singular, falling somewhere between the human and alien
ones as a result of her change, her energy much stronger
than a human's, yet not as brilliant as that of the others.
And Jared's reading was the strongest and brightest of any
he'd ever seen, even Thea's. It had always been a great
source of annoyance to Veckus that even with all his power,
he had never once registered anywhere near as strongly as
Jared on an average day.

But that wasn't the most fascinating thing. What Marco
was watching unfold now was an image he'd witnessed
through these binoculars hundreds—perhaps thousands—of
times before, and it never failed to awe him. He was observing the way Jared's and Kelsey's thermal energies altered when they came into contact with each other.
Whenever they were within proximity, their body chemis-
tries and heat indexes literally changed in composition, assuming entirely different levels than each held on their
own.

Over the years, he'd trained his eye to instantly recognize
their own peculiar heat impressions so that he could track
them, but he'd also quickly learned to follow their secondary register—the unique one they created together. Quite
simply, when Jared and Kelsey were near each other they
blended, their energy becoming one. He wondered if
Kelsey could feel how close she was getting to Jared, because he could certainly see it in the way her thermal energy was beginning to escalate, as was Jared's where he
was crouching just behind a nearby rock. Marco couldn't
see him completely, could only catch a glimmer of his thermal register, which was intensifying by the moment as
Kelsey approached him.

Marco's reflections were cut short when he saw another
familiar radiation, that of an Antousian hybrid who was
now flanked by two Refarians. That team was moving up
the eastern trail, the same one he'd sent Kelsey down. He'd
been so busy tracking her that he'd nearly missed their
approach. It had to be Scott Dillon accompanied by two
other soldiers. What the hell did Scott think he was doing?

He'd always liked Scott a great deal and had no old scores to settle with the man. Marco looked around quickly, trying to choose a course of action.

But when he gazed back through the binoculars again, he saw something much more disturbing on the path below: three Antousian hybrids off to the side, also tracking Kelsey's movements. His pulse raced as old instincts came sharply into focus. They were in terrible danger—all of them—and he had to do something.

Jared crouched in their hidden position, waiting beside Anika. Ahead of them in the darkness they heard a sudden noise, and a ripple of silent tension spread throughout the unit. Each of them raised their weapons, all senses on alert and ready to move.

The sound came again, almost directly upon them now. Perhaps it was an animal? Jared spread his palm on the cool rock where he crouched, steadying himself—and felt his chest begin to burn. It was only then that he focused on a background sensation that had been subtly building within him over the past few moments. His energy had begun to escalate. He hadn't even keyed into it—he often felt this way in the midst of a battle. It was a natural part of his D'Aravnian nature, and his other self often came to the fore when he was in danger. He'd been so caught up in the moment that he hadn't grasped the true source of the fire building within him: his mate.

He felt a golden thread begin to weave between the two of them, joining them. The connection became a living stream of impressions and sensations, a gossamer trail of fire leading her straight to him. She was almost on top of him; she was that near.

Not physically. It was her energy, teasing at him, urging him to open their mating bond. His hands burned with the power of it, the heat radiating into his forearms instantly. *Love, where are you?*

Oh, thank God. Listen, Marco let me go. The connection solidified between them, causing his body to tighten with awareness of her. He trembled in reaction, and leaned against the rock to steady himself.

Set you free?

He seems to have had . . . a change of heart. But I'm

*trying to find you in the dark. I've made it down this trail—
he showed me one the Antousians weren't guarding.*

She knew about the Antousians now. She knew all about
his enemies, he realized with a sickening spasm of his stomach. *Try to tell me where you are,* he urged. *You're near
me; I sense it.*

Me too.

His wrist began to throb with a dull, painful ache. *You're
hurt!* he cried across their bond. *If that bastard so much
as—*

It's nothing; don't worry. I fell.

Again the sound from just beyond their position. Anika
crouched, cocking her gun, but Jared caught her shoulder,
shaking his head. *It's Kelsey,* he mouthed.

I'm going to call like an owl, he told her. *Follow that
sound.* Cupping his hand to his mouth, he released the
bird's cry.

I heard that! You're nearby, really near.

Cupping his mouth again, he prepared to cry out, when
searing, bone-shattering pain exploded through his arm. He
processed the accompanying sound of gunfire a moment
later—as if he were a distant observer of the event. In the
background of his mind he heard Kelsey crying out to him,
communicating, but he couldn't focus enough to answer her
because of the mind-numbing pain that radiated through
his arm and shoulder and on into his chest like a shock
wave.

Anika leaped to her feet, followed by others. He tried
to do the same, but his legs buckled weakly beneath him.
Only then did he realize he'd taken a shot not just to his
shoulder, but to his upper thigh as well.

Kelsey, I-I am . . . injured.

*Oh, God, Jared. Be careful, be careful. I'm coming. Be
careful!*

Stay! he rasped.

"Sniper!" Anika cried as he collapsed to his knees. "Protect our commander." Orders spun about them, and he
tried to work his mouth, tried to see anything other than
the blinding red haze of his pain. His people took hold of
him, forming a ring about him with their own bodies. Clawing at the frozen ground, he gasped for breath, unable to

find it. The sniper had aimed well, hitting only places where his body armor left small vulnerabilities.

Kelsey. She was out there, in danger, and now he couldn't protect her. That was his last thought before he collapsed face-first in the snow.

All she could feel was the pain. Blinding her, crippling her, shattering them both into millions of pieces. Jared's, her own; it was all joining in some horrible, swirling dance between the two of them. She'd understood the precise moment he was shot because she'd felt every one of his wounds as if they were in her own body. Every one of his injuries was an assault on her because of their open connection at the moment of impact. And now Kelsey would be damned if she would let him go, not like this.

Clutching at her chest, she tried to cry out to him. *Jared, wh-what . . . ?*

No answer.

She couldn't move, couldn't think; she couldn't even cry out to him again. All she could do was lie on her back, dark forest overhead, and experience Jared's tormenting pain. Far worse than the physical sensations was her awareness of just how much he was suffering; one of the guns they'd shot him with wasn't any ordinary weapon. It couldn't have been, not with the massive electric shock it radiated through her entire body—and she knew she'd absorbed only a fraction of what Jared had experienced. Something close to an explosion had seemed to blast within her chest. Whatever they'd done to him, every sensation he was feeling ricocheted through their bond. She'd heard him cry out her name. Heard it in her heart, her mind. And then he'd just blacked out, leaving her alone in the midst of their connection. Alone without him!

But with the passing moments the pain hadn't waned— it had intensified. She knew she should break the connection, but she couldn't leave him, not like this. Not when he needed her so much. And so she'd allowed the bond between their two souls to remain open. She felt the dazed stir of his waking consciousness amidst the agony as the connection became more vibrant again. Then something significant altered, something within Jared. *What's happen-*

ing? she wondered in utter panic, and yet she couldn't seem to look up; the pain was that immobilizing. Or maybe it wasn't just the pain that had incapacitated her. Maybe it was something more. It almost felt like a deadly shock was spreading throughout her entire body, her extremities. Then she heard his voice, terribly weak and distant.

Kelsey, you have to break this. He gasped.

I can't. . . . Everything felt hazy and unclear, and the pain had enveloped her entire body.

Kelsey! Listen to me. Jared's voice, just beyond a circle of light. He was trying to shove her out.

No. I will not leave you, Jared. I will not. . . .

Break it now, *Kelsey,* he commanded forcefully.

Why? She sobbed, afraid for his life.

Because I can't. They've done something to me and I can't, Kelsey, and . . . *I won't let you suffer.*

And I won't break the bond while you're injured. I will not leave you!

Kelsey, he pleaded. *If you love me* . . . *let go* . . . *please, love. Just let me go.*

And not because she was willing to leave him did she do it, nor because he asked. Not even out of fear or physical pain did she relinquish the hold the bond had over her. But because she *did* love him, she allowed their connection to slip away.

Marco heard the spattering of gunfire and pulse weaponry coming from the direction of the lake. He flung himself down the trail, stumbling and catching his hands on loose rocks and dirt. With his intuitive skills he sensed Kelsey nearby and in pain. He'd lost sight of her through the night-vision goggles after spotting the Antousians positioned near her. It was imperative that he get to her before she was captured.

Then, slightly ahead on the darkened trail, he saw something, a crumpled form. It was worse than any of his imaginings in the past moments; his queen lay on her side, unconscious and curled into a tight ball. He immediately dropped to the ground beside her. "Kelsey," he implored, lifting a hand to her cheek, "tell me where you're injured."

No answer. She was unconscious, but as he skimmed his hands over her body he couldn't seem to find any injuries apart from her wrist, which appeared swollen. Radiating off her body, however, was the pulsing aura of immense pain.

He tried calling to her again, brushing a thick auburn lock back from her face. Her features were twisted in a mask of pain. His queen in such torture; it nearly sucked the life out of his body.

Scooping her into his arms, he knew she had only one hope: He had to get her to Jared and the others, *now*. She stirred slightly in his arms, moaning. "My queen, I will get you to him," he vowed, and took off running down the trail.

Chapter Nineteen

Marco carried Kelsey in his arms toward Jared's position and almost had her there when a massive exchange of gunfire and pulse weaponry exploded all around them. Dropping to his knees, he laid her on the ground and engaged his own energy to protect her. It was one of his skills as a protector, manipulating his personal reserve of power to form shielding perimeters. He couldn't do it for long stretches of time, but in life-and-death moments like this one, it had more than once saved his sovereigns' lives.

Kelsey stirred beside where he knelt, his hand extended and his power emanating in concentric waves from his hand. Kelsey bolted upright, crying out at the chaotic gunfire from the battle that raged about them, alarmed and then instantly alert to her surroundings. She quickly grasped Jared's predicament: He was under attack by the Antousians, and his soldiers wouldn't be able to keep the advancing enemy at bay much longer.

Veckus arrived, moving in on Jared. The other Antousians had the Refarian unit surrounded, ordering them to drop their guns. Marco watched in horror as Jared was wrenched from his own people and shoved gracelessly to the ground at Veckus's feet. Jared doubled over face-first, one hand clasping at the gunshot wound in his upper thigh, the other scrabbling for purchase in the snowy ground to keep him from collapsing completely. The snow beneath him instantly began to darken with his blood; Marco could see the pooling stain grow by the moonlight.

"Marco, you've got to let that . . . shield down so we can

get to him!" Kelsey begged. "You can protect him if you let me go."

"Your safety is paramount," Marco bit off without ever looking in her direction.

"No, *his* safety is paramount—he's the king," she argued, giving Marco's arm a forceful tug. "Jared still has a chance if we can get to him soon!"

Marco's protective boundary surrounding them never wavered, but his hands trembled visibly, and although Kelsey knew little about the Refarians, it was obvious that both the perimeter and his physical strength were depleting before her eyes.

Beyond the boundary, Veckus continued to taunt Jared cruelly, circling where he knelt in the snow. "So, the king bows down before me now," he said with a sneer. "Oh, Raedus will love that detail. I'll share it with pleasure."

Who was Raedus? Kelsey didn't even know the full host of Jared's enemies, and staring at his fallen, brutally wounded body, she ached to know everyone who had ever wished him harm. She'd take up a gun and go after them all herself.

Jared struggled with every breath he took, his chest rising and falling with erratic gasps. "We've been in this situation before, as I recall," Veckus hissed at him, giving him a hard shove that sent Jared tumbling sideways. His hands splayed against the cold ground, and he barely managed to catch himself, panting and gasping for air.

"We've been in this moment before"—Veckus paused, giving Jared a hard poke in the ribs with the butt of his rifle—"but no matter what we do, you just keep *repeating* yourself." Veckus laughed at his own joke until Jared raised his head weakly and met his enemy's eyes.

"You're going to lose," Jared rasped. The snow beneath him was soaked with his blood, and Kelsey knew that if they didn't get to him soon his life would be over. How was he even holding his form at all after losing so much blood? And if he *did* shift, would he be able to escape? Or maybe he *couldn't* shift because of his injuries. She frantically wished she knew more about him, anything at all that might help save his life. Thinking of their first meeting, she recalled that his injuries then had necessitated his Change— what about now?

"You will . . . not have . . . me." He gasped. Kelsey closed her eyes when she heard the agony that edged his weakly spoken words.

"Oh, I believe that I do, in fact, have you already, J'Areshkadau. Or should I call you *my lord?*" Veckus sneered. "That seems appropriately ironic, in view of how this little drama is ending, you bowing on your knees before me." Veckus glanced at Kelsey pointedly, across the barrier. "And of what will happen to your queen *this* time?"

"Wh-what?" Jared managed to stammer, trying to raise his head to see her. "What . . . Kelsey?"

Why hadn't she told Jared everything she'd learned about their future selves when she'd had the chance? Obviously Marco had told this Veckus all about their future, about what he'd done to her in the mitres chamber in order to travel back through the time portal.

Veckus stared at Jared in genuine surprise. "You don't think it will turn out differently for her this time, do you?" he asked. "Just because that crazy Refarian is trying to protect her? I'm stronger than all of you. The Madjin Protectors are long dead anyway."

Kelsey could feel Marco seething next to her, his energy building. He glared at Veckus, black eyes narrowing. "You know it's a damn lie," Marco shouted, his throaty voice taut with rage. "You've always known Jared holds the true power. It's why you're so afraid of him."

"But he's barely learned to use it yet," Veckus corrected, raising a finger. "And that's where I can thank you for bringing them both to me at just this point in time."

With that, Veckus turned to Jared, urging him to change in a low voice. But not so low that Kelsey couldn't hear what he said as the man spun upon him, putting a strange alien weapon to his temple. "Go on and *change,* you fool."

And for the first time Jared cried out, collapsing on the ground with a groan. Still, he refused to transform. "Why won't he change?" she asked Marco in a panic, but he shook his head. "He won't let Veckus take him captive in his Change."

"*Can* Veckus do that? Take him prisoner in that state?"

Marco's outstretched hands trembled. "Yes, but Jared would die before he let him do it. To be controlled in his Change . . . it would be the death of him. If he were uninjured, his D'Aravnian self would be formidable. A terrible weapon against Veckus. But if he were captured like this, the torture would be unthinkable."

Kelsey grabbed Marco's arm again, determined to get through to him. "You have to go to him," she begged. "Now, Marco."

"So I can leave you unprotected? So Veckus can kill you, too? That's what he wants, you know." He paused and looked at her, his dark eyes flashing with emotion. "You heard it yourself."

"He wants Jared."

"No, he wants the king *and* the queen," Marco stated firmly.

"I know you hate Jared," she began quietly, standing as tall as she could. "That much is obvious. But I also know that there was a time when we could trust you. That *I* could trust you. I'm begging you. He's dying out there."

Marco closed his eyes for a moment, and Kelsey couldn't read his expression. Finally he glanced at her, his dark eyes full of . . . compassion? She couldn't be sure.

"Kelsey, I'm doing what he wants me to do," he said. "You love him. You know it's true."

A sob caught in her throat. She did know it was true. Jared wanted her safe, not falling beside him. She felt hot tears begin to stream down her cheeks. "There's got to be some way," she whispered in a defeated voice, the sobs coming more quickly now. "Why can't you do what *I* want you to do?"

Marco bowed his head solemnly, hesitating for a brief moment. Finally he spoke. "Because long ago I promised him that I would protect you at all costs," he replied softly. "Above his own life, if need be. I forgot that pledge for many years." He glanced at Kelsey sadly. "But tonight I intend to honor it."

Kelsey turned from Marco slowly, and her gaze fell upon Jared. He lay slumped forward on the ground as Veckus continued his assault with the alien weapon. Slowly he raised his head, and for the briefest of moments their eyes met. Across the barrier, through the night, something flickered between them. Not their connection, not precisely. Something more. Some sort of understanding, a unity of minds.

He seemed to say something to her, only his lips didn't move. Even without their connection, she heard his words. They echoed outside of the moment, through lifetimes. So simple, so pure, they rang within her the very moment he thought them.

I love you.

At that precise moment, from the surrounding darkness a full battlement of Refarian troops appeared, weapons flashing and firing. Kelsey thought she recognized Thea very briefly in the fray, her rifle releasing a loud burst of ammunition, and then she glimpsed other Refarians; the action was unfolding so fast in the darkness, she could hardly make out anything. But she could hope. Dear God, she could hope they reached her mate in time to save his life.

Scott came up from the rear, firing with all his might. He'd be damned if he would let Jared die this night, and he'd sure as hell be damned before they'd take his king prisoner again. Not after what they did to him last time. He waved another unit of soldiers forward from where they crouched in the wooded clearing. "Now, now, *now*," he ordered, trying hard just to breathe. As a group they pulled up alongside a giant boulder, one that gave momentary protection. Ahead of him Thea had led in the first wave; now he would lead in the others.

"Go, go," he urged, and in they went. He had his night-vision goggles on and could see Jared slumped in the snow. God, he'd lost too much blood. It was a dark circle about him. He had to get to his commander. *Short, staccato breaths, farther in, closer.*

On the far side of the clearing Kelsey was being held by a man with a Refarian energy register. It had to be the one called Marco, and he was keeping her in . . . what? A protective perimeter of some kind. *No time, no time,* he thought, trying to remember to breathe as he sprinted to the end of the path, leaping over a fallen log that blocked his way. Soldiers were firing everywhere; some of his men were down. Another desperate glance. Jared just lay there in the snow. Unprotected, no one holding him. Did any of their enemies even have him anymore?

But then a pulse rifle, aimed at Jared—someone Scott

hadn't seen, obscured behind brush. Bearing down on his friend. Scott leaped without thinking, fired without rationalizing, and the assailant went down.

Marco stared in disbelief. From where he stood it appeared that Veckus Densalt had just been taken out by Scott Dillon. His heart clenched inside his chest, as he watched the Antousian crumple to the ground. Everything had happened so quickly; was the warlord only wounded? Or dead? Marco blinked, watching the action unfold, hardly believing that one of Jared Bennett's greatest enemies might lie dead practically at his feet.

But there wasn't time to contemplate the repercussions, not just yet. With Veckus down, Marco knew he had just one chance to reach Jared before the surrounding troops took him out. He turned quickly to Kelsey. "On my mark, I'm dropping this shield," he called out. "I'll go to Jared, but we have only a moment. You will stay behind me. It's the only way I can protect you both." Kelsey gasped softly and nodded. "Three, two, one," Marco counted off, then dropped his hand, and the purple barrier dissolved. He felt the energy surge as it reentered his body.

The two of them moved in fluid motion to Jared's side, and he threw his hand up again, circling both Jared and Kelsey. When he did so, he felt a slight sense of panic. His energy was seriously depleted, and he was getting too weak to keep this up much longer. Then what would he do—and how would he protect them?

Just beyond the purplish glow, Veckus staggered from the gunshot, but quickly rose again. His eyes flashed angrily as he turned to the man who'd fired the gun on him—Scott Dillon. Marco felt a surge of excited adrenaline, because Scott was a consummate warrior. He wondered if Hope Harper might be here somewhere too, though perhaps she wasn't part of their team yet. Scott and Hope had been a formidable fighting force, until she died. Her death, of all the ones Jared's forces had suffered, had always seemed the cruelest and most unfair. Maybe Hope was bringing up the rear.

Marco turned back to pinpoint Veckus's position, and found the Antousian aiming at Scott, preparing to fire. Marco flinched, knowing what was about to come, but

Scott's eyes brightened to laser points, momentarily blinding the warlord. Although barely more than a heartbeat, it was long enough to give Scott the advantage; he fired on Veckus again and again, until the alien slumped to the ground.

That was the first moment Marco could actually glance down at Jared; the gun battle had unfolded so quickly, he'd never had a chance before now. What he saw caused his breath to catch in his throat. Jared was soaked in blood, the snow beneath him stained with it. His eyes were closed, his breathing shallow. Was he going to remain alive? Marco couldn't tell, but a sick feeling began to grow within him.

Kelsey clung to him, burying her face against his chest, sobbing. "Hold on," she murmured over and over, refusing to let go of him.

If Marco could only figure out some way to fix this nightmare he'd created for all of them. And as he stared down at Kelsey's sobbing form, a plan began to form in his mind, a way he might be able to save all their lives.

Jared lay dying beneath her in the snow, but Kelsey no longer cared if she perished with him. With a hopeless cry of anguish, she buried her face against his still-warm chest, listening for his faint heartbeat. She heard it, the dull, uneven thudding of it beneath her ear, and the weak sound terrified her. His naturally dark face seemed pale in the moonlight, and she wasn't sure if it was because of his injuries or just a trick of the light. Lifting a weak, shaking hand, he barely managed to touch her hair, his dark eyes meeting hers. He didn't possess the strength to speak; that much she grasped. There were no words anyway, nothing to say; both instinctively understood his fate. He'd lost more blood than seemed possible and still lived; Kelsey felt it sticky beneath her fingertips, in her hair from where she'd leaned against him, soaking her sweater.

The moment seemed a cruel mirror image of the night of his crash, almost at this very spot. He couldn't possibly hold his physical form much longer; it was only a matter of moments until he shifted to his true state.

"Don't try to hold on," she choked, tears streaming down her face. "Just let go if you need to. Okay?" She released a sob and buried her face against his chest again.

"Just let go, sweetheart. I'm here. I'll hold you until the end."

She willed him to live, to stay with her, no matter what his form, even as she willed his passage to freedom. Away from Veckus and the enemies who hunted him—who, apparently, had always hunted this beautiful man she loved.

Behind her she felt hands pulling at her, urging her apart from Jared, but she would not relinquish her hold on her mate. Nothing would separate her from him, not even death. They were bound in every imaginable way; she'd be damned if eternity would step between them now.

With a gasping cry, he reached for her face again, stroking the outline of her lips. "Love," he whispered in a rasping voice. "Sweet love."

She nodded, showering his face with kisses, tasting the metallic warmth of his blood. "I'm right here, Jareshk," she promised him through her tears. "Don't worry; I'm here." In the distance she heard the receding sound of gunfire as the battle moved farther away from where they were. Closer around them it had grown still and quiet. She had the sense that people were gathered about them, watching and keeping their respectful distance.

"Let go of me, Kelsey," he urged, closing his eyes for a moment.

"Never."

"M-my energy," he tried to explain, but then swallowed and gasped for breath.

She covered his mouth briefly with hers, a kiss that she hoped conveyed all the love, all the regret, all the pain she felt at losing him. "You won't hurt me," she promised him, sobbing those same words she'd spoken at their very first meeting. "You could never hurt me."

His eyes flew open, locking with hers; then she felt what would happen before it actually did, the subtle shift in his alien form. Heat and power and roiling steam passed over his body and into hers.

And they became one.

Marco grabbed Kelsey firmly by the shoulder, while with his other hand he continued to maintain the shield. He had to get her out of here or she was going to die next. Jared had lost form, yielding to his natural, energized state, and she wouldn't be pried apart from him. She would be ash in moments if they couldn't separate her from him. And Jared would be dead; he would die anyway, but did he have to take Kelsey with him? Marco knew exactly where to go if he still hoped to save Jared and the others, but he didn't want to leave Kelsey behind to perish in the process. Yet the harder he pulled on her, the more she clung to Jared—and it tore him apart.

Marco had seen her in many tense situations before, had even seen her face down death, and she'd always been heroic. Sometimes she'd been stronger than the rest of them. But never once, not in all the years he'd known her, had he ever seen her this distraught.

But what had he thought Jared's death would do to her? The answer was simple—he hadn't allowed himself to think about it, to imagine it at all, because if he had they wouldn't be here now. He'd never have been able to go through with Veckus's plan.

That was why he had to fix this, had to try, and he knew exactly what had to happen. But could he get where he needed to go without being struck down himself? And could he get Kelsey there with him?

"Kelsey," he whispered, and gently shook her shoulder again, feeling Jared's power burn his hand a little. Yet she survived intact, clinging to her love, her husband, her king.

But she didn't respond at all; she was that lost in her grief. A little shudder passed through him when he realized how familiar this all felt, how much it reminded him of the way their connection would sometimes leave them completely unresponsive to their surroundings. Then it hit him with the full-impact force of a pulse cannon: Kelsey wanted to die with Jared, was even willing it to happen somehow. And he didn't have time to fight her will, or it would be the end of them all. He raised his binoculars and took a quick reading of the landscape. The sound of gunshots hammered the night—total chaos was erupting. But so far no one seemed to realize he'd dropped his shield.

That was the precise moment Jared's energy cooled. First it turned from its usual fiery golden color to a softer yellow—and then a muted green, all the while Kelsey clung to him, her body atop the roiling cauldron of energy that was his natural D'Aravnian form. Then Jared's power retracted visibly, growing smaller and cooler, fading to a cool blue-green until only a cold, soft cobalt blue remained. Kelsey was lifeless atop him, facedown and immersed in his fading energy pool. She would dissolve right along with him if Marco couldn't get to her!

Soft blue yielded to gray then gave way to black. Until nothing, nothing at all remained of J'Areshkadau Bnet D'Aravni except a large red stain in the snow. And Kelsey had been consumed right along with him.

A piercing scream raged within his soul, but Marco quelled it. He had done this. He had killed them both. Marco felt his energy waver at the thought, and made a risky decision. He could make his move now if he acted quickly. Glancing at the stain in the snow—all that remained of his king and queen—he made his decision.

And he ran with all the life left in his soul.

Marco's hands trembled as he took hold of the coiling device. He'd gone over every setting and adjustment three times to be certain, and yet using the mitres still scared the hell out of him. He understood exactly how much rested on his getting this right—and also that what he was attempting was far from an exact science. The energy within the unit still glowed the vibrant orange-red that it had attained when Kelsey began powering it an hour earlier. It appeared to remain at full power.

Marco prayed it would work without her here to link with it; they'd left it in midlaunch, which meant that he at least had a chance. It seemed a miracle now that, in trying to help her open an exterior portal during their connection earlier, Jared had misguided her in the mitres' usage. Instead, he had unwittingly instructed her in the opening of a *time* portal. None of them knew yet—in fact, it would be several years before they did know how to precisely use the weapon anyway. Yes, that fortuitous turn of events had created an instability in the dimensional space that might just save all their lives.

He tapped in the codes, they locked into place, and Marco stepped back, waiting, and hoped with all of his protector's soul that this mission would succeed; that he would be catapulted back a crucial five hours in time.

Chapter Twenty

Five hours earlier . . .

Jared's bedroom took shape, the vibrant blue of interdimensional space dissolving into the familiar landscape of Jared Bennett's chambers. Marco's skin and muscles and sinew tingled all over. He stared down at his trembling hands and cautiously moved his fingers, surprised to find himself still solid and alive. The experience of traveling through time and space had been beyond disconcerting; it had left his body feeling thinner somehow. Transparent. Insubstantial. Perhaps these sensations were the cumulative result of making two journeys so close together through a portal, or maybe it was just traveling to such a relatively close place in time. Five hours was a much less stable leap backward than the ten years he'd bridged on his first journey.

Shaky and nauseous, he felt as if every cell in his body had been shuffled and randomly rearranged. And yet here he was. Taking a tentative step, Marco felt his feet almost give out beneath him before he collapsed on the edge of Jared's bed. In the bathroom, he heard Kelsey splashing and humming in a light, joyous voice. Sweet Kelsey, blissfully unaware that in *this* time his other self had already manned the interdimensional weaponry to its full power in order to transport himself the short distance from Mirror Lake to Jared's compound without detection by security patrols.

It seemed inconceivable now that he had believed himself capable of hurting her, the only woman who had ever truly claimed his heart. Burying his face in his hands, he let his thoughts travel ten years into the future, to their last moment together in the mitres chamber and to the vicious battle they'd fought. Pressing a hand to his eyes he tried to blot out the image of how he had hurt her there. With bone-shattering clarity, he recalled the feeling as he stamped down on her hand, knocking Jared's strake stone from her grasp. She'd thought him her enemy, feared him her killer. Even worse, he'd given her nothing but proof of those beliefs.

She knows now, he reassured himself. *This Kelsey knows the truth.* Only that wasn't actually true, he reminded himself. The Kelsey who knew the truth had died as a result of his actions. Thick bile rose in the back of his throat as he recalled watching her dissolve to ash before his very eyes. His body shook with tremors as he pictured Jared's energy fading to cold blue, and then to nothing. Dead, both of them dead, the two he'd pledged to protect above all others. Tears came to his eyes, ones he'd choked back for more than four long years. Gods, they'd trusted him once. How had it all come to this?

You serve them now, his protector's voice reminded him. *You're here to save them, to shape their destiny.* Marco dropped his hands away from his face, resolved. He had come for only one reason: to prevent these other, deadly futures, and to stop his own role of betrayal in them.

A glance at Jared's bedside alarm clock revealed the time: 12:04 A.M. Only twelve minutes left. Upon his first arrival five hours earlier the red digits had burned like the hatred he carried in his heart. The display had read 12:16 A.M., which meant that if everything played out exactly as it had the *first* time, Marco would confront the other version of himself at exactly 12:16 A.M. Twelve minutes. Twelve minutes to unfurl a destiny, to remake a ruined future. All their fragile hopes now rested on his lone shoulders. It was what he'd been born for, bred for, this moment alone.

Of course, he couldn't be sure he had arrived on the right day. A quick glance around the room revealed the same casually discarded clothing, the rumpled throw pillows on the floor, the cooling fire in Jared's hearth. Everything seemed exactly as it had the first time, and he'd been so careful in his calculations—he had to proceed in the hope that he had succeeded.

Jared had been highly determined in sending her back to this time—and yet Marco still had no idea as to *why*. Not really, though he imagined it was to stop them from meeting each other at Mirror Lake. Jared had likely hoped to prevent the mitres data from fusing with Kelsey's mind. But, gods, when had Jared gotten so stupid? Marco wondered wryly. Didn't he know that without Kelsey by his side he was incomplete, a mere shadow of the leader he was meant to be? That he needed her—the connection he had with her—in order to stay in balance and be the king he was meant to be? Had he thought to prevent their falling in love, or had the plan been even simpler?

Marco could waste his precious twelve minutes endlessly speculating, but none of his imaginings would matter to the Jared and Kelsey who would soon enter this room. Future Jared's plan had failed, as had his own murderous one.

But something else niggled at Marco too. Had Jared perhaps intended to send Kelsey back to Thea, to avert her own betrayal? Jared had always believed that if Thea only understood who she *really* was, she would rise to her destiny. She was royal-blooded, with unique gifts and abilities, and possessing strength of will matched only perhaps by her king and queen's. He grimaced, recalling who Thea had become after Jared had mated—and then married—Kelsey. *Gods, what Jared's rejection has done to both of us.*

Marco stood cautiously, but found his feet much steadier beneath him now. He strode to Jared's small corner desk, pulled open a drawer, and fumbled through his books and papers. His hand settled on a small, leather-bound volume of Shakespearean sonnets, a collection Jared had treasured for as long as he'd known the man—not just the one poem inscribed in their matching wedding bands, but an entire treasure trove of human language that the king had valued. In the poems, Jared had once told him, he found a reflection of the species' beauty, something he could hold on to as he fought to defend the humans. Jared had always been a king with a heart of compassion—until the day he had turned his back squarely on Marco.

Marco shoved the book aside and rummaged through the drawer quickly, seeking a decent sheet of paper. When he found an open notebook with a clean page, he grabbed a pen. He pulled the chair out, sat at Jared's desk, and began writing a letter he had not believed possible earlier today.

My Dearest Jared and Kelsey . . .

Marco had been writing furiously for a good five minutes. He'd never tried to pen anything so quickly in all his life, and hoped they would be able to read his scrawling words. One consequence of being left-handed was that no one could ever read his damned writing. Jared had told him so dozens of times—Kelsey, as well. He glanced back over his hastily scribbled words, and hoped the letter would be at least somewhat legible. His message would be shocking enough to all of them.

He jerked his head in the direction of the clock: 12:11 A.M. Five minutes to go. *So much left to explain.* He'd give anything for just a few hours with Jared and Kelsey, time to sit with them and answer their inevitable questions. But he hadn't dared borrow that kind of time, lest he risk missing the other version of himself, which meant his only choice had been to arrive as close in proximity as possible to when he'd *first* appeared. It was the only assurance that he could subvert his own betrayal.

He glanced at the clock and resumed his furious scribbling.

Marco slipped the letter into an envelope he'd found in Jared's desk drawer, and sealed it firmly, pressing his thumb along the backside for good measure. He wrote their names on the front of the envelope, and propped it against the book of sonnets. He hoped that Jared would notice it there immediately when he returned to the room.

Twelve fourteen a.m. His heart began to hammer within his chest. He felt as much trepidation about facing this other version of himself as he would any enemy. But it would be swift. Easy. Without bloodshed or incident. But not painless. When they encountered each other both of his selves should disappear. Two versions of one person could not exist at the same place in time, so he hoped he wouldn't actually have to battle . . . *himself.* But he was prepared to do so, to the death, if necessary.

How could a heart change so thoroughly in a mere five

hours' time? He'd begun this day filled with so much hatred and roiling resentment toward Jared, and he was ending it . . . someplace else entirely. All the intervening years had evaporated. Seeing Kelsey as such a young woman, younger than he'd ever known her to be, and Jared, before his years of Antousian captivity, had opened Marco's eyes again. Made him remember things he'd long ago cast into a well of forgetting. This was not the legacy he wanted to leave, no matter what Jared had done to him four years ago; nor was it the man Marco had been designed and trained to be, and that was the true lesson of this day.

Marco stared down at his hands again, and turned his right wrist over slowly, feeling with his fingertips for the quickly beating pulse. Lifting his other hand, he allowed a tiny beam of light to flow upon the underside of his wrist, and allowed himself to see what he'd believed would no longer be there—couldn't possibly still be there after so much betrayal.

And yet it leaped to life just as it had eight years ago, when he'd first explained to Jared who he was.

A holographic image appeared in the air just above his wrist. It was Marco's seal, marking him as a royal protector. He wasn't the only one—there were a number of them— but his mark proclaimed his place in an elite and ancient line, branding him for life as primary protector to the royal family.

He stared at the swirling pattern where it hovered in the air just above his wrist. Magenta, gold, purple. Such beautiful colors. Royal colors. And he smiled softly to himself; Sabrina would be so pleased to know that he hadn't disappointed her in the end.

He allowed his other hand to drop away and the seal vanished.

Twelve fifteen a.m.

He took a deep, steadying breath.

One minute left. A single minute that seemed to last an eternity. It had hung in the air for so long already, he thought he'd go mad with the waiting. All his senses were on edge, and he was ready to face whatever happened. He had come out on the other side of something today, a journey that had begun four years ago, in fact. He smiled faintly to himself, knowing that he had won this siege, waged by some unseen force against his very soul. He had reclaimed *himself* in the course of battle this day.

And now he was going to die.

That much Marco did know—but as strange as it might seem, he didn't mind. He was proud to do so. Proud to walk out his destiny, to be the man he'd been called to be.

He closed his eyes for the briefest moment, his last moment. And thought of Kelsey. Her beautiful smile, her luxurious, flame-touched hair. The air around her had always been electrified for him, different from when she wasn't with him. That feeling had intensified incredibly when he'd begun to feel her connection with Jared, as he'd caught those brief glimpses of what the two of them shared. Their bond had begun to seep over to him somehow, and he'd had the tiniest glimmer of what it would have been like if Kelsey had loved *him*.

In hindsight, Marco understood what had happened with their connection, how he had begun to intercept it, his natural gifts of intuition playing havoc with his mortal emotions. It had come first in tiny gossamer shimmers, later in huge powerful waves. What had been intended to better equip him to serve—that he should have been able to connect with them whenever they were in danger—had instead transformed into something twisted and tormenting. He'd felt all their love, all their amazing passion for each other, and yet been left without a single recourse. Marco had been left standing outside, gazing in at something beautiful that he could never be part of, and could only yearn for in the deepest recesses of his heart and mind.

He opened his eyes again and his thoughts floated to Thea. That relationship had been a poor imitation of love, yet he'd felt *something* in her arms, those few times they'd been together. She had come to him that horrible night four years ago, just after Jared had thrown him out and offered comfort, a place to stay. Thea had seduced him that night—in every possible way—and he'd been more than willing, because he'd never felt so desperately alone. Only later did he understand that Thea wasn't just seducing him physically, but was leading him to the darkest side of his nature, and straight into the enemy's camp. By the time she offered to take him to the Antousians' highest realms, he'd been happy to follow her lead.

And in the process he'd lost what was left of his soul. Until tonight.

Perhaps if she hadn't already lost herself so thoroughly . . . perhaps if things had played out differently. But things hadn't been different, and she'd used him completely. It had never been love for her, even though somehow he'd felt a dim reflection of it in his own heart.

He shook the thought aside, clearing his mind.

Twelve sixteen a.m. The time was at hand.

He felt a quake within him, and drew in a sharp breath. There was a throbbing pain in his head, pounding now, demanding and incessant.

A vaporous form appeared just in front of him, an apparition that quickly took shape as hazy edges became solid boundaries. And he found himself staring into the dark eyes of his other self.

Gods, those eyes. Was that what he'd really looked like just five hours ago? So lost, so cold—so very dead?

His other self became more concrete, totally solid; the deathly eyes widened, the mouth opened, and then both he and the other man collapsed simultaneously to the floor of Kelsey's room.

The pain was unbelievable. His other self reached a hand out to him weakly, as Marco struggled for breath, gasping over and over in a desperate effort to fill his lungs. But he couldn't seem to draw in any air at all.

"You . . . will not hurt them," Marco choked out, staring into those other black eyes. "I will not allow it."

His other self opened his mouth to speak, his jaw working to form words, though only a hollow, "Oh," sound escaped his lips. The man staggered to his knees, crying out— and again opened his mouth to speak, but before he could, he disappeared before Marco's very eyes.

Marco crumpled to the floor, unable to breathe.

And yet I am still here.

He clutched at the floor, clutching at life itself, aching to go back and change so many choices. His head hammered with excruciating pain. Why was he still here? Shouldn't he have disappeared at the same moment as his other self?

His very last thought was a quiet, gentle answer: *Because you now have a greater will to live. A reason for being. Your other self did not.*

Marco rested his cheek quietly against the floor, knowing he'd achieved his destiny. He had given everything to protect his king and queen; they were safe now. He was restored.

With that thought, and gasping desperately for air, Marco felt himself begin to fade away one second, one cell, one molecule at a time, until only a shadow glimmered in the darkness, an echo of the soul who had once stood in that place. And then, fixing his memories on Kelsey, he disappeared completely.

Chapter Twenty-one

Jared descended the stairs to his quarters with the quiet stealth of a mountain lion. Often one of his soldiers could be found in the media room, and he hoped to pass by undetected tonight—or at the very least without arousing gossipy interest. Word of the royal mating would travel throughout the ranks faster than a forest fire, and the last thing Jared wanted or needed was to be the one who struck the first match.

He reached the first landing, and released a tightly held breath: It seemed fortune was with him and that he was all alone this night.

"I've been saving that bottle," came the husky voice of his best friend from the deepest shadows. So much for luck.

Jared paused on the landing, staring into the dark media room. "I'm good for it," he replied with a sheepish grin.

"Pretty tacky to go swiping the thing, don't you think? Especially since I've been saving it for *your* victory day." Scott's irritation was undisguised.

Jared took a step inside the media room toward Scott. "No disrespect intended, Lieutenant."

Scott studied him in serious appraisal, leaning back in his chair. "It's not your respect I'm worried about, Jared."

Jared folded his arms across his chest. "Then what?"

"It's not often I find you slinking about at this hour"—Scott's eyes narrowed sharply—"up to no good."

"I'm fine," Jared said, gritting his teeth at the suffocating protection. "You knew that I had to be."

"This human has bewitched you, plain and simple."

Jared laughed aloud. "Ah, so this is about my attraction

to Kelsey." He knew he was downplaying the matter to a ludicrous degree, but he was not yet ready to discuss his mating with his lifelong friend. "You're bothered by it?" he asked in his most offhand manner.

"Attraction is one thing, Jared," Scott said with a visible look of distaste, "but you can let it go only so far. Sex is sex, my friend, and best to keep it that way."

"This isn't that simple." Jared thought of how it had felt to be inside of Kelsey. The soft curve of her hips beneath his, that cascade of jewel-toned hair across his cheek as they kissed, the thrilling sensation as her soul brushed against his. How could once ever be enough with his sweet human? Never. A lifetime would be needed. "It's about far more than attraction," he finished huskily.

"She's hot, the end," Scott said, raising his eyebrows in challenge.

Jared nodded in unequivocal agreement. "She is beautiful; there's no question."

"For a *human*." Scott's keen eyes narrowed with almost laserlike intensity, but he made no further reply.

Jared cocked his head, studying his lieutenant. "You don't find her attractive?" He was genuinely interested in Scott's appraisal of his new lifemate.

Scott scowled. "Humans are pale and round faced." Now *this* comment—coming from Scott, of all people—made Jared snort with amusement.

"That is laughable, friend." He dropped into one of the large leather chairs, kicking up his feet.

Scott continued, "She's freckled and very pale—paler than most of her kind, especially compared to you, my lord—even you'll admit that." Jared's own high cheekbones and rich-colored skin stood in sharp contrast not only to Kelsey's, but to Scott's as well.

Jared grinned. "You have fairer skin than my human's, Lieutenant Dillon."

He smirked back at Jared. "But I'm dark blooded in my heart."

"Ah, the old racial questions," Jared said with a smile, "raising their heads once again."

Scott raked fingers through his raven-black hair, which seemed to respond by shooting out in every possible direction. But he said nothing. Scott's hybrid DNA had troubled him throughout their boyhoods and on into their early adulthood. Guilt, anger, shame—those silent emotions were his constant companions, and he spoke of them to none besides Jared.

He gave a shrug. "I wish I were Refarian."

Jared leaned forward in his seat, eyeing his friend with a forceful, kingly gaze. "Lieutenant, you *are* Refarian," he insisted. "You hold the second highest place in my army. *That* says everything about who you are."

Scott lifted his eyes to meet Jared's. "Have you seen my DNA markers lately?"

Jared raised a finger, thrusting it at Scott. "You lead this army," he reiterated. "*That* is your pedigree. *That* is your identity—not some useless genetic map."

Scott shook his head, staring into his lap. "Jared, please."

"Am I incorrect, soldier?"

"I wish . . ." Scott blew out a weary sigh. "I wish I respected the humans more," he finally said, "and I wish I didn't hate my Antousian blood so damned much."

Jared leaned forward in the near-darkness, eyeing his best friend intently. "S'Skautsa," he said, calling him by his most intimate, rarely whispered Refarian name, "think you not of the importance of your heritage? Think you not it is key?" Jared continued speaking in hushed, idiomatic Refarian. "Who better than you to rally all three of our races under one treaty?"

"You, my lord!" he said, burying his face in his hands. "You are the one they will follow."

"And if something happens to me?" Jared persisted, serious. "Would you still carry out my mandate?" His mandate had always been simple: to protect the humans from the Antousians' genocidal ways, to prevent the harvesting of more humans—or the taking of more life—until a peace treaty could be crafted between all three species. "Would you honor my wishes?"

Scott dropped his hands from his face in shocked concern. "Are you planning on dying, sir?"

"Of course not," Jared said, "but I'm not certain you're planning on leading if I do."

"I will lead," Scott pledged, giving a vigorous nod. "I will protect Earth. Should anything happen to you, I'll pro-

tect all those you love, and I know you love this species—
even though I don't understand it. They hunt you. They
want you dead; they do their level best to destroy you at
every turn, yet still you champion them."

"Because they do not understand either."

"They still hunt you, Jared," he insisted. "Don't be
fooled about that."

Jared grew quiet. "Only a few," he finally agreed, thinking of Kelsey and how tender he knew her heart to be.
Such vulnerability counterbalanced by strength—such fear-
lessness in the face of the unknown—the qualities he'd discovered in the woman had changed his opinion of the
humans, even more so tonight.

"What are you doing with this Kelsey?" Scott asked,
staring at the muted television. "You obviously think she's
gorgeous—you're half-crazed by your damnable bond with
the woman. Have you slept with her now too?"

Jared exhaled, a soft, electrified sound of pleasure that
caused Scott's mouth to fall open.

"Oh, no. Tell me I'm wrong," Scott said, his dark eyes
widening. "Tell me I'm imagining that look on your face,
sir."

Jared felt warmth flood his features, and wondered if the
blush was visible by the dim light of the television. "You
sleep with women, many of them," Jared contended, and
Scott rose to his feet, glaring down at him with thinly disguised impudence.

"I *sleep* with them. Yes. I don't hide that fact," he said.
"Our army has many beautiful Refarian women in it. *Refarian!* For All's sake, Commander, you could have had
your pick! Any one of them would have been honored."

"You've slept with humans too."

Scott shook his head in denial, wandering to the other
side of the room. "That's not true."

"I've heard the rumors." In fact, it was Anika who'd
reported that over the past year, Scott had developed quite
a taste for human women, often leaving camp in the late
hours to seek their companionship. In Anika's words, he
liked them "blond and small and well-endowed."

"Rumors," Scott dismissed, tilting his chin upward. "And
you believe them?"

"It's my job to track my chief officers."

Scott folded both of his strong forearms over his chest. "This dismal planet hardly makes a decent shore leave, but I'm determined to find my way here."

"Why won't you just admit it?" Jared gestured at his friend, frustrated by the man's refusal to acknowledge the truth. "You have a taste for these human women that, pardon my saying so, I'm told can hardly be satisfied!"

Scott gaped back at him, wordless. At first, his fair human skin blanched, but then reddened, high blotches of color forming on both of his cheeks. Yet he said nothing.

"As I thought," Jared continued, answering for both of them. "My intelligence is accurate. Which would make your 'round faced and pale' remark seem a bit hypocritical." Truth was, Jared had wondered if it might actually be a genetic compulsion that had been driving Scott toward the humans, if his Antousian mating urges weren't coupling with his human DNA, trying to pair him physically with his similar kind here on Earth.

"Human women are delectable as hell," Scott spit, his eyebrows furrowing with dissatisfaction. "But I won't pretend I like that fact."

Jared beamed in victory. "Kelsey is quite so," he agreed, feeling the burn for his lifemate begin anew. He glanced down the stairs, toward where she waited for him, probably in his giant sleigh bed. "I'm sure you understand," he said, rubbing his palms together in anticipation.

"No, I don't understand," Scott said, pacing the small room. "The attraction, yes. Sleeping with their kind for an hour or two, yes, I *more* than comprehend that, believe me." Scott paused, meeting Jared's eyes meaningfully as he made his full confession. "But not taking one as lifemate— no, my lord, that I do not understand at all, not when you're titled and destined to lead the Refarian people."

"Our destiny is woven together with the human one," Jared answered, gently rebuking his lieutenant. Scott knew the prophecies—understood them as well as Jared did—if not better, given his dedication to the mystics' teachings. "You know this, soldier."

"I know this," Scott grumbled, shaking his head. "But there is no edict about your mate, J'Areshkadau."

"Yes, there is a prophecy."

Scott regarded him, his face still flushed deep crimson. The black eyebrows shot up in unmasked curiosity. "Go on, my lord."

"I will share it sometime," he promised, feeling his heart thunder at the memory. The mystics had whispered over him the night they'd left Refaria on the royal battle cruiser. Boarding the craft, they'd entered his small quarters on the lower deck and whispered their thoughts. Then, as recently as last spring, they had spoken over him via the council chamber, whispering cryptic predictions of a "fire child." The elders, gathered for the prophesying, had immediately interpreted these prophecies to mean a royal heir from a mating with Thea, whose natural state was so similar to Jared's own. Jared, on the other hand, remembered the secret prophecies from six years earlier, and believed this promise of a fire child was a reference to the results of a love mating.

Scott tapped his foot impatiently. "My lord?" he prompted. "You were saying?"

Jared deliberated about telling Scott something so personal, but in the end, his deep trust for the man won out. In a quiet voice he admitted, "Six years ago, on the battle cruiser, the mystics spoke over me. They foretold a love match."

"You never told me there was a word about your mate," he breathed, dropping onto the sofa across from Jared. Scott was nothing if not curious about everything the mystics had to offer them.

Jared bowed his head, his voice filling with emotion. "It was private, for me only." On one hand, he had never believed himself capable of mating—had viewed his life as too dangerous for companionship, and been resolved to remain unfettered by that kind of attachment. But, in the most secret chambers of his heart, he had longed for the words to be true. "Not even the council elders knew."

"If they'd known, they would have pressed you even harder about Thea," Scott observed, obviously trying to guess Jared's motives for keeping the word secret.

Jared snorted with sarcasm. "Hardly."

Scott planted both hands on his knees, leaning almost out of his seat. "Did the mystics foretell a human?"

"They foretold love."

Jared swore that naked envy appeared in Scott Dillon's eyes. "You are luckier than I thought."

"I mated with Kelsey tonight," he admitted in a hushed voice, putting into words what he knew Scott already suspected.

Scott nodded. "I know."

Jared's hand flitted self-consciously to his chest. The smooth skin, exposed at the robe's opening, still burned hot. One glance down and he could see that the glow had only intensified over the past hour—the longer the bond had simmered between him and Kelsey, the brighter the mating aura over his skin burned. "I should have dressed," he reflected in embarrassment, tugging the robe collar over his chest.

"No, my lord, you wear the mating well," Scott observed, assuming a formal tone. "I wish you every happiness, sir."

Jared watched Scott sink backward into the sofa opposite him, his shoulders slumping into a weary posture—as if the whole conversation had taken all his energy and siphoned it. Jared whispered, "I wish you approved."

Scott's black gaze grew wistful. "I wish I had someone of my own," he admitted, sidestepping Jared's remark.

"You will—when the day comes."

"Oh, Jared, please." He yielded a bitter laugh. "I'm cranky and difficult, and none of the women in this camp will have a thing to do with me." He reached for the champagne bottle that stood on the table between them, turning it in his hands reflectively. "I'm good in bed. That gets me about an hour's worth of *human* attention—if I'm lucky, that is."

"You run from yourself," Jared whispered, knowing it was truer than Scott could ever understand. "Who can follow that hard?"

Scott laughed. "You're sounding pretty prophetic yourself now, J."

Then Scott blessed him with one of his warmest—rarely seen—smiles, and tossed the champagne cheerfully into Jared's waiting hands. "A thousand years of happiness for my king and his mate!" he thundered, and it even sounded like he meant it.

"A thousand years!" Jared agreed, accepting the traditional Refarian blessing over a mating union.

Scott watched as his king strode down the steps, a proud, cocksure measure to his naturally confident gait. A king walked like a king, no matter what he tried to call himself, Scott reflected. Jared was the most humble *powerful* man he'd ever known. The kind of power his king carried in his genes equated to that of a mini nuclear reactor, yet his commander would as soon go hiking for three days in the backwoods as call himself ruler of any people.

Still, he radiated all that power—all that heritage and purebred Refarian bloodline, and yet the one thing Scott Dillon would trade his life for was what he'd just seen in his best friend's eyes: true love. The man had found and claimed a lifemate, whereas Scott had forsaken that hope years ago, long before they'd even left Refaria. He was wed to soldiering and warfare and the nomadic way of life. Even within the ranks, he had no prospects of finding a suitable mate, not when he'd heard the gossip and realized the hard truth of his reality—none of his fellow soldiers considered him the least bit physically appealing. Among the Refarian ranks, *he* was the one with the round face and the pale skin and the low cheekbones and the wide-set eyes.

Scott caught his reflection in the long mirror that graced the hallway opposite the media room. The man gazing back at him had large, doleful eyes—almost black, he'd been told—and black hair to match, worn a fraction too long for a soldier. But Jared never complained, understanding that the long hair helped him blend in outside of camp, and so he dressed like a local, wearing knit caps and his hair long on the nape. And, not surprisingly given his Antousian-human genetic heritage, Scott appeared fully human—both in dress and physicality. Like the humans, his face grew ruddy when the wind kicked up, blotches of red standing out in stark contrast to his fair skin, like bloodstains on the wintry mountains. That didn't happen to the Refarians, of course; their own dusky-copper skin had evolved on a planet prone to extreme conditions—hot sun, frigid winter, briny oceanscape. Anna had nicknamed him Snow White, which just pissed him off on principle, plain and simple— .

it made him feel like the outsider he always was among this crew, not to mention the implied insult of giving him a feminine designation.

Anna—the same woman he'd once tried to kiss on a recon mission, who had instead laughed in his face. Was he hideous? He stared at himself in the mirror. He didn't think so. He just didn't look like the others in this army. So he'd begun to seek out the company of human women; at first not because he desired them, but because they wouldn't laugh at him, as Anna had. Ah, but then he'd gotten his first taste of the creatures. Lolling his head back against the cushion of the leather sofa, he closed his eyes in aroused appreciation.

Humans were delicious: their crazily gyrating energy, their frenzied bedplay, their emotionalism. He liked to believe that human women were his own well-kept secret, a kind of blessing for having to live among these ranks as an alien—until now. Now his secret had been revealed because Jared had discovered the delectable allure of human women. Of course, Jared *would* trump him; he always did, Scott thought with an ugly flash of jealousy that he quickly battled away. How could he begrudge Jared Bennett any happiness? His king had no life of his own to speak of— from the moment he'd been born, a baby brought forth in the midst of a bloody, tragic revolution, the D'Aravnian heir had been required to grow old. No, Scott could not begrudge his beloved king and best friend even one moment of happiness.

Still, Scott had "gone native" because he had been given no other choice; none of his comrades would have Snow White. He'd tried to broach something with another woman, a tech down at Base Seven. She'd been polite, but embarrassed, and told him it didn't seem like a great idea.

Two nights later he'd gone into town on the hunt, determined to go home with a human woman that night. That had been the first time. And the shocking thing wasn't that he'd been successful, but rather just how easy his conquest had been. Juliana, she'd been named, a leggy girl with straight blond hair that had fascinated him almost as much as the sex had. After he'd left her sated in bed that night, a new craving had been birthed inside himself—one that could seemingly never be satisfied.

But why had Jared chosen to mate with a human? Upon meeting Kelsey Wells he'd had no idea about human powers when it came to mating, even for the briefest unions. Or was it the sway of the soul bond over the man, working its subtle mysticism? No, the look in Jared's eyes had been unmistakable; the prophecies were true—Jared had made a love match. Was it really possible, then, that they still had a chance of finding love on this forsaken outpost of a planet, despite being aliens completely?

Scott gazed at his reflection in the mirror, and felt his racially inherited need for humans flame hot yet again. Curses on his mixed blood and his human-Antousian hybridization, he swore, even as another part of himself wished it weren't too late to head back out on the prowl once again.

Chapter Twenty-two

Stepping out of the bathroom wrapped in only a plush towel, Kelsey wriggled her toes on the hardwood. The cabin floor was cold against her bare feet, and she'd give anything for her thermal-lined bedroom slippers, but then again, they weren't exactly the sexiest items in her wardrobe. Now that she'd taken to the bed of a king, she'd have to start thinking like a royal lover. Mentally she searched her drawers back in Laramie, fingering cotton panties and simple camisoles. What she wouldn't do for that foam-green thong from Victoria's Secret right about now. Well, considering that Jared had already ruined one pair of her panties tonight with just the flick of his wrist, he might very well incinerate her little green thong thing.

Thong Thing. It sounded like a creature from another planet, or a bad B-grade sci-fi movie, where Amazonian redheaded women dominated alien lords by simple use of their magnetizing lingerie. She giggled to herself. Yeah, one day really soon, she just might have to see how Jared reacted to Attack of the Thong Thing.

She was still giggling when, stepping in front of his hearth, she shivered, despite the radiating heat. A sweeping chill settled over her skin, one that contradicted the giddy happiness welling within her heart. She glanced about the room. It had no windows—and the bedroom door remained solidly closed. Still, she trembled, tightening the towel about her body for protection. A crawling sensation along her arms reminded her of a feeling she used to get at her father's two-hundred-year-old brick row house back in Vir-

ginia. She'd always sworn that place was haunted; she had
the exact same sensation right now, as if some unseen person were moving all around her. Staring into the fire, she
decided to shake off the feeling. The cabin, after all, was
obviously a much newer construction, and surely no ghosts
hung around here.

When the door to Jared's bedroom creaked, she almost
jumped right out of her towel, spinning to see who entered.
Jared laughed, his dark eyes crinkling with warm amusement. "Who were you expecting?" he teased, nudging the
door open with his broad shoulder. His hands were filled
with a tray—champagne and glasses, chocolates. Basically,
the alien lord was bogged down with all manner of gifts
for her, and she felt her face flush in reaction.

Her creepy imaginings forgotten, she turned to face him,
biting on her lower lip. Ridiculous, but she felt shy with
him now that he'd returned.

With a proud gesture, he deposited his small banquet at
the foot of his bed. "Would you like some champagne?"
he asked, and then with a sudden frown added, "Do you
even *like* champagne?" She heard his unspoken thought—
in a certain way they barely knew each other yet, even
though they already understood each other's hearts very
well.

"I love champagne—but do you like it?" she wanted to
know. Just as she wanted to know his favorite music, what
books he loved, his favorite colors—other than red—his
birthday. Her questions about the man were endless.

He fingered the label of the champagne absently. "Ah,
yes, I've a weakness for many human things."

She raised a flirtatious eyebrow. "Quite obviously."

His eyes darkened, dusky with sexual heat. "Yes,
humans"—he paused, letting his gaze slide down the length
of her body—"humans are special to me. They've always
been."

"All humans?"

His face flushed visibly. "One in particular, now."

He reached for her and his bathrobe fell open, revealing
his smooth, bronzed chest—and it glowed. Literally. A soft
luminescence emanated from his skin, and now she noticed
that even his hands seemed to exude subtle power and

light. She didn't mean to, but she gaped at his exposed
chest a little. And he noticed, lifting a shy hand to finger
the collar of his robe.

"I-I suppose you're wondering . . ." His voice trailed off,
and she had to smile at the burnished red color that flooded
his cheeks. "Well, you must be wondering about the light,"
he finally finished, rubbing his chest self-consciously.

"It's all part of the mystery, Jared." She laughed gently.
Then she cast a very quick downward look at her own
half-concealed body. No glowing. No corona of golden heat
ringing her skin. Oddly enough, its absence left her with a
hollow feeling in the center of her chest.

He seemed to read her thoughts. "It's because of my
other nature," he explained softly, stepping closer toward
her.

She looked deep into his eyes. "What does it feel like?"

"Warm. Tingling. Alive." His lips formed a slow, seductive smile. "*Arousing.*"

She opened her palms toward his chest. "Can I touch
you there?"

He swallowed visibly and nodded his agreement. She
slipped hungry fingers beneath the collar of his robe, and
met the velvet warmth of delectable skin. God, she loved
the way Jared felt. The smoothness of his chest, only the
downiest black hairs dusting his warm golden skin, the allure of it beneath her hand. She slipped both open palms
beneath the terry cloth, exploring, rubbing until he gave a
soft gasp of pleasure, the robe falling completely open.

"You're right. It's nice and cozy in here," she whispered,
and he leaned in close to her until his hot breath fanned
against her cheek. He smelled like the earth, all natural
and touched by the mountain air. His large hands closed
about the center of her back, drawing her closer against
him—with her hands she edged his robe farther open until
it slipped off his shoulders and he shrugged it to the floor.
Before her he stood, a glorious warrior gleaming with otherworldly power and barely restrained sexual heat, and she
found herself simply staring, transfixed by the sheer beauty
of the man she'd taken as a lifemate.

She took a step backward, but he grasped at her. "No,"
he growled low in his chest. "I need you in my arms—not
separate from me. Please, mate, I beg you."

"But I want to *see* you," she explained, her voice a husky shadow of what it normally was. And she did want to see him—desperately wanted to see his fire, displayed all across his skin. But what met her gaze, as she staggered backward momentarily, was the hardened length of him, jutting out toward her with the same kind of devouring hunger she glimpsed on his face. With a single graceful motion, he spun her back into his arms, and with a possessive kiss, he took her. Until his golden-brown chest pressed hard against her collarbone. Until her towel slipped to her ankles. Until she felt swimmy and weak legged from the rippling sensuality of his embrace.

God, she had never wanted a man so much in her entire life. The shattering passion they'd shared earlier had already managed to multiply many, many times over.

"Look at me, Kelsey," he begged. He cupped one hand behind her head, tipping her face upward toward him. "You needn't fear me. Not ever."

"I don't," she said, but the look in his eyes was so fevered, she knew this mattered to him. She lifted a hand to his face, feeling the sandpaper of new stubble beneath her hand. "Jared, I would never be afraid of you," she assured him.

"But you're trembling," he whispered in a soft voice. "Look at you."

And she *was* trembling—but definitely not from fear. She smiled at him, a little embarrassed, wanting to convey every bit of love she felt for him. "Trust me, Jared. It's not fear that's making me shake," she answered with an awkward laugh. *Dang it.* Even her voice was all fluttery.

His dark eyes narrowed, his face warming visibly. "It is desire," he said in a knowing voice. "Yes, I understand this feeling."

"Besides, you don't scare me. If you did, I would've run at the beginning."

He bowed his head, still holding tight to her, but clearly wrestling with something too. "Perhaps you felt compelled then."

"Compelled to what?" she cried. "To love you? To follow you any damn place you'd lead me?"

His mouth turned upward in a sideways, grudging smile. "Well, when you put it that way . . ."

"Why does this keep coming up?" she asked, wanting him reassured once and for all. "I feel so safe with you, Jared. You always make me feel that way."

"I am fearsome, Kelsey. You have seen it." He dropped his head again, his jaw tightening, but he said no more, and instead lifted both hands to cup her shoulders. Heat radiated from his palms. Genuine power. She could understand another woman potentially fearing him—but not when his wilder nature was tempered by such uncompromising strength and goodness.

"No, what I've seen is a man who is beautiful," she told him. "Handsome. So many things I never even dreamed about. My heart's desire, Jared. That's what you are."

He dropped his hands from her shoulders. "For so many years, I didn't believe I'd find a woman like you," he whispered, emotion glinting in his dark eyes. "I didn't remember you, so I couldn't let myself hope. Not with my life the way it is. Who would stand with me? Who would love a man who'd done the things I have?" He gazed downward at his open palms, shaking his head. "You still have no idea—not really—of what or who I am, Kelsey."

"I know your heart, Jared," she whispered. "I've seen your soul. That's all I need to know right now."

His eyes widened, ringed with emotion for a long, silent moment, and then with an almost pained cry he captured her mouth roughly with his own. His tongue sought hers, his hands moving all over her body as if needing to learn the shape of her.

Jared wanted everything about Kelsey. Her body, her mind, her soul, her spirit, her hunger for life and learning— everything he could taste across their newly formed bond. But if he didn't have her *physically* again, now, he thought he'd absolutely explode with pent-up need.

"Kelsey." He panted in her ear, stroking his fingers beneath the soft curve of her bottom until he found her wet heat. "I need to join again." Even as one part of his mind reminded him that he spoke of Refarian ways, another couldn't silence the need. To join—in body, soul, and mind—was the height of satiation for a Refarian.

"So do I," she agreed without hesitation. Did she even understand what he craved more than his next breath? Now as full bondmates he could lead her into deeper places—things she'd only begun to glimpse in their lovemaking.

He dragged her back toward the bed, avoiding the tray and champagne bottle. With a deft move, he spun her so that she fell backward beneath him, her hips settling right on the edge of the mattress. Not a bad strategy, he commended himself, nudging her legs apart with his upper thigh. She lay on her back gazing up at him, and he positioned his erection right between her legs, barely able to restrain himself from plunging deep inside the woman. *But not yet,* he cautioned himself. *Pleasure her, ravenous king. She longs for it. Take her to an unknown, sweet place. . . .*

Hitching his hands beneath each of her knees, he lifted her thighs around his hips, drawing her tight around him. With a painfully gentle gesture, he pressed against her opening—so warm, so ready for him—and teased her. Nudging, stroking her with his length. Beneath him, she gasped her urgent need, but he planned to take his time. With a shiver of desire, he lifted his open palm and slowly rubbed it across one of her breasts, the nipple beading in reaction to his caress. She squirmed beneath his stroking; he felt the aching crescendo of her lust wrapping itself around his mind—impossible *not* to feel it across their bond, its pulsing heat slamming into his every awareness.

Take me, he heard. *Jared, just do it!*

He bent low over her, leaning heavily on one forearm, and showered her chest with kisses, suckling on first one breast and then the other. *You are ready?* Her hot breath warmed his cheek as she reached to cup his face in both of her gentle hands.

Oh, God, what do you think?

I think you are enjoying yourself very much. He groaned across the thin barrier separating the two of them. *I think I should not rush things,* he teased.

She gave him a playful slug in the shoulder. *Do it!*

He laughed softly, climbing past her and into the center of the bed. "Not yet, love." With a dramatic gesture, he reached beneath her and folded back his dark bedspread, revealing the edges of pale cream satin sheets. His people were always insisting on some modicum of royal treatment for their king, and for once he didn't disdain their showy pampering.

Kelsey sat up, her mouth swollen from his kisses; her messy hair spilled to her lower back, tumbling evidence of their passion. She reached with one hand, gingerly stroking the top edge of the satin sheet. He felt a surge of pride: That he could offer her something indulgent and sensuous here in his war camp gave him a thrill of heated pleasure. She was his mate. Here, in this chamber, he could worship her as such.

He drew back the covers in silent invitation, and with the sweetest of smiles she slipped her bare body underneath. "Ooh," she whispered huskily, "these feel nice, Jared."

He growled his own pleasure, sliding his heated body beside hers. Whenever he was around her, he couldn't seem to constrain his soft growls and rumbles of desire, even though he knew his Refarian expressions had to be alien to her. Still, as he nestled down beside her, tugging her hips flush to his, another long, heady growl escaped his chest.

She giggled, narrowing her eyes at him. "I have an idea," she said.

Nuzzling her collarbone, he suckled at the tender flesh there. "Um, does it involve interspecies bedplay?" he purred, ready to take her at any moment.

"Here," she instructed, giving his shoulder a light shove. "You roll onto your back."

He blinked up at her, curious, and did exactly as she guided him to do. Closing his eyes, he shivered in anticipation. He heard the rustle of covers, the shifting of her position, and then something light tickled his thighs, causing his abdomen to knot with fevered expectation. *Oh, gods!* Her mouth! The unexpected soft warmth of it closed over his shaft. He cried out, his eyes flying open, and found her head bent low over him, her thick curls spread across his thighs. He dragged his fingers through that auburn hair, desperate to hold himself back. Groaning, he squirmed beneath her licking and sucking, his hips thrusting upward, desperate for more. He wanted it deeper, harder. Gods, if she didn't stop . . .

She didn't stop. The sensations increased in their fury and intensity, and it was all he could do not to release himself right in her mouth. "Kelse," he half begged, writhing convulsively as her warm mouth drew in even more of him. In all his days, no woman had ever pleasured him this way. No woman—not even in bed—would dare be so intimate with the king. *Kelse, please, love, please. Please!*

What was he even begging her to do? To stop or to take him deeper still? Even he wasn't sure of what he really wanted. With an agonized gesture, he tugged at her arm, and she released him, sitting upright. She blinked in confusion and he explained shakily, "You . . . must . . ."

"Danger zone?" she teased, rubbing her mouth with the back of her hand.

His only reply was a trembling groan of delight. This lit her up, from the inside out. Leaning onto her side next to him, she began her next temptation—she took him within her hand and began rubbing him back and forth until he nearly came right within her palm.

"Kelsey!" he cried, placing a stilling hand over hers. Gods, it killed him to stop her, that heated friction she was creating, the back-and-forth over his erection and the soft folds of his skin. "Kelse," he groaned in her ear, and she pulled back, staring up into his eyes. A low growl rumbled out of his chest, and he squeezed his eyes shut. Sucking in burning gasps of air, he wrestled to still the tremors that shook his whole body.

He cursed low in Refarian, shaking his head. To even lay hold of any English seemed impossible, so he reached for her, pulling her right against his side. *"L'bashata,"* he groaned, sure that if she so much as touched him again down there, he would let loose everything he had, right in her hand.

"La Bashta?" she repeated, almost getting the word right. He groaned, leaning back into the pillows, smiling.

"No good . . . translation," he managed, then rolled her onto her back. The words meant roughly "hot-blooded, fast-handed woman." That was one phrase he'd definitely be keeping to himself.

"Why'd you want me to stop?" she asked, daring to again slip that warm, highly arousing hand between his legs, which caused him to release such a loud, shuddering cry that he feared the whole camp would know the king was being pleasured in the most arousing of ways.

"Because I don't want to spend outside of you." He gasped. Burying his face against her neck, he pulled her scent into his body. "I-I want inside. Outside is . . . good . . . but-but . . ." he stammered helplessly.

She studied him in surprise. "Don't Refarian men like being . . . touched?" she asked, suddenly unsure of her seduction routine. What if it were somehow painful for him? Or too much? She'd never seen a man respond so strongly to her touch.

"We like everything!" he blurted, and she giggled until he flushed in shock at his own bald remark. With a self-conscious gesture, he lifted his hand to his head, rubbing his open palm over the short, spiky hairs.

"Everything, huh?" she whispered, languidly moving closer, like a mountain lion considering its prey. "Just precisely what qualifies as everything, my lord? Hmm?"

"Am I your king now?" He panted as she hovered over him, turning her head first one way, and then another as she studied him. "For if I'm your king," he said, "then I may instruct you as to my pleasuring, may I not?"

She cocked both eyebrows upward in mock surprise—enjoying his flustered reaction to her flirtatious sexuality. "Is that what you did before I came along? You issued royal orders for this sort of thing?"

He shook his head, swallowing visibly. "No, love." She closed one hand around his shaft again, slowly stroking and rubbing, increasing her friction, until with a shiver he arched back into the pillows and growled his pleasure.

She'd never met a more physically sensitive man in all her life. It had to be a Refarian thing. Earlier they'd been so focused on other activities that she hadn't had time to realize his extreme reactions to her touch.

This could prove most interesting, she realized, and reached for the corner of his silken sheet. Drawing it down over him, she draped his hips, slowly sheathing him in the slick material, slipping it back and forth over his erection. Each time she caressed him, he released a rumbling sound the likes of which she'd never heard from a human man before. It was a low-pitched howl of desire that made every hair on her body bristle with answering lust.

"I thought you were going to command me," she teased, sliding the cool satin between his thighs, parting his legs with it until he spread wide for her with a satisfied sigh. She enjoyed watching the painful play of ecstasy on Jared's face—and most especially knowing she was the cause of it. "Don't you have some royal orders, my lord?" she asked, increasing the pressure of her stroking just enough to elicit yet another war cry from her mate.

His eyes tightly closed, he gave an almost imperceptible shake of his head. "None necessary." He gasped.

"Shall I continue?" she purred, but his only reply was to throw his head back in lusty enthusiasm. That was a definite yes. Again she wrapped his erection in the sheath of material, stroking him with a fevered pressure. "Ah, Kelsey." He said nothing more, simply repeated her name like the most joyous of chants, over and over, lost in the pleasure she offered him.

At last, he clasped her by the wrist, shaking his head. "Stop, love!" he cried out. "You must cease." Or he would obviously spill himself all over that satin sheet, and never get inside of her. She understood. And she had to agree with his assessment of their predicament. She lay there on her side, her head propped on one elbow, feeling mightily pleased with herself.

"So, Jared, what else should I know about your people?" she asked in a throaty voice. She was only partly joking.

Opening his muscled, dark arms to her, he wrapped her against his side. "Not now," he said.

Now this had her curious—apparently there *was* something more she needed to know, but with both of his large, golden-skinned hands he grasped her, urging her closer. "Please, mate," he moaned in a tight voice, "let me bed you."

With a flash of barely concealed energy, he flipped her onto her back. In that half second, he moved from being the pleasured to being her master. God, he was heavy—she hadn't felt the full weight of his large, solid frame either of their earlier times of making love, but now—*oh God,* she thought, feeling his hugeness atop her—the alien nearly knocked the breath out of her lungs.

Easing himself between her legs, Jared settled his hips atop hers. There were so many ways he longed to join with her—ways he knew she didn't yet understand. His own people's ways. There would be time for such. Right now his most pressing hunger was to plunge deep within her warmth, to feel her all about him. He lifted a hand to her cheek, brushing curls away so he could gaze into her clear, lovely eyes. He yearned to take her to the same ecstatic pinnacle she'd been drawing him toward.

"Now *you're* shaking," she whispered, capturing his unsteady hand against her cheek. Her eyes narrowed with concern, as she held his palm flat against her soft face.

Swallowing hard, he nodded. "The . . . intensity," he managed to get out, though some distant, Refarian-accented voice told him his body's reaction to her was far more complex than that. Only an hour had passed since they'd initially mated, and already swaying heat swirled through his body.

For a silent, profound moment, they just stared into each other's eyes. He searched her face, sought to believe she accepted all that he was. God, she had no idea. No true notion of all that his alienness might mean, especially in their marriage bed. As if reading his thoughts—which, perhaps, she had done—she lifted silencing fingers to his lips.

"Come inside me, Jared," she urged, bucking her hips upward against his. "Don't keep teasing me."

Burying his face in her hair, he released a pent-up growl of yearning, and thrust within her. And then they stilled, lost in each other, as his soul met such an explosion of color as he'd never known before. Purest gold showering over him, brilliant magenta caressing him. "Ah! *Kelsha, nyaat lansvari!*" A cascade of love pledges tumbled through his mind, none in English. He was a dolt at translating his love for her when they were in the throes of lovemaking.

He gave a gentle thrust of his hips; she threw her head back, crying out her pleasure, the smooth, creamy skin of her neck exposed to him. Nibbling her there, he kissed and licked her, feeling her warm hands cupping him from behind, urging him deeper. Fuller.

Flashes of golden-eyed purples, wavering teals. His lover's soul was a beautiful otherworldly tapestry. He wasn't sure what brought him more rapture at the moment—her soul joining or her lovemaking.

Warm hands pulled at his upper thighs, holding on for a harder ride. She seemed to be demanding it, requiring it; he let all gentleness fall away, pushing and thrusting and driving into her with his unrestrained warrior's needs.

She met every thrust. Every dip of his hips, she answered with a thrilling charge upward, her cries keening across his mind. And then suddenly, she shoved at his chest, both open palms forcing him apart from her—as if she meant to stop him. Shaking his head dazedly, he stared down at her. "What, love?" he asked, panic teasing at the edges of his awareness. Had he been too rough? Too hungry? Too alien? "What've I done, love?"

She settled into the pillows beneath him, fingering both of his nipples as she studied him. "I just wanted . . ." She stared up at him, blinking her eyes, which glimmered like royal jewels, and shook her head. A strange smile played at the edges of her full mouth.

"More? Or was it too much?" he rushed. "I can go slower—faster?" Gods, he was in a full-throttle shambles. It had been too damned long since he'd taken a lover; he was useless in bed—that had to be it.

"Shh," she whispered, giggling as she ran her fingertips over his neck, his chest. "I just wanted to slow down a little."

"I am sorry for being so clumsy," he apologized. "Too much time in warfare—" he began to lament, but she lifted upward, covering his mouth with her own to silence him. Her tongue teased his lips open, twining and mating with his own. She tasted human. She tasted like no other woman he had ever lain with in his life. She tasted and smelled like his *mate*.

I wanted you to slow down, Jared, she explained, the words a gentle sigh across his soul's edge. *That's all. You know how perfect this is—you are. All I've ever felt is your perfection.*

Panting, he broke the kiss, "I-I have never felt this," he blurted, hardly able to breathe for the tightness their bond had formed in his chest; he was reminded of a hunter's bow, strung impossibly taut.

"Hard to breathe," she agreed, swallowing hard.

"Need to . . . finish." He gulped, his voice hoarse beyond recognition. He was all but begging her now. Warm hands clasped his hips, taking hold again. Burying his face against her cheek, he slid his own palms beneath her, cupping her full, round bottom. With his mouth, he nuzzled her collarbone, nipping at the soft, exposed skin there.

Kelsey felt the enormous hard length of him and she struggled to breathe with every fevered thrust he made. His body was on fire—ravaged by fever—and he didn't even seem to realize it. It was just as when he'd first returned to the bedroom, his entire body blazing golden, only now the raging heat had pooled most intensely within his groin area. It felt as if a blazing sword, lifted straight from a forge, were being dipped within her, over and over again. A sorcerer's sword, capable of bringing light and pleasure and love beyond knowing.

The alien was just so damn big! She'd never had a lover so large—Refarians were definitely built to last. And last and last and last. He seemed never to tire, as he led her to the highest crescendo of pleasure, only to send her soaring even higher the longer he tumbled with her in her bed.

They rolled in each other's arms, panting and crying— real tears at one point in both of their eyes. They grew still, tangled in his satin sheets at the singular moment when their souls—which they'd already felt touching and pressing against each other all through their lovemaking—seemed to weave together, blazing so hot between them that for a full minute, neither could speak or breathe or even move.

"Oh, gods," he finally moaned with a shuddering reaction inside of her, rolling her atop him again. Yet still he forged ahead strongly, hard and full and raging hot, their souls clasping as tightly as their physical bodies did.

Atop him, she had a quiet, centered moment to gaze upon her mate. To take in his lean, dark face, colored the golden red of Native American skin as much as it was the dusky olive of an Italian. Beautiful beyond comparing to any race on this planet, Jared's exotic, Refarian features made her blood burn. Made her feel feral and untamed; maybe that was what happened with his people in bed. She wasn't sure, and raising herself up slightly, she reached between her own legs to stroke the man while rocking atop him. Now, this . . . this touch finally did her king in.

With one blinding cry of pleasure, he arched his back, pressed his eyes shut, and let loose the rumbling growl of a warrior-beast, shuddering all the way up inside her core. He squirmed and bucked upward so hard he lifted her right up with him, murmuring, "Gods, Kelse, gods . . . never so sweet. So beautiful. Never before."

"Me neither," she agreed, feeling tears of joy fill her eyes.

Collapsing atop him, she lost herself in all the royal colors that sped through her senses—Jared's colors, blazing within her soul.

Chapter Twenty-three

Kelsey woke to the remains of a slight champagne headache. She couldn't believe Jared loved champagne! The man had definitely embraced Earth culture. Not only that, but last night, when they'd finally started to drift into a warm, hazy sleep, wrapped in each other's arms, he had unexpectedly bolted upright in bed. "Hang on a second," he'd said with a boyish grin, and fumbling with something on the nightstand, she suddenly saw he had an iPod. (An iPod! Jared had an *iPod*?) Her mouth had snapped open, but before she could laugh or tease him or even say anything, Jared had rolled back close to her, enfolding her in his strong, warm arms. And Duke Ellington had begun to play from a small speaker in the background.

Jared Bennett loved Earth. It was a strange realization. One she was considering as she lay beside him, not quite willing to open her drowsy eyes yet, despite sensing that he was already awake. He didn't seem to need much sleep at all. Maybe a couple of hours a night. With a quiet sigh, she nuzzled closer against him, tucking one hand beneath his muscled bicep.

"You're awake," he whispered, slipping a large palm down to the small of her back and snuggling her closer.

"Almost," she murmured against his chest. Beneath her ear, his heartbeat quickened, its steady beat sending a thrill through her whole body. She lay curled against him on her side, one of her legs tucked securely between both of his. She loved the tickling feel of the hair on his legs. Not too much hair—she couldn't stand that in a guy. But just enough. The similarities between his body and that of a

human male were astounding. Almost as if he *were*
human . . . but not quite. There were a dozen different
ways that he seemed . . . well, for lack of another way
to describe it, just a click off. Not quite human in some
fundamental way that seemed just beyond her power to
explain.

"Ah, Kelsey, please wake." The near-plaintive tone to
his voice made her giggle. She leaned up, blinking at him
through sleepy eyes. He grinned at her, a boyish, lopsided
smile that almost made her heart stop. More than any other
time since they'd met, he seemed free. Unfettered by tension or concern. His eyes almost always had a driven intensity to them, a kind of worry haunting them. This morning
it was as if every single care had been swept away from
him; he'd been washed clean. Renewed by her love.

He lolled his head back into the pillow, studying her. His
room had no windows, and she wished she could see him
like this by golden morning light, reclining all gorgeous and
nude like some sated Greek god. "I've been waiting three
hours for you to wake," he complained, reaching one dark
hand to cup her breast. Instantly, her body tightened at
his touch.

"Three *hours*?"

"Yes, it is already past seven a.m.," he said and she had
to laugh at his idea of "sleeping in."

"You don't sleep."

"I do, some," he disagreed languidly, taking his rough
fingertips and stroking them just as languidly across her
right nipple.

"Not"—she gasped aloud as he tightened her nipple between his fingertips—"enough!"

"There is far too much to accomplish," he answered with
a wicked, kingly grin. "Now more than ever, in fact. I shall
save the sleeping for other men, while I"—he cupped her
breast firmly within his palm again, causing her whole body
to tremble in pleasure—"occupy myself in more valuable
ways."

"Yes." She gulped. "I'd like that."

"Then I shall continue," he said courteously, with a
heavy-lidded look of appreciation, his rough fingertips teasing her to greater arousal.

But as much as she ached to make love with him all over

again, she'd woken needing a few answers. Very gently, she covered his caressing hand, stilling the action. "Let's just talk first," she whispered breathlessly. She smiled at him, hoping he wouldn't be offended—she didn't actually know if he was the kind of guy who *got* offended when a woman denied him what he wanted, but she was betting on the fact that he wasn't.

"Something is bothering you?" he inquired, reaching for her hand. He lay there, gazing up at her as she sat beside him in the bed. She fingered the edge of the satin sheet, searching for words. Finally, she managed, "We don't really know each other very well yet."

His eyes widened, and one elegant black eyebrow shot upward in question. "You're not breaking it off with me already?" he said with a husky half laugh. Yet his eyes betrayed a seriousness that belied the humor. She just rolled her eyes at him, and he blew out a sigh of relief. "Ah, good," he said, smiling again. "You panicked me for a moment there, Kelse."

"You're the one who told me there's no going back."

He offered her a gentle, tender smile. "Not much recourse at this point, I'm afraid."

"I don't want any recourse." She snorted, swatting him on the arm. "I want you."

"That you have, my love. Always."

"It's just . . ." She drew in a strengthening breath. What she wanted to ask wasn't easy, but it had been niggling at her during the night, even to the point of entering her dreams. "You said something when we were making love that kind of got me thinking. When I asked what more I needed to know about your people." She paused, looking down into his eyes; he said nothing, but nodded his encouragement. "Actually, I think you said 'not now' about telling me more. That's what you said when I asked what I didn't know," she added, feeling her face flush.

"That's what I said," he repeated softly, a slight smile playing at his lips. But despite the smile he didn't *look* all that happy, she noticed.

"So, it got me wondering," she continued, forcing her voice to sound upbeat, even though the inscrutable expression on his face was starting to making her nervous, "about what all I *don't* know about you. Of course, there are obviously tons of things, but I mean, well . . ." She sucked in a breath and blurted the rest. "I'm talking about *in bed*." There, she'd put it out there. And—dang it all—the man blushed. Terribly. With a cough into his hand, he rolled onto his back and a little bit away from her.

"Is it okay if we talk about it now?"

Throwing an arm over his head, he blew out a heavy breath and stared at the ceiling. "You may ask me whatever you wish, Kelse," he said, his voice husky with emotion. "I'd never deny you anything. Never. I love you and I want you to know everything about me. Gods, *I* want to know everything about *you*." His roving gaze lighted on her meaningfully. "Everything. So, yes, of course you should know."

"Know?" She waved her hand between them, urging him to continue.

"Our species are definitely very different," he allowed, his gaze resting on her for a beat before he stared upward at the ceiling again. Both of his cheeks were still a deep reddish hue. From emotion? Embarrassment? Maybe even from arousal—she couldn't be sure.

She wanted to put him at ease, though, because he was way too self-assured to seem unsettled like this. "But we're a lot the same," she reminded him gently.

Again his gaze rested on her. "You've seen what I am, both sides of me, and you've seen the change I'm capable of. But you've no idea all the things I've done in this war—"

"You've already said that—"

"Or the people I've killed. *Killed.* With my own hands, Kelsey, and my own power. If you only understood, truly understood—"

"Are you trying to scare me?"

"I'm trying to make you understand that you don't know what I *really am*. I am an alien species; don't fool yourself that I'm human." The coldness from last night had returned, as if he dared her to believe him what she *knew* him to be: a good man.

"You're fighting a war," she said, thinking of her father and all the endless political fracases he'd been involved in. "I'm not naive about all this stuff, Jared. In a war lives will be sacrificed, and it's part of the cost—"

But he cut her off. "As a Refarian, my sexuality is different from yours," he whispered in a voice so quiet, she nearly missed it. In fact, she leaned closer toward him to be sure she really had heard him.

"Wh-what?"

He set his jaw for a moment, his black eyes narrowing to slits, and then hissed, "I said that my *sexuality* is *different* from yours." He closed his eyes in what appeared to be mortification.

"Uh, I don't think so."

"Think so!" he cried angrily, his eyes flying open.

She lifted the satin sheet that covered the length of his body and made a point of staring down at his groin area for a long moment. Then she swung her gaze back to his face. "It went in just fine, thank you very much. Repeatedly, I might add. Very human in its functions, I've gotta say. Or perhaps *universal* might be more accurate."

"Kelsey, it's not the, uh, equipment that I'm speaking of." He groaned, staring up at the wood-beamed ceiling overhead. "Don't you understand?"

"Not even remotely."

Jared blew out a frustrated sigh and rolled over to the edge of the bed, putting his back to her. In All's name, he'd never found himself in a situation quite so uncomfortable and complicated and *sad* in his life. And he'd lived through quite a host of situations; from being captured by Veckus to losing his virginity at seventeen to being lost in his Change for a full day once and unable to shift back. *That* had been more than awkward, to have his soldiers wonder why their commander seemed determined to stay in his most natural state. Fortunately no one had mentioned it when he finally found his way back to his other self's form.

But *this* . . . this moment eclipsed all of those previous occasions. And it didn't help matters that the woman was just so determined, so frank and unconcerned about his royal status. Everyone he knew had been intimidated by him at one point or another. But not Kelsey. Behind him he sensed her waiting, and it only made what he had to tell her all the more horrible. She would hate him. If she'd been angry about his seeing inside of her without her per-

mission, what would she now think about this new revelation? Forget the horrid shame of it—she would feel
betrayed. She would have to. He should have revealed everything last night before taking her across the bonding
threshold. *But you loved her; you wanted her . . . you were
afraid of frightening her off.*

Silence, you idiot! he told himself. *You are a fool, frail
king, and you never last at love, so why offer your wretched
advice now?*

She stirred on the bed behind him, edging closer. He
raised one hand over his shoulder to halt her progress.
"Please," he begged.

"I'm lost here, Jared."

Well, he thought, *that makes two of us.* He buried his
face in his hands and prayed to All that she'd understand
him, and that his genetic differences wouldn't send her
shrieking from the bedroom. He reviled the part of himself
he was about to unveil to her. It was the one thing about
being D'Aravnian that he'd always loathed. He loved his
Change—it was peaceful and blissful and sated every craving in the entirety of his nature.

But this—this that he had to tell her—he despised in
himself.

And yet she had to know. It was only fair that he tell
her everything. She would learn it inside their bond soon
enough.

"I have cycles," he blurted, then lunged to his feet and
bolted as far from her as he could possibly get, all the way
to the distant side of the room, by his reading sofa in the
corner. Keeping his back to her, he stood there like a cornered animal. *How appropriate,* he thought with a pained
laugh. He heard her bare feet, quiet on his hardwood floor
as she edged closer to him. Of course she wouldn't let it
go, but would pursue him all over the damnable compound
until she squeezed out every ounce of truth about his sexual makeup.

When she'd almost reached him, he moved again—to the
fireplace where he braced his hands on the mantel. He
wished he weren't naked; he felt totally exposed,
vulnerable.

One warm human hand settled on his back—over his
terrible scar, of all places. He flinched, but she didn't move,

saying, "You saw everything in me, remember? It's only fair that I know whatever this is about *you*." Her soft, melodious voice was like a balm to all his lifelong wounds. He'd always been exotic, no matter where he went, always different—a warrior, a king, a killer, a changeling—when all he'd secretly wanted, for so many years, was to be normal and loved. To be common, of all things. To be a simple man, a writer or a builder, perhaps.

But this one touch from an alien woman had him shaking from the crown of his head to the very tips of his toes. "Cycles," he repeated unsteadily. "My kind experience them." Still he refused to face her. The shame was too overwhelming. Gazing into the fireplace, he wrestled to find words, but none seemed to offer themselves.

At last, it was Kelsey who spoke. "What kind of cycles?" she asked in a soft voice, reaching a hand to stroke his hair. Black hair turning silver; hair that proved what he was about to tell her. "Jared?" Kelsey prompted when he did not answer. "What *kind* of cycles?"

He took a deep, stilling breath and turned to face his mate. "Refarian mating cycles," he answered in as even a voice as he could muster, and as cryptically as he could phrase his reply, even though he was certain Kelsey would never back down, not his determined human.

"But what does that mean?" she asked. Dropping her hand to her side, she faced him. "And don't tell me you don't know, because I can tell it means something, Jared."

He glanced down at her, standing there just beside him, and slipped one large palm around her waist. "Come closer." She leaned against him, her face open and waiting. In the past few nights he had yearned to cycle with her. For the first time in his life, he had opened—ever so slightly—to the idea. Now his face burned with the absolute humiliation of it. Bowing his head, he whispered the truth, a barely audible sound. "Mating urges," he told her.

She pressed closer, slipping one arm around his neck to draw him closer toward her. "What?"

It took everything inside his brave warrior's heart to meet his love's gaze, but he did so, and their eyes locked in the half darkness. She'd heard him—she simply hadn't understood.

"My line experiences mating cycles. Body heat, urges,"

he answered, forcing a clinical tone. "It is the way with my kind. Mating fever, blood fever. It has many names. All mean the same: We rut like animals." He spit the words, unable to mask his horrible self-derision. She frowned, her auburn eyebrows hitching together into a tense line of concentration. Even now, he could see the scientist in her making calculations, attempting to comprehend. Finally, she nodded, crimson blush creeping upward from her own neck into her fair face.

"Well, Jared," she said, licking her lips thoughtfully, "that's certainly an interesting detail to your species."

"Shameful," he snarled.

She slipped both of her arms around his neck, nuzzling closer against him. Instantly he felt more secure with the woman; he felt loved. She laughed softly. "You obviously don't *need* mating cycles." She glanced meaningfully toward his bed. "I mean, honestly, Jared!" She lifted a gentle hand to cup his face. "You're on fire when it comes to, well, *that.*"

"I appreciate the vote of confidence." He coughed, still feeling an outrageous amount of embarrassment, but somehow breathing easier all the same.

"How often?" she asked, cocking her head sideways.

"I've no idea, actually," he answered honestly, blowing out a heavy breath. "To date, I have never experienced one. Which is"—he paused, wondering how to frame it to her—"well, more than a bit concerning. It is the only way in which I might sire children. The only time I'm fertile, Kelsey." Here it was—the next revelation, the one she might find unpardonable.

"Oh," she said, a soft, swooshing sound of realization. "Oh, that's . . . not good."

"Not good," he agreed. "And it doesn't take a scientist to realize that, does it?"

"Maybe you have to be mated—"

He cut her off. "You don't."

She tried again, her eyebrows lifting hopefully. "Or of a certain age—"

"I passed it long ago."

"Or maybe it takes, I don't know, *practice,*" she tried, her voice rising in frustration.

"Thea has been through at least seven cycles already, and she's four years younger than me."

"Oh, crap," she said, her shoulders sagging a bit.

He drew a deep breath. "There's more," he cautioned, praying in his heart that the next revelation would not crush her—or send her fleeing from him.

"Okay." She nodded, swallowing visibly. "Go on."

He lifted a hand and stroked the length of her curling cascade of auburn hair. So beautiful—more beautiful than he deserved in a lifemate. "I am at my peak of fertility right now. That is, if I *were* to actually cycle, the chance of conception is at its highest point," he answered solemnly. "But very soon I will pass into maturity."

"Maturity?"

He coughed again, avoiding her gaze. "It's a euphemism among my people. It means I will grow infertile," he explained, reaching a hand to his own hair. "This silver that you see? It is a first indication of my maturing."

"Maturing," she repeated, running her fingertips over his short, bristling hairs. As if she needed to inspect the evidence to truly believe him.

"It happens quickly for the male of my species." He swallowed hard and added, "Usually."

"So you enter this maturity, your hair turns silver and you . . . can't reproduce any longer?" she asked nervously.

"You have the gist of it." He wanted to pretend that his voice hadn't sounded nearly as mournful as it had. But she'd noticed—of course she had; her intelligent eyes were alight with questions.

"It can't possibly be that simple," she said, but after he'd stared at her for one intense moment, she frowned, whispering, "Can it?"

"You never ate your chocolates," he said, reaching around her for the unopened golden box where it rested on the mantel. "Perhaps now would be a good time?"

"I don't want chocolate." She scowled at him. "I want the truth."

His hand tightened about her waist—anything to hold her here with him, to keep her from fleeing. Finally, in a low voice, he gave her the truth she sought. "I am on borrowed time," he said, tugging at his short hair by way of explanation. "Do you see now? For my kind, this is not a small thing."

"You're only *thirty*!" she exclaimed, her eyes ringed white with what seemed both shock and something else he couldn't place. Horror? Frustration?

He dropped his voice to a calming timbre. "This disturbs you."

"You're young, Jared." She shook her head adamantly. "You're very young. Not an old man. And what does it mean, 'grow infertile'? This doesn't make any sense. You're a guy! They stay fertile until they die."

"Men of my species experience the change," he answered. "Not the women. And men of my *line* experience it very prematurely. *Very.* It will come upon me soon; I feel sure of it. Months, perhaps. Not years. We're a hot-blooded, strange lot, the D'Aravni. Some say ours is a pure bloodline, closer to the true Refarian nature than most Refarians now."

He sighed, hating the unfairness of it. He'd never bothered with the idea of heirs or children, had never wanted them until now, with her. Now, he finally understood—he had been waiting for her. His heart had belonged to her, even if his memories had not. His sweet, precious Kelsey; he ached to give her a child that would somehow weave their two utterly disparate genes together in the form of one beautiful baby. Maybe her auburn hair and clear eyes with his darker skin? Or her fair skin and his black hair and dark eyes? Any child of theirs would be perfectly beautiful—and perfectly loved.

In a very quiet voice, staring at the floor, she asked, "Can you still have sex? After this change? Because if not, you can tell me that—"

"Gods, yes!" he roared, laughing and blushing painfully at the same moment. "Much vigorous and pleasing sex, I am told—no concerns about that. In fact, some say . . . well, that the desire increases afterward, and the joinings become far more . . . passionate."

She teased him with her eyes, but he didn't miss how her face had turned a lovely pink color. "That doesn't sound half-bad."

He gave her a shy grin. "Maybe it's some sort of gift

from the gods to compensate for the loss of . . . well, the other."

Her eyes darted about the room as she thought about what he'd told her. "But they could bank your sperm," she reflected clinically, the scientist in her coming to the fore. "I mean, *couldn't* they? They can do that with human men—easily."

"Yes, they can, ah, bank my sperm," he agreed, smiling at her directness even in the midst of such a painful discussion. "But it wouldn't remain viable for very long."

"That makes no sense whatsoever," she exclaimed. "With your technology—"

"It's because I'm D'Aravni."

"Explain what you mean."

"The fire can be passed only by natural conception." He hoped she could understand something that even among his own line had always been considered mystical. "My other self—the energized one you first met—the only way we pass that along is by the act itself. And that is the part of me that is Arganate D'Aravni. It is the part of me that requires an heir."

"Jared," she said, her blue eyes focused, "we have no idea if I could even carry a child like that. I'm human. And you're . . ."

"Of an alien species," he finished, his heart swelling with the possibilities, both of joy and of crushing heartbreak. For a moment, holding her about the waist, he noticed the golden-hued darkness of his skin juxtaposed against the alabaster beauty of her own. There were dark men like himself on her planet—much darker ones even—and fair-skinned ones on his own, but holding Kelsey this close, he noted that even her scent was exotic. Dark to light they stood, as different as any two creatures could be, yet every cell within his Refarian body yearned to cycle with the woman, to give her babies and an unbounded future, just as any normal human man might.

Glancing downward, he realized that he'd placed a protective hand over her belly—an unconscious gesture of both promise and faith. "My heart believes it's possible, Kelsey. Maybe it's illogical, but I have to believe you could carry our child."

"But what if I can't?" she said in a soft voice. "How will you produce an heir?"

He wrapped his arms about her, drawing her flush against his chest. "I never worried about it before I met you." He sighed, cupping a hand about the back of her head. "The council constantly urged me to mate with—" He caught himself, halting. "Well, to mate. To produce an heir to the throne."

She leaned her cheek against his shoulder, sighing. "With Thea," she finished.

"Yes, with my cousin," he agreed. "Because of her bloodline."

"They won't be pleased about this." She drew in a nervous breath. "Your joining with me." She pulled back to look him in the eye. "They won't be happy about this at all."

"But it is my decision," he said firmly. "I am the king, and while they advise me, they don't control me." He swore he saw relief wash over her features. "Besides, I have a theory as to how our memories were erased, and if my suspicion is correct, it will make winning over the council all the easier."

"But now that you've mated, producing an heir has to be important to you." Her voice had become plaintive, and he swore she trembled against him. "I mean, why would you have mated with me, Jared, when it almost guarantees the end of your line?"

He shook his head emphatically. "The line would have ended even if I'd not joined with you," he said. "I would never have mated with Thea."

"But it *is* important to you now, though?" she pressed. "Right?" He glimpsed hopefulness in her eyes—the hope that perhaps now, with her, he would finally yearn for a child. Clearly she still did not understand their predicament, but he would make sure that she did.

"Kelsey," he whispered fiercely, "all the odds are stacked against us, love. Don't you see that? You are human; I am Refarian. I have never once cycled in all my years, which means it is hardly probable now. It is unlikely that we will ever conceive—that is what I am telling you. Do you understand? I will probably never give you a child. It is unforgivable that I didn't tell you this before now. You should have

known last night, before you lifebonded yourself to me.
If you regret the decision, then I shall seek the council's
permission to—"

"Stop it," she cried, and jerked out of his arms. Beauti-
fully naked, like pure porcelain grace, she moved all about
the room. Agitated, but gorgeous, she rounded on him.
"Jared Bennett!" she almost shouted. "Stop it! We are not
parting ways here. I want you. I took you. I accepted our
bonding willingly last night!"

Then silence. She stood before him, her chest heaving,
her full, supple breasts rising and falling with every labored breath.

"What, precisely, are you saying?" Jared asked after
what seemed forever.

She flung her hands before her, spreading the fingers
wide in an exasperated gesture. "I'm saying to *shut up*!"

"And you understand?" he asked, unwilling to relent.
"Everything?" His nonexistent cycles, the terrible odds—
could she really grasp it all?

She stepped close, placing one soft hand on his shoulder.
"I understand that whatever it takes, we're going to make
sure you *have* one of these cycles."

How did she intend to trigger that which had never come
upon him? He loved her for her faith, he blessed her for
her determination, but he grieved the unlikelihood of it all.
Still, he found himself whispering, "How?"

"By tempting and coaxing and seducing you into it,
Jared," she said, wrapping her arms around his waist.
"*That's* how. We will make this happen—together."

"Together," he repeated in a murmur, searching her face
in an effort to find some measure of faith there for himself.
He wanted to believe, and that alone had to mean something.

"I love you, Jared," she insisted, fire flashing in the
depths of her blue eyes, almost turning them golden green.
"And nothing will ever change that. Because I love you,
I'll do whatever it takes. And I mean *whatever* it takes."

Strange, but he felt a slight thrill chase up his spine at
her words, as if she'd just thrown down a sexual gauntlet
of sorts. Or maybe what he heard was the first whispered
call of something ancient as it stirred in his loins: the very
first, distant murmurings of a blood fever, awakened from
slumber at long last.

Chapter Twenty-four

Everything in Jared's life revolved around logistics, he thought with an irritable grumble. His council, Thea, Scott—he couldn't perform so much as a bodily function without ten people expressing their opinions on the matter, so why should his mating with Kelsey be any different? She had, of course, been right—the council wouldn't be pleased about his choice of a human for his wife and mate. Whenever he was called to chambers, they inevitably brought up the issue of his succession, which made it difficult to imagine the elders embracing Kelsey Wells, their first queen in more than twenty years, he reminded himself, and the first non-Refarian queen in hundreds more. And perhaps it was that thought that caused his champagne headache to swell behind his eyes anew.

Oh, yes, the council meeting would make his head ache for certain. It would be arduous and long and exhausting, but in the end he would force their hand, and they would accept Kelsey as his chosen one. In fact, they would even perform the union ceremony—today, if he had his way with things. While a formal ceremony wasn't required by royal tradition, he knew it was important to Kelsey, and more than that, he wanted the elders' official seal on their union. Besides, it didn't make sense to have a protracted bonding period. They'd completed their joining, and in the compound's tight quarters the rumors would soon begin to fly if he didn't solidify Kelsey's place in front of the council as soon as possible.

Which brought him to his other significant hurdle—and one he dreaded even more than the council—Thea. They'd passed each other briefly during breakfast this morning, and she'd averted her eyes, feigning great interest in her bowl of cereal. She'd left soon thereafter, hurrying off to her research down here at the guesthouse. She'd been reviewing a set of maps and journals sent to them on the latest transport from back home. They'd belonged to the earliest Refarian explorers sent to Earth, those pioneer teams who had come to Earth centuries earlier and mapped the rugged terrain until they had located the ideal hiding place for the mitres.

Jared pushed against the wooden front door to the guesthouse; warped long ago by the elements, it required an extra shove with his shoulder just to get the thing open. Ducking his head so he wouldn't smack it on the low door frame, he entered and found Thea standing in front of a table with both her hands spread wide. She squinted at the antiquated notations, never so much as acknowledging his entrance.

"Hello, Thea." The front door to the small guesthouse creaked as he closed it behind him.

"Cousin." She said nothing more, not once pointing her gaze in his direction. He strode toward her, a small bouquet of narcissus in his hands. He hated that his palms had grown damp around them, and hated even more how difficult this conversation was going to be. He loved Thea—he truly did—just not in the way that she loved him.

"You're reviewing Prince Arienn's maps," he noted, seeing his ancestor's elegant, spidery handwriting on the paper before her.

"Yes."

"And you're angry with me." It was a statement, not a question.

She blew out a heavy sigh and moved a measurement calculator over the map. "This just isn't a good time," she finally answered.

He placed both hands behind his back, standing at parade rest with the bouquet of flowers still in his hand. "When would be better?" For a moment she tapped her finger against her lips, seemingly lost in thought, and finally he pressed her. "You won't answer me?"

"My work here is"—she sidestepped to the far end of the table to examine another map—"important."

"Tell me of it then," he encouraged, ambling to the other side of the room along with her. Perhaps if they could focus on what they shared in common, that would help break the ice between them.

At first she said nothing, but then very softly she began to describe a few new details she'd uncovered, becoming more animated as she spoke. She believed there were other gateway entries to the mitres, an entry beyond the one Jared had unsealed a week ago. "Prince Arienn recorded everything very methodically," she explained, waving her hands excitedly over the open maps. "These journals are the key, Jared. I don't know why we couldn't get them before."

Well, he knew exactly why: They'd been locked in the palace vaults, and it had taken one very clever spy to sneak them out. The Antousians held his family's palace now, not Jared, and that included all their possessions, the jewels in the vault, his parents' crowns. All of it. "I remembered seeing them in the vaults years ago," he told her. He'd been captivated to discover his ancestor's tales of this far-away planet, Earth, and had sequestered himself one rainy afternoon, flipping through the pages for hours on end, reading in the man's own words how Prince Arienn had led his Earth expeditions shortly after the war with the Antousians began. How Arienn's father had entrusted him with their newly developed weapons system.

Prince Arienn had been chosen for several reasons: his complete trustworthiness at a time of great unrest on Refaria; his cultural sensitivity; and, most important, because of the power that coursed through his D'Aravnian body. Like Jared and Thea, Prince Arienn had been a dual being, and once the mitres had been fully installed, he had fulfilled his true mission by seeding some of his own power into the shielding unit. Last week, Jared had seen that remainder of his ancestor's essence when he stood within the mitres. It had been a hushed, eerie feeling to realize that the long-dead prince had successfully managed to leave a portion of his energized self behind.

"I saw his energy," he admitted in a hushed voice. Her gaze snapped upward, her clear eyes locking with his. "It was in the coiling unit, cool now, but it was still there." He hadn't told anyone else of his discovery; no one else could possibly understand. "It was a soft blue-green, but it still glowed."

She nodded, one hand fluttering to her throat. It was a tremendous revelation for each of them, to know what their power had the potential to do. If this ancestor had seeded it that way, then they might do the same with the mitres if the time ever came. If the need became great enough. "He wrote about it in . . ." She turned from him, rifling through a stack of aged, bound volumes. "Here! In this one. He meditated for three days in the chamber, praying and seeking guidance before he did it. None of our kind had ever attempted something like that." She paused, flipping through pages until she arrived at one with a thin slip of paper marking it. "Right here," she said, tapping the page. "You should take it with you and read it." She handed the book to him with a genuine smile of excitement.

He took the proffered volume. "There's much to learn from Ariennn's journals. Thank you for studying them."

Just like that, the smile died on her lips. "You don't need to try to placate me," she said with a heavy sigh. "Just take it, Jared. Take it." She moved away from him, turning to the stack of journals, and painstakingly straightened them into a neat stack. "Look, I have a lot of work to do here today, so if you don't mind . . ."

He paced toward the fireplace. "We need to talk."

"I know that you mated with her, Jared, so don't bother trying to let me down gently."

His fist tightened about the flowers. How in All's name had she known? Everyone in the damnable compound seemed to know. With a quick downward glance he checked himself for telltale signs of the mating. The day had turned quite warm already, and he wore only a light turtleneck, the sleeves pushed halfway up his forearms, but one quick inspection confirmed what he already knew: Nothing glowed. The luminescence of his mating with Kelsey had faded by morning, or he would have thought twice about even leaving his chambers. He didn't exactly want to parade the evidence in front of all his soldiers, even if he would soon be married.

She answered his unvoiced question with a shrug. "I knew the moment she arrived that you would mate with her. I just didn't know how long it would take, although I certainly hoped it would be longer. But this morning when you came upstairs, I could tell it had happened."

"It doesn't show," he argued lightly.

"Jared"—she cut her eyes at him—"I'm an intuitive. Trust me, it shows. Your energy has altered, it's surrounding you differently. It shows. And it shows all over her."

"I'm sorry." It seemed ridiculous to apologize, and yet there was nothing else he could say. He knew it had to hurt her.

She kept her focus on the maps, hiding her eyes from him, and for a long stretch of moments they were each silent. Jared dropped the white bouquet on the table between them. "Those are for you."

"I get the flowers and she gets the guy?" she said, spearing him with her gaze. He made no answer, for there was none to give. At last Thea spoke again. "I won't pretend you're here for my approval."

"I'd still like to have it."

"Why bother?"

"Because you matter to me a great deal, cousin. You know that you do." She sniffed in disdain. "You matter to me very much, and I also believe that you and Kelsey could be friends—very good friends."

"Oh, please—"

"She's strong and spirited like you, and filled with life, like our kind has almost forgotten to believe in."

"I won't ever accept her or welcome her here. You should know that, Jared. I won't make this easy for you," she said coldly. "Not when it's the end of your line. One thousand years of unbroken succession, Jared—have you really thought about those consequences? Or at least thought about your people? You have an obligation to them, you know, and you've utterly disregarded it by mating with that human!"

At last, his temper flared. It was one thing if she admitted that he'd hurt her, but quite another to insinuate that he'd failed his people in any way. "Disregarded my people?" he hissed, circling the table. "Shirked my obligations?"

"You still have—no, excuse me, *had*—time to provide them an inheritor to your throne. But you chose your own path."

"I have lived every day of my life for the Refarian people!" He pressed fists into his thighs to try to quell his hot fury. "I've never once lived for myself. Never—"

"Except in this that mattered most of all," she said softly.

Jared slammed his open palms down on the wooden table, and the entire room shuddered at the impact. "I have served none but my people," he gritted. "In kingship and war and battle and torture and life and death, I have served them." She stared at him, her hand pressed against her cheek, obviously waiting for his explosive tirade to continue. He shook his head. "I never thought to hear such things from you, cousin—even when you were hurt."

"You've always wanted the truth from me. Good leadership requires honest advisers."

"Sometimes"—he hesitated, meeting her gaze to be sure she truly heard him—"it would be nice simply to be a man. Not a king. And sometimes, cousin, it would be nice to have my only living family member treat me like a mortal, not a god."

With those words he spun from her, storming out of the room.

Didn't he understand that she loved him? Thea wiped at her eyes, staring at the door Jared had just slammed. She wanted to shout after him, to run up the trail, crying it over and over, *Don't marry her! Love me, as I have always loved you.*

She shook her head and slowly turned back to the worktable. Jared had never understood what he was to her— well, to any of them, really. Because if he truly understood her feelings for him, he would never have treated that love so lightly, and he certainly would never have disappointed his people. For him to allow his line to end, and in the midst of such war and turmoil . . . it didn't even seem true to his character. His heart of compassion was one reason they all served him with such ardent devotion. And yet on this one topic he had never relented, not once in all the years that they'd fought together, and no matter how much pressure the elders applied, he refused. Plainly, unbendingly, he always refused.

She wiped at her eyes again, pacing this way and that about the small lodge room. There had to be some way she could stop this wedding. Perhaps if she spoke with the elders herself . . . Yes, that was it. She could use her persuasive powers with them, and they would then talk sense into Jared!

Reaching for her sweater, she made to leave, and only then did she notice the small bouquet of white flowers that Jared had left behind. She'd been so upset with him, she'd never bothered to ask about it, and had forgotten until just now, when she noticed it where he'd knelt by the hearth. There lay a small bouquet of white narcissus, obviously tossed aside in anger. She dropped low and carefully retrieved the haggard blooms, and a wave of intuition whispered in her ear. He'd held them tight in his hand, almost crushing them, he'd been so upset. Closing her eyes, she lifted the tiny flowers to her nose and smelled them. *Fresh as the morning air all around these mountains,* she thought, and maybe it was the purity of the bouquet—maybe it was the intense separation she felt from her cousin—or maybe it was just realizing that she truly had lost him forever, but she pressed them against her heart and began to sob. Flowers. Why did he have to pick a bouquet of white flowers?

When Thea had been but a small girl, her mother had brought her to the capital city of Thearnsk, where the main palace stood in the city's center. She'd been eight that day, much too small for her age, and with unusual fair coloring, qualities that often made her feel alone even in large groups. Her mother had held her hand tightly as their transport had stopped inside the royal compound at a security checkpoint. Only two years had passed since the assassination of Jared's parents, and with the war reaching a bloody crescendo, the palace—the whole city, actually—remained under a very high security warning. Their transport was brought below the palace guard station, and at least seven of the king's military guard questioned them, searching the gifts they'd brought, opening them and ransacking them, much to Thea's youthful disappointment. And even though both she and her mother bore the D'Ashanian royal seal on the inside of their wrists, it took retinal scans and other identification before they were finally allowed inside the palace to visit the young king.

Thea's heart pounded and she clutched the only present

they hadn't ruined, at least in her tender estimation: a bouquet of white flowers. *Cessanaram,* they were called, and she'd cut them from her mother's country garden. She was, after all, a country girl. It was her first visit to the sprawling, mammoth city where her cousin made his home. Everything she'd seen on the way to the palace had awed her, frightened her, thrilled her. But nothing about that day could possibly compare to finally meeting J'Areshkadau Bnet D'Aravni. She'd been promised to marry her cousin and king since she was just a baby. Everyone knew it. One day, she would be his wife.

The guards ushered her into the throne room, and there by the window, high atop a dais and seated in an engraved silver chair, sat the most beautiful boy she had ever seen. Unlike her, he had shiny black hair, straight and worn just to his shoulders; black eyes to match; and lush, dark skin. But the thing she noticed most of all, even more than his flowing robes of D'Aravnian purple and gold, was the way he stared out the window, as if transported away to somewhere else, a place so special only the king himself could see it.

The guards cleared their throats to signal their arrival with quiet whispers of, "My lord, sir," and when he realized they were waiting for him he stood abruptly. The embroidered robes billowed around him like a regal cloud as he took the steps down to where they stood waiting. Thea clutched the *Cessanaram* blooms in her small hands, praying that she'd be able to breathe. He was so beautiful. Special. The king! Her fingers trembled, her throat went dry, and from behind her she felt a slight nudge from her mother.

"Darling," her mother whispered under her breath, "you must go to him."

He continued in his path toward her, a gentle smile on his lean, dark face, but she could think of nothing to say, not a single right thing to do, as he closed the distance that separated them. All her protocol training seemed to fly right out of her mind until at last he stood just before her. And then, unbelievably, he bowed to her! The Refarian king placed one fist over his heart and dipped low.

"My l-lord," she stammered, bowing herself, unsure how to respond. Then, for lack of a better idea, she dropped to her knees before him, trembling from head to toe. "It's an honor to meet you, my king," she managed thickly. She noticed that he wore boots of the softest, most perfect leather, high up to his knees. No one, not even her father, had boots so polished and fine.

With an elegant flick of his wrist, he waved her back to her feet. "Please, my cousin," he urged, his voice as warm and peaceful as the hot-spring brook that ran behind her parents' home. "I am quite pleased to meet you." She gaped up at him, feeling so very small next to him. She was only just eight years old, and everyone knew the king was nearing his thirteenth birthday. At last he extended one graceful hand. "Here," he offered gently, and helped her back to her feet.

When at last she stood before him again, speechless, he reached for the flower bouquet she clutched in her hand. He must have known she was struck absolutely speechless; otherwise he surely would have waited. "Are these for me?" he prompted gently. "I love *Cessanaram,* you know. My mother used to grow them in our garden." His eyes filled with sadness for just a moment, his gaze wavering from her face as he lifted the buds to his nose. But then he smiled. A glorious, true smile, the sort little girls dreamed of when they imagined kings. "They smell like my mother," he said, closing his eyes for a long moment.

She smiled too, because while so many agreed that the young king had lived a life of only tragedy and loss and hardship, she'd done something to make him *happy.* And for reasons she couldn't begin to fathom, she was glad that she had. It would be years—many long years—before she understood exactly why.

Chapter Twenty-five

The silvery-blue image of Jared's lifelong mentor and adviser, Councilor Aldorsk, wavered before his eyes, finally taking shape in the council chamber.

"My lord," the elder said, his deeply lined face breaking into a genuine smile. "Are you well?"

"Yes, Councilor," Jared answered coolly, "I've never been better, but we've business to discuss."

Gray eyebrows shot upward in curiosity. "Just the two of us?"

"It is private business, Aldorsk."

Jared detected an almost imperceptible dark shadow passing across the elder's features before he answered, "I am here to serve you, my king."

"Fourteen years ago, you accompanied me on a mission to this planet—I wish to know what happened then, that summer I came of age." Jared hadn't soldiered for so many years without being a preeminent strategist. In this case, he would not hesitate or back down simply out of respect for his mentor; he pressed forcefully ahead. "And I wish to know why I remember so little of my time here on Earth."

"I-I am not sure why you do not remember more, my lord." The man's voice quavered, and he blinked rapidly. "You were still quite young."

"Oh, Aldorsk," Jared whispered with a melancholy sigh, "I never thought to hear you speak lies to me. Not *you*. Not ever."

For long seconds they simply regarded each other in silence; Aldorsk knew now that Jared had discovered the truth, but he clearly wasn't sure just how *much* of the facts Jared had ferreted out.

"You erased my memories of Kelsey Wells—did you not?"

Aldorsk dropped his head, but made no answer.

"*Did* you *not,* Councilor?" Jared allowed his fury to gain life. "Answer me!"

"Yes, my king," came Aldorsk's hoarse, quiet reply, his eyes still downcast.

"I could expel you from this council for treason." The elders had violated him—and Kelsey—by this act, which was all the more shameful because Jared had never allowed his heart to guide him in life, had faithfully served the Refarian people. Except in this one thing: his love for Kelsey. It was the man before him—the man he'd trusted more than any other—who had taken that love from him.

"I had to protect you. It was my role to watch over you."

"You were not my *protector*—you were my councilor."

Aldorsk dared to lift his head, and Jared glimpsed something in his eyes, but only for a moment, before he quietly said, "Sabrina was gone and you had no other protector—it had to be me."

"So this was not the council's doing?" Jared asked.

"I acted alone."

Jared sat up in his chair. "I loved Kelsey. If you wanted to protect me, then you should not have stolen her from me! All these years, all this time . . ." Jared sputtered for a moment, dropping his head into his hands. A terrible wave of grief crashed over him, and for a brief moment he recalled sitting with her long ago by the lake, when they'd been on the brink of his awakening.

"You have found her?" Aldorsk asked, his voice solemn.

Jared dropped his hands away from his face. "Yes, I have found her. I might never have done so, if it were up to you. How could you think that was protection? What sort of protection steals love? Takes my heart, where it's beating in my chest, and yanks it out of me . . . ?"

"You were young, so very young. Your awakening was a delicate time, what with the need for an heir—"

Jared slammed his fist down onto the armrest of the data portal. "A need that remains unmet to this very day!"

"Looking back, I have come to consider that my decision

was not in your long-term best interests. I have had cause to reflect upon that."

"State your meaning." Jared ground his back teeth together, the swell of anger almost more than he could bear.

"I believe you never married Thea because your heart recognized that another waited for you. Even if you did not remember, you knew it intuitively."

"Marrying Thea has never felt right," he said softly.

Aldorsk nodded gravely. "The memory tie between the both of you was more powerful than even I realized. I apologize, my king, and beg your forgiveness. I was wrong—but I did it because I cared for you."

"You cared only for the succession!"

"No," Aldorsk answered quietly, "I cared for you. I have no sons, as you well know, and have always regarded you as such."

Jared slumped back in the chair, suddenly exhausted by the volatile discussion. "Then you will champion our marriage before the council," he said with a sigh. "It is the least that can be done."

Aldorsk shook his head, confused. "You plan to—"

"We are lifemated. Already. I need someone to speak for us in chambers today, to support our union."

"There will be extreme opposition."

Jared speared him with a glance. "And fervent support from my chief councilor."

"You can expect nothing less from me."

"Good," Jared said, still angry, but finding somehow that the fuel behind his fury had dissipated already. After all, nothing could bring back those lost years with Kelsey, and nothing—except perhaps time—could heal those missing memories.

Right now, he had but one remaining concern: to rally the elders to his side so they would sanction his union with Kelsey.

Jared paced nervously outside the meeting chamber, attempting to put on a brave face for Kelsey while they waited for the elders to call him back to chambers. She was obviously trying to do the same for him, yet every time she tried to smile at him, her mouth instead pulled into a tight line of worry.

"Stop it," he urged under his breath, reaching for her hand and giving it a light squeeze.

"What's taking so long?" She glanced at the closed chamber door. "You said they would do whatever you wanted. You're the king, right?"

"Um, yes, Kelsey," he agreed with a smile, "I *am* the king." His soft laughter died on his lips, though, when he saw tears swimming in her eyes.

"What if they won't let us? I mean, can they *not* let you? Can they somehow refuse to marry us or something? Or make it really hellish and horrible so that we'll wish we never wanted to get married? They might do that, right?"

With a quick glance about them, he drew her into his arms. "Kelsey, this is a formality. It is wartime; I am in exile. What do traditions even matter anymore? Beyond that, the council may voice its objections, and I will hear them, but it is *my* choice. Mine. They follow me, not vice versa. Our elders, while sometimes aggravating, are good people."

"They tried to separate us," she reminded him softly. "And they might have gotten away with it." She reached out and slowly stroked her fingertips along the warm skin of his wrist, reminding him of his royal emblem—their one pure memory they had both reclaimed.

"Elder Aldorsk acted alone—it was not the council's doing."

"Still I can't forgive him for stealing you from me for all those years."

"I haven't forgiven him either, but today I have only one concern: my marriage to you, and he has promised to argue on our behalf before the council. For that support, I am grateful."

"So we have one supporter? Only one?"

"He is the most powerful of my councilors," he reassured her, "and despite the evidence, he *is* a very good man. He has always served me very faithfully."

"But then why did they want to meet in private?" she asked, her pale eyes ringed with panic.

"Because royal marriages are always quite complicated— not just on my planet, but here on yours as well, from what I've seen of your history. My council isn't happy; we should prepare ourselves for that. But they know as well as I do that Thea might yet marry and produce the heir that I have not." He hesitated, staring at his booted feet. "Well, that *we* might . . ."

She slipped her hand into his. "We've talked about this," she whispered intently, her eyes saying far more than simple words ever could. Oh, yes, they had talked about it, and just thinking about that conversation caused his groin to tighten in lustful reaction. He growled a low warning, certain that tumultuous desire must flash in his eyes, but said nothing.

Her hand tightened about his waist, and she stepped even closer. Tilting her face upward, she looked him in the eyes. "I *will* give you an heir, Jared. I don't know how it will happen, but I will. We're going to have a baby, maybe even more than one. *They* may not know that, but if you do, it might help today."

"Y-yes, it helps." He swallowed. Hard. Her assurances that she would lead him into heat did nothing to ease the mad desire that had him quaking in her arms. At just the mention of cycling with her, his whole body quivered with a craving so deep and so ancient, he nearly howled his longing down the corridor where they stood waiting. Thank the gods he had better sense than that.

She studied him, her blue eyes widening as she understood how she'd just tantalized him. Her wide mouth spread into a very wicked grin. "Why, my lord, you're blushing again," she teased, staring up at him through thick auburn lashes.

"It seems to happen quite a bit in your company," he agreed, glancing anxiously toward the chamber door. "Won't those damnable people reach a decision?" he barked irritably. He wanted to wed her. Wed her and then promptly bed her—what a perfect way to spend the day.

Kelsey laughed, watching the way her husband-to-be licked his lips, his dark eyes darting maniacally, his gaze flicking first in one direction, then another. He thought she hadn't noticed what their talk about his mating cycles did to him, but he was sorely mistaken. She knew she had a lot to learn about the unique sexuality of his species, but even so, it didn't take a *Gray's Anatomy* of alien species to recognize a seriously turned-on Refarian. When they'd first discussed the topic Jared had blushed and stammered in obvious shame and embarrassment—but ever since they'd brought the subject into the open between them, he'd begun to change. An unnameable thing in the man had been set loose, and he now seemed barely able to restrain himself whenever the topic came up.

In fact, she'd begun to wonder if the only reason he'd never experienced these cycles before now was a pretty simple one: because he'd never taken a mate. He'd tried telling her that couldn't be the case, pointing to Thea's own situation, but Thea was a woman, which meant her physiology was different from Jared's. Beyond that, as a leader and king, Jared had lived a life of careful restraint. It didn't take one of his Refarian intuitives to realize that he'd kept his personal desires tamped down pretty tightly. No wonder the poor man hadn't achieved one of these cycles. He hadn't allowed himself much of anything, so why should his physical needs be an exception? That fact, together with the obvious mortification he'd felt about what he'd referred to as "animal instincts," and she had a pretty clear picture of the problem. Had it even occurred to him to consult one of his medics for a diagnosis? Or had his deeply held sense of shame run that deep?

"What did your doctors say about your, uh, situation?" she asked in a quiet voice meant only for his ears.

He gave her a blank, vaguely annoyed stare. "What situation?"

She twirled her finger in a circular loop. "The"—she leaned closer toward where he'd taken up position against the wall and stage-whispered—"cycles."

He folded both strong forearms over his chest, looking as disagreeable as he could possibly make himself. "You're obsessed," he muttered, huffing peevishly.

"You've given me my first wifely task, *remember*?" She fluttered her lashes, and with a slow, suggestive flick of her tongue, ran it over her bottom lip.

He stared back at her, his dark eyes wide and filled with lust. "Damn it all!" he suddenly blurted in frustration, glancing at his watch for about the fiftieth time since they'd been waiting. He hit the comm button on his arm, speaking in clipped, urgent Refarian. She didn't need to understand his words to recognize the irritation in them. "Stay here," he growled at her, stalking off to the end of the corridor.

She smiled to herself as he barked something at a group of engineers out in the breezeway who had been working on one of his fighter planes when they'd stridden in. The entire group scrambled back into the hangar. Then, rounding back toward her, his face a grim line of determination, he hit his comm again, issuing yet more commands. Almost immediately a pair of female soldiers materialized in the hallway at Kelsey's side. She looked curiously at the women, but it was obvious they'd been summoned by Jared to wait with her—and it was equally obvious that he planned to barge in on the elders' meeting.

"Wait here, please," he asked her formally, and then in a thunderous sweep, vanished behind the chamber door.

Jared's fingers twitched against the arm of his chair. It was all he could do to remain in the seat and listen to the council have their say. They'd spoken one after another in turn now for nearly an hour, when all he wanted was to get married and set about the business of the procreating they seemed so eager to describe. And describe and describe. Right now they were elucidating in painstaking detail the particulars of the D'Aravnian mating cycles and the attendant high-powered sperm he would release within his mate. He in turn had a raging hard-on that he would rather be experiencing in the bedroom than here inside the council chambers.

He shifted uncomfortably in the chair, glancing among the wavering holographic images of the elders, and wondered if the sizable bulge in his pants was visible all the way back on Refaria. Nothing quite like an intergalactic erection, he thought, shifting yet again in his seat while the elders discussed the particulars of his tricky sexuality in a heated volley of possibilities. He pressed a hand to his brow and forced himself to listen.

After a few moments Dalnè stepped forward, her manner as unassuming as ever. He'd have sworn she hated this process as much as he did. "My lord, it is just that we need an assurance of your line's succession." She extended her hands in a placating, calming gesture. "With this human woman and your looming infertility—"

That was it. Enough was simply enough.

"*Looming* infertility?" he roared at the youngest member of the council, nearly rising out of his seat as he did so. "Looming? I am thirty, Councilor. Young by any species' reckoning, and yet you've now exaggerated my problem into a state of such urgency that it is all but towering over me. Are you privy to aspects of my own body that I am not? For last I checked I was the one living in this form. Just as I'm the one who best comprehends its behaviors and my own complicated physiology."

Dalnè bowed her head, trembling visibly, but said nothing. Neither did the other objecting elders who had spoken so freely all morning. His furious gaze swept over each of them. Aldorsk gave him a small nod of encouragement—he had argued for a full fifteen minutes on Jared and Kelsey's behalf, but had been alone in his support of their marriage.

"As I thought," Jared said. "None of you dares speculate on what might transpire between the sheets of my own bed." He heard a slight gasp, though from precisely which one of his councilors, he couldn't be sure. "My private life is not for public consumption. I have made my choice, and you will marry us this afternoon."

Dalnè's eyes lifted, meeting his—she stood closest to him of all the elders. In her expression he saw a touch of rebellion as she dared to lock gazes with him for a beat longer than appropriate. "You will disavow your line?" she asked in a tight voice.

"I am an exile. Not a king."

"With all due respect"—her eyes remained trained on him, blazing in unexpected challenge—"I beg to differ."

"If I fail to impregnate my wife, then the line will shift to the House of D'Ashani. Thea is younger than I, cycles like mad, since you seem hell-bent on studying our unique sexualities, and is sure to find a mate in the coming years."

Then Graeon, his other beloved mentor from so many years past, spoke, his voice quiet yet firm. "But D'Aravnian succession has been unbroken—"

"What, dearest Graeon, do you propose?" He ground his back teeth together in order to speak respectfully to the aging Refarian elder. "I will hear your propositions so long as they include my marriage to Kelsey Wells, whom—I should obviously remind each of you—I have already mated with. It is a finished act. The marriage is but a formality."

"So you've not yet begun to display the early signs of your maturity?" Dalnè ventured, and although the truth enraged him, he had to admire her brave tenacity. "Is that what you are suggesting, my lord?"

He blew out a frustrated breath. "You know that I am not. We've had enough conversations in this chamber that you know better."

"And if we were to estimate the time before full maturity has come upon you . . . would it be another five years?" Dalnè pressed. "Or would even that be far too optimistic?"

He growled a furious complaint at her frankness, but said nothing.

Aldorsk and Dalnè exchanged an uncertain and uncomfortable glance, and then, with a slight bow of her head, Dalnè retreated into the circle. Aldorsk took her place center stage, dropping his voice into a quiet, calming timbre. It was as if his mentor were speaking privately only to him. "My lord, I would propose a simple solution. One that would accommodate both your heart's desire and your wishes, while protecting the succession." The older man paused, searching Jared's face for permission to continue. Jared waved him onward, though his belly clenched with dread at the prospect of what the man would say next.

Aldorsk nodded, taking yet another step closer toward Jared. "I propose that you marry this human, sealing your union with a formal acknowledgment by this council. She will bear your mark, the mating rights will be solidified, and she shall be queen of Refaria." But then he paused. It was a dreadful, horrible pause, and Jared knew that the man's next words would be dreadful too.

"Go on," Jared ground out.

"But you will lie with Thea—not the queen—during your cycle. She will give you the needed heir and the problem will be solved."

"Gods preserve us!" Jared shouted, throwing his head back with a bitter laugh. "Enough is enough."

Aldorsk pressed on, ignoring his outburst. "If you cycle with Thea, the succession is guaranteed. There will be no doubt as to your ability to conceive with your cousin."

Jared leaned forward in the chair, leveling Aldorsk with his most regal gaze. "Elder Aldorsk," he said, making his words like a deathly vise about every gathered elder's throat, "I have a revelation that may startle this council, but it's time that the truth be made plain to every one of you gathered here. I have never—not once in all my days— cycled. Not once. Not even the first inkling of fever has overtaken me, not the briefest touch of our heat. Nothing." There was an audible intake of breath from someone, per- haps Dalnè. "And so you see why I chose to mate based on, shall we say, other considerations. I am not your man. Nor, it would seem, the man you have long thought me to be. Although I am certainly still *a man,* one with all the inherent desires of my kind, and I have found the woman I love—the woman with whom I care to spend my days in exile." He stood and brushed his hands off, the meeting finished. "And so now you finally see. The line will fall to the D'Ashani," he announced with an air of finality. "Far better for Thea to mate with another, one who might actu- ally give her children, than be with a man of *looming infer- tility* such as myself."

Every elder gazed at him, shock and pain mingling in their expressions, but not a one of the gathered council in the room dared utter a word. So he would. With a proud smile, he lifted his chin and declared, "Now, fair council, if you do not mind, I would like to marry my mate."

It was always the unexpected small things that created tremendous snafus in any military operation. In the end, it wasn't the council's approval that interfered with their wed- ding day after all, nor any last-minute outbursts from his people, nor even the nervous stomach that had been plagu- ing Jared for the past hour. It was the simple fact that Kelsey had never been retina-scanned and approved for chambers transmission before today, and no matter what the techs attempted, the elders simply could not *see* her. Which made having Council Aldorsk perform the ceremony a trifle problematic.

"Perhaps if the lady would take *your* seat," one of the techs suggested in a gulping, uncomfortable voice. "We could attempt to scan her and then load the data by super- seding *yours,* my lord."

Jared shot an impatient look at the young man, who in- stantly fell silent. A flurry of other suggestions tumbled forth from the other two techs who labored diligently within the room, and none of them worked. Jared paced, waited, and generally lost his composure as time continued to progress. Kelsey sat patiently on the side of the room, offering him that lovely wide smile of hers—the one that seemed to fill her whole face and lit him up in the process— whenever he dared glance in her direction.

He paced, shook his head, and didn't bother wondering exactly why he was so irritable about his pending nuptials. Fear wasn't an emotion he ever liked to acknowledge.

When he was just about to throw his hands up and head for Las Vegas, a soft knock came on the chamber door. Then it slid open, and Thea filled the brightly lit doorway. The chamber always remained dark so that the transmissions could be viewed, and he had to squint as he looked at her. He covered the distance that separated them quickly, praying against any other obstacles that might further interrupt his wedding day.

"May I speak with you, cousin?" She kept her voice low, her clear blue eyes darting about the room. He knew she was searching for Kelsey, but because of where his mate sat on a settee to the left of the entry, Thea didn't see her.

"Of course," he agreed, touching her arm affectionately.

Her eyes shot about them nervously. "Alone?"

"They're working on the console unit right now. It's a good time," he said, and she nodded, then led the way back into the corridor outside.

Now that Thea had him alone, she wasn't sure what she wanted to say. Well, she had a general idea, but the words she'd rehearsed had fled her mind now that Jared stood before her. She felt for the bouquet she'd gingerly tucked inside her jacket for safekeeping.

Taking a deep breath, she began. "Cousin, I love you," she blurted. Jared's eyebrows narrowed sharply, and he opened his mouth to say something, but she pushed ahead. "I love you more than you will probably ever know, and I understand that you don't return those feelings."

"Of course I love—"

She placed a silencing hand on his forearm. "Please, cousin, let me finish."

His mouth snapped shut and he nodded, folding his muscled forearms over his chest.

This wasn't easy; it was even harder than she'd imagined as she'd trudged over from the guesthouse to the base. She continued, "You deserve to be happy, and I know that from the day you became king, your life has not been your own."

He dropped his head, but she could still see the quiet pain that appeared in his eyes.

"You have sacrificed a great deal for all of us, and we love you for it, Jared. We honor you for it. It is only right and fair, therefore, that with all that you've sacrificed in your lifetime, you should be allowed happiness in at least this one thing."

He gaped back at her, blinking rapidly. "Why would you do this?" he asked hoarsely. "I don't understand."

Even though her heart was breaking, she gave him a weak smile. "You are a tremendous leader and an even better man. I shouldn't have said what I did earlier at the guesthouse." Tears welled in her eyes, blurring the image of him before her. He wavered, and she blinked until the tears began to spill freely. "But the thing is, Jared, I always thought you would be mine. You were meant to be, for all those years."

He opened his arms and without a word pulled her close, right up against his chest. So close that she could feel the natural D'Aravnian heat that emanated from within him, the energy that resonated so very clearly with her own. She would never find another man, not on any planet, who could understand who and what she truly was like this one man did, her king, her beloved cousin, her friend. She cried against that strong chest, and one warm hand folded about her back. Wordless, soundless, they stood like that for a long while.

At last, muffled against the top of her head, she heard a quiet pledge from him. Something she knew she would replay and replay for years to come, would rehearse in her head and imagine ending differently. Words for a lifetime. He said, "I am yours, Thea. Just not like you thought I'd be."

He pulled apart from her, tenderly brushing one of her errant blond curls away from her cheek. But she wasn't finished yet.

She slipped a hand inside her jacket and retrieved the

bouquet. "Here, these are for you," she said hoarsely. "For your wedding day."

"No, Thea, I brought you those," he tried to argue.

"You should have them. To remember your mother today."

"My mother—oh, the *Cessanaram*." He lifted the bouquet to his nose, closing his eyes just as his younger self had done so many years ago. "I can't believe you remembered that."

"I want you to be happy, Jared," she said, recalling the first day she'd met him as a young king all those years ago. He was meant to be hers, then and now. But he was also deserving of happiness. She bowed her head and dropped to her knees. "My lord, this is my wedding gift to you." She trembled there, kneeling before her king. Her hands grew clammy, the tears stung her eyes anew, and she waited. Waited for him to urge her back to her feet. But all she heard was silence, and still she waited—until there was a soft rustling sound. She glanced upward . . . and instead found Jared kneeling, eye-to-eye with her.

"I predict," he whispered, gathering her hands within one of his, the flowers in his other, "that one day we will assemble here for your own marriage, someone you love far more than you've ever thought to care for me."

"So you're a mystic now?" she teased, wiping her eyes with the back of her hand.

"Times are changing. I feel it, and I feel it for you too."

She wanted to accept his words; she truly did. But deep in heart she believed the only thing different about today, the only thing that set it apart from every other day they'd fought this endless war, was that Jared Bennett had found love—and it wasn't with her.

Chapter Twenty-six

They were connected now, and in every conceivable way. Their hearts, their minds, their souls and spirits—every aspect of their selves was tuned to a unity of one. Even their bodies; Jared held Kelsey so closely in his arms they might as well have been in the privacy of his bedroom, not in front of eight council members and his best friend. She almost wondered if he feared she would bolt from the room. The tempo of his heart was frighteningly fast, his chest rising and falling with ragged breaths.

When they'd first taken their place before the council, he'd sought their bond by shooting his energy toward her like one of Zeus's mighty thunderbolts, electrifying her on the spot. Damn the guy, but her hair had instantly stood on end with static electricity. That was how intense a single jolting dose of her lover's powerful alien self had been. He'd smiled at her sheepishly, and she'd quickly patted down the flyaway hairs (wishing for a cling-free sheet), and then the formal ceremony had begun.

She was using the word *formal* pretty lightly, since she wore only a slinky red dress; sleeveless (well, spaghetti straps kept it from sliding off her body) and backless, it would have qualified as *formal* on, say, a cruise ship. Or at a New Year's Eve party. But it wasn't exactly a wedding dress by any usual standards of the imagination. Kelsey had borrowed it from Anika, who offered no explanations as to why—or how—an alien soldier came to have a postage stamp of an evening gown in her possession. Miraculously, the gauzy fluff of material had fit Kelsey perfectly—and gauging by the way Jared's dark eyes had narrowed to slits upon first seeing her in it, she wondered if the gown's fortuitous appearance in Anika's room might be in no small part because he'd wished it so. And wished it to be so in his favorite color—red.

As for Jared, he seemed determined to be as devastatingly handsome as he could possibly manage on such short notice. Translation: He wore his military uniform, all black and sexy as hell. He couldn't have chosen better even if he'd been wearing some kind of kingly formal wear. For a moment, she wondered what his traditional garb would have been if they'd been married on his planet, and decided to ask him later, when they were alone.

She had no understanding whatsoever of the meaning of the elders' pronouncements over them, but as they rambled on endlessly in Refarian, Jared's hold on her tightened anxiously. Speaking within their bond, she promised, *I'm not going anywhere,* in exasperation. She sensed his confusion, so she explained. *You have a death grip on me.*

I need you this close, he whispered across their connection.

She sensed an unsteady emotion within her mate. Was it . . . fear? Was he really afraid?

Yes, came his resonating voice.

Why on earth?

Because I'm getting married, he cried, the words practically jarring inside her brain. *Sorry,* he muttered.

You'd better listen to these people, she cautioned with a quick burst of humor, *because I don't have a clue what's being said.*

He pressed a kiss against the top of her head. *Traditions, rites . . . It's boring; don't worry.*

When does it get exciting?

When I start translating it for you.

O-kay, she teased. *No wonder you're holding on to me with the Vulcan death grip. You're bored, so you're trying to imagine life beyond this moment.*

I'm imagining all manner *of things with you.*

Don't do it.

Do what?

Try to give me a midceremony orgasm. She laughed and felt him grip her even more frantically. *What are you doing?* she asked as he shifted her in his arms.

Hiding my erection.

It's your own fault, you silly king.

And on their banter went, as all the while they kept their faces as neutral and placid as possible. She wasn't sure they ever *really* listened to any of the ceremony—not until it reached a critical turning point. Jared released her then with a satisfied sigh, allowing his gaze to sweep over her, and turned to face Scott, where he stood slightly behind Jared. The other man, she noticed, had worn a permanent scowl throughout their ceremony—right up until the moment he glimpsed Jared's face. And then Scott's stern expression dissolved into one of the warmest, gentlest smiles she'd ever seen, a smile that told her she *liked* Scott Dillon—immensely. And from that moment on she knew she would always like him.

Scott slipped something into Jared's waiting hand, and the two of them exchanged quiet words in their own language as they embraced.

And then at last Jared turned back to face her and grasped both of her hands. "Mate, it is time—time for the sealing of our bond, the solidifying of that which already exists." Jared's dark eyes fixed on her, narrowing with emotion. "For the taking of us, one heart to another, one body and soul." *One man, his queen,* he finished softly across their bond. *One lover, his lifemate. Oh, gods, Kelsey . . . I hardly want them to hear what I wish to say.*

It's okay, she promised him, as much within their bond as with her eyes.

He nodded, then very slowly continued. "It is the tradition of the D'Aravni that the royal mark be passed upon the moment of the wedding seal. Our royal mark"—he released her hand, exposing the underside of his wrist to her—"that signifies our lineage." He opened his other hand, allowing a warm golden beam of his energy to fall upon his exposed skin. The familiar spiraling burst of light appeared between them, just above his wrist in the middle of the air. Magenta and blue and golden red spun and wove together like a mystical helix of energy. His energy. His mark and seal, she realized, and even though she'd seen it before, her hand flew to her mouth. It was a wonder! He bore a hidden mark that set him apart from all others of his species, at least the ones who were not of his line.

Very slowly, dangerously even, he lifted his dark eyes until their gazes locked. The colors of his emblem reflected in the black depths of his eyes, and she knew he was calling to her. Summoning her. Making a gift of something exquisite and rare that was a crucial part of himself.

What did he want? What was he offering to her? She didn't understand, and shook her head.

Love, he breathed, *take it.*

Take what?

I'm giving you my royal emblem. Take it, love. It belongs to you now, not just me, so go on and take it.

How? she cried in confused frustration. Leave it to this man to confound her at such a crucial moment on their wedding day.

He bowed his head, a lopsided, charming smile appearing on his lips. *How do you want to take it?* The words were whispered with all the thrumming seduction he might utter during lovemaking.

I-I don't know. I'm not sure.

Actually, you do know, he corrected, his voice husky and teasing. *Tell me what you feel inside. You're bursting with it, Kelsey; you just haven't quite figured it out.*

She stared at the floor between them, then swung her gaze about the chamber. One young elder, a woman, gave her an encouraging nod. They all expected her to know this answer! And he hadn't prepared her at all by telling her anything about what was expected. Panicked, she shook her head again. *Just tell me.* It was hard to conceal her annoyance, and of all things he only smiled more. So did Scott Dillon. So did every single other person in the room, except for her.

Just tell me! she shouted, staring again at his spinning colors between them, mesmerized by the beauty of such a mark, and knowing that he bore it hidden within his body. The swirling, coiling light was almost a kind of multidimensional tattoo, she realized. And what did you do with a tattoo? You wore it someplace sexy. Someplace where your lover might lick it and kiss it and play with it beneath his hand.

You're starting to understand, he teased.

I'm mad at you.

No, love, you are crazy for me. Wild with it.

He took hold of her shoulders and spun her away from him until she faced the other side of the room. Behind her, she felt the warming of his energy as he pulled back the clingy fabric of her dress, and then the light brushing of his fingertips against the small of her back.

He knew. He knew *exactly* where she wanted his mark, and she'd never even so much as expressed it to herself. The skin at that small dipping curve of her spine felt like fire—as if something had stung her, setting the skin to burning and itching and crawling all at once.

"Y-your m-mark?" she managed to stammer, though her mouth suddenly felt very thick, as though gauze were smothering her words. Her legs beneath her wobbled, her vision swam, and he slipped both arms about her waist, pulling her close.

That's why I've held you so near the whole time. The sealing ceremony is quite powerful. I didn't want you fainting during our wedding.

And I-I just thought . . .

Me a terrible seducer of human women?

Yeah, that too.

"It is done," Jared pronounced aloud for all to hear. "The human, Kelsey Wells, is now marked as queen, taken by me, J'Areshkadau Bnet D'Aravni, king of Refaria. We are mated. We are married. It is done."

From behind her, he slid his large hand over her smaller one, cupping her palm against her abdomen, and before she realized what he was doing, he slipped a simple gold wedding band on her finger. "Now *you* say it," he whispered against her ear, sending a chill up her spine. "Tell them that it is done."

"It is done," she repeated, feeling herself in a daze. "Th-the . . ." he gave her the words quickly within her mind, and she continued. "The queen has taken the king as mate. I have accepted his mark and he is taken by me, Kelsey Elizabeth Wells."

"Tell them, 'We are mated,'" he prompted her softly, brushing his lips against her ear with a light kiss. She repeated the words, her voice strong and sure and resoundingly joyous, even if it did quaver a little.

"The king and queen are one," one of the elders pronounced in halting English.

And with that simple yet ponderous phrase, she began her journey as the Refarian queen.

Sometime during the day—probably during the long wait outside the council chambers, or perhaps during the ceremony itself—the late-November day had turned unexpectedly cold. Dark clouds had blown over the mountains, hovering over the land like a tight blue-gray fist. And then, as sometimes happened even in July in the Grand Teton area, a heavy snow began to fall. Even in the middle of the summer, a serious snow had been known to extinguish forest fires in Yellowstone. So it came as no real surprise that on her wedding day, of all days, she found herself on the back of a four-stroke snowmobile hanging on to her new husband for dear life. Because *of course* Jared was a snowmobile hotshot; what else would the man be? He gunned the engine on the thing, tearing off up the mountainside away from the base, and she flung her arms around him, giggling with joy even as the wind whipped her hair and stung her eyes. She was a natural-born snowmobiler, and though she usually preferred to be the one doing the driving, today it suited her perfectly to ride up the snowy mountainside on the back of Jared's sled. Even in a slinky red dress—though thank goodness Anika had loaned her a long winter coat to go over it.

After only a few minutes of rip-roaring joy along the fresh powder, he pulled up at an overlook. Down the mountainside and into the valley spread a moody panorama, just the kind she most loved about her home.

"Gods, your land is beautiful, Kelsey," he said, removing his helmet with an appreciative shake of his head. "It suits you."

She smiled, handing him her helmet as she swung off the back of the snowmobile. "I'm glad you like it." She felt shy, as if he were remarking on her breasts or the shape of her figure or the shade of her hair. It was deeply personal to her, hearing him talk about his love of her world.

The soft whisper of wind whipped about them both, winter's early chill already riding the mountain peaks down into the valley. Along the ridge where he'd brought her, the brilliant late-day sun pierced through the snow clouds and drew its hand over the low land, painting a spectrum of blue and crisp gold and white. With a proud smile, he stepped up onto the rocky cleft and nodded to the view. "Awe-inspiring, isn't it?"

"Yes," she agreed, feeling the mountains' ancient hush weave a mystic spell between them. This was *her* land he offered like the most priceless of wedding gifts; the land her father had taken her away from, refusing to acknowledge its importance in her life—the land she'd missed every single day she'd lived away from it, in D.C. "It's a part of me," she said.

He cocked his head sideways, watching her. "I understand that feeling."

"About Refaria."

He shook his head in disagreement. "No, about *this* land, Kelsey." He crouched low on the ridge, tracing his fingertips over the jagged, snow-covered rocks. "I feel this land of yours is my trust, somehow. That it's been granted to me, same as my home world. That hundreds of years ago my people chose this place, this portion, so that I might know its beauty. That I'd understand what it is I'm to protect. The air, the mountains here—you have no idea how the war has ruined my home. But then here," he said, sweeping his hand around them, "here I can know the possibility of restoration. The beauty of your world, and the destruction I'm meant to prevent."

He sifted snow between his fingertips, thoughtful and quiet for so long that she wondered what more he might say, and then he turned to face her. "Now I know why else I've loved this land so passionately, Kelsey," he said, rising to his feet. Brushing his hands together, he continued, "I was sent to protect your people—that was part of it, I am certain. But there's always been something more that I could not place my hands around. Like a word beyond speaking, or an English phrase that I could never seem to learn."

With his hand, he cupped her chin and tilted it upward until their eyes locked, his black Refarian ones meeting her own human ones. Their bond flared, opening like a river of fire between their two bodies and hearts, causing her legs to almost buckle with the twined rush of alien power and sensual desire. "Shall I tell you what I've finally learned, dear Kelsey? Shall I tell you this word beyond my speaking? It was you, love. You were the place my heart longed to know. You. You are this land; you are my love for it. The feelings are inseparable for me."

He had no way of knowing the hurt she'd carried inside after being wrenched from this place by her father, nor for how very long she'd endured that pain. Her father, as much as she loved him, had left her feeling abandoned and cheapened by the simple fact that he wouldn't *keep* her here after her mother's death. Now, on her wedding day, the man she had chosen as husband and mate stood on this precipice—a king in every way—declaring that the worlds belonged in her hand because he had given them to her.

She bowed her head, unable to stanch the flow of warm tears. Husband. This man at her side loved her, would protect her at all costs. She wiped at the tears with the back of her hand, unable to find her voice.

"Kelsey," he said, turning to her in deep concern, "I'm sorry—have I bungled my English again?"

She burst into laughter. "No," she said, still wiping away tears, "that was very elegant, Jared."

"Perhaps I should have kept to Shakespeare?"

"You've given me a wonderful wedding gift," she said.

"You are worth it," he said, pulling her close against his chest. She felt his heart beating beneath his powerful rib cage. Closing her eyes, she marveled that the pounding she felt was that of an alien heart, of one born galaxies away, born to lead a world, to helm a revolution. And yet it beat so simply when he held her this close.

"Actually, I have another gift for you," he promised, his warm breath on her cheek causing a shiver of desire to snake down her spine.

"What's that?" she asked, curious.

He cocked his head sideways, a most lascivious grin forming on his face. "Ah, no, love. Not here."

"Where?" she blurted curiously.

His hot gaze swept over her form. "To my chambers." He laughed. "Where else?"

It must have been another one of Jared's alien powers that was to blame, because otherwise Kelsey couldn't account for her near-instantaneous nakedness once they were inside his bedroom. With a deft move he had her out of her clothes, flipped onto her belly on his bed, and had begun kissing the small of her back. More than kisses, she amended dreamily, feeling his tongue flick and outline the curve of her spine. He was owning her. Branding her. Marking her with his mouth the same way he'd apparently marked her with that alien tattoo of his. With every taste of her skin he was doing exactly what she'd fantasized about him doing while they made their vows.

He took hold of her hips, digging his fingers into the soft flesh of her belly. With his mouth he kept on kissing, outlining, laving. What *wasn't* the man doing to her back?

"Now," he purred.

"Hmm?" she asked dreamily, grinding her hips against the mattress with pure desire for him.

He halted his explorations and kept her pinned beneath him, panting against her back breathlessly. "Time . . . to let me . . . see," he cried, moaning softly as his fingers pulled at the skin he'd been showering with kisses one moment before.

A thrill shot through her center. She got it now. Jared was crazily turned on by the presence of his royal emblem on her—and that it was in precisely the place she'd longed to have it.

"How do you, well, see it? The royal mark?" she asked, turning her head sideways so that her cheek rested against the mattress. She studied him through her lashes. He hadn't even stripped out of his uniform. A black-clad soldier had her facedown on his mattress and was licking her to pieces.

He stood there at the mattress edge gazing down at her, cupping her bottom in both his hands. "You amaze me, Kelsey," he whispered in a wondrous voice.

"Is the mark showing already?"

"Always so curious. One of many things I love about you, wife." He laughed.

"Well, *is* it?" she persisted, and he pressed one knee into the mattress, never relinquishing his hold on her hips.

"Not until I bring it to light," he purred in a voice electric with promise. "It wasn't revealed during the ceremony—only placed on your body. But it's been there ever since, simply waiting for me to reveal it."

"Then do that," she urged him breathlessly, aching for

him to proceed. "Go on, Jared. Please." She didn't care that she was practically begging the man; he was her husband, after all. Surely a little bedroom begging was a given in any marriage.

His fingertips trailed down her backbone, touching her with fire. Carefully, painstaking in his slowness, he stroked her bare skin. "I thought I was fulfilling your fantasy."

She squirmed as he bent low, pressing his full, warm lips against the small of her back. She felt the rough texture of his tongue flick against her body yet again.

"The first part of my fantasy was for you to lick it, kiss it, and whatever-else it." She gasped, squirming beneath him. "The second part was to know *exactly* how it affected you."

A low, rumbling growl erupted from his chest, and she felt his heat sweep over her bare skin as he cupped his palm over her lower back. The growling became a piercing howl, and then all she heard was his harsh breathing as he pinned her, facedown against the mattress again. "It is true," he rumbled in her ear, lapping at her cheek with his tongue. "You are all mine now. No one shall ever take you from me. Mine. Mine. Mine."

Oh, how he loved to possess her—she'd known that from the very first time they made love.

"I can't pretend anymore, Kelsey," he continued, kissing her behind her ear, slipping both of his palms beneath her hips and holding fast. "I love this belonging. It makes me half-crazy; truly it does."

She smiled to herself. He had no idea yet, did he? Her smile broadened as she wondered how long it would take her husband to recognize the beautiful change that had begun in him not even twenty-four hours ago.

"I love it too," she agreed huskily.

"I don't love this uniform," he complained, easing off of her.

"Hey, I have a question," she said. It was something she'd wondered about in the midst of their ceremony. "What would you have worn if we'd gotten married on Refaria?"

She heard the low rumble of sexy laughter. "Not a military uniform; that's for sure."

"Then what? Tell me."

"No," he said in a slow, seductive voice, "I believe I'll show you."

When she rolled onto her back to get a better look at him, she gasped. Jared stood before her clad in skintight leather pants that outlined his muscled thighs like a second skin. As he moved toward her, the black pants hugged every ridge and furrow and dip in his very masculine body. A white shirt was laced from his navel to the middle of his chest, where it fell open to expose the golden-brown skin there, hinting at the dark peaks of his nipples, just visible through the thin white cotton of the fabric.

"Th-that's your traditional wedding outfit?"

One dark eyebrow shot upward in question. "Would you have preferred a tuxedo?"

She stretched on her back languidly, watching him step closer. "Not on your life."

He laughed softly. "Perhaps I should have worn this and not the uniform?"

"I would have expired during the ceremony. Besides, I could never have competed with"—she paused, swooshing her hand in the air—"well, with *that*."

"No, love, you would have held the room in your hand, just as you did today," he said. "Now roll over."

"That sounded like a command."

"It was."

She sniffed, but grinned wickedly to herself as she flipped over onto her stomach again. She felt his warm hand against the skin of her back, his fingers roaming and exploring—almost as if he were searching for something. His leather-clad legs pressed between hers, parting her thighs as he climbed onto the bed, all the while his fingertips were caressing and stroking the small of her back until he made a soft cry of exultation. "There it is," he said, his voice full of hushed amazement. "Oh, gods, you're beautiful."

The skin beneath his hand began to burn, an explosion of fevered fireworks all along her skin. The sensation was at once erotic and wicked as much as it was majestic. She was marked forever as a D'Aravni.

Brushing his lips against her spine he breathed, "Mine. Incredible."

"I want to see."

"Later. But right now . . ." he paused, swallowing audibly. "I-I just want to look. Besides, I still have that gift for you."

"And I still wonder what it is." She felt something warm and solid press into her back, right where she'd been sealed with his royal mark, almost like a heavy, warm stone or coin. "Is that your strake stone? I already know—"

"I'm giving it to you. *Really* giving it to you, this time." She felt him remove it from her back, and he pinned her beneath the full length of his hard body. "Only it's more now."

"How could it be more?" It took effort, but she managed to roll over until she found herself staring up into his dusky eyes. He hovered atop her, bracing himself with his forearms to keep from flattening her with the full weight of his body. Without a word, and without ever dropping his gaze, he reached for her hand and slid his strake into her open palm, slowly closing her fingers around it. She drew the stone against her face, awed by the hush that had settled over the two of them. This moment meant far more than the giving of a simple gift; she knew it as surely as she knew the Refarian heart beating heavily against her own. She knew it just as she recognized that something fundamental had changed within her during their ceremony earlier today.

She *knew* it because of the way her husband's unwavering gaze fixed on her, his near-black eyes blazing like midnight suns.

"Look at it," he breathed, and she slowly opened her hand that held the stone. "I-I had it set for you," he continued. She'd noticed before that he stammered slightly when he was filled with emotion; perhaps because his facility with English became less precise when he was overcome with feeling; she wasn't sure. She gazed into her palm, and gleaming there was a golden ring. Not the kind you wore on your finger, but the strake now resided in the center of a polished golden circle attached to a delicate chain, its obvious power practically setting the golden band afire like an amulet. She'd not imagined it possible for the ebony stone to become even more beautiful, and yet offset against the bright golden circle, it seemed somehow newly radiant and mystical. "It's like a wedding band?" she asked uncertainly.

"Yes, love, and it's also a symbol of where it once resided. It came from my father's crown, you see, and it was the only jewel smuggled out of the palace that ties me—well, us, now—to our rightful position. It's an emblem of everything we fight for as a people, and all that we believe in for restoration. I wanted you to have it."

She pressed it to her lips, tears burning behind her eyelids. "I don't know what to say."

"My wife, dumbstruck? I shall mark the date," he teased, but his eyes narrowed with extreme emotion and pleasure.

"Why did you choose a ring? I mean, I get that it's like my wedding band, but—"

"The ring is a crucial icon to my people. It signifies the cyclical nature of our life, the triumph of good, our rhythms with the universe. Like water—water is very critical to my people as well. It's not just for sustenance or survival; it's considered arousing to my kind."

"Water? No way!" Immediately her mind supplied many very wicked ideas about seducing her new husband in the shower. No wonder he'd been so hot and bothered in the bathtub last night!

She stared down at the strake again and noticed something that she'd not caught on first glance. "It's inscribed. Is it English?" She couldn't tell in the semidark of his room.

"Yes, just like your ring." He hadn't told her that her ring bore an inscription either. "It's Shakespeare. A sonnet that means a great deal to me, actually—"

"The one you quoted last night," she whispered, realization dawning. "You had it inscribed inside my ring and in this pendant."

He closed his eyes, blushing slightly for reasons she didn't fully comprehend, reciting the poem to her: " 'For thy sweet love remember'd such wealth brings—that then I scorn to change my state with kings.' " He opened his eyes and slowly began to link the gold chain around her neck, the stone and ring dangling from the end of it, and continued. "I-I wanted to mark our day with something permanent. Beautiful. Something from your culture."

"You don't have a ring from me."

"It's not our way to wear one," he explained. "Only males of our species give them."

"Hmm, I could get used to a culture where the men are expected to drape their women with jewels. Not bad, Bennett."

"Could you get used to a culture where men are meant to make love to their wives all day long?"

"Aha! You held out on me. Now the truth is revealed."

"True, true. We're actually a pleasure race. It's all we do, in fact." He laughed huskily, dipping low to kiss her breastbone right where the strake rested. "Make love, give jewelry, eat, and drink. It's quite the thing, you see. Now you understand why it was imperative that I take a mate."

"I'm glad you did," she whispered softly. She stroked his bristling black hair, feeling the give and play of it beneath her hand. For a long moment he rested his head against her breast, the two of them lying quietly together.

"I'm dying of curiosity," he suddenly pronounced, pushing up off the bed.

"About what?"

"About making love to a woman," he said seriously, "who bears the mark of D'Aravni on her bottom."

"It is *not* on my bottom!" she protested.

"Almost." He laughed, stepping across the room, where he shrugged out of the soft cotton shirt he wore, revealing the ripples of his abdomen and the hard planes of his muscled chest. She lay on her back, watching his catlike grace, and felt warm heat swirl in her body. Pressing her eyes closed, she allowed the sensations to crescendo, her abdomen knotting with waves of desire.

She heard the unsnapping of buttons and the soft rustling of discarded clothing. Still she kept her eyes closed, savoring her husband's energy as it pulsed across her skin, sang through her body, infused every bit of her soul.

Then he was atop her again, the bed yielding beneath the weight of his lean body. But he was gentle with her, oh, so gentle, whispering soft Refarian words in her ear, words that she recognized even if she didn't understand them. They caused her soul to thrum with need for her mate; they caused her whole body to tense like a musical string that only he could pluck.

"Jared," she purred in his ear, repeating his name over and over again. She ached to make him know the depth of her feelings in his own language. With one graceful movement, he rolled with her, and she found herself atop him.

"Call me J'Areshkadau," he urged, grasping her hips within his palms and steadying her atop him. "Please." His voice quavered slightly with the request.

She smiled, pushing up so she could stare into his eyes. "Please?"

"I-I long for it," he admitted, blinking up at her, then moaned something in Refarian before adding, "It is difficult . . . to express."

That was when it hit her—all this time, she'd been calling him Jared Bennett, which was really only a sort of nickname, or a false name—not his true one. It was such an easy gift to give her mate on their wedding day! She bent down until her lips brushed against his left ear, and blew out a husky, arousing breath, kissing him lightly on the cheek. And then she waited. She waited and drew the moment out—and hesitated just enough to cause him to rumble his desire back against her cheek.

Only then did she whisper, "I love you, *J'Areshkadau.* I think I always have."

These words seemed to awaken her alien husband completely, and he began to tumble with her on the bed amidst a tangle of covers and discarded clothing, until after a moment's lustful tussling, he emerged atop her once again. She lay bucking beneath him, and he gave her a wicked grin of satisfaction. He'd pinned her like any creature would its chosen mate, as if he'd bounded upon her in the wild and simply determined to *take* her.

"I wish to have you now." He panted breathlessly, kissing her full on the mouth, and then with a playful nuzzle of her cheek added, "And—of course—for you to have me."

"The king wishes it?" she teased.

He bowed his head against hers, and in a voice filled with emotion whispered, "I wish it very much."

She cupped his face within her palms, drawing it upward until their eyes locked, and said, "J'Areshkadau, I can't deny you anything. All you ever have to do is ask."

With that, he thrust into her with a joyous, shivering yelp

of pleasure, bathing her with kisses drawn from the very heart of the man's soul.

Long into that night they made love, stroking and caressing every inch of each other's bodies. Sometimes they paused at the pure joy of discovering some hitherto unnoticed aspect of the other, perhaps a freckle or scar or luscious curve—sometimes they stopped because they needed to rest. Never did they stop because their souls required it. No, their souls touched until there no longer seemed a separation, until they wept in each other's arms at the mystical connection possible between two alien hearts such as theirs.

Never did they stop to notice the world around them, for if they had, then surely they would have discovered an envelope—a plain envelope, extraordinary only for its appearance seemingly from nowhere—that lay on the other side of the room waiting for them. For if they'd noticed it, they would have seen that in scrawling, nearly indecipherable handwriting the envelope read:

My dearest Jared and Kelsey . . .

But they didn't notice it. For that one night, the world consisted of only two people, the king and queen of Refaria, which was as it should have been for the newly joined and bonded lovers, lost in a universe of two.

There would be time enough for the universe to expand once a new day dawned.

About the Author

Deidre Knight is a literary agent, mom, wife, novelist, and Southern woman, and proud to answer to all of those titles. She began her writing career at age nine, when her award-winning essay on Barbie was published in her hometown newspaper, and since that time has always written in one form or another. After selling hundreds of romance and women's-fiction novels for her clients, she's delighted to bring her tales of aliens and adventure to someone other than her own family—although she still hopes to convince her daughters and niece that present-day aliens really do live in Wyoming.

You can visit Deidre on the Web at www.deidreknight.com and www.deidreknightbooks.com.

Read on for a sneak peak at

Parallel Heat

by Deidre Knight

Coming from Signet Eclipse in October 2006

FIRST TIMELINE—THE FUTURE

There weren't many places a dead man could go if he hoped to survive; at least, that's how Marco had always regarded the matter. Fighting in the royal army, and back on Refaria in the midst of the revolution, he'd learned that soldiers who embraced the afterlife had an uncanny way of finding it. Right now he wished he could lock in on some eternal, mystical wormhole that would shoot him straight out on the other side of his current hell.

He was literally in the middle of nowhere, hunkered down in the back corner of some dive on Highway 189, the perfect geographic location for him after everything tonight. *He* was nowhere, nameless, lost. He didn't even know which bar he'd landed in, only that there were a half dozen pool tables and a haze of cigarette smoke shrouding the place. And beer . . . racks and racks of beer, and Marco didn't give a damn about his protector's vows, not now, not tonight. He was going to get drunk and free-fall into a painless state of oblivion if he had anything to do with the matter.

His waitress returned, her low halter top revealing a small butterfly on her right breast, and slid yet another bottle of Heineken toward him across the scuffed wooden table. He nodded mutely at the woman before staring down mutely at his swarthy hands. He'd already lost count of how many bottles he'd tossed back since his arrival, and the cut on his forehead hurt like hell, but that hardly mattered. Taking another heavy swig of beer, he felt the world around him grow even hazier—the dark bar was so cloaked in cigarette smoke, he could hardly tell if it was the effect of the alcohol on his system or just the cloud hanging over the place. His eyes burned, and for a moment he closed them, feeling the world swim woozily all about him.

Yes, let me forget, he thought. *In All's name, just let me forget tonight.*

Throughout the barroom were positioned rough wooden picnic tables, little more than graceless constructions of two-by-fours slapped together at haphazard angles—as if the working-class regulars who populated the place required nothing more than basic stalls for their drinking pleasure. In fact, Marco had been lucky, managing to land one of the only real booths in the joint, and even then, the garish red leather beneath him was ripped and cracked, at least ten years past its prime.

Through the din of loud honky-tonk music, he could hear the phone at the bar ring, jarring him from his dazed state. The bartender—a burly guy with tattoos up and down each arm—grabbed it off the receiver. After listening a moment, he cupped his meaty palm over it. "Eh! Jordo!" he called out. "Your old lady wants you home!"

Around the nearest table, a group of men erupted in bawdy laughter, slapping the man who was obviously Jordo on the back, making crude comments.

Even he has someone who cares about him, Marco thought miserably, sinking down into the booth. *But not me.* Not that he'd ever had a woman of his own. No, he had always led a solitary existence when it came to matters of the heart. Still, people had cared for him, important people. But not now. He was utterly alone—without his unit, without his king and queen, without his homeland. He was, quite simply, a protector without a protected. And maybe he did deserve to die as payment for his crimes. At least that would end the torment that had hounded him for the past year as he had secretly loved his best friend's wife.

Marco leaned his head back heavily against the wooden booth and glanced around the bar through slanted, half-opened eyes. Jordo and his pals were gone—most everyone was gone, as a matter of fact. He'd probably been here, sopping up his sins with booze, for at least three hours. He'd have to ride his Harley somewhere before the night was done, but where? He had no home anymore, not after tonight.

Alone, alone. The only way for someone so vile.

After a sluggish, dizzying moment, he raised his eyes at last and saw someone who looked vaguely familiar. A golden-haired angel stepping out of the haze straight toward him. Why couldn't he place the woman moving so easily toward him? And then, within a heart's beat, she was standing just in front of him, smiling faintly. She was blond, beautiful, and seductive as hell. Someone else's lover, not his.

"Hi, Marco." Her high-timbred voice was throaty, and she clasped his shoulder as if they were old friends. "We meet at last." She trailed her fingertips down his arm familiarly, and a shower of electricity shot through his arm and chest. No way was she human.

He lolled his head forward again, narrowing his eyes. "Do I know you?"

"Well, let's just say you know of me." She slid uninvited into the booth beside him. "You've certainly seen me before, though not up close. Never like this."

He inventoried her features: wavy golden hair, blue eyes—*lots* of hair, he amended. Long and shimmering.

Small frame . . . "Thea," he said finally, taking another sip of beer. "Thea Haven."

She smiled in satisfaction. "You have been watching, haven't you?" Her voice seemed to trill in victory.

"It was my job," he answered dully, refusing to rise to his enemy's bait.

What was Thea Haven after? And why was she suddenly here tonight of all nights? It made no sense at all. His thoughts were clouded and dim from the alcohol; that had to be it.

"Right," she replied slowly, drawing the word out for effect. "Yes, I hear Jared really respects your hard work on his behalf." Her voice was tinged with bitter irony.

He raised his eyes again and found her staring at him meaningfully, flame darting in her pale eyes. She knew. Somehow the woman knew everything that had happened tonight! Or maybe it was only his drunken mind playing tricks on him. Suddenly the dozen beers seemed like a really bad idea. He leaned his elbows forward on the table, burying his face in his hands for a moment. Anything to stop the torturous spinning of the bar around him.

"Why are you here?" He groaned quietly. "What do you want, Thea? Really?"

"Well, that's simple enough," she said seductively. "I want *you.*"

Marco slowly lifted his head, and met her eyes—and swore he heard her call his name somewhere within his mind. He couldn't fight, not like this. Not tonight.

Jared's enemies had planned their attack extremely well, and all he could do was surrender.

He lay back naked on the bed, the frayed hotel bedspread on the floor in a tangle. Thea peeled off her underwear, climbing in after him. Her eyes took in the length of his body, the sinewy bulk of it and his solidly muscled torso. She had never seen a more beautiful man in all her days. His dark skin was incredibly rich beneath her fingertips as she traced her hands across the silky black hairs that dusted his inner thighs, then between his legs. He shifted his hips in reaction, causing the cheap mattress springs beneath them to creak and groan in reaction.

His eyes were shut tightly, an expression of painful ecstasy dancing across his features. She began trailing kisses down his firm abdomen, lower . . . then even lower still, taking him into her mouth. He cried out, and she drew him in deeper, then eased him out again. He gasped her name, cupping her shoulders firmly within his large hands.

Thea liked the feeling that she was pulling this Refarian soldier toward the brink, a man trained for every potentiality. A man sworn to resist all his king's enemies—and for the briefest moment, she simply liked being with Marco McKinley, period. But she quickly buried that thought. She couldn't afford to feel anything for this man, and yet the emotions radiating off of him were so strong, so intense. It was hard to resist, especially since his gift of intuition left him wide open to her. If Thea chose to, she could feel everything happening within him. *Maybe just for a moment,* she thought breathlessly. *What harm can one moment bring?*

As she opened herself ever so slightly to him, she had a strong flash—and it was something she found nearly impossible to believe. This was Marco's first time with a woman. Any woman. *That* was certainly something she could use to her advantage. She pulled away, gasping, and he opened his nearly black eyes. She could read the undisguised pleasure in his lazy gaze. *Yes,* she thought with a wicked smile, *this plan is working to perfection.*

She rubbed her thumb over the swollen tip of his erection. "You're a virgin," she breathed huskily, and tightened her grip.

His dark eyes flashed—with what she wasn't sure. He seemed almost to panic for a moment, then, just as quickly, the emotion passed, replaced with something much harder. *Colder.*

"Who would I have ever made love to, Thea?" he asked wearily, letting his hands drop away from her shoulders. His face became guarded, and she couldn't read his expression.

He was pulling away from her—and that simply would not do.

She climbed on top of him, straddling him as she drew her face within a breath of his. "A beautiful man like you could have his pick. Any woman would thrill to pleasure Marco McKinley, sovereign protector."

At those words, he closed his eyes tightly shut again. "No," he groaned, "they would not."

"You are beautiful." She pressed her lips against his ear, even as she squeezed her thighs around him, and felt the sensation of her toes against the hairless place behind his knees. "Anyone would be a fool not to love a man such as you."

Oh, Marco, she thought, *I could love a man such as you.* Quickly she pushed that thought from her mind. *Never!* She had a mission here, nothing more. *Don't buy into your own words, Haven.*

Slipping one hand between his legs, she trailed her fingertips over his hardened length, teasing him. Seducing him. Controlling him. A virgin who'd never lain with a woman in his life? Well, this had certainly played to her advantage!

She'd seen the look of pleasure flare in his eyes when she'd called him beautiful. Good. Then that same quiet voice whispered in her mind again. *He is beautiful . . . unbelievably beautiful.* He'd taken her breath away when she'd first seen him tonight, his black hair windblown from the motorcycle, and his smoldering good looks perfectly offset by his black leather jacket and faded blue jeans. She'd been keeping him under surveillance from afar for months, but tonight had been her first really good look at him. For a fleeting moment, she'd found herself disconcerted by his dark Refarian features: the rich black eyes, the olive skin brushed with a touch of gold, the formidable size of his body. And then she realized why his appearance unsettled her so badly—Marco reminded her of someone, someone she had strong feelings for.

Their kiss continued and so did her swirling emotions, spiraling crazily inside her mind and body. *Someone familiar. Someone important. Gods, of course!* she realized with a shocking jolt, and for a moment she pulled apart from him, gazing into his black, slightly slanted eyes. He blinked back at her, his face ruddy with emotion. His full lips parted, waiting for another of her kisses.

Of all the men in the universe, why did Marco have to look like her cousin Jared Bennett, the only man she'd ever loved? But before she had time to react to that association, Marco cupped her face roughly, pulling her close for a much hungrier kiss, his tongue heatedly exploring her mouth. She could feel his heart racing wildly against her chest while her own hammered out a twin crescendo. *These feelings—this attachment—will not do,* she reminded herself. *You are here for one purpose only.*

And with that she silenced the unexpected, quiet voice of desire this man had spoken within her . . . once and for all.

She'd laughed at him, at his virginity and inexperience. That had been the final humiliation of this day. He had felt so damn powerless against her as her hands had kneaded his thighs, as she'd rubbed and teased his rock-hard erection until he ached beyond expression. And now their kisses grew rougher and fuller as she cradled her hips so perfectly against his, teasing him into a thrusting motion—letting him know what would come next beyond any question or doubt. He met every gyration of her hips, and he knew one fact for certain—he was totally losing control in the arms of his enemy, going over the edge, and there would be no coming back. Never again, not after tonight.

This woman didn't just have him in the palm of her hand—she had all of him, his very soul even. No one had ever taken his body and simply pleasured it. He'd been a servant, a warrior for so long; he'd always thought of himself as the property of others. Yet tonight she was worshipping his body, and it felt achingly, powerfully, disastrously good.

The gash on his forehead throbbed painfully, and as he became aware of it, her finger traced it lightly. Had she felt his pain? Their kisses stilled, and he stared up into those blue eyes as she touched his wound. Everything about her was the opposite of him. She was all lightness, golden hair, blue eyes—where everything about *him* was so dark. Even in the half-light of his room, he could see how olive his skin looked next to her fair complexion. She traced the throbbing place on his forehead with the tip of her finger.

"Let me fix this," she breathed. She lifted her hand to help him, and he captured her wrist roughly. He knew Thea Haven had been gifted with healing abilities, but he didn't want to be healed.

"No," he growled.

She raised her eyebrows in surprise. "Why not?"

He released her hand slowly, and she resumed tracing her fingers lightly across the wound until he flinched slightly in pain. The cut was physical proof of his crime—he'd kissed his queen tonight, even when he realized the advance was unwelcome. In return, Kelsey had sent him sprawling headfirst against her bookshelf.

"I want the scar," he breathed. "I want to remember tonight from now on."

"They really got to you, Marco, didn't they?" She began trailing hot kisses across his jawline.

He groaned softly. "Yes, but now you're getting to me in whole new ways."

"You've been lonely." Her tongue flicked softly against his earlobe, then she tugged on it between her teeth.

How could he stand up against this? He didn't care what she really wanted with him: This was all he needed tonight.

"Yes," he moaned quietly into her hair, taking her full breasts in both of his hands.

She nuzzled his cheek. "You need this. Me."

"Yes," he agreed softly, raking his hands through her luxurious blond hair. There was so much of it, and it was all over his face.

"What will you do to have me?" she teased, straddling his naked body with her own. God, she was so close to him; he could just slide inside her easily. He let his hand find the warm place between her legs. Earlier he'd caught a brief glimpse of a soft tuft of dark blond hair there. She was incredibly wet for him. Did she want this as much as he did?

"What . . .ever," he gasped, "I need to do." He thrust upward clumsily, trying to push himself toward her, but she lifted, holding herself away. He had no idea how to get what he wanted, not without seeming as inexperienced as he was. His face burned with shame, and he tried to work his way into her again—she raised her hips coquettishly, lifting just out of reach.

"No, no, Marco. Tell me," she urged with a wicked smile. She was hovering over him now, straddling him. If he wasn't careful, he might lose control before he ever came inside of her. "Tell me what you will do."

"I'll make love to you," he gasped unsteadily.

She ran her fingers through his hair and laughed, a quiet, seductive sound—the sound of a devil temptress—and said, "That's not what I want, Marco. You *know* what I want."

He didn't understand at all what was happening. Not what she wanted? She was so wet for him, so seemingly full of desire. But in his heart, he did know what she was after—had known since she'd first appeared in the bar tonight.

"Then what?" he asked, sucking his breath in quickly. He felt like he was begging her now. He let his hands wander roughly across her backside, cupping her bottom, pulling her closer to him.

"I want you to make love to me, yes. But that's not all." She hesitated, sitting up on top of him until she gazed down at him seriously. "I want you to come to our camp. I want you on our side. Jared will never take you back—you do know that, don't you?"

He felt something turn over in his chest, and for a moment he thought he might be sick. She had put voice to the words that he hadn't yet allowed to fully form in his mind.

Damn her.

She did know everything about tonight; he was certain of it now. That he'd kissed his queen, and afterward Jared—his protected and king—had banished him from camp forever. Did their enemies have the compound bugged? How else could they have known what transpired in the king's chambers, in private?

"Raedus is the true king," she continued, softly stroking his hair away from his forehead. "Jared is only the leader of a tiny little rebellion; it's not his destiny to rule anymore. Someone with your"—she paused, brushing her fingertips over his lips to emphasize her point—"exceptional talents belongs with a real king, Marco."

Suddenly she captured his hand in her own—so quickly that he couldn't stop her—and a small beam of light emitted from the palm of her hand, falling upon his own wrist. Immediately his royal seal appeared in the air between them, the one true proof that he was part of the most elite circle of royal protectors. He was among the last of the Madjin Protectors, one of a dying breed.

"This is who you are, Marco," she said, gesturing at the undulating royal emblem where it swirled in the darkness between them. "Jared never respected it, never appreciated it. But Raedus will—he needs you. Our alliance needs you," she whispered, and began trailing hot kisses across his forehead along the edges of his painful cut. Her kisses ended on his eyebrow. "And *I* need you. Badly."

He closed his eyes as he felt her stinging kisses along his forehead. They seemed to electrify his pain, intensify it. He tried to pull away from her, and she raised her head slightly, meeting his gaze. Those blue depths were so empty, but somehow shot full of passion, just like the ocean at Mareshtakes could be—shining, tempting, and treacherous.

She touched his forehead once again. "Why would you want this scar?" Her voice was surprisingly gentle and sympathetic.

He steadied her face within his open palms, studying her thoughtfully; when he did finally answer, his voice was an electrified hush: "Because it's who I am now, Thea."

In the near darkness, she smiled faintly. "Good," she breathed, tracing her finger along his eyebrow. "So you know, then."

He could only nod. He wanted inside of her . . . now. No more toying with it. *Mine,* he thought. *She can be mine. . . .*

She can never be yours, the voice disagreed, *but now she owns you—all of you, from your body to the depths of your soul. They all do. For eternity.*

And the worst part was . . . he no longer cared.